SARABAND FOR A RUNAWAY

Robb White
Ashtabula, OH
29 Sept. 2017

SARABAND FOR A RUNAWAY

A Thomas Haftmann Mystery

Robb White

NEW PULP PRESS

For information contact:
Publisher@NewPulpPress.com

ISBN-13: 978-1945734120 (New Pulp Press)
ISBN-10: 1945734124

Printed in the United States of America
Visit us on the web at www.newpulppress.com

To Jack E. Smith, one of the Chosin Few

SARABAND FOR A RUNAWAY

PART 1

What man can live and not see death?
                    - Psalms Bk. 3.89.48

MID-WINTER, JEFFERSON-ON-THE-
LAKE, NORTHERN OHIO

CHAPTER 1

Alligator mississipiensis.

A real mouth-filler. That's how the dictionary, the battered one on top of the fridge, defines one of these great lizards.

There is a word for a fear of these beasts: *herpetophobia.* I don't have a problem with snakes and lizards. It's just alligators, although you can throw crocodiles into that bracket too, even if they are supposed to be different creatures. I'm not a zoologist. I'm a private eye.

I named my fear of alligators and crocs my Captain Hook syndrome. Before I went to Florida in search of a runaway, I could watch those National Geographic shows where these fifteen-foot animals lay in wait for the zebra and water buffalo herds fording the Zambia River on their annual migration. The same narrator with his plummy British accent and Oxbridge degree always described in eloquent terms how these big reptiles "assist nature" by thinning the herd. I was pretty sure that pinhead would change his mind in a big hurry if he found his own boat upended on that very same river.

Micah, my ex, used to tell me there is one for everything in life that you can name, including a fear of dust, but I have never troubled to look it up myself. When we were first married, I was a cop in Cleveland and I had to chase a few knuckleheads through backyards all over the east side, and they do love their pit bulls, these guys, so I've been bitten a few times. That's called *cynophobia.* But I like dogs. When I was a very young boy being raised by a religiously nutty grandmother, I had a fear of thunderstorms. That's called *keraunophobia* only if you include both lightning and thunder. During a terrific storm one summer over Lake Erie, she told me that was God's wrath roaring from the heavens.

She was good with books, my ex-wife. Often she would read passages to me in bed or quote lines, especially from psychology texts, although she was a lawyer by profession. She used to say that I was a classic underachiever. Even after the divorce, there would be books lying about the house with bookmarks in them. I once bought her a set of laminated ones for Christmas that she never used; instead I'd see scraps of papers, hairpins, and anything that lay close to hand fulfilling the task of keeping places for her. In the way that your memory has its own way of bookmarking events in life with its own reminders, I recall it was the same day that we had that brief conversation about alligators that she mentioned splitting up.

"Look it up," she'd say, in that librarian tone of hers whenever I asked her something about what she had read to me. She showed me a picture of one of these oversized lizards lolling fatly in the sun, snout forward, sprawled in the mud, its snarled, crooked teeth poking out stupidly every which way from its trap-like jaws. It lay on the banks of some bayou or swamp beneath clusters of Spanish moss. "Crocodiles have the pointed snouts," she said.

Alligators, crocodiles – whatever. I occupy my time as the proprietor of a one-man investigative office in this resort town. My lawyer-wife liked to rub it in my face that the difference between my occupation and her profession was that what I did for a living did not qualify as a real profession because it didn't come with "a public avowal of beliefs." I told her that's fine for lawyers, doctors, and the rest of the white-collar crowd, but people don't line up to take vows to deal with the kind of reptile my business involves. In my experience, the two-legged kind can have blood just as cold.

Latin was an aphrodisiac to her. She was not only a lawyer but she left me for one. She studied law at Case Western in Cleveland and moved to our little burg where she acquired the reputation as a tough prosecutor. We met when our paths crossed over one of her early cases. I know almost all the lawyers through my cases; sometimes I work parallel to theirs; sometimes I need them to defend me. My friend Reggie is a judge of the Western District now, and I'm sure he's relieved about that because he often lamented how much he'd hate to throw the book at me if he ever saw me in front of him. I was pretty sure he'd have recused himself if it came to that, but sometimes I think he's serious. Knowing me hasn't helped him in the social circles he frequents. Micah herself is living in Portland, but is moving to Salt Lake City in the spring. She's divorcing the lawyer she left me for, and is dating another one from Utah.

But I digress. On the day alligators and crocodiles came up, we were leaving for Naples, Florida, where her parents owned a small house worth a quarter million – just a squared-off cinderblock job with a red-tiled roof and some stucco for ginger-breading. The realtors down there called it "a chic bungalow," but up here in my neighborhood, it would be called shabby and wouldn't get a bid over $50,000. Location, as they love to say.

Our vacation plan was to drive across Alligator Alley to Miami, follow the old Tamiami Trail, and then take the A1A up from Delray Beach and catch I 95 and ride back north. It was familiar turf despite my being an Ohio boy born and bred. For one thing, runaways love this place. It isn't just the aging snowbirds who make a beeline for Florida. My last skip-trace job ended with a suicide in a motel not ten miles from Delray Beach. I knew how the guy must have felt. The state depressed me too. It was like nature at constant war with itself, with exotic strains driving out domestic. Australian pines, orchids, and mimosa taking over with redolence and beauty against the native species. Sea grape strains to find purchase in sand, insects fight everything in their path like all the young hustlers without money go after the geezers with it, as bad a combination as matter and antimatter.

But it would turn out we would return from Naples without driving into Miami. For some reason, I wanted to take a different route home, pick up 77 in South Carolina and take the Shenandoahs for a change. I was tired of lowlands, the humidity, the everlasting sunshine.

Later on I would learn the reason for Micah's moodiness. She had just begun her affair with this corporate lawyer of hers, a tax consultant for Price Waterhouse and a few other big outfits in Cleveland. He showed Micah how to do the books for my business on the Strip. Then he showed her another kind of business. He had written to tell her he was leaving his wife, and he was begging her to make the trip short. I remember with such clarity that icy feeling in the pit of my stomach when he got around to describing parts of her anatomy that I assumed I alone had seen, let alone caressed. His passion seemed unlawyer-like, unreal to me, but then, I must have been in a kind of shock to discover her treachery. He also told her he was fondling a locket of her pubic hair and counting the days until they could see each other again.

I knew all this not because I'm such a crackerjack investigator, but because I came across his letter to her after I was released from hospital, my head no longer swathed in bandages but my vision still blurry, and

4

migraines were jackhammering me to the point of blindness. Astoundingly, Micah had used his letter – a half page of letterhead paper with the law firm's name across the top – to mark a place in a book. In an era of facebooking and sexting, it turned out to be an old-fashioned letter that exposed her. Weighing less than a feather, but as I held it in my hands, it felt like something with the mass and weight of a bag of hammers. I remember nothing at all about the book, not the title or the subject, color or size, but I can still see the words she had underscored in pencil when I came across the folded paper: *Fear is the parent of all cruelty – J.A. Froude.*

Maybe she wanted me to find it. At first, it seemed nothing more than the casual malice of a cheating spouse, one more stab into the heart, or maybe the balls. I now think she was reaching out in those final days of our marriage for some kind of – response, maybe. Micah had too many intellectual weapons against me to need to justify her infidelity. There was no pettiness in her character, yet this quotation haunts me worse than anything lewd in the lawyer's letter. To leave it behind for me to find like that, like a cheap Freudian slip. I put the letter away inside a tiny panel in my grandmother's old secretary downstairs. It's in there now, pulsing with its own secret life.

Convicts have an expression: "running through the gears." It's a slangy way to describe slamming a shiv into a guy's chest – in and up, over; in and down, over. Just like driving stick when I was a kid. Froude, whoever he is, is right about cruelty. I remember watching her once as she lay curled up on the sofa in a winter shaft of light reading a thick biography of Stalin, and she told me he personally crossed out the names of his victims. The ones who had done him a kindness or a service used to cause him to tremble when it came to their names on his death list.

"Why?" I asked her.

"Sexual sadism," she answered in a bored tone.

That's always been my Achilles' heel. I never identify with the killers or the psychos. It's the faces of the victims I always see first.

~ ~ ~

I never actually saw an alligator in the wild until I went to Florida to bring back a runaway named Raina Toivela. She was almost twenty, beautiful, with these high Finn cheekbones, piercing blue eyes, and hair that must have been white-blonde in her childhood but which time had darkened to a buttery caramel.

One teenaged photo showed a strikingly pretty girl smiling behind a kind of sheepdog hairstyle that had been in vogue back then. You noticed the eyes because they were out of sync with the smile, a kind of Micah-smile, I thought then, with knowing eyes. She came from a good home, large family, both parents who stayed together. Both wept throughout the interview I had with them about the details of their daughter's running off.

My office is halfway down the Strip, as the locals say. It used to be a realtor's office before me and before that it was a beauty parlor. Not much to see inside: a desk perpendicular to the plate glass with my name – Thomas Haftmann, Private Investigations – in a style of script that's supposed to be Baskerville Old Face, according to the drunk I hired in Tico's Place to etch it there, my computer and printer, a phone with a landline, and a big stain on the ceiling above the fluorescent tubing that isn't so much the Rorschach designed to plumb the observer's psyche – as Micah claimed when she spied it on the day she co-signed the papers for me – but a bloodstain with the blood and sere separated, as if leaked from a bled-out corpse. An old timer, an ex-con who liked to paint ore boats, once sat across from me and looked up. He called it a ghost drop, which is prison slang for the aspirated blood convicts with tuberculosis spit up because it has a bubble of oxygen in its center.

Raina's father was an accountant and a county commissioner for Jefferson, the county seat and big brother to our crappy little resort town of Jefferson-on-the-Lake. The wife was a vision of Raina in twenty-five years: similar features but fewer angles; her face was pretty but not as stunning as her daughter's, more as if a sculptor had used his thumb too much to blunt and round the places where the planes of the daughter's cheek would catch light. They were twins in the eyes, however – that same penetrating blue like Arctic ice.

I'm used to people sobbing at me. Being in homicide in Cleveland has helped.

The mother kept mumbling *why, why* into her handkerchief as if she expected to find the answer there. Mister Toivela cleared his throat every few minutes while he gathered his thoughts – a logical man trying to cope with the dark forces of irrationality.

This job, I thought, *will be easier than most.* I was to retrieve her from a state psychiatric ward in Dade County. Toivela gave me a paper with the hospital's name and address on it. Since I was just an errand boy and not a detective on this one, I didn't ask why she had run off, nor did her parents go into detail. She was already enrolled for her senior year at the Dana School of Music in Youngstown. Her performance of Satie's *Lent et Doloreaux*, they said, had won her the scholarship right out of Jefferson High School.

When I returned her to her parents at the end of that August a few days later, she was surrounded by crying siblings who came out of the house in a rush to greet her and throw their arms about her.

I had called the father earlier to say I was driving, but I didn't tell him the reason I wasn't flying back with her. She was too incoherent to be strapped into a plane, even if her disheveled appearance got her past the airport security. Besides that, I needed time to clean her up. When she got out of the car that afternoon, she was coherent again, twitching from withdrawal from whatever drugs she had been dumping in her system. But she was recognizably the daughter her parents had shown me when they had pressed various photos on me that day in the office. Raina, a golden halo of fractured light above her head, intense at the piano; Raina smiling with her prom date beneath an arbor of artificial flowers; Raina playing with her siblings or seated at table during Thanksgiving; Raina eating popcorn or playing with the family cat. I was embarrassed not to take them, but I didn't know what to say.

Still lethargic and too thin, she would resume her life in a loving family. Her hair needed better combing than she was able to manage on the road. Her body weight would come back in time; after all, she was young. I had seen it happen before.

On the morning of the day I drove her home, she sat slumped against the passenger-side window and dozed. The air-conditioner in the rented Toyota blew air that smelled of banana oil. I pulled off the exit ramp at the first Jacksonville exit to get some food into her but she threw up out the window before we had crossed the state line. Traveling through Georgia's red hills at dusk, I felt calm, relaxed, some of the day's prickly heat dissipating like the mirage squiggles of the highway stretching north. I'm an existentialist, but I had such a powerful flashback to a case that had me running in circles in downtown Los Angeles under that filthy brown haze they call air out there. I remembered another broken-down air conditioner on the Santa Monica freeway; it made my neck hairs rise. For a moment I had that California smell in my nostrils all over again. *Just a synaptic misfiring in the brain,* I told myself, *the déjà vu effect of a road-weary brain.*

The country air wafting outside my car was scrubbed clean by the stands of loblolly pine, cedar, and black maple. The sloping hills like green waves in the distance were absent the chrome and steel high rises of the big city. It was nothing like my time in Los Angeles, dealing with a hopeless case beneath the "murder winds" of the Santa Ana that never stopped blowing for three days, and kept the coyotes in the hills baying all night.

Raina offered little conversation throughout the trip so in the end we barely spoke, except for my periodic announcements of food, gas, or piss stops. I asked her why she never called her parents and she said her cell phone was stolen on Biscayne Boulevard.

"What were you doing on Biscayne?" I asked.

"What did you say?" She looked at me blankly.

By then she was resigned to coming home and wasn't going to give me any trouble about it. Whatever demons drove her from her safe middle-class life to a rundown motel and drugs were her business. I'm no Dr. Phil and the last time I saw him on television I threw my shoe at him. That annoyed Micah, who seemed to consider her Texas shrink a cross between Deepak Chopra and her hero Siggie Freud.

"Idiot, why'd you do that?"

"He used the word issues *twice in one sentence."*

As we wound through West Virginia, I realized that the air in the car was rank with the coppery smell of blood. Her period had come upon her and she'd soiled herself. I pulled off the interstate at a Motel 6, checked into a room, and pointed her toward the shower and told her to wash herself. I thought she was going to fight me. She stood in front of the mirror holding her towel across her breasts and tried to smooth out the tangles in her hair with the other hand. I watched her arm drop and she stood there staring at herself. Her face wrinkled and I thought for a second she was going to cry. Instead, she spat a gob of phlegm at her image.

I told her I was going to get us some sandwiches to eat. I had seen a sign for an Applebee's a few miles back. I was afraid to leave her alone, however, so I ended up taking her with me. At the restaurant she couldn't eat anything I ordered for her. I caught a cook and a waiter smirking at me through the food transom. It didn't look right, I knew – a middle-aged man and a disheveled blonde girl who looked half-stoned. I drank my coffee and we left.

At three o'clock in the morning, she awoke screaming from a nightmare. The gown she kept from the hospital was soaking wet and her eyes were wild. I had to slap her face twice to make her stop clawing at me and screaming. I decided to hit the road right then and hoped that her family could find out what her problem was. I could see none of the classic signs of abuse in Raina's situation: parents who clearly loved each other, sisters who loved her, a future of promise – sometimes I would quibble with Micah about this very thing. People, I told her, almost never add up to the sum of their parts. As a homicide cop in Cleveland, I saw human nature at its vilest, whereas Micah always found her answers in books. I don't know what makes people tick or why people do what they do to one another. Some runaways I've fetched home tended to be hardened after a few weeks on the road because it either toughens them up or it sends them running home in a hurry. Sometimes I go get them for a fee.

The eyes she cast over me when I met her in the

Dade County psych ward were dulled. *Drugs*, I figured. At the motel, when I was helping to clean her up, I saw the bruises when she pulled her shorts down over her hips. I was prepared for it because the supervisory nurse told me she had been thumped around. I wasn't prepared for the sight of her beaten breasts and scored backside, much of her exposed flesh was livid, purpled or mauve with dark rosettes of past beatings – deep bruises. The worst, however, were bite marks on her inner thighs, some healed and yellowing beneath the broken skin. Her body was a grotesque study in colors and splotches. Maybe that was when I should have knocked off the silent shit and demanded to know what had happened to her. That's a regret I'll have to carry.

When I pushed her into the shower, she turned to snarl at me like an animal, her eyes feral, hot with anger, and the look accentuated her prominent cheekbones. She scowled when she noticed me looking at a trickle of blood worming its way down her thigh. She cupped one of her breasts where teeth marks circled the areola, touched the rose-tipped nipple and began to sob. I put the washrag in her hand and gently closed her fingers around it and then backed away. I left the glass door open and water sprayed across the carpet. When she came out of the shower, she was calm again, but we never exchanged another word until we crossed the state line into Ohio.

~ ~ ~

A month after I returned her, her father emailed me. I was coming back from breakfast at Tico's Place across the street. He had sent me the check for the remainder of my bill for finding his daughter and said he was sorry he was so late with this payment because funeral arrangements for Raina's grandmother last month had taken up all his time. Would I please resume our prior arrangement...?

What the hell?

I looked at the date again. I had just returned from Phoenix the day before, back to my routine skip-tracing work for a local bondsman. I had not been back long enough to keep up with local news. I had to root for the right *Star Beacon* issue from the stacks piled on chairs: *SCHOLARSHIP STUDENT MISSING FROM CAFARO HOUSE*

DORM. The article mentioned that Raina Toivela had been enrolled for fall classes at the prestigious music school, but had not attended classes in a week and her advisor had called her parents when she failed to show up for recitals. She was then reported missing officially. The Youngstown police were taking over the investigation from the campus authorities. It did not mention that Raina had run off before this.

I had a flashback of her strangled sobs coming from the bed in the motel room in Georgia. A pang of shame swept across my mind like drifting cobwebs at the memory of the dirt-encrusted fingernails, her body's welts and bruises. Gurgling noises under the covers like someone drowning in a sea at night. That's when she said the word *saraband*. Very softly but distinctly. Just that: *saraband*. I asked her what it meant, but she only looked at me with those strange blue eyes and kept silent. I thought it was a girl's name, maybe one of her sisters. When I got home, I looked the word up in Micah's dictionary. It said: *a stately court dance from the eighteenth century in "slow triple time."*

~ ~ ~

I don't like runaways. Private investigations don't make much money from them as a rule, and I have grown weary of dickering with parents, fathers usually, about my fees for returning their wandering, sullen children. Besides, you can get a reputation as a one-trick pony in this business. Trouble is, with computer IP addresses and 4G LTE smartphones nowadays, anybody can do skip-tracing work, check a credit rating, find out where your boyfriend/girlfriend's working, how much you owe your doctor, who holds the mortgage on your house, and a thousand other personal kinds of information you used to have to dig out with shoe leather. There will be an app for wiping your ass someday. I get calls from worried parents all over the state, not owing to any particular finesse but just because my office is located at a crossroads of the Midwest. We're a magnet for runaway teens. Kids can get lost for a while, do some drugs, hang out on the Strip, and maybe make a little pocket money. Some sell themselves as entrepreneurs or at the end of a tether held by some biker thug.

The chamber of commerce turns a blind eye to the prostitution. It's not as wide open as it used to be in the days when Millimaki was chief of police and high-profile johns used to leave envelopes for him at the substation – no police department gives prostitution a priority bust. We would do the occasional vice targets off Little Minnesota where the kids sell themselves and fulfill the "zero tolerance for prostitution" sound bite of the big shots who run the town, but that was just official lingo repackaged from the annual station-house directive issued to the local citizenry. All strictly for local consumption. Complaining about vice when you put three million people through this sausage grinder of a town in summer means you have to take the bad with the dollars.

Fact is, Tico serves a few cops and cops talk as well as drink. That chamber of commerce hype doesn't apply to businessmen and wise guys up from Youngstown, or gamblers and drunks stumbling out of the Windward Lounge at two in the morning. When I worked a short stint at Vice for the county sheriff's (this was just after I left Cleveland PD), I used to spend half the night rousting local businessmen and fifteen-year-olds of both genders blowing them in parked cars.

"That don't mean shit," said Tico. "Just so long as dey ain't so many chicken hawks or fudgepackers hangin' about. Bad for the town's image, man."

In high summer there are too many teenagers out there, too many runaways from the dying coal towns of West Virginia and Pennsylvania. Too many closed factories in Youngstown and Sandusky, Toledo, north as far as Detroit. Some wind up calling the Strip home. Most leave at the end of the season. A few stay lost for good. There's a methane probe that we used to keep handy for the occasional death-by-misadventure or the infrequent murder. The Lake, as locals have always called it, caters to families, although there have been two serious riots in my time here, and its fine reputation is exaggerated. The local windbags love to preach family values and moral rectitude like the good citizens they are, but let me tell you, they know to a decimal point by Labor Day any given day where the town's financial thermometer stands.

The crap and corruption finally got to me and I gave it up for private work. Whether I want it or not, much of my business comes from runaways. It's simple economics: if they're here, I can find them; if not, I won't make a dime, and I'll spend my time chasing leads to nowhere and back.

There were three messages to call Paul Toivela on my machine. The following day he caught me in the office; it was also our wedding anniversary. Micah had long since walked with her lawyer in tow. I was hoping she would give me a call for *auld lang syne*. I don't brood, as a rule, but I don't see the harm in remembering, either. They say memory is only a defense mechanism, something which blunts self-awareness – an unnecessary emotion in the jungle. I get bad feelings about phone calls in late afternoon. They usually mean someone has thought too long about something and couldn't make the decision before then and can't wait until tomorrow. It was close to five o'clock and I was hungry. I usually have supper at Tico's Place unless I'm working the phones or staking out some dive or lover's lane.

Toivela's voice sounded itchy with impatience, one of those who expect you to be right there when they call you. My blood sugar plummeted.

"I want you to find my daughter, Mister Haftmann."

"I'm taking care of some old business, but I'll call you back in an hour or two. Better if I call you in the morning."

"I'll pay any amount you ask – that is, within reason. I'm not a rich man, and I'll expect results. She's probably in the Miami area – "

"Your daughter is a few months short of being a legal adult, sir. She won't need anyone's permission – "

"You're obviously not a parent are you?"

I was losing sympathy by the second. "No, sir, I am not."

"Then you don't understand. You can't possibly understand what her mother and I are going through right now."

"I'm sure you're in great distress, Mister Toivela, but I can give you the names of some reliable agencies in Dade or Broward County, and they'll be happy – "

"I want to blame someone. Myself, anyone, but I don't understand it at all. Her mother and I love her! Her sisters worship the ground she walks on. Why is this happening to us?"

"I don't have the answer to that."

"She was a wreck when you brought her home in August. You saw my sweet little girl. You saw what she looked like – " Sighs like bubbles popping punctuated his words. "She seemed so happy to be herself again. Christ, Oh Christ – " A gulp and then a chest-racking sob. Click.

Fuckola.

He would call me back, I knew. I hoped he would take my advice and call a Miami operative. I was sorry for him, but getting sucker-punched by sentimentality has done me no good. Too many years as a cop listening to the sordid catastrophes of people's lives mean there's a shortfall of compassion in my character that I can't change. My mood turned sour. Part of me hoped that it would go no further, and Toivela would not foist his grief or guilt onto me; let him go off into some dark corner of his own mind and brood about the whys and wherefores.

The numbers on the check in the mail changed all that. It was for nineteen hundred dollars, a retainer, and the letterhead paper with Paul Toivela's name in cobalt blue at the top expressed a contractual arrangement between us, setting forth the conditions under which I might consider myself his employee until such time "as the association should be terminated by the party of the first part." I was the party of the second part, but unlike my ex-wife, I take cold comfort in the language of the law.

There was no denying one thing, however. I was about to whore myself again for money and scruples be damned. Micah and her tax lawyer had cleaned me out. I was bleeding money at every orifice and I needed to stop the hemorrhage. The extra jack after some overdue bills got paid wouldn't hurt, and my office needed a makeover. I had a computer riddled with Trojan viruses, a car that was a piece-of-shit, held together with duct tape and the magic of my trusty mechanic, a dour saint whose face took on an anguished look the last time I asked for a tow to his shop.

Besides, South Florida in December isn't exactly hard duty, come right down to it. I didn't mind asking a few questions, shaking a few doorknobs for a week or so to justify the check. *Doing it under a bright sky in a balmy eighty degrees could be managed,* I thought.

I looked outside the office window and dispelled the last doubt: typical Northern Ohio midafternoon in early winter with a pewter sky shifting by the minute to blue-black.

Catch a few rays, lie on the beach, listen to the surf ... why the hell not?

I keep Zeiss binoculars close by to watch over the lake when I'm bored. I saw a few hardy gulls oblivious to the bone-aching cold, wheel and dive over a patch of slate water where a couple of ice fishermen had dug their holes in the dun-colored ice and pitched flimsy tents. Perch and Coho salmon frozen solid as bricks lay a few yards from the holes. Close to shore, I zoomed in on one fisherman bundled up like the Michelin Tire Man. He tossed a barracuda-shaped pike onto the ice where it flopped about, fighting for oxygen and arcing its back. It was too far for my one good eye even with German-engineered field glasses, but I knew it would be dark green against the snow with gold and candy apple-red flakes dotting its back, razor teeth opening and closing in a gaping jaw. When I next looked, the fish gave a few more sporadic shudders and lay still.

Lacy sweat-streaks of condensation marred my windows and showed dirt from late-autumn gales. I read the thermometer, barely nudging ten degrees, and made up my mind. Existentialists must choose, so I was on the phone booking a flight out of Cleveland

Hopkins.

Afterward, I called Toivela and told him he was only renting a private investigator, not buying a miracle worker. I told him I carry no gun or weapon of any kind, a useful lie. I'm legally barred from owning one, but that's as enforceable as blocking a thirteen-year old from a porno site. I said that, if I found that there was personal danger involved, I would back off immediately and report what I knew to the local authorities.

"The odds aren't that good I'll find her soon, Mister Toivela," I said.

"Get whatever information you can," he replied. "Her mother and I would be grateful to know she's — she's been seen and that she's all right."

"All right?" I thought. *Jesus Christ on a pogo stick.* A pretty female without money and a masochistic bent on top of a drug habit in a wide-open city is not ever going to be all right.

"I'll do my best," I said.

I told him I'd be over in an hour to make arrangements before leaving town. I needed some new information about Raina since the time I had dropped her off. Only the family would have the answers to my questions about her second vamoosing. The last thing I said to Paul Toivela was about my standard contract and the retainer fee for services to be rendered. I heard silence as he pondered my repudiating his contract in favor of mine.

"Well, if it must be," he said with a sudden archness of tone, the father replaced by the accountant.

I had a couple photos of Raina still in my files. I took them out and began to gather some equipment and clothing for surveillance for the trip south. Years ago when I was first starting out as a private investigator, I blew half my cop pension on fancy stuff like shotgun directional mics, pinhole cameras, digital voice recorders, and all kinds of gee-whiz bugging devices. I keep most of it in a couple cardboard boxes in my closet and rarely take any of it with me.

I looked outside at the icicles hanging from my low office roof and a wisp of old memory twitched somewhere in my brain. When I was a boy, I used to walk out on Lake Erie where the ice got thin as window glass. Once I looked through at a speck between my legs and watched it get bigger. It was a fat golden red carp, and it had chosen that instant to float to the surface. Fascinated, I watched its fat rubber lips make kissing motions in the mint-green waters beneath my boots. Mindless of my boot soles inches from its head, it seemed like an ancient visitor, something from another world. A memory was scratching away but couldn't break the surface. *What is it*, I thought? A premonition? An old cop's phantom reflex maybe. I didn't know, but I didn't like the sour taste in my mouth.

~ ~ ~

I still had a cop's nose and the olfactory memory that goes with it: the smell of her unwashed body and the rancid odor of menses. I figured she was free-basing. Corpses of drug abusers I had known in my homicide days carried a lingering scent to the skin. Like the whores Jack and I used to bust on Broadway on Cleveland's west side; they had that same citrusy odor of cheap perfume, held the same stuporous look of zombies. Dope fiends in the throes of "kibbles-and-bits" time can get vicious. Jack and I held one of these thrashers down on the shitty brown rug of his living room when I heard the sound of strangled sobs coming from a bedroom. It turned out to be his three-year-old girl. The junkie did a tracheotomy on her throat with a serrated kitchen knife because he thought his little girl had accidentally put a piece of rock in her mouth and he was determined to fetch it.

I wondered what was in Raina Toivela's mind. Like all my other cases, when the check is in the bank, I mentally quit the case. My losing Micah was canceling everything else out. Memories of our past became open sores. Sometimes I'd awaken in the middle of the night talking to her as if she were a phantom pain from a missing limb. Raina and I had become silent driving companions from different generations in a car heading north. *That's all,* I thought, but one last flicker of my flyblown memory came back as I was packing up. On the express lane of 271 past the east suburbs of Cleveland, as we were barreling into the teeth of a sudden lake-effect thunderstorm with gale force winds and zero visibility, a mosaic of lightning erupted across the horizon and left ghostly shadows in the passing landscape. I watched the road disappear in a whiteout sheet of rain and had to concentrate my vision even harder, the muscles around my bad eye straining so hard I thought my eyeball was going to pop out of my skull.

"Saraband," she said again in that quiet way, as if she had discovered some essential truth about life. I was too focused on the road and the storm sweeping us into a white oblivion, and so I didn't saying anything.

Then the memory came back clear: she looked at me and turned on a smile that melted all the irritation between us of the last two days. She was truly a stunning young woman, unselfconscious of her physical beauty in a way that few girls are in this wretched hook-up culture. Did I smile back or was I too obsessed by my poor vision and the poor road conditions? I soon turned off the ramp at Jefferson-on-the-Lake. *Home, sweet hell. Would it have made any difference,* I wondered, *if I had asked her what she meant by that word?*

I had the one clue, not much else. The inpatient form I had asked the nurse to show me when I retrieved her from the Dade MetroHealth psychiatric unit. The name *Toni DeCamillo*, in fat, schoolgirl handwriting was written on an index card given to me by a psychiatric nurse who answered the few questions I had about Raina's condition and how she got there. The nurse made me show her my private investigator's license and Paul Toivela's letter of authorization. Nothing else, just that loopy signature and a Coconut Grove address that I copied in my notebook. I figured right off the name had to be fake.

The veteran nurse I had spoken to down there said that the reasons for running away seemed to get less serious with each passing year. It didn't take an abusive father or molesting uncle, contrary to popular belief, nor did it take much at all nowadays to send young girls off to Miami or Los Angeles. She mentioned Raina's bruises with clinical disinterest, even the bite marks around the genitalia. I said to her that I didn't know why Raina Toivela had run off.

"They go for their own reasons," she said. "What's strange is they'll stay with someone who abuses them rather than return home to someone who never abused them." I told her about Raina's family and her home environment.

"Some rabbits," she sighed, "don't need reasons to run."

She handed me several patient-release forms to sign. I shrugged but said nothing. Was it in Micah's blood too, I wondered. Micah was sleek as an otter, every hair in place, as lithe as a cat stretching, not to mention aggressive as a badger in a court of law – no rabbit blood there.

Was I, however, imprisoned in my own hop? Doing

what I did for little money and not much in the way of thanks or good in the long run? No particular animal came to mind when I thought of myself, but I knew it would be something nocturnal and missing the social graces that would get it invitations to hang out in burrows for any clan get-togethers.

CHAPTER 2

I caught the redeye out of Cleveland; the big silver bird was delayed an hour for de-icing. Watching the steam billow from the wings, I tried to stomp out images of the plane stalling in flight and plummeting to the ground in a death spiral. High in the air over the frozen checkerboard of farmland, I remembered when Raina had called out what I first thought was a girl's name, half-heard, its soft sibilance like a beckoning from ancient mists.

A thin whistle indicated the oxygen valve overhead was turned on full, and I cracked my jaws to unblock the pressure in my ears. There was nothing to see outside the smeared window but blackness interrupted by ragged shreds of cirrus whipping past, reminding me of torn bed sheets. Occasionally the cabin lights winked on and off as we hit turbulence, the plane bucking as it crashed into mountains of crazy air.

To be so helpless in a hollowed sheet of aluminum tubing has the opposite of a soothing effect on me. *"Associational denial,"* Micah called it. I have a bad memory of one case and anything that sounds like a pipe hissing takes me back there. Back to the containment building, and the broken steam valves in the water loop on that summer day years ago. Back to Lonnie Dale Nelson, the man who lifted all two hundred-twenty pounds of me, put a massive hand over my face and dug his thumb into my left eye socket until white-hot pain brought a roar from my throat. I still hear it in my dreams.

A hand was shaking my shoulder, nudging me awake. I came to and saw the look in the flight steward's eyes. I must have dozed off. I knew, without turning around, the eyes of the other nearby passengers would be boring holes in me, wondering about the kook making strange noises.

Great, I thought. In a jittery post-Nine-Eleven world, I have to be the one to act like an asshole on an airplane. Micah used to shake me awake in the early hours of the morning like that, so I knew I was moaning in my dream. I grabbed a *Skymall* magazine in the holder in front of me and for the next twenty minutes became avidly interested in packable wine glasses.

The reverse thrust of the engines jolted me back to reality. The plane angled its nose toward the concourse and I heard the *whump* of the plane made on its scissor lift. The same flight attendant looked weary behind her lusterless eyes. She issued dozens of monotone farewells to the deplaning passengers with minty breath, varying the formula once or twice. She didn't look at me, however.

The concourse was in plastic with the obligatory pastel colors and tones. *Welcome to art deco Miami. No fumar in el aeropuerto, por favor*. Through plate glass, I saw Hispanic and Haitian males leaning against their liveried taxis advertising various products and dot-com businesses that waited beyond the baggage area in search of fares. I slung my bag over my shoulder, tripped the beam that opened the sliding glass doors and walked into warm nighttime air; not only warm but moist. The smell of bougainvillea and diesel fuel made me sneeze. I found a car rental and aimed a slightly dinged, gray Camry toward Coconut Grove. Old habits, like aging men, die hard.

I found a Day's Inn on West Flagler and looked over a city map of Greater Miami before bunking down for a few hours.

~ ~ ~

The desk clerk woke me at seven as I had requested.

The air from the motel parking lot was ripe from uncollected garbage in bags lining the street. I was in northwest Miami, close to Liberty City, far from the salty tang of Miami Beach. The radio jock intoned that the air was a nippy fifty-five degrees and the water temperature off Miami Beach only a couple degrees higher, while the natives in the coffee shop were talking of the possibility of frost tonight and the citrus crop peril. I ate *huevos rancheros* doused with hot sauce and drank a pot of black coffee. My hands itched for a cigarette, another old habit that died hard, and left grudgingly.

I would bask in the rolling surf later; one of Haftmann's rules is to earn the paycheck first.

My lead was at home. Toni DeCamillo turned out to be a real name. I got her on the third try, ninth ring and, better yet, heard her say she was *"happy"* to talk to me about Raina Toivela. She sounded raspy from being awakened, but agreed to meet me at her place.

She lived in one of those Spanish-Mediterranean apartment complexes off the Palmetto Expressway. Most of the colors strove for a white and baked-earth-tone effect. *A. DeCamillo* was scrawled on the white card below her apartment number in the foyer. *Toni, from Antonia*, I guessed.

I buzzed and heard a woman's voice. She said to go through and knock on her door, the third on the left side.

Toni was about thirty – big-boned, fleshy – with a square jaw that just missed being mannish but looked at me from a pair of striking amber eyes like the color of tea. There was a prison pallor to her skin and a few tiny craters of old acne scars. Blonde hair from a bottle that delivered okay on the yellow part but was losing the battle against the dark roots at her crown. I found her claims of professional work at odds with the

25

unkempt place and time of day. She was a single mother, she said, working for an outfit that designed offices, and explained that she worked on commission, although at the moment, the season was in a slack period. I told her I knew all about slack periods.

She prattled with words like *feng shui* and *ergonomics*, and I knew I was dealing with a bullshitter. She plucked at the front of her bathrobe – a frayed orange terry cloth cinched with a leather thong that might once have been a man's belt. Her small hands and bare feet belied her physique. She stopped tugging at the robe long enough to dart hands into the pockets and fish out a pack of cigarettes.

The brand was Pyramid. I'm impressed by any woman smoking unfiltered cigarettes nowadays. She offered me one. I declined, saying I'd live vicariously through her.

"Real funny," she said in a tone that said it wasn't.

She said she should have family like that woman in Jacksonville whose lawyers were suing R. J. Reynolds – or Liggett, was it? "I'd never live to collect it probably," she said, and her amber eyes deepened a shade. I flashed to Micah's bio of Stalin; he'd had yellow eyes and a mottled complexion too. She said it like *prolly* and I placed her accent.

The room was small and littered with newspapers and trays of TV dinners. The front of her robe was crusted from a purple wine stain. I'd had plenty of time to cut my eyes around the room but saw no obvious evidence of a male's presence. She showed me to a Naugahyde chair in a mustard color. The armrests were dotted with bullet holes of past cigarette burns.

Suspects use a stream of patter to distract. I asked her to go back over something she had said just to see if her story changed slightly. She changed a few tiny details about time and day, as if a little uncertainty were normal to recollection. That's often true but even a rusty homicide cop like me rings those three cherries: you have a liar in front of you. Something in her tone, the pitch of voice, was telling me she had this canned ham of a yarn waiting for me when I showed at the door despite the dishabille.

She stopped her chatter and stared at me. "How come one eye looks different?"

"I got into a fight," I said.

She snorted. "Come on, man, that don't change your eye color. Who you tryin' to kid?"

Pure Bronx honk. Toni from *New Yawk* had come a long ways south.

She sensed I was on to her. Too late for nicey-nicey, but we played on anyway. She crossed her legs and I held my gaze on her face instead of dropping it to the exposed backs of her thighs where she expected. She fumbled with the front of her robe where a whole lot of cleavage was playing peek-a-boo with me.

I kept nodding my head, playing it easy, scratching away into my notepad, my prop. The whiff of mendacity grew to a stench like somebody's fart at a formal dinner party. I would check her out, if I ever got the chance to cultivate a connection with a well-placed cop. *This,* I thought while doodling nonsense, *was not how a citizen of Florida explains to a citizen from Ohio how a young lady, also from Ohio, got herself checked into the county boobie hatch.*

DeCamillo said that Raina had spent a couple nights at her place when she, Raina, first arrived in the Grove.

Still playing Captain Obvious, I asked: "Why, Miss DeCamillo, would you take in a stranger, a girl with a troubled past, into your home?"

"I dunno, ya know? Like, I just felt sorry for her, you know? She was panhandling in front of the apartment, and I thought she could use a meal, poor kid. She looked like she needed a friend." She added a little grimace for effect.

Old big-hearted Toni from the Bronx. I wasn't buying.

"She said she was from Lantana at first," Toni said. "That's all I remember."

Lantana was where the *National Enquirer* was published. Rednecks, geriatric Jews from Manhattan, snowbirds from the Midwest – everybody's from somewhere else in this state. She let more cleavage out, maybe to enhance the fib. The taut skin at the tops of her breasts suggested pneumatic enhancing. I imagined it would feel like touching a dolphin's back.

I told her why I was looking for Raina. Toni shrugged her shoulders, as if to imply *What's that got to do with me?* She played with the front of her robe some more – enough to cause a slight commotion behind the cloth. I decided my best tactic just then was money, so I mentioned I was able to provide "assistance" to anyone who could help with my investigation. She shrugged again and asked how much.

"Two hundred if the information is good," I said. "Five hundred if it leads me to her. One hundred right now for whatever you know that I don't."

She cocked her head and gave me a sideways look. "How do I know what you know?" she asked.

"Talk first, Miss DeCamillo. Then we'll see. I'm sure the family would expect me to express their gratitude," I said. I winked at her. "Besides I can always goose the bill."

I waited while she fired up a third Pyramid and took a long drag, assessing me. She crossed her legs again and checked to see if I followed the movement.

The longer she talked, the more familiar it started

to seem from countless interrogation rooms in my past – voices raspy from fear or, like Toni's, the committed cigarette fiend's overlaid with something else. Sometimes the whine of women who feel life has habitually given them the short end of the stick. Cops can play that card for all it's worth and crack them like eggs. Toni DeCamillo, however, was made of tougher stuff.

Right then, the fingers of blame were pointing directly at her and we both knew she wanted them pointed elsewhere. The Good Samaritan story was as weak as rooster soup. There had been cops asking questions before in her life, I was sure, and I smiled as I wrote the words *why lie to me?* underscoring it several times. The rest of my note-taking comprised variations on *Mary had a little lamb*, sprinkled with obscenities and stick figures.

I wrote down a couple more lines of gibberish and smiled at her, the hick p.i. from Ohio. There would be time for another interrogation later.

She offered me coffee, and I accepted. I followed her into a kitchen designed for the vertically challenged. The laminate flooring was scratched and speckled with crumbs. The sink, like the rest of the place, was overrun with clutter: dirty dishes stacked on every flat surface, a garbage can in the corner needed emptying. No feminine bric-a-brac near the splashguard behind the sinks. In this climate, it amounted to a cockroach feeding frenzy.

"It's just decaf," she said over her shoulder. "That OK?"

"That's great," I said. "I prefer decaf." *Liquid filth* was what I thought because I take my coffee seriously.

She was talking about her life and job, the non sequiturs and evasions piling up faster, little lies on top of little lies. She paused long enough to blow twin streams of smoke through her nostrils. Our conversation moved on to the great themes of her life. She affected a girlishness belied by her dirty sensuality and big-boned physique. I tossed in the noncommittal grunt to keep her going. How much of this simpering was designed to keep me off balance I couldn't tell. Some people can't tell the truth even when no reason exists to lie. If you listen to enough muttheaded lies, you do lose faith in humanity's aptitude for truth-telling. I kept playing the game, however; this was still act one and it was a long way from getting me closer to Raina Toivela.

The mug was some kind of souvenir from Key West, and I looked for a place to set it on the Formica table, littered with nylons and old newspapers. The floor around it was strewn with discarded grocery bags and glasses. A chipped mug, the match to mine, was lying near my shoe. A large beige futon, newer than the furniture we'd sat on, rested against the opposite wall in its factory cellophane. "I bought that for Raina," she said and waited for a compliment.

One lie too many. "You expected her to move in with you?" I asked.

"Uh, sure, why not? She was a good kid and she needed help."

"So you and she bonded over those two days she spent with you?"

"Yeah, so what?"

"Did you socialize together?"

"What do mean by that, you implying I'm a lez or something?"

"I mean, did you go out to lunch, go shopping together, visit museums – "

"Yeah, I took her with me sometimes."

She arched an eyebrow at me. It had been shaved off and redrawn a couple centimeters to extend the length.

"Where did you go, together?"

"Like, I don't know. We went out to eat a couple times, to the mall, like that."

"Did you do girl stuff," I asked, "like go clubbing, go to bars?"

While asking, I extracted one of Paul Toivela's crisp hundred dollar bills and my card with the motel address.

She eyed the bill, her eyes going green-gold like a cat's watching a sparrow with a bum wing.

"Yeah, couple of times," she said. "Have a seat," she said and pointed me back to my ugly-looking chair. A second ago, she was about to show me the door. Nothing like money to grease the social amenities.

Her nails were bitten down to the quick, crimson where the polish had not been worn off. I sipped the dregs of the bitter fauxcoffee and caught her staring at my bad eye, that arbiter of dubious veracity, as Micah used to call it. She mentioned bars and bistros I had never heard of.

"I like to drive up to West Palm after work once in a while," she said.

"What's in West Palm?" I asked, lost in the thread of where she was leading me.

"The Au Bar," DeCamillo said. "Sometimes I go to the Taboo in Palm Beach."

DeCamillo began spinning me a story of a girls' night out with Raina in tow. It bothered me on several levels. I'm an existentialist, as I've said, and that precludes kismet, karmas, intelligent design, or divine intervention. There is nothing to explain anything except what the physicists proved about strong and weak nucleic forces, electromagnetism, and good old gravity. Find a grand unified theory and they'll give you the Nobel Prize. Now that they've proved the Higgs boson exists, that subatomic quark that enables mass so that we don't go flying off into the vacuum of space, there's just the fact of coincidence. Angels or demons aren't going to show up to explain why anything exists.

She expected me to believe that she trotted a mentally unstable blonde ten years her junior, a girl she'd found out front of her place who could be an axe murderer for all she knew, into a swanky bar in Palm Beach. It was a wrong number, just as wrong as a slovenly ergonomics expert living in the cluttered filth of a cramped apartment.

The late Senator Kennedy's nephew, last I heard, was a successful socialite doctor in New England. Aside from my scrupulously honest ex-wife, I rarely dealt with lawyers of the caliber that were drawn by powerful people and old money. Most I knew could have come from firms called Trickem, Dickem, and Dumpem. I see a celebrity lawyer show up on TV now and then whenever an expert legal opinion from a white-shoe law firm is needed. My German grandmother had a name for a good old boy of this caliber, somebody who had the power and clout to make things happen the way they wanted: *gemutlische önkel*. Toni DeCamillo wasn't one, but she implied she knew some by dropping these trendy names and locales. That expensive villa on North Ocean Boulevard belonged to somebody else after the Kennedys, but money keeps the same green color and works the same way it always did.

Then she mentioned someplace where they served a really *fantasticó* veal parmigiana. The day after Raina showed up at Toni's apartment complex, they were already fast friends. They got to talking – *you know*, Toni said – the way girls do in a bar or a restaurant.

"We were like sisters," she said and smoothed the front of her robe over her mounds.

I wanted her to explain the transition from benefactor to big sister.

"How so?" I asked.

"Two gals enjoying themselves, ogling the good-looking men in the place, you know."

I smiled at her. "Maybe bashing the ones you knew?"

She looked at me and the smile slipped a notch. "I don't have men trouble," she said and leaned her body backward.

"Did Raina?"

"How the fu– how should I know?"

"Oh, I see," I said. "Just two girls out on a toot, knocking back a few."

"Yeah, like, so what?"

I didn't look up from my notes to see whether her lips were pursed, suspicious; the tone said it.

"Oh, that kind of sisterly stuff," I said. Me: dim bulb, typical male, not understanding. I hoped she was buying it because I needed something to take with me out her door and I had nothing.

I gave her a chummy smile.

She felt "sorry for her," DeCamillo did, because she herself knew what it was like to come to a strange city all alone. "It's tough on single girls down here. The places that do hire don't pay jack shit."

"Did you worry, Toni, that Raina might be just another hustler on the make?"

"No, no, Raina wasn't like that," Toni said. "She was real sweet."

I noted the past tense. I knew from tracking runaways how many girls worked their passage south down Interstates 75 and 95, the big arteries all the way from Panama City, the "Redneck Riviera," to the exclusive places along South Beach. Plenty of long-haul truckers will trade rides for sex. Using CB, they hand them off to one another at various truck stops en route. Some of the cruder males had nicknames for the veteran runaways. I had found a couple not long ago just from listening in on their conversations and decoding their smut-laced slang.

Raina had a birthmark an inch below her left earlobe just under her jawline. I noticed it when she brushed back hair from her face. Its port-wine color was prominent. Distinguishing features help in this line of work; big-city cops love gangbangers for their tattoos and all the helpful information they get stitched on their bodies. People rarely recall eyes, for some reason. I have seen many young faces with glazed eyes with irises swallowed up by the pupil staring out from under the white lights of Doc Harris' steel tables in the Jefferson mortuary. Female faces and settled flesh where the highest part of her body isn't the breasts but the pudenda.

While my dyed-blonde tipster blew more smoke around me and tried to blow it up my ass, I had a pang of anguish at one memory of that steel table back home: the soft gurgle of water that ran in tiny rivulets down either side of a child's stick-like legs. The patter of thick raindrops hit the windows and I thought of Raina at the piano, performing a Chopin etude, only to see that image disappear and reform. I saw her face bent over the lap of a trucker, lips engulfing a spade-shaped glans... then Micah's face replaced Raina's, and the trucker became the lawyer. *Fuck.* She loved to talk about the id-driven part of the psyche after sex. She told me aging was a product of emotional abuse. I figure that's why my face looks the way it does.

I came back to the monotone of Toni DeCamillo and her pug face. Compared to the classical beauty of Raina Toivela, she was an oompah-pah band. She was convinced I was buying her line. One Friday Raina asked Toni about finding work. She said she was thinking of dancing in a strip joint close to Overtown. Somebody on the street told her table dancers earned a couple hundred a night especially if they didn't mind dancing "for, you know, them, the moolies." Blacks, she meant, African-Americans – *them.*

Raina was afraid, according to DeCamillo, because the Latino bar owner was said to be pimping the girls on the side. Most of the girls were stoners, burnouts, not even getting paid anything except in drugs. An old scam: crack keeps them docile until they start looking too bad and a new girl is brought in and it starts all over.

We used to call them Strawberry Girls in Cleveland PD. One bad summer the Cuyahoga County Medical Examiner stacked them like cordwood. We were finding them in vacant lots mostly, skirts up, murdered, shot, and stabbed. Dead eyes full of the final moment's agony. The coroner wrote some of them off as overdoses – burst heart valves from the jolt of their last hit, no evidence of foul play. The D.A. used to scream at him to sign the goddamned things. Doc Harris in Jefferson, by contrast, was an ego trip, a man whose florid signature on a death certificate was a prosecuting attorney's nightmare according to my ex. That bad memory came back: the dead child on the steel table had been strangled to death by her mother's biker slob boyfriend. The livid bruises made me suck in my breath. Doc Harris called it a "neck compression event."

Raina had spoken to Toni of a Cuban pimp whose name might have been Angel or whose surname might have been Angelista. He ran some girls from taxicabs servicing Miami International. He hung out at the espresso shops in Little Havana and hooked the girls out of Eighth Street. He stopped her on the street when she was cadging quarters and asked her to dance in his club.

"Where is this club?"

"I dunno. Raina just, like, mentioned it the one time." *Goddamn.* I saw another lead go down a rabbit hole.

Toni pitched another story of Raina being stalked on the street the week before Toni found her outside her complex.

"Raina was real scared of this guy," she said. "She said he used to drive up to the curb wherever she was and try to get her into his car."

She described the man to me.

Poor Ohio farm girl terrified of leering spic pimp with gold tooth and a twenty creased in his palm. *Yeah, pull the other leg*, I thought, *the one with bells on it.*

I let her ramble, embellishing the story with more sordid details while I jotted away like a brain-dinged stooge.

I threw her a question: "Anybody else show an interest in her?"

"A boxer ... name of Emilio."

A long pause afterward; she was rethinking the wisdom of letting that out. Maybe a real slip there – something, anything.

She said he trained out of a gym right here in Coconut Grove. "Just one more question. Why Dade County?"

"Huh?" A scowl, perplexed.

"I mean it's quite a distance from here," I said. "Wasn't there anything closer like the local hospital? The Yellow Pages lists several detox centers in Coconut Grove alone. Why not use one of them?"

"A friend recommended the one in Dade to me."

"Who's the friend?"

"I forgot, some guy I met in a bar."

"I see. OK, thank you for your time. You have my card in case Raina turns up."

"Yeah, I'll call you if I see her," she said.

She flicked my business card with her fingernails, now showing impatience to see me go.

I stepped around a pile of newspapers and walked over to the wall where photos of a child graced an otherwise bare wall. Toni's place had nothing else to show she had put down roots. She picked at a thread on her robe as I pretended to admire the portraits of the little girl. They looked like a set, taken at the same time, like some package deal from J.C. Penney's. She said over my shoulder, "My little girl. She's at my neighbor's right now. Us working moms, we have a kind of babysitting co-op here."

I nodded back, all smile and teeth, and asked, "May I?"

"Sure, why not? Her name's Takiya." "Pretty name for a pretty girl." "That's what it means. 'Pretty One.'" I eased the photo gently from the wall.

"I hope you find Raina, Mister Hoffmann."

"Haftmann," I said. "It must be tough with a child to support.

How old is she?"

"She's, uh, gonna be six next month."

Her girl was in a crinoline party dress with bows and ribbons in the tight curls of her hair. I replaced the picture.

"The INS doesn't believe our marriage is legitimate. They sent her father back to Jamaica six months ago. I'm working two jobs to pay for a lawyer." Her voice trailed off, she hugged her robe about her, looking as demure as a stevedore.

"A very pretty little girl," I said. I left her standing there, arms akimbo, one large breast suddenly exposed right to the shell-pink areola, a curious smirk on her face.

She reminded me of Tico's favorite kind of barfly back home: a brassy, uncouth chain smoker with a little deep-dish cleavage to keep the drinks flowing along in the tide of male lust. "One good-looking' bitch with nice melons pays the light bill for a month," he liked to say and then he'd wink at his scowling wife wiping down tables.

Tico's wife Marta bore a resemblance to Toni; she'd been a doe-eyed beauty when he first introduced her to me and Micah, his chest puffed with pride, his bride fresh up from Guatemala. Tico had saved every dime he made picking grapes after climbing out of the garbage pit of Guate, as he called the capital. I thought again of Tico's harried wife just then, her hands busy in a work apron behind the bar of her husband's establishment. Chin wattles and triceps quivering like Jell-O as her meaty forearms washed down the tables.

Some associational logic set me to thinking of Micah as I walked down the foyer of Toni's apartment building, to our Florida vacation where her treachery was even then building to a crisis. I could see her in my mind's eye, walking the white sandy beaches of Naples, holding my hand, but distant, bored. I had thought a drive up the coast to Sanibel Island off Fort Myers would help us, open the lines of communication, as they say. I wanted to break through that brooding silence of hers.

"Micah, look," I said to her as a pelican hoisted itself aloft with a mighty flap into the cerulean blue air, "Marta."

Walking that beach in silence beside me, she looked at the bird struggling to get lift, a flicker of a smile passed her lips. Of course, that was also the day Micah's lawyer had sent her the letter, and I have always wondered whether it was me, not Marta, she was secretly laughing at.

My reverie ended outside in the bright sunshine. I decided to jot down the names of DeCamillo's apartment dwellers: McQuarrie, Thompson, Mahan, Strbac, Markwright, Siegel, Corapuna, Marovitz, and Cruz. Names are destinies we are forced to live out, according to some pop guru of my ex.

A tagger had sprayed some indecipherable gang logo in orange paint across the opposite complex. I could make out the triple crown of the Latin Kings.

The air was fuggy, liquid-warm, tainted with marshy odors and piercing fragrances, a slight breeze carried the tang of salt water. No matter how I turned my head, the sun's brilliance thrust knifelike spasms around my bad eye, making it weep. Along the near horizon I saw wide shafts of light strobing thick taupe clouds like in those religious pictures that show God's beneficence above us.

As I was getting into my Camry, I saw a gull pecking at something under the stairwell – a dead kitten with its forelegs stiff. It reminded me of the last house I shared with my mother before she dumped me on *her* mother. A bunch of white-trash hillbillies lived next door, and the old man of the brood used to toss any unwanted cats onto the second story roof for the hawks or owls to catch. I would listen to those kittens mewing for hours.

The gull was still a fledgling, mottled with brown speckles but big as an adult and as voracious in appetite. It canted its head to watch me, wondering if I were a competitor for its prize. Birds have tightly packed cones in their heads that make their vision so sharp. A bird's eyes take up most of the room in its skull. Try losing or damaging one; you'll find eyes become an interesting subject.

I drove to the address in Coconut Grove where this Emilio was supposed to be training. I found a gym sandwiched between a black and-white art deco bar and a theater where DeCamillo told me it would be. I wasn't confident this would pan out after the tall tales that preceded it, but DeCamillo's lies told me she had something to hide and her hesitation about this Emilio told me she wanted to walk back what she had told me about "the fighter guy" that seemed so enamored of Raina.

I parked the rental on Bird just off the South Dixie Highway.

Entering, I saw a fight card taped to the glass advertising Emilio Vasquez's bout as the main event in an eight-bout fight card. Emilio's fighting name, *El Lagarto*, was written in stylish italic script after his name and stitched diagonally across his sequined, knee-length silk trunks. He had those scalloped flaps like a Davy Crockett cap running along the seams. He wore his fight face in the photo, a cresting wave of black eyebrow bisected the smooth plane of his forehead.

He was in the ring when I entered. Some hangers-on were watching and shadowing his punches from ringside. His sparring partner didn't look happy to be in there. He was in his twenties and wore trunks cut from gray sweats. A short, stocky, older man with an old-fashioned crew cut held a stopwatch in one hand and the bottom rope with the other. He wore an expression that alternated between boredom and irritation.

"C'mon, you fuckin' tomato can! Punch! Move! Ain't paying you two hunnert a week to dance, Alshamoon."

Some of the men standing ringside added their support. One black with his Dodgers baseball cap backwards showered a running commentary of mocking abuse on Emilio's sparring partner. The ring action continued to show a one-sided affair as Emilio's flurry worked the head and jiggling belly of his adversary with mechanical precision. Emilio's heavy opponent glistened with sweat. The air was spongy and smelled of bodies and liniment. Fluorescent lights made the perspiration from the black fighter's rubbery fat rolls gleam as he twisted and turned to avoid Emilio's punches. Emilio's gloves made a staccato popping sound after every flurry. He danced backwards, spat out the mouthpiece and looked at his trainer.

"Manny, this punk ain't fightin' back. I tole you to get me a sparrin' partner I can work with. How'm I spose to work? This fuckin' guy, he ain't throwin' no punches."

The abused Alshamoon, a weary slit of smile creasing his face, lolled against the ropes, seemingly immune to the critique of his skills. He shook his head from side to side to shake off fat drops of sweat like rain. Tributaries of sweat on his back formed a Mississippi down the center of his spine.

"Alshamoon, you hopeless, man," said one of the young men at ringside; the bill of his cap had been spattered with sweat.

"Fuck you, you fuckin' motherfuckah," said Alshamoon. "I in here, you out there, nigger."

A different bystander said to someone in a loud voice: "Why you lyin' on me, cuz? I paid you that shit already."

I heard the word *punk* and then a scuffle erupted that sent metal folding chairs clattering and banging in all directions; some men scurried over to separate the combatants.

Emilio seemed oblivious to the action outside the ring. He danced around on his toes, twitched his neck. His ropy muscles bunched around his shoulders and chest; he had too much muscle mass for a cruiserweight. I wondered if his manager was bulking him up with steroids for the next weight class, the money rung of the fight ladder, heavyweight.

The trainer swung his head in disgust and said, "Aw right, take a break. Emilio, hit the bag."

Emilio, all eyes from ringside on him, danced across the ring and exited while one of the hangers-on stepped on a ring rope to let him through.

I walked over to Emilio who was swaggering in front of the timing bag, his hands loose at his sides, as if they were taped to his buttocks. "Hey, Emilio, I'd appreciate a word with you."

"Who the fuck you, bitch?"

He barely cut his eyes toward me and turned back to glower at the speed bag.

"I'm a private investigator. My name is Tom Haftmann. I'm looking for this girl."

I held out one of the photos Raina's father had given me the first time she ran away.

"Dunno her, man."

"She ran away from home a couple weeks ago."

"Where she live at, man?"

"Ohio."

"Thass up north, right?"

"Have you seen her?"

"Cute little bitch like that. Some nice pussy."

"Do you know her?"

"I was speaking, like, in general, you know? Makin' a observation, you might say."

"I'm looking for any information about her I can find."

"I don't know nothin' about nothin,' man. Like, fuck off. Hey, Manny, this motherfucker's botherin' me. Manny, *pendejo* motherfucker, where you at?"

"Tell me anything you remember about her," I said. "It'll stay between us."

"You fuck, you hard a hearing or what? I tole you I dunno the bitch, ain't never seen the bitch, en I don't give two fucks where the *puta* is, you got it?"

Several heads swiveled in our direction now. *Trouble*, I thought. If he wanted to grandstand for his crowd, this wouldn't be a good thing for me.

"*Ivate a la mierda*," Emilio spat out, building to a higher pitch. "I'm onna flush you like dat piece of shit in the ring."

I had him by three inches and maybe thirty pounds, not much of that muscle, which height and reach advantage means zero against a professional fighter. Before I could open my mouth to apologize for bothering him, he hit me. He whistled two punches at my head before I had my hands up. Both landed, one solid to the side of my face; the other glanced off my neck, but hit enough to stun me.

I threw a right hand with nothing on it, but he stepped aside easily and dropped me with one to the rib cage. I struggled to my knees, gagging. Somebody must have pulled him away because I was aware of the scuffling of feet. A blinding shock of pain in my head still had me groping on my hands and knees trying to find the center of gravity.

Then somebody, or a couple of men, jerked me to my feet and rushed me toward the door. I half-turned to see Emilio swagger off, laughing and punching air. Manny shook his head at his fighter in disgust. Emilio, now surrounded by admirers, was explaining what had happened – flexing for his homies.

I was back outside in the bright light and I knew what that kitten being savaged by the gull would have felt like; a pungent whiff of oleander, funeral flowers, on the breeze, pushed my brittle stomach over the edge. I made it to the street before a tan stream of my coffee splattered against the curb. Giddy, I remember thinking I didn't even see that second body shot.

A taxi drove past. I saw the bemused smile of the

driver watching me reel about on unsteady pins. Passersby on the street all of a sudden gave me a wide berth and parted like two sides of a single wave separated by a bow: *Morning drunk. Disgusting.*

I stood, holding my tender stomach. The scent of perfume wafted past. Micah's brand: *Obsession.* I was too empty to heave again, but the spasm sent tiny shockwaves of pain rippling across my forehead.

A few minutes and I felt well enough to lean against somebody's Trans Am at the curb; my legs were still wobbly but I had my bearings. I saw a patina of bruising on the side of my neck where his glove had scraped skin when I glanced at the sideview mirror. I spat a gob of blood out and sat down. In high school, I spent one summer roofing, and after a near fall from a roof with a steep pitch, one of the older guys told me to sit down. It's what you do after a scare.

I stopped carrying on the job a long time ago. I made it one of my rules. Guns are more a nuisance than anything to a private investigator. One of my colleagues in the business told me they're strictly for hot-dogging in front of prospective clients. When I got off the street to work homicide, I sold my Sig to a cop named Luke, and went back to a .38 because it was departmental regs to be strapped. I didn't need a gun then and I don't want one now. The temptation to draw one on that punk Emilio would have been too great. What I needed was a higher threshold of pain, maybe a left jab. Even an out-of-shape cop in uniform could have thrown Emilio over the hood of his patrol car, but as a private investigator in a state where I had no license, I had zilch-point-shit juice, and it was like being at the wrong end of the siege of Masada. My old street partner would have said it simpler: I was a shield somebody brought to a shit fight.

~ ~ ~

I staggered past the theater and crossed the street to a fern bar just opening for business. In a corner booth with a view, I took a chance and ordered coffee, and swallowed two aspirin I kept in my wallet.

I picked up a discarded paper. *Surveillance time. Get my wind back.*

The coffee kept coming and soured a stomach still queasy from Emilio's bodywork. I placed a five-dollar bill in front of me to keep the waiter from bumrushing me and waited. Waited for something to happen, something to click, something to get me moving in the right direction.

I read the local paper front to back again. The crossword was half-filled. A memory imprinted itself against my eyeball: Micah, gloriously naked, knees up, doing the crossword in bed. *What's another word for 'recalcitrant,' eight letters? Never mind, you wouldn't know...*

Her eyes lit with joy when she discovered her word had an embedded Latin word: *calyx* for "heel."

"I got it," she said, with a light kiss on my nose, "*stubborn.*" That was her word for me.

I read a brief piece about a woman who arrived at her home in Florida City and found an alligator chasing her West Highland terrier in the backyard; then it went into the house through a screen door, all twelve feet of it, and chased the woman through her house, nearly catching her in its pink, toothy grip when she fell and skidded across the kitchen tiles. A ranger from the Florida Park Service described it as a typical "nuisance" alligator, one which made its way along drainage ditches, eating small animals and family pets. They aren't afraid of people and thrive in canals along the highway and will stay put once they've been fed, he told the reporter. "Giving food to an alligator is its death sentence," said the ranger at the end of the piece.

The booth had a clear view of the gym. For two hours and nine minutes I watched people coming and going. Shoppers, women with every color hair, older men in flowery Hawaiian or pastel Polo shirts with pants cinched to their nipples; lean, sun bleached-kids on skateboards cruising past, tourists in bright clothes sporting their new carcinogenic tans; professionals and office workers jamming the streets. These people never did get that memo about the recession. Even their Gucci and Ralph Lauren shopping bags looked expensive.

A girl with slim legs wearing a kimono over a thong bikini stepped out of a black Mazda Spyder convertible, her skin the color of cinnamon except for the tan lines. I watched her adjust her bra strap in full view of the street and expose the fishbelly white undersides of breasts that rode high and had no bounce when she walked into one of the small shops lining the street. A man with a wrinkled face and greasy yellow-white hair pulled behind his ears in a ponytail walked by with two Colt 40s in his hand grinning like someone who had found the elixir of happiness.

Several young men of mixed race in their teens and early twenties, some toting duffel bags, entered the gym in singles and small groups. A few whites, mostly blacks with do-rags and a couple Hispanics with gothic-lettered tattoos at the nape. One sported a pigtail.

At 1:20 I saw the fat trainer walk out the door.

I left the bar and followed him from my side of the street. He walked west down Bird and soon the chic boutiques were replaced by fashionably poor bohemian quarters and then we were in a neighborhood most unfashionably rough. Manny looked neither left nor right but kept his pace unabated.

"The little hump can motor," I thought. He wore a

lavender *guayabera* that stretched taut over his huge belly. Worms of sweat jigged down the center of my back as the temperature rose steadily. I left my shades in the car, but there was little point in disguise now.

Squalid brown houses with blistered paint and porches missing rails inserted themselves between the coral and buff-pink most favored; realtors' signs lined both sides of the street. I was a long way from the tiled-roof villas on the city's perimeter. Coconut Grove's Chamber of Commerce would not have liked the word *slum* bandied about, I was sure, but I was sure I was entering one.

A liver-spotted pit bull barked from behind a steel fence. I was closer as we walked tandem from opposite sides of the street. Too late to go back for my wheels.

Short, stout arms pistoning like an emperor penguin, he suddenly turned into one of the shabbier houses. A broken Big Wheel with a low-rider profile and angled handlebars lay in the handkerchief-sized patch of chickweed lawn. Gangsta rap blasted from an alley nearby. I noted the number as I made my way past and then turned abruptly back in the direction I had come from.

My bad depth perception has changed even my stride nowadays. I have this loping scissor-walk, something between a jog and a trot, and it makes me as conspicuous as a guy wearing an Eskimo coat to Miami Beach. I didn't know how long he'd be inside. A white man can't walk around a black neighborhood without being eyeballed from a dozen different windows. Five more minutes, and I decided I'd go back for the car, sit on the house, and wait.

I was a few steps in that direction when he came out, his pudgy arms swinging from side to side. I did a Michigan-left just past him and cut him off so abruptly that his momentum doubled him over the hood of a nearby car. I was on him fast, my left hand rucked inside the material of his shirt and I had him pinned.

"Wha'th'fuck? You, shee-it!"

"I had to play punching bag for your El Lagarto, Manny," I said, "but I won't for you."

"I know you ain't a real cop so get the fuck outa here."

"What I am is a citizen who just got his ass kicked in your gym. That's criminal assault because it was done by a professional boxer. I can make trouble with your boxing commissioner. Get your fight show canceled."

His facial expression told me he considered that a bluff, which it was, but I hoped he'd choose to get me out of his hair and avoid any cops by cooperating. Gyms are ideal places to plant C.I.s and scope out the local riffraff or see who's new in town. One of boxing's most reliable matchmakers operates out of Cleveland and we used to check his stable from time to time to see who might have shown up dodging a felony warrant.

"Aw, leggo my shirt, man."

Beads of sweat dropped from his nose. It was like looking at a quadruple bypass waiting to happen. He said *fuck* about five more times, and I let go of him.

"Stop stalling and talk."

He eyed me. "Clappy-eyed *chulo*, I get your fuckin' balls cut off!"

I could thank Tico back home for a wide vocabulary in Latino curses. Without craning my neck about, I knew we were observed. No one in sight, but the air rippled with news that something was happening in the street – maybe some good old street justice.

I rabbit-chopped him with the edge of my hand along the right side of his jaw, and before he could recover, I had his shirtfront gripped so tight a couple buttons popped free.

I shoved a photo under his nose. "Look at her. Where did you see her?"

"Listen, you fuckin' with some serious people."

"Where ... did ... you ... see ... this ... girl?"

"I ain't never seen that fuckin' girl before this second!"

"The cops will be pleased to hear it because that's what I'm telling them. I guess they'll know what to do, the cops." He straightened his *guayabera* over his big stomach.

"Hey, what's this 'cops' shit? You dint say nothing about no crimes."

I slapped my forehead in mock dismay. "I must have forgotten to mention that. How about 'missing' as in 'missing, presumed dead'?"

"I tol' you. I ain't seen that girl before, man."

"Maybe an extra deuce tacked on for reckless endangerment," I said. "That'll mean your boy will be doing his fighting in the joint. You, Manny, I figure you're good for three to five, procuring. Her old man's a big-shot back home."

"Fu-uck you!"

"You'll be wearing these little plastic diapers for adults they give you when you can't control your sphincter after those badass boys in Raiford get done reaming you..."

His face was mottled. Rage and fear jostled for first place. He looked about to swing on me.

"Talk to me or to the cops," I said. "Would Emilio stand up for you, Manny? Or you think he'd cut a deal for himself?"

The flush that began at his neckline moved steadily upward toward his jaw and deepened his olive complexion to ochre. Then the dam burst.

"*Estoy hasta los cojones*! I'm fuckin' fed up babysittin' that shit! He's popping these *gringa* bitches faster than I can pull them off his *pito*. I tell Mister Pavelic, I tell everybody Emilio don' train, he chase pussy all day! I can' watch his sorry fuckin' ass every five minutes! Let go a me, you fuck."

Then I saw it: jailbird art in blue indigo, a thumb tattoo. Lowest rung of the human ladder, short eyes.

What would a multimillionaire developer be doing with a Cuban child molester?

I had read of Raymond Pavelic in the papers. Two columns' worth extolled his neighborhood renovation project on the west side of Coconut Grove. That would explain the near-deserted look of the streets; the other was a smarmy chez-Pavelic piece that worked up a lather over his being an avid sportsman, philanthropist, and all-around business genius. He bought struggling companies, retrofitted them for profit by downsizing employees. The article made me think of those corporate raiders of the eighties. The writer of this schmaltzy brew, somebody named R. Gersack, gushed in the final sentence that stuck in my head: *"Raymond Pavelic is this generation's Ted Turner, Bill Gates, and Donald Trump rolled into one."*

According to Gersack, he was currently building condos off the Dixie Highway, and the article concluded with a reference to the new marina Pavelic had been instrumental in promoting. All of this miracle-working in the face of Florida's burst housing bubble.

"What's Pavelic's interest in Emilio?" I asked.

He looked at me warily. "You some flake lookin' for trouble?"

I took a calculated guess. "Pavelic owns a piece of Emilio"

"He owns half this fuckin' state, man! You from fuckin' Mars?" "Close enough," I said. "Ohio."

Manny grew still and looked at me with something besides contempt. He was getting braver by the second. Raymond Pavelic was a name to conjure.

"I take it people don't mess with him," I said. "I assume he owns cops and judges, right?'

"Thass fuckin' right, loco. So you joost go runnin' your mouth off. What Emilio done to you is nothin', man. Any guy fucks with that man is gonna get his face changed in a big way, make you look like a *cagadera*."

Cagadera. I racked my brain for a second: *OK, got it, thanks to Tico, my poor man's Rosetta Stone. Cagadera, latrine.*

I was running out of time. "How did Emilio get to know this girl?"

"Man, you are wastin' my valuable time. Nobody give two shits about no runaway bitch."

This time a jab, same spot.

"Ow, you cocksuckin' fuckface!"

"Talk, hurry up. We're being watched," I said.

"That girl, she showed up one day at the gym with some guy knows Pavelic. She seen Emilio. Dick, meet cunt."

"This guy, he brings in girls?"

"For the fighters, sometimes. Little *concha* to take the edge off, you know? These guys aren't faggot priests."

"Who 'gave' her to Emilio?"

"Some dyke name a Toni."

"How much?"

"Fuck I know."

"How much?"

"Three hunnert, four hunnert."

"Toni gets a finder's fee for the girls, right?"

"So? She useta dance in some sambo dive off Calle Ocho."

"Who pays her?"

"Same guy I gotta check in every other day about

Emilio's progress. See if he behavin', sparrin' like he spose to."

Fuckola. The nape of my neck prickled. Several pairs of eyes were scoping us now.

"Looka me, asshole," Manny said. He had one ham fist balled and cocked.

Macho time, better book, I thought.

I let go of his torn shirt and loped off in the direction of my car. I was half-afraid Emilio's trainer was going to clock me from behind. I was relieved when I heard his spit-flecked torrent of Spanish curses.

Inside my vehicle, I burned rubber like a goofy teenager. I missed the back end of a dumpster by inches. A parking ticket was sucked off by wind action, but my foot on the pedal was light, the air was a little sweeter, and my teeth were grit for action. My heart was beating a tattoo thanks to the adrenalin jolt of my little dust-up back there.

It was a selfish thought, but it pleased me immensely. *I had a real case.*

~ ~ ~

I sped through the manicured streets of a neighborhood I didn't belong in, imagining a dozen blue-veined Caucasian hands reaching for their phones to report an unshaven galoot buzzing around their beautiful streets.

Maybe DeCamillo didn't expect the hospital to call Raina's father so soon. I debated half a second whether I should call the local heat, a friendly check-in from an out-of-town private investigator. Sometimes I could use my ex-homicide credentials to hook up with a cop who wouldn't mind sharing information about the local scene. Some departments just like it when you check in so they know who's on their turf. My partner Jack hated to be pissed on that way. When we worked dogwatch in Cleveland all those years ago, he'd roust p.i.'s sitting on houses where unfaithful spouses were, just to kill the boredom. Now I was the one getting looked over by suspicious cops.

I put that idea on hold for the time being and finally found a pay phone off Grand near a Duke & Duchess. Pay phones were as rare as canaries with teeth in cities nowadays. The directory gave me the *Coral Gables Courier*. I was patched around to several offices including maintenance and wound up talking to the voicemail for a man named Gersack in sports. The electronic voice said to leave a message. I said I'd like to meet him and that I had information. I gave the address of a Denny's on South Bayshore. I would be there, I told the machine, in two hours. "It's worth your while," I said and hoped he'd take the bait.

What the pudgy trainer had said about Pavelic made me think hard about my next step. "If you kick a tiger in the ass," Jack reminded me often enough, "you better have a plan for his teeth."

~ ~ ~

At two-o'clock I was sitting in a booth at Denny's opposite Roberta Gersack. An intense woman, she had a pretty oval face and a short hairdo, the kind that looked good on petite women, with graying bangs frosted at the tips. She wore trousers and a styled poplin blouse with those frogged closures on the front. I told her that my ex-wife once told me that women's buttons were on the wrong side because their servants used to dress them in the morning.

"What did your last servant die of?" she asked. "I'm busy today,

Mister Hoffmann." "Haftmann," I said.

"Whatever," she replied.

When I saw her approach, I immediately began to apologize for my male chauvinism in assuming Gersack was male. She brushed it off as not worth her time to listen to. I imagined many people had made that mistake before. She drilled me with a pair of light brown eyes the color of rust, contacts, I guessed.

The biography Micah was reading before the one on Stalin was about Josef Mengele, Angel of Death at Auschwitz. He used to dye eyeballs various colors like purple, yellow, and red in his laboratory. No particular reason. A Czech doctor who survived the camps because she was assigned to work for him once stumbled into a darkened room where hundreds of these eyeballs were pinned to a wall by their stalks. They glowed with an eerie phosphorescence because of the dyes Mengele had injected into the viscera. She said she thought at that very moment she was in hell.

Gersack had an honest face. "That teaser of a phone call," she began. "Look, I need to know what this is about, whoever you are."

She refused coffee with another wave of her hand and said she had a story over in Coral Gables and not much time to spare. She checked a thin silver and gold wristwatch. Being a private investigator means you get used to busy people treating you like the shit on their shoes.

"Another alligator get into a swimming pool?"

"What?"

What the hell, I might as well go for it, I thought.

"I want you to consider writing something else about Raymond Pavelic," I said.

She bristled. "Listen, if you're one of his lackeys, you can bite me. I did that piece as a favor to a colleague and that's all I'm going to do. Get somebody else to write it. I don't do hagiography."

She grabbed her notebook and stood up. I asked her what that word meant.

She looked at me as if I'd asked her to go dumpster diving for cherries jubilee. "You're serious."

"I want you to write another story about Pavelic but I want you to tell your readers the truth this time."

"You go tell that rich prick –"

"Just hear me out, please."

She stood glowering at me – all five-foot, three-inches of her.

"The truth? Who are you and what do you know about the truth of Raymond Pavelic?"

"I'm a stranger," I said. "I might be wrong, but I think one of Coconut Grove's leading citizens has the morals of a pimp."

"What's – what did you say your name is?"

"Haftmann."

A long, searching look, assessing. "I think you're lying, Haftmann. Goodbye."

I reached for her wrist.

"You let go, buddy-boy, or you'd better be prepared to pull back a bloody stump."

I let go. I said to her back, loud enough for the woman in the next booth to turn her head to look at me: "Raymond Pavelic employs a man who served time for child molestation."

That froze her in her tracks. She turned slowly and looked at me. "What the hell are you talking about?" Her eyes zeroed into mine, a cop's auger.

"Emilio Vasquez's trainer."

"I wrote the police beat column for the *Tribune* for five years," she said.

"Start talking." *Music to my ears.*

She sat, we talked. I liked her. I wanted her to like me back.

~ ~ ~

Lucky for me, she was no friend of Raymond A. Pavelic. She was the kind of listener who burned energy without moving. When she settled back into the booth opposite me, I got the impression of a force field taking over empty space. Compared to her stillness, a cigar-store Indian sizzled with kinetic energy.

She asked probing questions and didn't comment while I spoke.

What I had used to tease her over the phone had not piqued her interest, she said. I asked her why. While it wasn't common knowledge that Raymond Pavelic had secrets, those in the loop knew he was not kosher. "This might not be Louisiana, pal, where we send the governor to prison every five years, but we can recognize a turd when we're doing the backstroke in the toilet bowl with one." She said her story was a greasy favor somebody owed Pavelic and this somebody had the clout with the managing editor to get it published. She happened to be next in rotation and her boss was a good guy who had let her go home for her mother's funeral so... "So you wrote it," I said. I wasn't being sarcastic.

"So if I didn't, the next reporter in line would have had to do it," she snapped back.

I raised my hands in surrender, palms up. "Not judging you," I said.

"What's that look on your face for?"

"This look? It's my alienating women look," I replied.

"You're not married, are you?"

"You guessed."

"I *know*. There's a look married men have."

"That should please," I said. I was thinking of words like *undomesticated, virile, free.*

"It's from being alone too long," she said.

"Let's return to our friend Mister Pavelic, shall we?"

"Pavelic," she said, rolling his name and giving it a European spin, "is a very prominent citizen, and that, Mister Haftmann, is why I'm here with you sipping this iced tea that tastes like somebody wrung it through a dirty dishrag." I told her why I was here.

"Look," she said. "You come stumbling down here into the Grove looking for some girl from Iowa – oh, pardon me, Ohio. You get a pasting from a fighter owned by Pavelic before you've even been here twenty-four hours –"

"– and you smell a great story that will put your name in Pulitzer lights," I finished.

"I hate when people finish my sentences when I'm talking. I don't smell anything here but the odor of hurt male pride."

"Then why are you here?"

"I despise men like Pavelic. It has nothing to do with playing Nancy Drew or polishing apples to move up to a bigger market."

"Then help me, Bobbie – for your own reasons. I have contacts in South Florida but nobody with the kind of law-enforcement credentials around here I can use."

"Something tells me you're used to being out of your depth.

What do you need?"

"I need a cop."

"Dial nine-one-one."

"Not that badly," I said. "I need one who can discreetly type a few names into a couple of databases as a favor to a friend of a friend."

"Whoa there, cowboy. We're not friends. Not *yet* anyway, and I'm guessing that hypothetical computer you just mentioned you want requires passwords," she said.

"You would be right about that," I said.

"I told you I used to work the crime-beat section, right?"

I said: "Yes, I do believe you did."

"Then it's done." *Thenk yew, Jesus.*

~ ~ ~

I asked if she would help me, first off, by filling me in on how the land lies.

She knew this burg top to bottom, she said, the way a piranha knows a wounded capybara is in the water.

I discovered that some of the primo acreage of that land lay firmly in the grasp of Raymond Pavelic, entrepreneur, respected businessman, developer, community leader, sportsman, and fight buff. Even by Miami standards, he was no piker. The new marina – according to Bobbie "Don't call me Roberta" Gersack of Coconut Grove via Minneapolis-St. Paul – was worth about 80 million. And, she added, putting enough sugar in her iced tea to make the spoon stand up straight, he owned or controlled jai-alai courts, a piece of a greyhound track in Panama City, strip malls, condos, and had come within a hair of getting a casino license for some riverboat gambling venture. This was last May, she said, and he was putting that on the backburner until he had the right people greased. She figured Pavelic easily "networthed at around 800 million." Give or take a few dozen million more the IRS probably didn't know about via sheltering dodges for the *über*-rich.

"Lots of people down here are wealthy on paper, Haftmann," she said. "There are a million millionaires in the US. Most of them take advantage of the fact that the United States Tax Code is over twenty-thousand pages long, nearly all of those add-ons exist solely for dodging taxes or sheltering money."

I told her my own income usually qualified for that easy form, the one teenagers working at McDonald's could fill out with a fat crayon.

"Raymond Pavelic," she noted, "is one of the really rich ones." "Any rumors of drugs?" I asked.

"Always that, but nothing that anybody can prove. You can't go to a night club in South Florida without hearing how some rich guy makes his money with the Mexican cartels."

She talked me into the jambalaya, the house specialty.

"So," she said between bites, "everybody knows and therefore nobody knows. This way it stays murky – rumor, gossip – but no one in the D.A.'s office is going to make political hay out of Pavelic anytime soon. Least of all with drugs." "Why not?" I asked.

"That's all the tourists think. It's not easy to get into drugs in a big way now. The cartels don't need Florida, for one thing."

That, I knew, was fact. There's a quarter of a million going through Juárez every week. You can't pick up a newspaper with reading about some death house regurgitating fifty bodies out of the ground. The US Department of State is obsessed with that pisshole of a Pakistan but we have a failed state right on our southern border.

"The man knows everybody," Bobbie said. "But the wise guys don't own him. He's too big to muscle. One of the guinea mobsters from New York tried to move in on his trash-hauling concession five years ago. Pavelic owns a big piece of the waste hauler who got the contract. Word was out he was not to be touched by any of the New York families."

I looked at the plastic menu and read it to her: "'A creole delight,' it says here, but the shrimp are missing." One boiled shrimp hung precariously from the side of my dish.

"Gee, you notice things, don't you?" "It's my curse," I said.

I asked her to give me her real impressions of Pavelic from her interview. "Cordial, charming, confident. I'll go as far as to say 'gracious.' Nobody can really say what he's like," she said. "The real poop is unavailable to little people like me. You don't get close to him, for one thing. He's got bodyguards twenty-four, seven."

"How do you know?"

"That piece I did had to be vetted by his people. Some big ape hovered in the background throughout my interview and never stopped glaring at me. You'd think I had an AK-47 in my purse."

"Does he have any known enemies?"

"None I know of, but I keep a file on Pavelic the editor doesn't know about."

"What about the other dailies?" I asked.

"I know a couple reporters on the big papers in Central Florida. Years ago they tried to scrape at the lacquer to see what's under the finish," she said. "Nothing came of it. Pavelic is squeaky clean as far as the public goes."

"That doesn't make him untouchable," I said.

"That doesn't make him untouchable," she agreed.

"He obviously likes his image."

"Granting an interview to tame journalists is one thing, but a real interview isn't likely."

"Maybe I'll try to ask him a few questions."

"Were you listening to me just now? Be careful how you approach him, Haftmann."

"What else?"

"Six months ago a rumor made the rounds that one of our senators – who has an eye on the White House – personally met with Pavelic and told him he couldn't accept his money. Scuttlebutt doesn't say, why but I can assure you that doesn't happen too often."

"Maybe gambling?"

"Oh heck, no. That means nothing down here, maybe where you're from. The thing about Pavelic, is he's very ... protective."

An odd word there, I thought. "So who is protecting

him?"

"I said *protective*. *He* doesn't need protecting. If anybody does, it's the citizens of Coconut Grove. He gives money away to local causes. He's buying up vast amounts of property for his condos and hi-rises. It all looks great. Urban renewal, Miami-style."

"I noticed you don't seem to have a Liberty City like Miami," I said.

"That's because Pavelic is cleaning out whole blocks of derelict buildings on the west side, and his money has been doing 'good' things – " She paused, drawing inverted commas in the air. "– in Overtown and even Liberty City."

"In your piece on him, you never said why. What's he after?" "You kidding me? You think he was going to tell me anything?" She was still bitter about having to write that puff piece.

Pavelic obviously had a pair of big fuck-you shoes and he knew how to wear them.

"He *tells* my editors what he wants printed," she said. "And what size type font he wants it in, and what kind of complementary copy he wants next to it. When we did the marina story, one of his people calls up, goes ape shit on the phone because we had this follow-up piece on a local drug murder. It was two columns from it."

"This sidekick, does he do promotional work for Pavelic?"

"I doubt it. He sounded like some no-neck thug on the phone. 'Put some air between it and them jigaboos murdering each other,' he says to the editor. I was in the publisher's office when the call came in. If you knew our publisher, you'd understand how significant it was that the big boss apologized to this schmucko."

She was oblivious to grains of rice falling off her fork halfway to her mouth. I had seen men in prison eat like that but never a woman in a family restaurant. Her nonchalance toward Emily Post's table manners didn't affect my own appetite. Besides those stylish bangs and her outfit that reminded me of the pantsuits women detectives wore when they wanted to be comfortable rather than fashionable, she had the kind of lips that gossip rags of the fifties used to call Cupid's bow and poets called bee-stung.

"Are you going to eat your shrimp?" I asked.

She stared at me. "You ought to get out more often." I wasn't sure she was referring to my shrimp question.

"Tell me this," I said. "Does he rig Emilio Vasquez's fights?"

That made her laugh. "You don't fix fights today. You bring in a stiff for your guy to knock over. Why would anybody do something illegally they could do legally?"

"What is it you think Pavelic's up to?"

"You ask twenty questions for every one you answer, you know that?"

I tried to curl my lip in a way that Micah used to refer to as *Haftmann's arch look*.

"Tell me more about this girl Raina," she said.

I told her the back story as far as I knew it and what I had done so far besides get beat up.

She didn't seem to like the possibility of a runaway story. "Jeezus-wheezus, Haftmann, Florida's bursting with them like overcooked bratwurst."

Pavelic was the real news, not some whey-faced runaway from Ohio, so I baited the hook. I told her about my encounter with Manny earlier, the tattoo below his thumb.

She sniffed at that, testing it. The aroma scents wafting back and forth with the waiters' trays reminded me I was still hungry. When she had cleaned her plate,

I asked her if she wanted dessert.

She declined. She cocked her head to the side for a second. "Listen."

"Listen to what?'

"Louis Armstrong's *West End Blues,*" she said.

"Bobbie, if you can get your ADD under control for a moment, we might consider what we have to do here," I said.

"Testy, aren't we, when our appetite isn't sated?"

"Sorry," I said. "I need your help."

"Look," she said, "I do admire your Christian impulses and all that, wanting to find this lost girl–"

I'm an existentialist," I said.

"Whatever. Look, Haftmann, I do this for a living. Corroboration is what I need for anything having to do with Pavelic. I have to lock it down tight with fact checking. Journalism one-oh-one, you know."

"I'll have eyewitness testimony for you," I said. *Jesus, was I dangling Raina as bait?*

"You better. They *say* Minister Farrakhan in his prime could bench three hundred pounds. Show me the YouTube video of him slinging iron and even then I want to spot him."

"I could tell you were a pro from the way you bit into that shrimp."

"It's called eating on the run," she said, "a dedicated journalist's habit."

Bobbie eyeballed me across the table, her animated face now serious. I realized she was older than I had first thought: tiny crow's feet webbed the orbs of her brown eyes.

"You're wondering if you can trust me because I flattered Pavelic."

"What's Pavelic done so bad to you?"

She ignored that.

I reached across the table to shake her hand,

partners in a risky business. The pain in my gut caused me to wince. Emilio's quick hands found my solar plexus and you have a whole bunch of nerves there you don't want violently disturbed. Same with the shoulder where all the movie heroes take slugs; in reality you'd bleed to death in three minutes from half those shots. Same as throwing punches at a guy's head – the human head is hard; you'll fracture a metacarpal and roll around on the ground blubbering in pain. "You all right?"

"Peachy," I said.

"Sorry, but you've been wincing like that every three minutes since I sat down."

"Sorry."

"And that one eye of yours seems out of kilter with the other," she said.

The palm of her hand was soft and her hands were pretty. I noticed women's hands. Micah never believed me when I said it was her hands that caught my eye first.

Bobbie smiled at me in a strange way, a moue of discontent maybe.

"Something you should know up front. I came out of the closet when I was fifteen," she said. "You do have gay women up there in Ohio, right?"

There was no point in telling her they were as pissed off as straight women, so I finished my coffee and we went our separate ways into another miserably hot, muggy Florida afternoon.

CHAPTER 3

I laid out my scheme for her the next day at the same place. She said she didn't play long shots.

I told her I had a long history of playing long shots – and mostly losing, a fact I didn't mention. I asked her for more details about Pavelic's boxing operation.

"Small potatoes," she said.

"You led me to believe from our conversation yesterday this is one guy who doesn't do small," I countered.

We talked boxing for a bit. I told her I once shook hands with James "Lights Out" Toney, who attended my matchmaker friend's show in Mexican Town in Detroit. He had a light handshake; boxers protect their hands outside the ring. I watched my friend count out the bills for each fighter after each of the bouts. He told me the entire show was paid for by one of the city's big drug dealers. They were only ones besides rich, stupid lawyers who could afford to take the financial beating.

"A guy from the paper, he does the sports, he tells me *El Lagarto*'s got a glass-jaw, a candyass who doesn't turn his punches in." "What does that mean?" I asked.

She threw a punch at my head. "Like this."

She left her fist hanging in front of my face and curled it to show me.

"He can't take a punch," she said.

Pavelic wasn't afraid to toss money away on boxers or beautiful women. My Detroit friend told me a lot of rich professionals liked to be seen hanging around boxers.

I said, "My friend calls that pants-on masturbation."

"Haftmann, before this partnership of ours ... before it goes anywhere, explain how this figures into this girl you're looking for." I told her what I had learned from Emilio's trainer.

"Too flimsy for me. Take advice from this journalist when I say you'd better believe there are very tough libel laws in this state and they do get invoked."

I asked her what she thought Pavelic's angle was.

"What is he going for? My hunch? Florida tourism is down since the housing bubble, and it's *way* down in Miami. We've always got local problems anyway, like foreign tourists getting jacked and murdered by thirteen-year-old gangbangers from Liberty City. The mayor and the governor have held closed-door meetings every time something like that occurs."

"That's everywhere now," I said.

"Everywhere doesn't depend on tourism like us. The airport goes right through the northwestern section of Miami. No problem if you take the expressway, but make one wrong turn, you get a tour of the ghetto and not many international tourists have that on their agendas first thing off the plane."

I said, "So Pavelic buys up a lot of city blocks in the northwestern section of the city."

"More than that. I've never seen the wheels move so fast for one man's self-interest."

"I thought that was Miami's problem?"

"We are Miami, Haftmann."

"Won't the people who live there try to put a stop to it?"

"Who gives a shit about them? Those aren't middle-class whites we're speaking of."

"People being screwed have a tendency to wake up every few years and burn the place down," I said.

"Really? There was no Occupy Miami, Haftmann," she snorted. "Throwing the rascals out just means letting the new rats in the other way."

"It doesn't sound as if he's doing much that's illegal to me." "Neither does insider trading on Wall Street, but it is," she said. "That kind of information is worth millions. Pavelic always comes up with the goods. One of my cop friends tells me they picked up a couple of brothers on BOLOS. Those are lookout notices–"

"We had those back in the Jurassic Age when I was a cop," I said.

"Right, well. These two are typical bangers, shaved heads and bling. I forget their street names, but my source tells me they do hits for major dope dealers. People turn up missing down here besides runaways."

"I'm aware of what human beings can do to one another."

"Does your little runaway? These two brothers were nabbed coming out of a condo owned by a company I traced back to Raymond Pavelic. He has more shell companies than a Russian oil billionaire."

"Do you have any real proof Pavelic is connected to these guys?"

"I have my... hunches, like you," she said.

"My old grandmother used to say a hunch and a dime will get you a stale donut."

"Yeah? Well, your grannie had something there. Pavelic's people don't go around manhandling high-profile people. He gets what he wants in other ways."

"That's where we need to focus," I said.

If what Bobbie said was true, then Pavelic would need a lot of layers between him and gangbangers with choppers.

"If Pavelic needs slum property, there's eminent domain. The next thing you know, there's another strip mall with a sign and his name on it. He knows all the big lawyers in Miami, ones with D.C. clout and more with international connections."

"Nothing illegal there, Bobbie," I said. "Money makes the world go round. Look at those greedy bastards in Washington selling out the country, stuffing lobbyists' money into their pockets," I said. "They're not even afraid to admit they do it."

"My point is this state can't seem to do enough for Raymond Pavelic," she said. "My own paper can't run enough tripe saying what a wonderful good old boy he is."

"There must be blacks and Hispanics in office who would stop him if they felt their power base threatened," I said.

"You would think so, but there's no opposition anywhere. Nobody trusts the system anymore. Entropy's taking over the country." "Who is entropy and let's go get him," I said.

"I don't think you're as dumb—"

"— as I look?"

"— as you might want people to believe you are."

"Now who's finishing somebody else's sentences?"

Micah used to say that when we talked cases together. I told her it was my protective coloring in the jungle. Micah said colorblindness was an atavistic throwback to hunters, an anachronism from the times when you were seeking prey who were seeking you. A colorblind man can distinguish beige from tan from khaki, she said, but he can't tell red from green.

"You said Pavelic likes to be sociable."

"Only to the right people," she responded. "He gives big parties at the Bal Harbour where all the beautiful people turn out, politicians, fixers, a kingmaker or two. He rents an entire stable of models from agencies for the night. I've been checking out rumors..."

I sensed she was retreating behind her journalist's armor, the need for secrecy.

"You must know the politicians he turns to."

"Nobody I can quote publicly. Last year's rumor mill said he was putting together some financiers to get a second NFL team down here and we're just a stone's throw from Joe Robbie. My guy in Sports said it fell through at the last minute only because one of the potential investors got reamed in a palimony suit."

That money stream that flowed round the world never veered in my direction.

"Where's his Achilles' heel?"

"Hard to say. His ego, maybe. Let's say he wants to destroy you for whatever reason. Let's say you've got a restaurant or some small business he doesn't want you to have. All of a sudden, you've got building-code infractions, labor problems – I mean, you just never see *him* pushing the buttons.

"Sounds like the Cleveland I used to know," I said. "But they clean house every few years and lock the scoundrels up."

She looked at me as if I had just wandered loose from the homeless shelter.

"I'm going to trust you, Haftmann."

I told her I wouldn't let her down.

How could I have told her that almost everyone who had ever trusted me in my past life got hurt? Part of me was sincere in what I said. Part of me was impatient to begin using her. I was down here to find a girl, not to make people like me. Even my sainted grandmother, who despised my own mother – her own flesh-and blood daughter – couldn't manage that one all the way.

Grandmother Haftmann went crazy after so many years. By the time I was an adult and indifferent to her religious dementia, she had come to believe I was the "spawn of Satan," which she called me often enough. I've learned this much: there's plenty of room on the escalators going both ways. The down escalator just seemed to suit me better.

Both of us now water-logged with coffee, I listened to her and watched her face the whole time she spoke. I asked her for the part she held back yesterday: what made her go after this rich man in the first place? She told it to me with indirection, the way you do when something hurts too bad to say it straight up.

"...Let's say you graduated from a top law school, OK? Let's say you're ranked at the top of your class, were named editor of your law review and all that jazz. Bright, beautiful, a great future. Moved here from Dade County and opened your own firm. Worked hard for five years. Brought in partners because the business grew so well, so fast. Great reputation. Then one day there's a matter of property litigation. Your partners won't touch it, won't say why. You take it on. Go to court. You win. Brilliant legal work, your law professors would have been proud. Suddenly your partners draw out their investments. Clients abandon the firm. Old clients too. Nobody new comes in the door to replace them. Word spreads. The bills aren't getting paid. You mortgage everything. A temporary reprieve until you can get through this bad patch, this run of bad luck. Just a fluke, you tell yourself. Nothing helps. Bankruptcy. Three months pass. Depression becomes severe. Suicide. A serrated kitchen knife in a tub of warm water. End of story." "Your sister," I said.

The crow's-feet around her eyes seemed to deepen like cracks in old movie film.

Her eyes blazed. All the bitterness of the memory lashed out: "She tangled with Pavelic's best lawyers and beat them. Pavelic was in court the day of the verdict. He smiles at her when he passed.

Even shook her hand and congratulated her."

The light bulb finally going off: not her sister, her

70

lover.

"Not your sister," I said.

"No, not my sister."

Then she broke, wiped scalding tears that wouldn't stop flowing.

I said, "Revenge can be a risky thing, Bobbie – "

"Don't condescend to me, Haftmann."

She dabbed at her running mascara. Streaks like dirty rivulets smeared her cheeks.

We sat there quietly thinking about our separate burdens. I knew I had to call Raina's father soon and report something.

I gave her the names I had copied from DeCamillo's apartment foyer and asked her to give these to one of her cops. "Have them run through the NCIC database first, I said."

"I know how to do it," she snapped. She tucked the paper into a purse bulging with paper. "Two more things," she said, with a noisy last slurp of lukewarm coffee.

"Go ahead," I said.

"Say this helps to get your missing girl back–"

"Yes?"

"Don't even think about fucking me over."

She held up a miniature tape recorder with the tiny spools still revolving.

I watched her go, thinking about my next move in the lemony whiff of scent in her wake.

An Hispanic kid with pimples entered just then and boxed the room with confident, surly eyes. He didn't look at me, but I knew he had taken me in with the rest of the diners.

An old couple rose to leave. The woman had a blue rinse and her husband, apparently, muttered something as they passed him. The kid was lip-syncing words to some song playing in his head, bobbing to the music.

The boy's silent music lowered a tombstone on my mood. As I made it past him, I heard the words *I'm a loser ba-bay, so why don't you kill me* and wondered whether this, too, like the dead kitten being pecked by the gull, was another portent to ignore at my peril. My existentialist armor failed me and I felt lost in the wonderment of symbiosis and chance, whatever dark forces ruled our lives and sneaked malevolence into our humdrum paths. But I had little time for reflection. The boy's lyrics were booting me in the ass out the door into the tropical night.

~ ~ ~

I got lost on the way back, the air conditioner on the fritz, the air soupy with moisture. My stomach still hurt and the coffee sloshing around in it wasn't helping. I found myself circling trendy Mayfair and finally worked my way back to the motel from Ponce de Leon.

Hot needle spray uncramped most of the muscles in my back. My face was bruised, a little puffy, tender where I touched it. I lay on the bed in a dark room that reeked of disinfectant.

I had put my tells, tiny pieces of lint and thread, in various places in my luggage. They were intact. I was hoping there would be time to buy a shirt while I was here, something with parrots on it. I slept uneasily, bad memories poking holes in my sleep and scratching like mice in the walls all night. I awoke with the night sweats and a thumping heart full of fear.

At dawn, a viscous light seeped under the linen curtains. I had been dreaming about being lost in a jungle – monkeys sat in trees and called out warnings as I made my way through the foliage. Streams of red and black ants fought in a war at my feet. Life teemed and shrilled. In Ohio it would still be dark and the cars would be rimed in frost. You'd find the paw prints of feral cats in your yard and sometimes the bigger prints of hungry coyotes.

I shaved, wondering if I should take up smoking again. I called the *Miami Tribune*, dropped Gersack's name along with a couple modest lies about needing information for a story I was helping her write for the *Courier*, and asked for the archives section.

I got a very young-sounding voice. I gave her Bobbie's fax number and hoped I could explain this requisitioning later. I had to interrupt the woman, who was asking how Bobbie was doing over there at the rival paper. Then I called her home phone and left a message on her machine asking her to retrieve the fax stuff from work and use her contacts with the local cops to check out Emilio's trainer. I missed the old reverse directories in print; it's all online now. Bobbie could find out if the name on the apartment was different from the name he used in the gym. She was to meet me at Denny's at ten o'clock tomorrow night. I said I would have something for her then.

The voice gave me one thing more when I mentioned that I was doing a follow-up on the piece on Raymond Pavelic. A lucky bit of confusion ensued because I learned someone "at the highest level," according to the voice in archives, had spiked a Pavelic story only last week.

"Which one was that?" I tried to sound five-clock bored, low in blood sugar.

"Oh, some of the guys were chatting in the lounge. Nikki Corchoran in Society, you know her? She no sooner got the assignment than the old man starts twisting her arm about Pavelic's right to privacy, et cetera, et cetera, you know?"

I said, "Oh, do I ever."

The gist of it was that Pavelic's private security had

a run-in over some calls to this section of Grapeland and South Dixie – all strip joints and palm readers. Pavelic owned some high-rise retirement condos there.

Then her voice rose one more notch to mezzo-soprano: "It's like – voilà! – no crime, no street people, no derelicts, no crack prostitutes – nothing, all gone. Cops are talking to Pavelic's people and these guys are packing more guns than those – those *whatchamacallems*, them Mexicans, you know, that chop off hands and heads and shit." "Zetas," I said.

"So what's Nikki think about this?"

"Well, you know, Nikki, right?"

I learned that Nikki's talent lay in her ample cup size, according to her colleague. Nikki could thank her big lungs for all the choice assignments. I heard the usual malice of mailroom gossip. Somebody had to pull strings high up because the next thing Corchoran knows, her story, "which ain't even written, mind you, has got the kibosh put on it."

"Who spiked it?" I hoped they still used that lingo in journalism school.

"All one to Nikki. She got a raise out of it and the old man's personal apology. Never told her who."

"Ha, good old Raymond Pavelic does like his business kept private."

"Say, who you say this is?" Click.

I parted the chintz drapery and looked outside. I was feeling claustrophobic suddenly. I saw hordes of people walking to and fro. Most of them didn't look gainfully employed like me. Street trash: druggies, burnouts, drifters, teenaged huffers with their painted nostrils, only they weren't gathering under the stairwell; now they met near the motel sign at the entrance to plot their next Day-Glo outing. Some would be turning tricks like the pros hanging around the intersections at dusk; some were runaways without an agenda. All of them could turn up missing and few, if anyone, would care. What was it Micah had quoted to me one day about people living on the risky margins? Homicide cops out of the earshot of reporters used to call the code for any Dead Body Found in the slums or projects of Cleveland exactly the right kind of population adjustment.

~ ~ ~

Bobbie Gersack hadn't changed her eating habits much in twenty-four hours; she dropped crumbs of cherry pie from either side of her mouth as if she had holes in her lip. Her eyes were a muddy brown. She dared me to comment. I didn't. She wasted no time with small talk either, shoving over papers as soon as she sat. Some of my coffee spilled when they hit the cup.

"Don't ever use my name again without permission," she said. "*Ever* again, hear me?"

I nodded and the look in my good eye was as sheepish as I could make it. The other one had a will of its own.

"Je-sus," she said. "You are one ridiculous-looking..."

"Flannel-mouthed, uncouth, unkempt son of a bitch? Lying, thieving, bastard son of a motherless neo-Nazi whore?"

"I was going to say *buffoon*, but those will do even better."

"Thank you, Bobbie. I mean that."

"I owe that cop of mine big time."

"Thanks."

"Stop thanking me! You don't mean it anyway. I'll eat, you read. I'm still working on the Gables story so I can't stay long."

She settled back in the booth while I read. I didn't even hear her place the order.

It was an interesting life but it asked more questions than it answered. One day Pavelic showed up, a second-generation son of the *Marielitas* of the seventies. I vaguely remembered the news articles from that time: Castro's boat people, some genuine political prisoners, the desperate and those disaffected with Castro's socialism, some the vilest scum scraped from jails and psycho wards and dumped on Miami – thousands became instant citizens under the Carter administration. One of Bobbie's articles gave an interview from 1982 in which Pavelic discussed his family, all lost or killed during *La Revolución*. His father was a German factory owner from Stuttgart and had held a post in the Batista cabinet. His mother was the daughter of an old Cuban family. Miss Havana in 1953." *La-de-da.*

"Pavelic's not a German name," I said. I knew that much from being a German kid growing up in an Irish-Catholic neighborhood. Kids used to give me the Nazi salute at school.

"The family's Croatian, originally," she said. "Spelled like so." She wrote the name on her napkin: Pavelić. She made a *ch* sound pronouncing it. "He was a little vague about his mother's side when I interviewed him," she said, "and I had a feeling she was less than reputable."

Back then, the late fifties, the mobs owned Havana and all the casinos. Fulgencio Batista took his cut from the mob – Giancana, Trafficante, Marcello, Lansky – all the time he was promising to rid the island of corruption.

"Then Castro kicked him out and the Pavelic family fortune declined," I guessed. "But how much of these news stories can you believe?"

"Don't remind me of that wretched interview," Bobbie said. "I waded through his bullshit for two hours. He went on for at least an hour about his heroic father fighting for freedom against Fidel, Raul, and Che." She mimed vomiting into her plate like a kid.

"One of my first assignments was to interview the great retired gangster Meyer Lansky having a pastrami sandwich at Wolfie's on Collins," she said, thinking of a happier memory.

"No shit," I said.

"Yeah, he was a gentleman, or so I thought at first. Soft-spoken, courteous. I had to lean halfway across the table to hear him until I realized it was a trick to look down my blouse."

"Pavelic could be mobbed up," I speculated.

"I don't know. There's more to it. I know this because I did a story on it. This government is still paying fifty million dollars a year to keep some of these aging creeps locked up in federal pens under charges so vague Jefferson would spin in his urn. This is three decades before the Patriot Act, too. They're just waiting for them to die in custody."

"There's always repatriation now that Castro's dead," I said.

"Raúl's still in charge so far, " she said. "Haftmann, does the Yiddish expression '*tsuris*' mean anything to you? Trouble, big trouble. The kind you don't want."

"You can check me out," I said.

"You want to know what one of these psychopaths did from those times? Sodomized a pregnant woman in a phone booth on East Flagler in the middle of the day. Cut her throat *and* her two-year-old daughter's because she witnessed the attack on her mother. The paramedics saved her life but she's still comatose in a Dade County hospital. If you lived in Miami then, you'd find a better word for those bastards."

I worried about that sometimes, the fact that depravity didn't shock me anymore. Her own paper had a story of a cop who shot a naked man eating a homeless man's face. He didn't even stop eating when the cop approached him.

I said, "Pavelic's apparently got a pretty effective public relations team on his payroll."

She glowered at me. "What do you mean?"

She thought I was referring to her kiss-ass story again.

"I noticed a tattoo on the base of his trainer's right thumb. Like this."

I drew the design on the same napkin, a pitchfork bisected at the handle with two lines and what looked like a teardrop beneath the middle tine.

"He's a convicted baby raper," I said.

Her eyes lightened a notch, expressive eyes. *Micah's gave away nothing: deep mahogany pools.*

"What are you implying?"

"Cuban cons used to advertise their specialties."

"So don't the boys in *Bratva*, the Brotherhood," Bobbie replied.

I thought she meant the Aryan Brotherhood, but she said, "Russian mafia. The Red mob, Japanese Yakuza, they all do it. I cut my teeth doing crime beat, remember? I can find you dozens of bikers wearing teardrop tatts on the beach right now. Neo-Nazis with spiderwebs. Doesn't mean they killed anyone and it doesn't mean they're contract killers."

"Yeah, but my friend owns a bar back home and he used to feed me information about some of these characters. This kind of pimp specializes in children."

"He has all kinds of people associated with him." Her face darkened. "It doesn't prove anything about Pavelic."

"Make a great story, though, wouldn't it?"

"Don't try to con me. It might *lead* to a real story. If, and I repeat the word *if*, a real story pans out – that's an *if* in forty-point type, Haftmann – we may have something."

"I'm only saying that one of the richest men in South Florida employs a convicted pederast to train a fighter and that this individual reports to him. You don't find that interesting?"

"There's no record, nothing, under the name he's using. Pavelic might not know anything of his real background, assuming that tattoo means what you say it does."

She was playing the skeptical journalist keeping my assumptions in check.

"There's something else. I noticed one of the hands hoisting me to my feet had a tattoo in the same place. It's another one I remember from my days in Vice."

I drew a quick sketch on the same napkin. "Like so: 'murder for hire'."

"Still isn't proof of anything."

"I've got a hunch to play. If I'm right about Pavelic and what happened to Raina, it'll be my... how does it go ... my *quid pro quo*." Micah loved that one. Damn lawyers anyway: you can't live with them and you can't kill them.

"So you were a lawyer in your past life, too?"

"No, but my wife ran off with one," I said. "Does that count?" "You should take your comedy act on the road," Bobbie said.

"Look, I've got to run. Places to go, people to see." She chugged the rest of her coffee.

Watching her guzzle, thinking of her words, I realized the one act I had brought down here with me wasn't working very well – at least not with one cynical reporter.

"I do know the difference between horses and horseshit, so ... don't play me..." I finished.

"There you go again, damn it," she said and turned

on her heel.

I watched her stiff-arm the door open. She had stuck me with the check again.

I had told her as simply as I could what I wanted her to do and when to do it. Something else I learned from Tico, himself an ex-welterweight, when I was eager to start life anew with Micah in a forgotten little corner of Ohio: *When it gets a little sticky, go slow.* Tico used to say that a fighter between rounds doesn't want to hear a lot of complicated instructions from his corner man. Something else I remembered Mike Tyson used to say when Tico and I watched his boy Cesar sparring at the Southside gym in Youngstown: *Everybody has a strategy until the bell rings.*

I wasn't eager to repeat my pounding from Emilio. Some men wrongly believe they are more courageous than they are because they have dangerous jobs or take more chances. Ironworkers, for example. You might be able to climb that high but once you're up there on the girders, you have to work. I lacked simple courage, and I knew it. I did reckless things at times but that's not courage. I let my toes hang over the edge just to prove to myself I wasn't a coward. Micah used to argue with me at times for this compulsion to take chances. She once said I would someday wreck our marriage because I didn't know when to stop.

Before she met the lawyer that she left me for, I had begun to suspect her of cheating on me with a colleague from her office, another assistant DA. The guy was a few years younger, a college lacrosse star, good-looking, single, a graduate of Columbia Law. He attended one of those New England rich-boy boarding schools with private golf courses. Micah was really impressed with him. I hated him. Worse, they spent hours together preparing big cases, sometimes at our house, sometimes at his. I grew jealous, but she scoffed at me.

One night I watched her slip a bottle of expensive wine into her briefcase and head to the guy's house. I waited an hour and followed, where I lurked outside in the dark of my vehicle and waited for her to leave. I spent four hours torturing myself with the image of her grinding down on his erection, the sweat from her neck trickling down her naked back all the way to her cleft. I could see the sacral dimples where her hips flared and that untrimmed tawny bush with its flame-like swirl as she stepped out of her panties... *What kind of man does that? Treats his own wife like a cheating-spouse case?* It never occurred to me to break in there and confront the guy.

Micah never knew.

"Haftmann, am I boring you?"

"No, why?"

"Because you haven't listened to a word I've said in the last five minutes. You were a million miles away."

"I don't know how this is going to work out," I said.

She stared at me, assessing in the way people did after they got to know me a little.

"Is it for the money?"

"Sure, it is," I snapped. "Do you people pay your bills with colored beads down here?"

If she thought I had other motives like playing hero, I was going to disillusion her fast.

"Let me talk to a friend I know in the Miami PD."

"Maybe it'll be a good idea to bring him in after tomorrow." She scowled, shook her head slightly but didn't say anything.

"I didn't take an idiot test to get where I am," she said. "I'll remember."

Those dark eyes with the flecks flashed at me again.

Now I knew what it was about her mouth I liked: she had a slight overbite, an imperfection in a near-perfect oval face. The symmetry was off by a touch.

I gave her the material back except for one color photo of Pavelic, a headshot; he wore a wide-brim black leather hat, a camel coat, and an oatmeal neck scarf, his eyes opaque above a toothy smile – the Beau Brummel of Coconut Grove.

She left me there, as my old white-haired grandmother used to say, chewing the cud. My thoughts were not placid, and somewhere in the murk of my psyche I had a prevision of shock and blood and disaster. It was as if those old days as a cop in tight places were coming back to me in a single, floodlit adrenalin rush.

Trouble was, I didn't know what the rules of engagement were. I was sure of one thing only: Raina Toivela had fallen in with a strange mix of people that ran the gamut of every demographic I could name from high to lowest of the lowlife rung of the criminal chain. I still hadn't puzzled out her connection to Pavelic. What I did intend to do was a follow-up interview with Toni DeCamillo.

This time without the stooge act.

~ ~ ~

The foyer to Toni's apartment was locked, so I sat in my car and chewed No-Doze and washed them down with the thermos of coffee I had refilled at a Vietnamese cafe on 27th Avenue; the place was redolent of garlic and the potted oleanders on the counter.

A single light burned in what I remembered was the kitchen area.

At four in the morning she came home, the sky bruised in the light of false dawn. A Cadillac that looked gold under the oval of a streetlight let her off a long way from her apartment and, lucky for me, she spoke a few words to the driver before turning away so that I could get out of the car and creep up from the blind side. I saw a bunch of keys flash in her hands like silver fish in the light above the door and she was in.

I was right behind her, a big happy smile on my face. She grunted when she saw me. "Who? *You?* You scared the–" "Hi, Toni," I said.

"Whadda you want now? No more quesh ... no more questions."

Word-slurring, weaving, reeking of alcohol, close to blacking out.

She waved her arms about elaborately as if she were bringing in a jumbo jet or fending off some invisible *paparazzo* with his camera lens.

"Sorry, I didn't mean to frighten you. I have a few more questions about Raina Toivela.

"This time ... of the ... night? Are you crazy?"

"I suffer from insomnia," I said. "I hope I'm not interrupting anything."

"Yeah, you are, man. My sleep."

Jumpy, but on her own turf. Soon she'd be confident as well as surly.

"Myself, I'm planning on snorkeling a coral reef at dawn," I said.

"You're ... funny. Whass your name, Half-something. Halfwit? I forgot."

She peered at a gold wristwatch and he-heed a giggle at me, swinging between coquettishness and turning malicious.

"Let's go inside, Toni."

"I've already tole – told you everything–"

"Not everything," I said. "Do you want me to tell all your neighbors you're a lying cunt who sells girls to Raymond Pavelic?"

This last part was spoken through the veins in my neck, very loudly. The empty stone walls gave off the echo in the lot. Highway traffic was sporadic, but two die-hard whores were out patrolling in their miniskirts and halters. The closer one to the motel looked our way.

"Shhh, sshh! Whatthefuck're you doing? Gonna wake ... gonna wake neighbors!"

I could imagine her confusion – all kinds of neurons snapping and misfiring over synapses. The smell of alcohol was powerful in the warm pre-dawn air. She was about to bellow something when I put my hand over her mouth. She reached for my hand and pulled it away.

"Getcher fuckin' hands offa me. You – you," she spluttered.

"Let's find out what I know," I said and shoved her ahead of me.

That provoked a surly grunt, but she lumbered down the foyer, and I followed her unsteady gait to her apartment doorway. She pointed a different key at the keyhole, this time like a fresh doctor inserting his first probe, but with much less skill.

I grabbed the key from her and opened her door.

"I know tough guys'll kick your narrow white ass, fucker." In case I didn't get the full import, she repeated the last three words with a slower alcoholic's pronunciation.

"I'm sure you do. I know something about the circles you run in," I said.

We were facing each other in the same spot as before. This time she wore no spotted robe. Her sequined evening gown was made of shiny material and her big protruding breasts distended the fabric beneath her armpits. Spiked heels rounded off the tawdry cheapness of the whole package. Toni in her finest was a sight to behold.

The apartment reeked of frying meat. Her eyes were wet, and smeary, with big pupils. If she were fried on coke, I'd be lucky to get anything from her. Drugs on top of alcohol gave a speedball effect to perception. I wanted her cocky and loose, not wired and paranoid.

"Ash – asshole," she hissed. "Jizz-gargling faggot. You better know what you're dealing with, chump-ass motherfucker."

Prison dissing. Got it down pat right to head wag like a baaaadass sister, letting me know.

"I know what happened to Raina," I said. "I can prove it to the cops."

Weaving a little more as she fumbled for a light switch, she walked toward me unsteady, a slight list to port. I couldn't see her face well enough, but I braced for a charge.

Toni might have thought better of it. She stopped a few feet from me and said, "These cops? Can't scratch their asses without – without permission...."

"Whose permission do they need, Toni?"

"From the man you're fuckin' with, motherfucker."

She stumbled backwards into a potted miniature fan palmetto.

She wasn't reaching for her cell phone yet, so I had some time.

I said nothing. I wanted it to sink in.

"You – you don't know what you're talkin' about," she said.

"You don't know what cards I'm holding, Toni," I said.

I reached into my wallet for a business card and sailed it at her. "Pick it up. Go on. Try not to fall over. The name on it says Edwin Booth, FBI, and he's a big shot in the New York office. Now why do you think I'd have his card in my wallet?"

"So fuckin' what? I know cops, loss a cops." She hiccupped getting it out.

"You'd be smart to talk to me, Toni."

"F-fuck you, halfwit. That's your name, ain't it?"

She found her own wit delightful. "Yeah, Tom Halfwit, thass you, enna?"

"Tell me about Pavelic," I said. "I can help you. I think you're in trouble."

"You think – you think I'm in trouble? You dumb shit motherfucker."

Getting all that out in a couple boozy breaths was too much and she burped up a rancid gas bubble from her stomach. I wouldn't want to light a match in the place just then.

"Sure," I lied. "People don't have much shelf life when you make trouble for the big man. You know that yourself, Toni, and you're a problem for him right now, aren't you?"

"Bull-shit," she spat out. "I'm callin' the real cops, you fuckhead."

"Let's swap information, see where we are. Then I'll go away, forever."

I figured I better step into the silence before that turnbuckle in her brain unknotted.

"What happened to Raina after you gave – after you *directed* her to Emilio?"

"I dint do nothin', faggot cocksucker."

I kept my smile fixed. Her anger was rapidly diminished only by the descending booze fog in her brain. She would soon collapse into a comatose sleep. She spoke in the drunken, truncated syntax of a real boozer; her eyes were less focused and she seemed even drunker. I thought of slapping her face but she started to talk.

"... hangin' around the theater ... the Grove. Panhandling. Gave her ... gave her chance, chance a ... chance to make some money." It's called pandering," I said, still the smiling clown.

"Hunh, whaa?"

"How did she wind up at the asylum in Dade?"

"The bitch ... she kept shoving every dollar she made up her nose, thass why."

"I'm not judging you, Toni. You tried to help her."

"Fucking-A, copper. She dint like ... money ... she ... goes home, right? Back to Shitsville. Ain't nobody stoppin' her."

"That's right, Toni. Pavelic, what did he do to her?'

"Used to ... watch ... Emilio and his pals. Likes to watch..."

Runaway girls, you buy them right out of bus stations like a commodity. "Did you watch, Toni?"

Blinking at me in her best dress, nostrils flared, wobbling on her thick legs. I tried again:

"Tell me what he did, Toni."

"Hunh, fuck're you doin' here ... "

Losing her fast now. "Was Raina forced into that?"

"Tired ... sleep ... get the fuck out, you ..."

The puzzle pieces were dropping and I could see some bigger pieces about to fall. Pavelic tells somebody to get her checked into the psycho ward in Dade. Wandering around like that, panhandling, goofed out, Raina would be a liability. You can't destroy too many girls like drowning kittens without some blowback.

I needed one more piece before I left her to sleep it off. The big one.

"She dead, Toni? Is Raina Toivela dead?"

She swiveled her head back and forth, slowly, and settled her gaze on her daughter's portrait. Her neocortex crackled with synaptic confusion unable to process much of anything now.

I ticked off a list on my fingers: "Acting in concert, access before the fact, pandering, coconspirator to a criminal activity, white slavery, abduction. You'll be lucky to get out in time for your little girl's wedding."

Bobbie Gersack had come through big. The father

wasn't in Jamaica and he wasn't having problems with Immigration. The DEA bagged him because he was a known member of a Jamaican posse. He was doing a deuce upstate in a maximum-security prison. Toni's rap sheet was sordid, pathetic. Grew up in East Morrisania; arrested twice at the age of fifteen for hooking in Hunts Point, the stool pit of the South Bronx. She helped her pimp rob the few elderly whites left behind; cops called these crib jobs because the geriatric victims are as helpless as babies.

"Portraits on a smoker's wall shouldn't have nicotine stains behind them, Toni. You steal babies, too? I'm calling Children Services as soon as I leave here." *That worked.*

She came at me growling, her hands extended like talons aimed at my face.

I grabbed her wrists and turned them out and away. She was a strong woman and if she hadn't been so drunk, I'd have had my hands full. She tried to butt me with her head. When that failed, she tried to knee me in the pills. Our faces were inches apart and sour fumes of her breath washed over my face. The wings of her nostrils flared and whitened while the rest of her face mottled with blood and turned sodden with fury. She stopped snarling long enough to blow spittle into my face. Hate boiled off her but her strength was undermined by inebriation. Her panting mouth opened wider and she showed bared teeth to bite any part of me within reach.

"Fuckin' bastard, I'll ... rip ... your ... fuckin' ... face ... off..." I hit her in the stomach right where Emilio had hit me.

She collapsed in a heap and rolled to her side. A geyser of vomit shot out of her mouth in three spasms. In seconds the room's foul odor became so bad I thought of breaking a window.

Instead I dropped to my knees and patted her back.
Christ Almighty, what do I do to women?

She made coughing noises for a long time. I held
her head; her eyes were squeezed shut. I shook her
gently.

"Is Raina dead, Toni?"

I don't know if she heard me. She was a long way
away but her retching had stopped. She tried to curl
away from me; dark pubic hairs curled up from the
exposed furrow of her panties.

Toni and I had a bond even though I knew she'd
want to kill me when she woke up. It had to be similar
to being a woman in prison except for the ersatz
families' woman created as substitutes with their
bulldyke daddies, mommies, and kids. Every prison is
a foul gulag of gray memories and sounds despite your
effort to will yourself away from your bunk and those
walls closing in. It's a never-ending clang of bars, grate
of metal on metal, yells, coughs, screams; the same
nauseous smells day after day: urine, farts,
disinfectant, sweat – all tumbling together in one
swirling stink of human corruption. The color of gray,
death and only two emotions left: fear and anger.

One dismal fact the men's and women's prisons
shared was that things around the cellblocks or pods
always changed for the worse when somebody went
after somebody else's bitch.

CHAPTER 4

Pavelic lived on Ocean Boulevard – with his manicured Japanese garden and his power boats docked on the Intracoastal and membership in the exclusive Palm Beach Polo and Country Club – like the rest of the billionaires and millionaires. The strands of the spider's web were vibrating all the way from DeCamillo's shabby apartment to his ritzy digs. If Pavelic was as connected as Bobbie said, he'd know by now some nameless private eye was asking questions. I was counting on it.

I played solitaire in my motel room, cheated every chance I had, and waited for the phone to ring. Waited for that second chance that almost never comes...

~ ~ ~

The motel phone burred in my ear at six-fifteen in the evening. It was Pavelic himself; he had a deep voice, confident-sounding, each spoken word counted. "Thomas Haftmann?"

"Speaking." I was still edgy from my night's vigil with Toni.

"You've been asking people about me. I don't talk to people who don't make appointments first."

"This situation would be mutually profitable," I said, "if you were to break that rule for once."

"How so, Mister Haftmann?"

"A simple business transaction," I said. "I'm looking for a missing girl named Raina Toivela."

"I never heard of her or you, Mister Haftmann."

"I spoke to Toni DeCamillo, an associate of yours."

"I don't know this person, either. But I'm chary of my reputation, and when a man comes into my town asking questions and making baseless insinuations

91

about me, I feel I have a right to know what's going on," he said. His voice stayed level.

"All the more reason we should talk," I said. "Not on the phone."

"Tell me where and when," I said. "I'll meet you."

He gave me the address and a time and then clicked off without waiting for me to answer. I was to meet him in the morning, at the same house where Manny had gone after my pummeling from Emilio. He didn't bother to ask if I knew the location.

I shaved around the swelling on my face, since the lump had not gone down much on the side where Emilio had rocked me. The bruise on my neck was yellow and purple, the size of a waffle. I had enough time for food but my stomach was sending little jolts of adrenalin around that made me queasy.

A chilly morning. The frost warning mentioned in the paper was destroying the citrus crops in the central part of the state. Five minutes before the time Pavelic had said, I got out of my car, went straight up the sidewalk, and hit the front steps, and rapped my knuckles on the door.

A few faces looked out their windows at the ruckus and I breathed easier. *Witnesses. I won't be rolled up in a rug and dropped into the Everglades.*

I tapped again, and waited before trying the doorknob. The door was unlocked.

Not a good idea, my older brain said.

I went inside anyway and let my eyes adjust.

I saw a stairway to the room at the left. It was unlocked as well and opened immediately, revealing the man on the other side: *Raymond Pavelic*, I assumed, *in the flesh*.

His smile was thin-lipped, brief, despite the wide mouth; he wore the hat I had seen in the photo. Big — about six-two, two-twenty, Pavelic had salt-and-paper hair cropped short, brown eyes, and an aquiline nose. Looked to be in good shape, but the knee-length cashmere coat obscured the physique. Shoes were glossy oxblood.

Three men sat at a table in the small kitchen. Two were big. One was a bodybuilder, the biceps straining the fabric of his coat.

Pavelic nodded toward the others.

"My associates," he said. "Meet Mister Amezcua and Mister Odio."

I noted the impassive gaze of the one identified as Amezcua.

The other man, Odio, looked straight at me.

Shit, piss, fuck. This wasn't going to be good.

"Well, Mister Haftmann, we meet at last." His voice was richer and deeper than his phone voice.

"Yes," I said. "Why don't the two of us go somewhere to have a private conversation?"

"Of course," he said. "Do you mind if one of my men pat you down first as a precaution?"

Micah's been right all these years. I do have a death wish. Even my grandmother knew it: '*The dog returneth to his vomit,*' she used to say after one of my teenaged escapades.

The stocky one with the Ben Franklin stove around his middle, Amezcua, giggled – the boss was cutting up for the troops.

"Did you say something funny?"

"I'm busy and your profession doesn't command more than a modicum of respect or very much of my valuable time. In fact, you have a sordid way to make money. Snooping in people's garbage, peeping through keyholes. Digging up dirt, hiding in bushes. *Tsk, tsk.*"

His voice was back in register, deep mellow tones. His eyes were moist and his tongue lightly darted about his lips as if to help his enunciations.

"I resent the part about hiding in bushes," I said. "I've taken precautions in case you were wondering about that too."

Pavelic barely nodded his head and I was patted down fast by his men, front and back. They even felt against the middle of my back where few bother to check. Odio gave my testicles a light squeeze when he finished and a big smile lit his handsome face, letting me know exactly how helpless I was.

Pavelic's men, their job done, moved away to give their boss room to operate for whatever was next. Odio yawned and took out his cellphone while Amezcua fingered the gold chain around his neck and kept his eyes on me, a fat owl on a limb watching a field mouse frozen in place.

The hackles on my neck could not have been more frizzed. I tried to put things back toward equilibrium, if not in my favor.

"You know what happens to kidnappers? It's federal, not state."

Pavelic sounded bored. "Why don't you enlighten me?"

"Hot House," I said. "Smack in the middle of a cornfield in Leavenworth, Kansas. There's another in Marion, Illinois. A whole complex of supermaxes in Colorado. Twenty-three hours of lockdown." "You seem to know some interesting places."

"They'll buy and sell you for commissary snacks," I replied. "You must be speaking of your past, not my future." He must have nodded again, this time I didn't catch it.

Pavelic's handsome features notwithstanding, his immaculate dress and mirrored shoes, were offset by one tiny flaw in the portrait – whitish pinpricks of dried spittle in the corners of his mouth.

Amezcua had taken a position behind me. I

94

blanched with fear: *Never let them get behind you,* they told us at the academy.

Pavelic tapped a Rolex dangling from his wrist. "I have important business. Accompany him down the stairs," he said to his men.

Two big bodies pressed against me. I heard the soft clack-clack of Pavelic's footsteps descending. *Christ, how stupid to think broad daylight could save me.* I was bundled down the narrow stairs and out the front door squeezed between these two massive sides of beef. Pavelic was waiting at the bottom of the steps.

"I own most of this block," he said. "I'm cleaning them out one at a time."

He looked at Odio. "Ten minutes, Miguel. No more," he said.

Fuck me. This was going to be bad, all right.

The last thing he said going out the front door was something that sounded like *no more talking to little birdies.*

A horn tooted in the distance. Minutes passed like glacier ice moving down a mountain. I was sweating hard, thinking with more concentration than I have ever thought. One riff played above the rest of my thoughts: Don't get in the car. *Don't get in the car ...* *Don'tgetinthecar.*

I decided to make a run for it on the street or cause enough commotion to get one of these lookie-loo neighbors to call it in —

But his men had my arms pinned so tight to my back that my lips opened in a snarl of pain and I could do nothing. I drew my leg to kick backward into somebody's testicles, but I was punched hard in the liver and my right thumb was bent back to the snapping point. I was aware of being thrown into the back of the car. I could barely hiss through the pain. I thought a bomb had gone off inside me.

I was pulled upright in the backseat next to Amezcua. I blinked through tears at Odio's broad shoulders behind the wheel. Amezcua sat beside me tighter than a tick and jammed a gun barrel hard into my ribs.

Odio hit the buttons of the CD player. I expected Mozart's *Requiem*, but I was amazed I recognized it: *La Forza del Destino*. Micah loved Verdi.

I can't polish a turd, Thomas. That woman could hit below the belt too.

I knew that if we got too far out of town, my chances of escape would evaporate to nil. The smoke-gray Lincoln turned down a side street and followed a dogleg that bumped into McFarlane. Miguel wheeled the big machine with expert turns out of the morning traffic of Coconut Grove and then we were gliding south on Highway 1 at a steady sixty-five.

Better try something, anything, I thought.

"You speak good English for a spic, driver. They teach you in jail while you were taking it up the ass?"

Miguel never bothered to look in the rearview.

"*Cabrón*," said Amezcua and dug the barrel in harder.

Miguel's head never moved a muscle.

Calm, calm. Think...

Bad vision or not, I saw everything in magnified clarity. Hopelessness turned my guts to water and acid sloshed inside my stomach so violently I thought my gag reflex was going to go off and turn me into a puking, shitting coward. Each second ticked a hammer blow against my temple where a vein throbbed like a fat worm ready to pop through the skin. Yet I sat there fixated on Miguel Odio's big hands clenching the wheel.

A blue Datsun suddenly appeared in my vision, cutting us off from a crowded lane; Odio's knuckles whitened in response. He said something in rapid, idiomatic Spanish.

Amezcua said, "That fuckin' moron."

A straw of hope appeared out of nowhere, dangling in front of my face.

Miguel's hands smacked the steering wheel as the Datsun slowed to a crawl in front of us. "*Imaricón de mierda*. Motherfuckin' bastard," said Amezcua.

The car juddered as Odio tapped the brakes and blew his horn. The driver of the Datsun had hair whiter than a Q-tip; he gave the big Lincoln behind him the middle finger.

"*Me lo paso por el culo*. Motherfucker fuckin' with his life now," Amezcua said.

"Easy, Luis, easy," said Odio. "*De nada.*"

I felt the gun dig another inch out of my flesh. "*Piensa sólo en eso,*" Luis hissed.

Miguel shrugged off his companion's simmering rage. He turned to me and smiled. "Don't make Luis mad at you. He has a very short fuse."

"Fuckin' right," Luis said in my ear. "I don' fuck around, *chuvallo.*"

Time, time. Not much left.

"You mind if I ask you guys something?"

"If he talks again before we get there, break his jaw," said Miguel without turning his head but with a smile for me in the rearview.

I was a long way from home and I couldn't change anything or do one thing to stop it.

"If you boys don't mind," I began.

Amezcua hit me in the jaw with his forearm. My magic triad of words couldn't ward off the black vortex opening in front of me and sucking me down.

~ ~ ~

Hissing noise, then a loud ringing of fire alarms awoke me. Sound of surf rolling up the beach: I had finally made it to the beach.

No, not the beach, I thought.

Something warm in my mouth. Wet, salt. My own blood.

I opened my eyes and wondered how long I had been out. A sign flashed by. In big letters it said *Leaving Florida City – Ya'll Come Back!* A long-faded *Fuck Andrew* had been spray-painted beneath it.

My eyes were blurry but I could see well enough through the pain. My jawbone tingled as if an electric current had been strung through it. I hurt right into my teeth.

My brain kicked in fast where it had left off. Soon there would be nothing but wide flat spaces and a few limbo-gumbo trees; brown scrub dotted the landscape where the sea grape had failed to root.

The heater's fan was blowing. *Florida, and I'm traveling in a car with the heat on* was the first coherent thought I had.

"Just about there," Amezcua said. He grinned at me: *no hard feelings.*

I was aware of piano and cello music rolling out of the speakers, but I couldn't recognize it.

We turned left onto a dirt road and traveled a couple miles and then turned again onto a smaller track scored with deeper tracks, the heavy chassis of the Lincoln bucking across the ruts. Amezcua said something in his rapid Spanish to Miguel and waved a ringed hand to emphasize it. Miguel slowed the car to a crawl.

We drove on and the foliage grew thicker. Kudzu and Spanish moss hung in green drapes from the tops of trees. The fronds of overhanging vegetation thwacked the windshield causing Miguel to wrestle the car back onto the narrow tracks.

The sun kept bouncing across the shiny surfaces of

the dashboard.

Then we stopped. I was hustled out as fast as I was thrown in. Amezcua lashed my hands together behind my back while Miguel held a Glock to my forehead.

"You move, bang," he said.

I felt a cord being wrapped around my legs.

"Not too much," Miguel said. "I'm not going to carry this son of a bitch."

My escorts gripped me on either side and rushed me along a tiny path that cut its way into what looked to be a mangrove swamp. Branches entwined with long vines were thick in places and once Amezcua let a branch whip across my face. He laughed when I stumbled to the ground.

"Get up, fuckface," he said. "It ain't gonna hurt much longer."

He reached down to grab the front of my shirt and hoisted me off the ground like a ragdoll. My good eye teared up.

"Stop fucking around," Miguel barked from up ahead.

We walked single file for almost a hundred yards. Red-winged blackbirds sent their piercing *scree-caw* alerts ahead as we passed clumps of cattails; once or twice something small skipped out of the path ahead as we came clattering through. The sun was well up in the sky but it was colder and darker where we were.

Amezcua stumbled in a rut and cursed. "*Heule a rayos.* Fucking stinks."

"Quiet," Miguel said.

From the treetops high above the scrub I could see ragged patches of blue sky. I gulped from the anguish of being so alone at that moment.

We came to a clearing of sorts; I could see the water's edge about ten yards away. Green-crusted like pond scum but lighter, almost phosphorescent. There were twigs and branches poking their bony fingers through the water. The fuggy odor of rot hung in the air, and sounds of the swamp echoed across the water.

A fish or frog jumped near a submerged tree with branches loaded down with yards of Spanish moss. Guanabana vines dangled into the water. Cerise orchids bloomed at the swamp's edge, their delicate pink and white flowers cascading down to the water's edge. I saw others with blood-red petals. A bubble of giddy laughter erupted in my throat; then I had a return of that feeling from the night before. I remembered Bobbie's slightly crooked smile as we parted from the restaurant.

"Quiet," Miguel repeated.

We followed the water's rim for another ten yards or so. I was walking like a man in a dream, one whose legs are mired in quicksand. The path had been cut through the bamboo that towered above us. Somebody had cut a path through it, or it would have been impenetrable. Amezcua went ahead and took out his automatic, pulled the slide back with a *snick*.

"Yo, snakes, man," Amezcua said. "Cottonmouths. Whew, hate them things."

The darkness inside the bamboo brake was claustrophobic. My shirt was ripped and I was soaked and dripping with perspiration. Miguel pulled me along. Crescents of perspiration beneath his suit jacket grew to half-moons. He breathed heavily.

Something small whiplashed through the saw grass and splashed into the water at our approach as we came to a clearing, a small space under a canopy of green.

Manny, the trainer, was nude, tied to a tree at the edge of the water.

"You just missed him!" Amezcua shouted and clapped his hands like a kid.

"He was right fuckin' there, man. Right there! Fuckin' bull gator, man. Huge motherfucker!"

I couldn't take my eyes off the man tied to the tree.

Miguel jerked me roughly over to where Manny seemed to be waiting for us. His white head was canted to one side as if he were asleep. I heard the drone of flies; a black column of gnats settled about his head in a moving halo. Then I noticed the busier flies and I saw what had happened to Emilio's trainer in the swamp.

Manny had no legs. Rather, he had stumps of legs and shredded ribbons of flesh and gristle exposed above one knee, where it was bitten off and showed pink and white.

Amezcua seemed exhilarated by the sight and smell of death.

He clapped his hands again and capered about Manny's corpse.

"You maniacs," I said.

Amezcua now had a MAC-10 in his hands and he was pointing it at my face.

"Shoot me, motherfucker," I said.

"Naw, man," Amezcua said. He grabbed my face and shook it. "Not so fast, homes."

"W-Why? Wait for what?" I had a hard time speaking around his fist clamped on me.

"We waitin' on the boss, see?" Amezcua said. "He gonna wan' see this too."

I suppose there's nothing original or unique left to feel or think. How can there be, with the billions of people who've lived and died on this earth? One human being's life, after all, is pretty much nothing if you take the long view. The trouble was, at that moment, I didn't have that luxury. Ask those poor bastards from Latvia or anywhere the Nazis had sent their *Direkt Aktion Kommandos* to clean out a village. What's it like to be frog-marched to a big trench and told to kneel down?

How long does time take then? What do you think about when you stare down into the hole you know is your grave?

I had told Micah when we first married, when I was the happiest I've ever been, that I didn't trust happiness. She told me I should have been born during the Dark Ages when Vikings, the Black Death, marauding thugs on horseback called knights, miserable poverty and hunger, dirt and disease were the lot of everyone but the privileged few. While the spit dried in my mouth and seconds slowed to molasses speed, I thought in clichés of hopelessness, *no escape, no turning back.* Just that, a coward's mantra.

CHAPTER 5

Pavelic stood back, nonchalantly appraising me as he lit a cigarillo. Coils of thin blue smoke wound about his head in the stagnant air. The sun was beginning to cook us. He turned his gaze from me to look out over the water. Amezcua, becalmed by his master's presence, swatted at a deer fly biting his ear and picked at his mud-flecked trousers.

"These Glades," Pavelic mused. "The *primitiveness* of this place speaks to me." He was examining an orchid at the edge of the swamp.

"Did you kill her, Pavelic? Tell me that much. Is Raina dead?" "Why should I kill anyone?" "You animals," I said.

Amezcua's blow to my chest knocked me flat. "Careful, *hombre*. Look what happened to Manny before you mouth off like that to Mister Pavelic again."

Pavelic smiled at me as if we were alone, two friends on an outing in the swamps to scope out flora and fauna.

"Ah, hibiscus. Periwinkle. The elemental nature of life. Life teems, a genetic soup."

I heard Amezcua say, "*Un poco putrido*, boss. It's all stink and flies out here."

Pavelic ignored him. He sniffed and peered down at Manny's torso.

Lying on top of the dense smells of swamp rot was something else like burnt meat.

"You think he went into shock first? The mind, apprehending death, shuts down. The amygdala in the brain squirts an enzyme to ease the transition. Like animals being devoured alive."

You sadistic fuck. My skin burned and itched. A

thousand nerves were tripped, all demanding attention at once.

"When I was a boy," Pavelic began, enjoying himself.

"F-fuck you," I interrupted. *Not like this, not like this.*

"Did you know a jackal doesn't bite the throat to strangle its victim? It prefers to eat it alive. The animal's big eyes watch its own intestines being pulled out. This is nature. This is history. It is what we are."

"It's what you are, and these two cretins with you."

"Haftmann, I'm going to make a tiny incision right here in your gut and have Miguel take out the large intestine, carefully, extracting it an inch at a time. He'll place the end of it near the water's edge. This will make things proceed faster, you see."

"Pavelic, look, listen to me. You don't have to do this."

"Don't beg. It's pointless and unbecoming. I imagine those settlers who pleaded with the Kiowas and the Apaches got the same answer when they pled with their captors. The only difference is that it won't be coyotes coming for your guts. Keep your eyes on the water."

The nauseating warp of his voice penetrated my mind and bowels despite every mantra I could summon. The first dead body I found in the weeds had been a runaway. Possums had burrowed up the anal passage, made a home...

"Alligators are discerning creatures," Pavelic, the classroom lecturer, droned. "But it likes its meal dead, soft and rotten, jammed under the water to decay faster."

Amezcua stepped over to Manny's corpse.

"That big old gator, he chomp your legs while you look him in the eye, eh? You lucky, man. We don't need no information or else I get to set your balls on fire like I did Manny."

Amezcua held up a plastic bottle of lighter fluid. That explained the smell of burning meat.

Then, to me: "Pretty soon he gonna bite through your asshole right to your fuckin' brain."

"*Au contraire*, Luis, he'll most likely tear Haftmann's limbs off first. Bull males like to rip their opponent's limbs to immobilize their prey."

Miguel and Amezcua were cutting cards to see who had to film my death with their cell phone. He'd need to hold that videophone close to its snout and that might not be so good a thing.

Prison gave me a different kind of mental discipline for dealing with pain and time but for horror, it wasn't working very well. One part of my brain begged Pavelic to stop talking; the other wanted him to chatter on forever.

He was saying something about murderers, but it was getting hard to concentrate. If I could, I would smash my head into a tree before that gator started chomping. That was my great plan.

"... because the act of murder forces someone to participate in the second of the two most important events a human being can know. It makes one special, different."

"You're different, all right," I said. My voice sounded strange to me, alien.

I tried to muster another *fuck you* but I was empty of defiance.

A chunk of ice crept up my belly and surged into my throat.

"Are you familiar with Ovid's *Epistulae ex Ponto*?"

"He pissed himself, the *maricón*," Amezcua said, pointing at me.

"Let's put things in order first, gentlemen? Get rid

of the garbage first," Pavelic said.

Odio went over to Manny's corpse and cut him down from the tree, cursing when the added weight of his burden sank his feet up to his ankles in muck. Amezcua found that humorous.

"Luis, tie our friend to the same place," Pavelic ordered.

Hobbled by the cords, I was pushed and shoved by Amezcua against the tree bark. My eyes were fixed on Miguel as he wrestled the body of Emilio's trainer toward the water's edge.

"Hey, Miguel, dat ain't no fireman's carry," yelled Amezcua, watching him struggle with the dead weight. "He lighter now without his legs."

"Fuck your mother," grunted Odio, high-stepping about the body as he rolled it in. He picked up a fallen branch and shoved the corpse into a blanket of green algae and lily pads with bright phallic stems.

An instant after the last ripple died away, two pairs of reptile eyes broke the surface of the water simultaneously and moved toward Manny's body, floating face down like a cork. I saw his back was a red and black crust where they had soaked his shirt in lighter fluid and set it on fire. The first hit of the gators jerked the body only slightly. The second took an arm and dragged the corpse under for a moment before it popped loose and surfaced.

"Yo, dese babies trained real good," Amezcua chortled. "Like fuckin' seals."

Not real, not happening.

Then the water beneath Manny's torso boiled and he nearly sat upright as one of the gators, all of the twelve feet Pavelic had described to me, took him in a death roll and jerked the body under water and rolled its white belly up: Manny and gator, gator and Manny.

Sickening. I lost it then – yellow spumes of hot bile

ejected from my mouth; hot watery shit burned my legs when my bowels loosed. ...*Too much, too much...*

My stomach spasmed again and I felt my esophagus on fire. The action moved under water and except for the massive scalloped tail breaking the surface one time, we saw nothing except the water lapping against the shore.

"They've been around a long time, and they do learn," Pavelic said. "We have provided many free meals over the years. They used to fight over the morsels. Now I've spoiled them."

Pavelic told me Manny was the appetizer; they'd pin his ravaged corpse under a tree limb at the bottom of the swamp until it turned soft, and they'd come back to eat it later.

I said, "I hope cancer eats your insides out, Pavelic. I hope you die screaming in your own blood."

"Seconds must seem like hours to you right now, Haftmann. All that pain to come. Like sitting in your own electric chair waiting for the switch to be thrown. All those receptors screaming into a brain that won't be able to receive them."

My voice cracked again. "Did Raina ... come here?" His voice sounded farther off than before.

"Why would I want to kill that girl? *'Passion cannot be beautiful without excess,'*" Pavelic said, stepping close to whisper in my ear.

"What will your last words be, I wonder."

Cop memory: murder victim's last words the same. Don't please don't.

He fondled a flower and plucked its petal. "That's what they call the pope – *Pontiff*, a builder of bridges."

Jesus, Latin. No escape from it, not even here at my death.

I felt hands grip me and drag me toward the tree where Manny had been. I could hear every twig crack, every insect noise as if magnified out of all proportion.

I was thrust against the tree, my hands still tied and nylon cord was wrapped about my body in tight loops. I smelled like a body farm. I tried one final time to will my brain to shut down, blunt the nerves so that I would not feel, would not see, the eyes, the snout ripping into me.

Amezcua shouting: *"Mira, viene." Look, he comes. ...Oh fuck.*

Fifteen feet from where my feet were stuck in the mud kicked up by Manny in his death throes, I saw a pair of eyes breaking the surface of the water.

Amezcua said, "Let me throw him in, boss."

"No," Pavelic said. "He'll have more time to think about it this way."

My breathing was loud in my ears – the short, shallow breaths of hysteria. I pressed the sternum of my chest hard against the cord. I tried to induce vomiting, preferring to choke to death. Veins in my neck throbbed with blood. Every second and particle of a second stretched out, spaghettified into Planck time. I was really fucked. I looked at that single pair of eyes looking back at me and imagined, in every possible acute detail, the brutal power of what lay hidden in those massive jaws.

Something gave a fraction of an inch. The ropes were still taut but as I dug my heels into the water's edge I found purchase against a trunk or branch.

Every sound tore at my ears. I strained. I wondered how much blood loss could I sustain before darkness numbed me past feeling.

Not that. Soft belly. Torn to shreds, blue intestines ripped loose, bones snapping.

Slapping sounds of palms against flesh, muttered curses at the mosquitoes biting them. I thought: *Was this how I was going into oblivion – with a paltry thought of mosquitoes?*

Like a broken stylus skipping over a bump in a record: *No hope, no hope, no hope.*

Then a sound of mosquitoes, a vast horde of them, crescendoing in the distance. It went from tinny vibrations in the still air to a ratcheting, ear-bursting whir. Then I knew it without ever having seen one up close: not mosquitoes – fan blades.

Fucking airboats. *Beautiful, I'm saved!*

The noise grew in decibels to become a loud, steady whine.

I heard loud male voices. I heard Pavelic's voice behind me bark orders. Scuttled sounds and breaking branches, crashing noises in the underbrush.

Pavelic said, "It's not your cavalry coming to the rescue, Haftmann. Glades tourists."

Steel against the throbbing pulse of my temple.

Amezcua's voice, spittle in my face: "You are a dead man no matter what happens, cabrón."

A motor cut on the airboat. Two men talking above the diminishing engine noise.

Shouts, voices.

This way ... this way ... I tried to beam my thoughts at them.

Then the staccato *crack-crack-crack-crack* of automatic fire in the distance beyond the canebrake to my left. Another swamp boat's engine drowned out everything.

Moments that seemed like hours later, a single pistol shot cut the air. Swamp birds flapped wings and wheeled overhead. More crashing through the underbrush. Coming toward us – I heard the wheeze of Amezcua's voice, laboring from his run:

"Miguel and me, we shot both of 'em!"

"Shot both of *what*, you fool?"

"P-park rangers ... dey lookin' for poachers ..."

Pavelic cool, assessing, ice for blood. "Where is Miguel *now*?"

"He coming ... right behind ... me." Amezcua gasped for breath, bent over, hands on his knees, his clothes a sodden mess.

"Imbecile," Pavelic spat. "Rangers have two-way radios."

Amezcua: "What about him?"

"Kill him."

Gator meat, insect food. Seconds to live.

Miguel came lurching out of the underbrush, stumbling, cursing.

More sounds, yelling. I couldn't see Pavelic's face, but I could imagine the spit gathering at the corners of his mouth. Amezcua, crazed, hollering something about his gun jamming.

A second spun on a new, weirder axis of time.

"Get moving! Now! Back to the car before we're spotted."

"*Teiene chorra,*" hissed Amezcua in my face spattering me with his saliva. "Now you get a bullet instead of a gator."

He called that luck, but I think I believed him at that moment and was grateful for it.

"Miguel, Miguel...!"

I heard Amezcua above and behind me, fainter of voice, wheezing something from far away behind me, running.

Raina Toivela, I'm so sorry. Micah: I thought love would last forever...

I was wrong about a lot of things in that split-second of eternity. I don't remember the gun firing when it was placed roughly against my head, the barrel at my temple near the hairline.

The second was stranger yet; I wasn't in any pain at all. I just wasn't there anymore...

I wasn't looking through a brightly lit tunnel at a flaxen-haired Jesus beckoning me. None of my long-dead relatives in a heavenly conga line. No choirs of angels. No demons with mottled faces and fangs and claws for hands eager to pull me down.

Just nothing – zero. I was missing from a universe that is never empty of force fields and attractive forces in atoms and particles of atoms. I was missing from gravity itself. This creature of flesh and blood and three trillion cells comprising him named Thomas Haftmann, born in a motel, abandoned by his mother and raised by his half-loony grandmother, once a deckhand on ore boats, then a cop turned private eye in a shithole town – well, that Thomas Haftmann had never been written into the book of history in the first place. It was the emptiness of oblivion my heart had been yearning for so desperately when I was tied to that tree.

PART 2

The most dangerous dog is a wounded dog.
- folk proverb

EARLY SPRING, JEFFERSON-ON-THE-LAKE

CHAPTER 6

It turned out I would have a lot of time to think about those moments.

Parts of my memory are gone forever. But I remember the barrel against my head before the explosion. Pavelic would have killed me. Amezcua, I knew to a certainty, wanted to kill me, would have killed me if he hadn't been ordered back to the car. I remember Pavelic shouting for Miguel, calling his name. Miguel must have been given the order to kill me, and I had him to thank for my life.

Rather, I had his stoic, humorless, amoral character to thank for it. He was the wild card, and my hunch at the beginning of my ride to the Everglades was right. Miguel could kill easily, too easily, so that my or anyone's death didn't matter as much to him. With Odio appointed my executioner at the last second thanks to those park rangers, I had that tiny fragment of a chance, and it paid off despite the bullet in the head he delivered.

I see it happening this way: he must have approached me on the run, blowing and puffing from his race back to the clearing. His expensive loafers would shimmy about in the slurry at my feet. That by itself could have put off his aim by the slightest bit to ensure that the slug he sent into my head wasn't a killshot. The slug didn't churn my brain to stew as it should have. Instead, according to one of my neurosurgeons, it took an angle that bounced off my skull with minimal damage to my brain. I have headaches on the Richter scale that reach an eight-point-seven at times, but I am still here making my stomach go in and out, taking in oxygen, expelling carbon dioxide.

There are days when I wish his aim had been true. The pain is beyond belief, worse than torture.

In all the time I had been tied up, I never stopped straining against the nylon cord. I had won an inch at most, more when Amezcua first roped me to the tree. Stretching my body as far forward as I could gave me a little movement, and when Miguel Odio pulled the trigger, I must have flinched just enough to help prevent a brain shot. Had Amezcua come back with that MAC-10, it would have been a different story. One more centimeter, my youthful medico at the Cleveland Clinic told me, would have meant the difference between Haftmann-mobile and Haftmann-vegetable, drooling in the corner.

Sometimes I awaken in the night screaming curses at my would-be killers: *Miguel, you toilet-licking maggot cocksucker* or *Amezcua, you weasel shit from your mother's asshole.* Those and other expressions of a dubious education give me small comfort.

My last image, obviously reconstructed from a damaged brain that never had the actual experience to record it and stamp it in there, is one that comes from pop culture or TV, I suppose. I see a whirling mass of red fire spinning like a child's pinwheel. I don't know how long it lasts but the blackness will always follow it to take me off. It bugs me deeply that Pavelic is always there somewhere observing but never the one I scream at as I do at his thugs.

~ ~ ~

The doctors in Cleveland love to talk about it. They're also under the misguided impression I enjoy hearing them talk about it. They like to bring young interns into my checkups and point at the puckered scar and describe in loving detail – in that Latin I detest – what might have happened if the bullet had taken a different path and smashed into the medulla oblongata instead of deflecting as it did and coming to rest against the occipital bone, that saucer-shaped bone at the base of the skull that allows the neck to swivel. I was stupid enough to ask one of my surgeons what would have happened if the slug had taken the first path, the one Miguel no doubt intended for it.

"Between the anterior median sulcus and the anterolateral sulcus, you have the pyramid of the medulla oblongata..."

"English, Doctor, English."

"The medulla controls a great many functions, you see. Respiratory, cardiac, vomiting, and vasomotor centers and deals with all the body's autonomic functions."

"And those would be what?"

"All the involuntary functions, of course, such as breathing, heart rate, blood pressure..."

Sometimes I think I can actually hear the slug deflecting from the skull bone, but the doctors tell me that's not possible.

My mind plays it over and over every single day, and I still don't know. Like an old-time film reel stuck in the same sprocket holes, I see myself roped and tied to that tree of death, I see Amezcua approaching from behind, I hear Pavelic calling Miguel's name, I hear the throaty whirr of the swamp boats' blades chopping thick air, I smell that swamp stink all over again, and I feel the metal jammed against my head before the lights go out. But no shot, no pain, no trio of killers fleeing to safety. My brain won't put those pieces back right, so I figure they're lost forever. No matter which scene comes first, it always ends with a mini-black hole that sucks up everything after that day into a chasm of darkness. My mind refuses to play anything past that point. The rest is the daily consciousness of pain, rage, confusion.

I keep it in my pocket like a worry stone – a little piece of metal, snubbed from its microsecond's trip through my flesh. The furrow is healed over with scar tissue, as is the entrance wound. The doctor said I will suffer headaches and memory lapses for the rest of my life. Had that .9 mm slug penetrated my skull, he said, instead of bouncing off, I wouldn't be here talking because my brain would have had the pulpy consistency of thick soup.

"Find another way to make ends meet, Mister Haftmann," he said.

Trouble is, I don't know how to make myself do that. I know other guys can see when something ends, pull the plug, walk away. I wasn't ready to lick the bottom of the glass.

At the academy, the instructors brought in the Cuyahoga County Medical Examiner, Dr. Elizabeth Bhargrava herself, Cleveland's legendary pathologist whose hands have kneaded more entrails than most grandmothers have cookie dough. She told us that a bullet doesn't have weight and mass to knock a human being off his feet.

"Look, it's just a small lead projectile," she said and held up a round for all to see. "You can take a lot of bullets unless it's a spine or a brain shot. Then you go down regardless. It's only television and films," she said in her pleasant sing-song voice; "it's the power of the mind and nothing more than that which makes you think you've got to go down when you're shot," Bhargrava said in her finale.

One dumb rookie next to me had to ask: "So what do you do if you're shot?"

"Keep running," this grandmotherly looking woman in gray braids said in her lilting accent.

~ ~ ~

So I'm alive. I had stopped believing in God long before that day in the Everglades. Just before I came out of the anesthetic, I was standing on a mound in the dark overlooking the night sky. I was naming the constellations and calling out the stars as I used to do silently when I had gone sailing as a teenaged deckhand on the Great Lakes.

Sitting on the boat deck alone on a clear night, you could see the constellations where they touched the horizon's edge. I was struggling with Taurus, its faint spackling of third-magnitude stars difficult to discern with a pair of good eyes, and I distinctly remember trying to say *Aldebaran*, a massive red first-magnitude star. In my head I kept saying it. One of the nurses, it must have been, shook me awake at that point. Then I knew I was blind. My worst, my darkest fear since damaging my eye.

A greasy salve in my eyes prevented the eyeballs drying. Knifepain shot back and forth inside my skull like a deadbolt being snapped – murderously intense from which there was no respite because they were afraid of brain hemorrhaging and drugs would obscure the symptoms. Nobody's idea of any god should allow people to suffer this much pain – no merciful god, at least.

I remember struggling, somehow, to put that bone-shivering agony someplace so that I could deal with it. The nurse chittered like a squirrel around my bed. *Please stop talking*, I said but it might have been merely a thought. She was trying to cheer me up. When Micah forced me to read Dante's *Inferno*, I found myself laughing throughout the cantos at the ingenious punishments doled out to sinners. I would have put the nurse in the circle where they bury you upside-down and all you see are the soles of their feet.

"Who is 'Saraband'?" the same nurse, her name

was Alice, asked me one day. I don't recall whether it was night or day; it was like doing jail all over again, but I remember I was moaning in my bed at that time.

The word, a deathly susurration in a time far away, started to make sense. Like those silver notes of the piano playing from the car stereo on my last ride. I had never heard Raina play the piano, so why, I wanted to know, was my brain insisting that I had? I made gurgling, baby noises, as she wiped the salve off my eyes. *Her hands aren't meant for a piano's keyboard*, I thought then. More likely they were destined for the dugs of dairy cows, a tough farmwoman in speech and manners.

"You were saying the name just now," she said. "She your wife or a girlfriend, Mister Haftmann?"

Claustrophobia, bandages covering my head and eye. Someone had pinned my hands to my sides. I struggled against the restraints.

"No, no, no, that's not going to help you. We had to keep you from pulling at the bandages."

I heard her say something about a Get Well card on the table next to me.

"Shall I read it to you?" She had this unnerving habit of asking and answering her own questions – another circle of hell warranted for that.

"What did you say, Mister Haftmann?"

I mumbled something I hoped sounded like *Nothing*.

She read it to me – a sappy greeting, signed Your True Friend.

"I'll put it … there. Feel it, hon? It's in your hand. It's from – let me see her – Leggett, I think," she said. "I can't read the signature."

"Never mind," I mumbled to her. El Lagarto. *The Lizard. Shit of alligators.*

When the bandage around my head finally came

off, her moon face rippled above me in a mirage of pain. My tongue was fat in my mouth. I think, in my confusion, I was being allowed to go home, so I struggled to get up to dress myself. The wrist restraints had been removed a day earlier. Somehow in the commotion I was causing the nurse, I was put down with a shot of morphine.

More days passed, long days, uneventful days. Days without visitors or cards. I was grateful for that. How could I have faced Raina's father?

CHAPTER 7

My recovery, if that's what it was, became a slow descent into the old-time hell of fire and ice. The pain grew less, my addiction to painkillers grew more, and my soul shriveled inside me like a wisp of paper in a dust storm. I was saturated with fear every day, and huge bouts of despair; every emotion that ransacks a weak mind afflicted me in the state I was in. I wanted to die, I wanted to murder. I found no peace. I read the newspaper account of the "incident" Bobbie Gersack sent me right down to the commas.

The article talked about poachers surprising park rangers. It never mentioned Manny's corpse or me or Pavelic or his two goons.

I felt like an open wound in a perpetual condition of festering. I smelled rancid to myself. For the first time in twelve years I drank. Hard booze with an occasional beer chaser. I wanted out of everything. The pain that awoke me as I lay on the floor beside my bed with an empty fifth of Jim Beam or Old Grand-Dad made me renew my vows to quit. I never want to feel that combination of vertigo and lightning in the *cabeza* ever again. I fainted twice and cracked an incisor against the toilet bowl. My heart was full of ill will toward everything that breathed or moved.

Micah called. I don't know how she heard. Tico might have gotten in touch with her, because the day I came back to the Strip on Jefferson-on-the-Lake, she called me at home. I doubt the conversation lasted three minutes, but I sobbed like a baby after it. For the first and only time since the shooting, I was indifferent to the raw nerves in my head twitching like worms dangled over a fire.

I don't remember much of what I said to her. I remember fracturing the plastic sheathing of my cell phone from squeezing it. She asked if I was OK. I said I was. She told me about her new job, her daughter's cutting teeth, but never once mentioned her husband. I asked her if she wanted me to send on her dictionary. She said no, she had a new one just as good. She said it too fast. I knew she didn't want me to have her address. She said she'd call again soon.

I had bills to pay. As soon as I could think straight, I called Paul Toivela and gave him an oral report, although I abridged most of the parts about my own incompetence. I didn't tell him about Manny's torture in the mangrove swamps. I told him how much I had spent, how much I had coming for services rendered, and said I would return the rest, about $1200. He thought for a while and then said for me to keep it and to consider it a partial payment.

"Why?" I asked, fearing the response.

"You know why."

"Mister Toivela ... I can't do that."

"As soon as you're fit to travel again, I want you to go back down to Florida."

"It's a police investigation now. Two Florida park rangers were killed."

"I don't care about that. All I care about is my daughter. You find Raina. You promised me, you promised us, her mother and me."

How do you tell a father a corpse is all there is to find and that's probably impossible?

"I'll give you the name of a good professional agency down there."

"No."

He terminated the conversation with that and I had the dead air of Ohio to listen to.

Fuck. Shit. Piss.

~ ~ ~

God damn it to hell. Every time I opened an envelope

or looked at my ravaged face in the mirror or changed a pus-filled bandage, I felt the pressure to call Raina's father back and refuse.

I have never had a problem with my own physical cowardice. Courage is for assholes, not existentialists. But the bills kept coming; the Florida hospital where they lifeflighted me sent me a detailed printout for every ace bandage, syringe, aspirin, and drug given to me in the thirteen days of my stay. My Ohio Blue Cross picked up $192,000, which still left me owing $24,000.

There was a number for someone in their accounting department for me to call as soon as possible to arrange payment. *Well, sue me*, I thought. Light, gas, phone bills for the house and office were past due. I had used every spare dollar from my credit union and was on the phone to borrow more.

Instead, I called Toivela. We spoke for fifteen minutes. He said he'd send a check for $2,500. I asked him to make it for $500 more.

He agreed without hesitation.

"I've got a question for you," I said.

"What is it?"

"Why didn't you take my advice and call an agency in Florida? I'm one man. I'm not licensed for any state but Ohio." I could have said that Florida law enforcement would wipe their collective asses with my credential.

"I did."

I let my silence hang there.

"I called every private investigator and every agency from the Miami to the Keys," Paul Toivela said. "Nobody wants to take on the job. They all gave me different reasons."

There was only one reason: *Pavelic. That motherfucker.*

~ ~ ~

I had a slim-to-none chance of finding Raina at this

point without help – big-time help.

I made a call. It was through no luck or skill of my own but through the mysterious workings of the federal bureaucracy – specifically, the federal investigative branch – that I hit pay dirt. An FBI agent named Edwin Booth owed me. Last I had heard from him he told me he was being re-assigned to New York City, a plum assignment if you have the bucks to afford to live there.

Unlike my own race to the bottom, Booth's career parabola was a marvel to behold. He managed to extricate himself out of the agency in charge of keeping Indians on the Pine Ridge Reservation from cultivating hemp, the lowest you can go if you're an FBI agent on the skids, which Booth has been from time to time. But the man has a silver tongue and the shrewdest sense of political maneuvering this side of the DC Beltway. He's worked the Southeast European Cooperative Initiative on Sex-Trafficking, Operation Sword in the nineties investigating corrupt banks, and even did a stint on the Bin Laden Task Force.

Booth was close to mandatory retirement, however, and I didn't know whether he would honor my request for his help. This same silver-haired, dapper man once convinced me into helping him find a psychotic serial killer operating in Northern Ohio, the case infamous as the "Jack-in-the-Box" murders because the killer liked to leave his victims' heads in cardboard boxes. This was after the first victim, whose head was placed carefully in the women's public restroom at Severance Hall during Yehudi Menuhin's last conducting tour with the Cleveland Orchestra.

I called the Manhattan office of the bureau and got the runaround when I asked to speak to Special Agent Booth. I finally got a receptionist in Cyber/Special Ops to tell me he was in Washington, DC at a conference and was expected back "soon."

"Please have him call me at my office number in Ohio as soon as he reports back," I said.

"And whom shall I say is calling?"

Her tone irked me. I can tell when people think I'm wasting their precious time.

"It's 'who,'" I snarled. "Thomas Haftmann. He'll have my number."

I owed that one to Micah. She was forever bitching at me about my bad grammar.

~ ~ ~

"I don't owe you shit, Haftmann."

Well, I didn't quite expect that.

Booth's language was normally as polished as his image. We did, I knew well, have our little disagreements. I had the feeling he didn't look at our time together in Boston as one of the brightest feathers in his cap.

"It's good to hear from you too, Booth. Long time no see."

"Listen to me. I have gone the extra mile for you time and time again—"

"I know, I know. You got me into that cushy prison in West Virginia."

"Don't think that was nothing. Those cons in Lucasville would have shredded an ex-cop like you into pulp inside a week. You were in no shape then, as I recall."

Booth, I thought, *you should see me now.*

"That's true, and I'm noting it that way in my memoirs. Meanwhile, I have this problem—"

"No, no, and again, no. Do you hear me, Haftmann? You are a practicing licensed investigator in Ohio despite the fact you are a convicted felon. Do you have any idea how much clout I had to use to get you that license back? I called in every favor ever owed to me and you have the gall to call me for another."

"May I interject for a moment?"

"The slate is clean. All debts canceled, all favors called in. Nobody owes anybody."

I heard a tinny *churring* that might have been an automatic monitor being activated.

"We got our man, though, didn't we, Booth? *You* got him. That got you all the way back to the Big Apple, am I right?"

We had to dance around like this for a while. I should have realized it. Booth was a go-by-the-numbers man until he saw an opening for himself, but he didn't like anybody like me getting ahead in his investigation. I decided to wait him out. I knew I was softening him up a bit by the time he mentioned he would have to report the call.

"Am I on a list?" I asked him.

"Don't be naïve, Haftmann. Everybody's on a list somewhere," he said.

"Is the name Raymond Anton Pavelic on one of your lists by any chance?"

"Goodbye."

The other noise I had heard ceased a half-second later. I was thinking my hearing had improved as compensation for my bad eyesight. Or maybe they wanted you to hear it.

~ ~ ~

He'd come round. Booth hadn't written me off as easily as that. It would take a little time to let the shock of hearing from me wear off. I had probably hurt his career in that he did do everything he said; he even came to see me in prison once when I was less than a cordial guest, but he took the credit for the case. Cops despise feds for that. They're always grandstanding for the kudos afterward, but it's the donkeywork of detectives that gets it done most of the time. One side plays by the rulebook and the other has to use intuition, which sometimes takes you past the line if you want to solve cases.

It took another week before the nausea and the headaches subsided to levels I could handle. I had little stamina though, and I had dropped twenty-five pounds. My eyes had the look of a raccoon mask and my wound continued to ooze. Still, I was feeling human again. The only thing that hadn't subsided was the murderous rage in my heart for what had been done to me.

I called Bobbie Gersack, kept missing her, and finally caught her at work between stories. She started to apologize for not seeing me in the hospital in Florida, but I brushed it off, and we were back where we were. Her smoldering anger for Pavelic vibed through my cell, pinged off towers between Ohio and Florida, not a whit diminished. I loved a good hater and told her so.

"I didn't come to see you for a reason," she said.

"Forget it," I said. "I know you're busy at the paper."

"It wasn't that," she said quietly. "I was afraid."

"Forget it," I said. "I wouldn't have wanted to see you even if I could talk."

"Do you remember me telling you about my cop friend?" "I remember everything up to the swamps," I said.

"She's willing to meet. She has some confidential information she's willing to share."

She: I had always assumed her source would be a man. I had also assumed it was about Toni DeCamillo's whereabouts. What she said next took my breath away.

"It's about your missing girl."

"I can't wait to meet your friendly cop," I said.

"I'll arrange it. You've got my home cell. Buzz me when you get back. By the way, just so you know, she's attractive and gay as a tangerine, too."

"I'll try hard not to do or say anything stupid, Mom," I said.

She clicked off before I could get another word out. It was always my sight I was terrified of losing, not speech. But I thought about it when Bobbie hung up. She wouldn't use ten words when none would do, and I liked that. If that bullet had taken away my speech, it would have killed my job, but good riddance, I sometime feel about that. Social networking is all gabble: it's all about the new pair of shoes somebody bought at Dillard's. Facile, superficial, egotistic, a quick-hit, thrill-in-the-moment but no time to think or read anything that isn't in text-English. It all adds up to the weight of a snowflake just like all the radio waves we've ever sent into outer space. It used to mean something to say goodbye, I reflected, but then I was thinking of Micah and how she left me. Breaking up today is another symptom of the times. We say our lovers' goodbyes from saddleback, like Apaches.

Why not? We kill like them, don't we?

~ ~ ~

Whenever my head would give me some slack from the pain I was able to give more thought to that day in the swamp. Pavelic's failure to kill me must rankle, and though I hated him, I respected his intelligence; he just was not the kind of man to take stupid, unnecessary chances. Yet he had wanted to see me die out there – why? What sadistic thrill-seeking had he compartmentalized somewhere in his own lizard brain that needed that? Maybe Micah's psych books had something to them, after all.

He must have figured I had gotten too close to something important to his security to allow me to go back to Ohio. Raina was alive, then. What did Toni DeCamillo know about Raymond's sordid side operations that would make her dangerous to him? No, it wasn't adding up yet. *What*, I racked my brains, *had I stumbled upon or found out that I wasn't even aware of?*

I had to get stronger. I had to make myself get past the headaches, nausea, fear and night sweats, past the dreams of the swamp, past seeing Pavelic plucking orchids like an indolent boy playing she-loves-me-she-loves-me-not. That roiling water and the turbulence beneath the surface. All of it, if I let it, would freeze me into a state of such fear that I would never find the courage to go back there and do the job right.

Even as shit-scared as I was, and no matter how many times I awoke in an empty room sweating in fear, I was going back even if Paul Toivela had not called. It wasn't the lack of money, and I knew it. It had nothing to do with testosterone or facing my own fears. I wanted to kill Pavelic. I wanted to put a bullet into his brain. I wanted to kill Miguel Odio and that other mustached bastard, Luis Amezcua. I wanted them to know my fear. Most of all, I wanted to look in Raymond Pavelic's eyes when I stuck the gun in his mouth.

As I told Bobbie, I do so love a good hater.

PART 3

EARLY SPRING, SOUTH FLORIDA

CHAPTER 8

The air inside Delta Flight 543 Cleveland to Miami blew moist and hot all the way down. I took some painkillers – Demerols – washing them all down with warm Coke from a plastic cup that gave me heartburn. I was going to lay off the booze. How much insult can a brain take before it packs it in? I didn't want to know the answer to that. A vision of me in that familiar dope-fiend lean at the county nursing home was waiting in a Tarot card I didn't want to turn over.

My ears popped all the way down and the two businessmen jammed beside me hogged all the view of blue sky the Plexiglas afforded.

I thought of Raina constantly. She had thrown another of fate's hoops around me and linked me to whatever destiny lay below this aluminum bird with a hundred twenty people lining the sides of its hollow belly. My own physical rehabilitation seemed to be coinciding with the onset of another chilly Northern Ohio spring in parallel course: rough-hewn, ugly, and reluctant.

Before I left town and locked up my office, said goodbye to Tico in his bar and downed a last shot of Johnny Walker Black for good luck, another Alberta Clipper was blitzing us with below-zero wind chills, and the locals were still cocooned in lethargic winter blues to care much about sloughing off another year. The scent of money from next season's tourists was still a long way off. Tico was still serving the same twelve customers and the same three perennial winos at Happy Hour and the same five addicts between fixes who made Jefferson-on-the-Lake home despite Tico's wife Marta's daily threats to bumrush the whole bunch out of town. I was sure she had me in her sights, too.

Nothing had changed for me except the battering inside my head. I had deep bruises under my eyes that refused to clear up altogether. The surgeon who had my post-operative care counseled me in his humorless way about avoiding "future head trauma," as if I were keen to take up rugby the minute I got home. I had more bottles, prescriptions, and medicines than my grandmother did when she died of cancer the year I came home from sailing the Great Lakes as an ordinary seaman. I packed up the painkillers in a small traveling kit Micah had bought me years ago, and left the rest on the shelf in the bathroom. In Florida, the rule is pack lighter.

I was met by Bobbie's cop buddy at Miami International. She was mid-thirties, intense with darting eyes, and had hair the color of wheat, which looked casual and professionally cut at the same time. Her name was Sonja Andersen and she worked Intelligence, not Vice. Bobbie had not lied about her "cop" being attractive, but she stopped short of the truth: this woman was downright gorgeous.

"Bobbie and I are good friends," Sonya said.

She walked fast, unusual only because I had a hard time keeping pace with her long stride.

"I helped her find an apartment when she got off the plane from Minnesota," she added over her shoulder with a warm smile. It was a full-lipped smile, rare for cops of either gender in my experience, and she had perfect teeth to go with a tan that *Cosmo* would have described with words like "golden" and "honeyed."

On the way to her car, she told me she and Bobbie used to chase the same girls in the same bars. She cast a quick look at me to see how that was going over. A little crinkling of flesh around her deep green eyes seemed to say she wasn't going to have any masculine nonsense.

"Bobbie told me not to get cute," I said.

"Bobbie still thinks I work Vice but I transferred out to Intelligence a few months ago."

"I'll keep that confidential," I said. "Bobbie must have told you about our little partnership, Operation Pavelic, before it got aborted."

"Not exactly," Sonja said.

Now I was curious. "What did she say?"

"Bobbie mentioned you were Homicide in a resort town up north, somewhere near Pennsylvania, I think." "Close enough," I said. "What else did she say?" "She said you had ... issues," Sonja replied.

She was far enough ahead by then, dashing between rows of parked cars where gray seemed to be the dominant color, that I was looking only at the swivel of her hips.

She drove a pearl-gray Celica and avoided expressways clogged with rush-hour traffic.

She was right to be concerned about my credentials. Coconut Grove is just a Miami suburb. Too small for an Intelligence division, but every major urban area in the country had one. Most of these were subsumed under Gang Intelligence Units nowadays, which is where the real business of intelligence is. Street cops gave them a wide berth because they were the ones in charge of secrets, and you never knew whose secrets they held. Even Internal Affairs tiptoed around them. They didn't concern themselves with crimes; in fact, few of them with rank had been near a crime scene in years. They were there to stop crimes before they were committed and the dirt they gathered was closely guarded from within. They were often distrusted by the average street cop.

I knew what a risk it was for Sonja to give me even

morsels of information. Nobody in Intelligence who couldn't keep secrets would last long.

"Tell me what you can," I said.

"Bobbie told me what happened to you out there in the Glades," she said. This time she turned to give me a look with those green eyes full-bore. "How long were you out there?"

She meant how long I was there, sagging against that dying twisted tree trunk with my brains leaking out of my skull.

"The cops told me twenty minutes. They thought I was dead but somebody got a faint pulse. They had to toss me onto an airboat and then life-flight me to Miami.

"You owe those dead park rangers your life."

The cops who interviewed me in the hospital said the one ranger piloting the airboat was shot through the sternum in his seat. The younger ranger bled to death before they could save him. He gave pretty good directions to me, though he didn't know about me. It was his partner he was thinking of.

"He was twenty-three, had a wife, a son," Sonja told me as we left the airport lot.

I didn't hear an accusation in that. Her sunglasses covered her eyes. "One of the slugs ricocheted off a rib and nicked his carotid. All the other wounds were superficials except for one T & T in his wrist," she added as an after thought. She knew the reports in the murder book pretty well: *through and through*. The poetry of homicide. She hadn't been off the streets very long, I guessed. Intelligence had to be strapped like all cops but they only drew a gun to qualify annually.

"Do you mind? We're close to my house. Let's go there, have a drink and talk. Then I'll take you back to the Grove where you can find a motel.

She lived in a tidy bungalow with expensive

landscaping. There was a wrought-iron gate with rusting fleurs-de-lis we had to pass through along a winding driveway bordered by loblolly pines. An oak festooned with Spanish moss in the back shaded a quarter of the house. The air was damp and threatened rain. My kidneys ached from the long trip down.

She drank some kind of party wine while I had pink lemonade.

She asked me how it was and I told her it was lousy. She smiled. "Bobbie said you could shift moods very easily."

I imagined that was a euphemism for "erratic," but said nothing. I must have put a scowl on my face.

"Did I say something to offend you, Mister Haftmann?"

"Thomas, or Tom, please. It's just that I can't drink and I hate the fact that I can't and am too afraid to drink anything but this circus water."

Her green eyes were flecked with gold in the iris and they were zeroed in on me. She sat across from me in a comfortable chair in her living room. I was sitting on the edge of a padded lounge chair. She had changed into a brightly colored wrap-around sarong. It was loose fitting but its material clung to the curves of her body.

She lifted her glass and checked it against the light. "I have some very light wines if you prefer to switch. A Bardolino or a Valpolicella? They won't make you groggy in the heat."

"No, no thanks. I've never seen the point of wine no matter what color it is."

"I need to get one thing clear before I tell you anything," she said. "If you're here for any kind of revenge, our conversation ends now. I'll drive you right back to the airport."

"No," I said. "Absolutely not."

My old grandmother died convinced I was of the devil's party. What did I have to lose by telling one more measly lie to a beautiful stranger?

She looked at me for a while, not a friendly stare. Then she said, "I'll believe you."

Meaning *for the time being*. I sipped my lemonade and we talked shop, cop to ex-cop.

In her home, Sonja Anderson was relaxed. She had a habit of puckering her lips in thought. I told her about my interview with DeCamillo. I soft-pedaled the details of my second visit later that night.

Sonja kicked off her sandals and rubbed one foot against the other. Some rain had begun to fall, a typical South Florida cloud burst. Her picture window beneath the awning was stippled with those fat drops. "It'll cool off for a while, but that heat will build up again," she said, continuing to look me over with a cop's gaze. We were in sync on the main points of planning moves and what order I should follow.

She brushed a strand of hair away from her forehead. I noticed a couple white hairs like spiky filaments working their way free from the part at the crown as she leaned toward me, elbows on knees, and asked me to tell her everything I knew of Raina Toivela. She never interrupted nor asked me a single question. When I stopped talking, she fixed me with a gaze that suggested she had resolved something. "What I'm going to tell you stays in this room," she said. "I want you to see something first."

She got up, walked into the other room and came back with three disks. She put a DVD in the machine and stacked the other two on top.

"She's in porno," said Sonja. "This first one came from a shop on Collins Avenue."

It was low quality, tinny sound and dubbed-over visuals. It reminded me of those VCR tapes from the seventies without the roller-rink music.

Raina looked younger despite the heavy make-up. She was in three segments in the production by a film company called Silver Cyprus Productions, Ltd., and it was copyrighted last year. The date was in Roman numerals instead of Arabic numbers. In the first sequence she was performing fellatio on two Hispanic men. The older male with a scarred belly kept up a steady patter of smut talk throughout. When he ejaculated on her breasts, he crooned in a basso voice with a soft accent something about "vitamins," and told her to "lick it up." The other, younger male had a smaller penis but ejaculated an unusual amount of seminal fluid. Once she brought him to climax with her mouth, she kept her eyes shut as he sprayed her breasts and then lifted his pumping organ to her mouth level and face. Her face, eyelids and hair were wet with his sperm.

"The film is called 'Pearl Necklace for South Beach Hoes,'" said Sonja.

"Classy," I said.

My stomach fell like an anvil through a trap door. I thought of Raina's parents.

"The group I work with calls the younger male 'the Marzipan Man.'"

"Not hard to guess why," I said.

"One of my colleagues thinks it's not seminal fluid but Ivory dish soap or something similar. The amount of ejaculate is ... freakish."

Raina in the film was thinner than I remembered from the time I had left her last summer; the last image was of her licking her fingers and opening her mouth right after the money shot. Her eyes cut to the side where someone was issuing commands off camera. It was so cheaply produced there was no credit roll. The fade out of her semen-smeared face, trying to look girlishly slutty for the camera, ended the film.

"You want to see the other two from the set? Just about the same except they change positions. It's mostly cunnilingus. The camera doesn't waste much time on her face."

"No," I said. "Are they dated the same?"

"Yes. These films have a distribution on both coasts. We found these in a shop in Naples, but the owner said he gets his film list from a distributor who wholesales the product from a variety of ordering sites online and doesn't place orders himself."

"What else?"

She ejected the first disk and put one in from one of those flimsy wallets she took from a separate pile of DVDs.

"The action gets a little rougher here, but it's still legal stuff – just kinkier. Some analingus. Toys. Inserting beads and other objects in the anus of one or the other partner, both male and female. Group sex. There's even a German shepherd in one scene."

"I don't know how to explain this to her parents," I said. "She plays Bach, Mozart, for Christ's sake."

"We have a file on some because of the drugs and organized crime connections to the porno industry. But some of these are amateurs, weekend partyers in motels, locals, mostly Miami. Some rich degenerates who think it's cool to be filmed like this."

"Or too stoned or too stupid to care," I said. "Look at the crazy shit kids put on their Facebook pages."

I was beginning to sense something, but I kept silent on it.

"This is different," Sonya said. "Taking photos of your fraternity brother puking into the toilet after a kegger or sticking toothpicks in your friend's hair after she's passed out is one thing."

It began with group sex, three women and two men.

The place looked like an expensive fuckpad with a sauna in the middle of a large wood-paneled room. Glass doors framed by sheer curtains opened onto a patio with a garden in the background. Potted palms and ferns all around. The action at the center of the screen wasn't choreographed by any offstage director. The camera would simply pick out the most intense action at the moment and zoom in. Faces were clear.

"I don't see her," I said.

"Watch," she said.

Raina was obscured by two of the men in the center of a heap of bodies; she was taking on two of them, anally and vaginally. The one having oral intercourse with her had grabbed hold of her hair and was pulling it back in his fist. He yanked so hard at one thrust that her mouth opened in surprised pain.

I sucked in my breath.

Sonja was watching me rather than the film. The contours of her face were shadowed by the coming on of dusk. The light was soft after the rain and had a yellow tint to it.

"Pretty much all we have. She's only in this sequence. The guy who pulls her hair is in real estate in Greater Miami. The man beneath her is a superintendent of schools. We don't know all of them but most are politically connected, one's high up in the Republican Party in Broward."

"I've dealt with enough lawyers," I said. "All of this is legal, as far as I know. Sordid, but First Amendment rights and all that." Sonja turned the audio off on the remote but let it play. She had given me a good lead to Raina, but I had mixed feelings about it. I knew there was more.

"The real-estate guy," Sonja said. "Rumors are he dabbles in small dope deals with Colombians but nothing we can prove."

I looked at the TV again. I was more interested in

the flatscreen plasma model in hi-def than the action. My own set back home was half the size and had a fuzzy black line that descended from the top. The real-estate man was just then going down on a different woman who inserted herself into the group action.

"He considers himself a player," Sonja added, "but he's really small time. He hosts these parties. He's the ringmaster of this sexual circus. See her? The one just coming from the sideboard, there? That's where he keeps the dope."

The woman was getting all her holes plugged, the camera action amateur but her face was clear.

"It's the cocaine in her nasal cavity that really turns her on," Sonja said.

When the male withdrew from her mouth, the camera caught her face up close. No money shots; all random fornication. When she got up to go off camera, maybe for more dope, her pubic area revealed whorls of spiky caramel hair. She was shapely, wide hips but narrow-waisted, and a navel button that protruded. Her breasts had large areolae and erect nipples.

"Who is she?"

"One of our more prominent local cougars. She's married to a county commissioner, a big shot in state politics. Got a couple kids. One's in law school in Columbia, the other's at Stanford in med school."

"She doesn't look old enough to have kids in grad school," I said.

"She's got the best figure money can buy. Have you seen boobs that large not jiggle?"

Actually, I had. Toni DeCamillo owned a pair like them just bigger. It seemed like years ago when I braced her in her apartment that night. But I said nothing.

On screen, the woman was stroking a hirsute, but balding man's scrotum from behind while a woman with cropped auburn hair fellated him in front. Every once in a while she would lower her face to the buttocks of the man and dart a pink tongue into the crease.

"Her husband thinks she's playing bridge every Tuesday night. He believes it's a Girls' Night Out and they all get tipsy on the sherry."

She uncurled herself and stepped over to the machine to eject the disk.

"This is about blackmail," I said. Rich people's sexual hijinks was not illegal.

"Wait," she said.

"If there had been a pile of cocaine on the dining-room table, nobody in Vice or Intelligence would care," I said. "None of this is worth prosecuting."

"I wanted you to see these to prepare you for this next one. This next one's a little rough in production values. Your missing girl's in the big leagues now. We think this copy's dubbed from an original made about six months ago. It's been circulating underground for about that much longer."

She placed the disk in the tray. It was half as long, very amateurish. In psychological time it took much longer.

There were children in it who didn't understand what was happening. It was hard to stomach. A man with nut-brown, hairless skin wearing a black mask with a zippered mouth frolicked on a bed with two of them. The camera was aimed at the bed throughout and it appeared to be the same bed in every sex scene. A bound and gagged blonde woman appeared in two of them toward the end; she was with a different male, who wore a black hood. He beat her on the torso and legs with one fist wrapped in what looked like sandpaper. The camera would zero in on the bruising as soon as it appeared on her flesh. Once he took a scalpel or stainless steel knife and toyed with her, feinting thrusts and cutting her delicately around the breasts and pubis. She squirmed throughout and arched her back under the worst of the blows but the overall effect was that she was prepared to suffer the ordeal.

I was thoroughly nauseated by the time a girl about ten years old came into the room and took direction, hand signals, from whoever was operating the camera because she kept looking toward the lens. Finally, she climbed over the blonde's face and sat down on it, grinding her small naked pelvis into the prone woman's face. There was a cut to a different time and the blonde was bound face down; she was spread-eagled on her stomach on the bed which was covered with vinyl sheets. She was ordered to raise her ass in the air and then her upended buttocks were whipped by a masked male with a cock ring to maintain his erection.

She was ordered by a second man off camera to urinate and the camera zoomed in on the stream issuing from her exposed vagina and splattering the sheet beneath her legs, drops glistened from her pubic hairs. Then the same voice ordered her to "make a shit" for him. When nothing happened to his repeated commands, he ordered the naked male to punish her more with the whip. In the end she was punched and kicked while tied down and released only to be turned over and retied to the iron bedposts with silk ropes. The male had taken off the cock ring and was masturbating over her face. When he ejaculated, he immediately reversed position and squatted, dropping his defecation over her face and stomach. She was ordered by the guttural voice to smear it on her face and eat it. The scene ended with the blonde's shit-smeared face blinking into the camera for a close-up.

"Turn it off," I said. "I'd like a real drink now."

"I'm sorry," Sonja said and got up to make me a drink. "There's no way to say this. I need to know you understand what we're dealing with here."

"You mean you don't want my little case to get in the way of your big one," I said.

She handed me a tumbler. I drank it without asking what it was, floor polish or whiskey, it didn't matter. My head was reeling from those images. Even I had limits. Raina, drugged and senseless maybe – but Raina, beyond all doubt. I remembered her wan face the day I dropped her off. I remembered how she came at me hissing and snarling when I had to clean her up.

Sonja had disappeared behind me into the velvet darkness of the room, leaving me alone with my thoughts. When I looked for her, I saw her on a different chair in the corner; she moved once, just to curl her legs under her. I heard the rustle of fabric as she shifted her legs.

"Nasty, isn't it?

"It's worse than that. My stomach is churning. I have new respect for you people in Intelligence," I said.

I felt the onset of another migraine. I'd have to get to a motel to rest in a blacked-out room or the pain would be brutal.

"Why don't you take the couch tonight? I leave early in the morning," Sonja said.

I told her I would be fine at a motel. I wanted to be alone. I felt nauseated, depressed, disgusted with the human race.

I got up and walked across the blonde wood floor where a streak of moonlight had created a silver shadow. I opened her front door and breathed in the smell of wet grass. The night air was humid and warm as blood.

I heard Sonja get up, watched her turn on all the lights in the room. My good eye wept from the sudden brightness. I shook my head to her offer of another drink. I asked for water to wash down a couple painkillers.

I knew better than to ask for an explanation of the films, so I crossed to my chair and sat down putting the cold glass to my head and feeling the sweat beads cool down the ache.

"Vice got us the kiddie porn tape about three weeks ago. We take in a lot of raw data in Intelligence because we don't know what's going to be useful in the long run, so we have to be careful until we know."

"What is it you know for sure?" I asked her.

"First, I'll ask you something. Why didn't you tell me she'd been here before?"

"The way her father explained it to me the first time, she had only just run off and would I go get her from this psycho ward down in Florida."

Then she dropped the bomb.

"We think the film belongs to Pavelic. His is the voice giving commands in the last part. He tries to disguise it but the voice specs match. Like a fingerprint."

"Pavelic," I said. *That voice, those words.* I could be in a grocery store buying bread and any man's voice that approached his in tone or pitch numbed me into a frigid stillness like one of those fainting goats that fall over dead.

"Your runaway found herself a prince all right," Sonja said.

"Why not leak it to Bobbie? She'd love to see him destroyed." "I can't do it."

She looked at me in a peculiar way: *lovers once*, it said, in case I were still being thick.

"You can end him with just the rumor of child pornography."

"The only thing I'd end would be my career if I did."

"Some things are worth it."

"Easy for you to say," she said. "He's a big fish and it's more complicated. And I'm already giving you too much credit for having the good sense not to want revenge for what he did to you."

"That's easy for you to say," I shot back. "As soon as I could speak, I told your cops everything that happened to me. Where's that report? Why hasn't anything been done?"

"It's called documentable proof in a court of law," Sonja said.

"I had one call from your homicide the whole time I was back in Ohio. Nothing in the papers down here."

"I know, but the case is still open." "You had a park ranger killed," I said.

"You were law enforcement once. You know we're basically a paramilitary organization. We follow orders."

"So the official story, as Bobbie told me, is some redneck poachers jumped a couple rangers, shot one, escaped, bullshit, bullshit?"

"That's true," she said. "But Pavelic can't control this investigation."

"He's doing a pretty good job of it so far," I said.

She brushed the same lock of hair off her forehead. Then she hit me with another bomb.

"*We* killed the investigation," she said matter-of-factly.

"W-who did?"

"Intelligence."

I just looked at her. I was suddenly in one of those thriller movies by Hitchcock where you start out, an ordinary guy on an ordinary day, and things start going off little by little, one little thing at a time. Your logical world is suddenly not so logical anymore. The weirdness starts getting worse and you get deeper into it while you're trying to get yourself out of it. We all have that same dream, right? The one where you're stuck in the mud and something bad is coming up on you fast. Mine's a variation of that. The people you trust or love are looking at you and smiling but they don't know you can see their thoughts. You *know* it isn't love you see in their eyes; it's a murderous, bloody hatred.

CHAPTER 9

I've learned not to be surprised by human beings, especially about what they're capable of. Nothing is pure evil or pure good. People, truth be told, baffle me and one person's compassion today, could be tomorrow's cruelty. There were rabid dogs like Luis Amezcua who should be put down. There are scarier people like his muscle-bound companion Miguel. And then there's a whole different breed like Pavelic. Beyond that, I didn't think about it.

Detective Sgt. Sonja Andersen dropped me off at the Holiday Inn in Coconut Grove. It was tucked inside the toney comfort of a Mediterranean-style enclave of hotels and boutiques, and I was miffed I didn't ask her to bring me right to a Motel 6 sooner. I was spending Paul Toivela's money recklessly and his ignorance of what Raina was doing down here stung me as if he were in some way responsible, too.

One fat German tourist in a shirt with small green chameleons chasing each other around his belly held an unlit cigar in his chubby hand. He was complaining to an elegant man with a goatee about the noise from his air conditioner until a leggy Hispanic woman in a chignon glided past. The hiatus in conversation resumed with the faint clacking of her spiked heels on the Mexican tiles of the foyer. She trailed a delicate lavender scent that was spoiled for me because it reminded me of those lavatory cakes in the pissoir at Tico's Place.

My room was on the first floor. I stopped for a Bloody Mary at the bar and canceled the vodka at the last moment. A hand-drawn sign on an easel near the bar said tonight was Karaoke Night. Dante would have loved karaoke. Imagine being tied to a chair and forced to listen to that for all eternity? Was it any better than heaven? Not even if Sumi Jo was leading the choir.

The bartender was a sullen twenty-five, untanned like a true native and pony-tailed. Three Japanese businessmen sat at the opposite end. The embossed floral wallpaper reminded me of my grandmother's bedroom.

The air conditioner in my room was running at low. I turned it up and peeled the shirt from my back. The window afforded a view of the parking lot and a hedge of yellow hibiscus. I imagined large Florida insects hidden away, waiting for dawn. I took three more aspirins and gulped tap water to bring down the radiating prongs of pain in my head. I felt weary, psychologically bankrupt and unable to get the ghost in the machine to focus on the case. My little stock of courage had abandoned me at the airport. I hated every ritzy, plastic motel in the state and everybody who dwelled in its corrupt maw. Mostly, I hated myself because I saw no chance of getting revenge.

I fell asleep watching television, listening to the weather forecaster talking about hurricane formations in the spring; he used some 3-D computerized projection to show how a spinning locus of hot air over Western Africa becomes a hurricane in the Caribbean. His map of South Florida was a parti-colored display of counties in pastel colors like a toddler's first puzzle set.

"The heat is back in South Florida," he opined needlessly.

I slept badly. In my dreams pit vipers threw their fanged heads at my legs as I raced across a meadow ahead of a darkening sky. A woman, backlit by a ball of red sun, beckoned me from a rocky ledge of promontory overlooking the sea. She pointed out toward the horizon, as if there, way out there somewhere, was an Ultima Thule of tranquility, without storms or marauders. When I caught up with her, she leapt off the cliff and I made it to the ledge in time to see her falling, white-blonde hair fanning out, her arms flailing horribly as if she had fallen from an airplane.

I stood there watching her shrink to a small black dot barely discernible above the white waves and crashing blue sea. That's when I heard the snakes before I saw them, thousands of them, hissing and slithering pell-mell at my back onto the ledge of rock, heading right for me. I was still deciding which way to go when the hisses turned into the sharp trills of my wake-up call at five.

I had forgotten to close the drapes. There was activity in the parking lot already, and traffic had just picked up a decibel on distant South Dixie. Joggers and senior citizens walking lap dogs moved across my vision. I shut off the air conditioning and headed out to find breakfast and a car rental agency.

Beyond the lobby, the air was bathwater warm, and sweet, the sky suffused with golden light. Banks of clouds streaked in colors of peach and canary yellow loomed in a broken crest over the Atlantic. It was neutral so far in my Book of Days, but I knew it would not stay that way.

I found a French Provincial style restaurant in walking distance from the hotel, drank expensive cafe latte and read the Miami papers on a couch next to a digital fireplace complete with hearth and burning logs. Some digital tropical fish floated by on a screen above me. Nothing I read hinted anything about Raymond Anton Pavelic, corporate benefactor to Coconut Grove, boxing aficionado, urban developer, Miami multimillionaire, killer extraordinaire.

I reasoned that Pavelic must have chosen Coconut

Grove rather than Miami to get a base, because it provided a foothold where federal agencies were scarce. True, Miami Intelligence would have picked him up sooner or later, but there's an advantage in putting a little jurisdictional distance between your base of operations and the state's biggest police department, FBI field office, Bureau of Criminal Investigations and Trooper headquarters that can target you.

I knew Sonja was holding back on me. Maybe Cuba was backing Pavelic in anticipation of Raúl Castro's demise. An oligarchy of powerful men hoping for a new relationship with filthy rich America ninety-three miles offshore the Bay of Pigs. Money talked, bullshit walked. Castro's younger brother would talk socialism until they lowered his withered body into a grave. Money went on forever; greed was permanently fixed into the spines of human beings. One of these days it'll show up in DNA.

Either way, it didn't much matter to the people in Pavelic's crowd. They were, according to Sonja, ruthless in achieving their ends, and citizens of no country when it came to their objectives. I was giving Pavelic too much credit. He was no Caligula. He might be a scout sent ahead to prepare the way for the next wave. Cubans had been recently linked to the Russian or Chechen *mafiya* in arms trafficking, the remnants of the Medellín cartel, and lately Mexico in smuggling artifacts looted from the Yucatán Peninsula. Mainly, it was illegals and drugs, principally tar heroin and *la cocaina* operations that involved everybody from border guards to assistant attorneys general.

"Who are these Cubans?" I asked Sonja on the way to the motel last night.

"Just names to you," she said, "but our files are growing thicker all the time. They haven't linked up yet, because these are enormously powerful people who have used every violent and subversive means possible to get where they are. They use one another's networks for smuggling drugs and girls from Eastern Europe."

It made sense: use the same routes until you have to change. Everyone in America, especially our politicians, knows drugs arrive on time no matter how they get here.

She told me nothing I couldn't have read in a Miami paper. Shiploads of automatic weapons traced to a factory on the Volga, all handled by Columbians. The documents were done by ex-KGB forgers, still the best in the world. International organized crime cartels without boundaries were the coming thing. The banks were all waiting for a piece of the action.

At seven, I called Sonja's cell as she had asked me when she dropped me off.

"I know where it is," she said. "I'll swing by on my way to the station."

"I'll be out front. I'll be the one not showing off his bony kneecaps and paunch or wearing colors you can see in the dark."

When I jumped in, she pulled into morning rush-hour traffic by blasting the horn at a Hyundai swerving into our lane.

"Damn tourists" she said as soon as the traffic settled.

"Pavelic, Sonja," I said. "Time to give to the needy."

"Let me put it this way, Tom. There are hundreds of millions of dollars, narcodollars mostly, floating around in very few hands. The people in his circle have had a lot of practice in eliminating competition."

"I'd say Pavelic's way is extreme by anybody's standards. Who am I that he'd want to risk a homicide conviction?"

"You're nobody, of course ... Sorry. I didn't mean to

put it that bluntly. Financial profit isn't the only thing that incentivizes him."

"Strange way of describing a sadistic sociopath," I said. "You make him sound like a businessman."

"Did we get up on the wrong side of the bed this morning?"

"A beautiful day with bright skies in the morning puts me on edge."

She filled in a few more details on his background. Pavelic had come out of nowhere, some rinky-dink factory his father built up as a German immigrant in the forties. He was fabulously wealthy as Bobbie had told me. The society pages doted on him. He had hundreds of millions in backing from hedge funds if he needed capital for major investments.

She drove fast like most women I knew. My stomach burned as if I had swallowed hot seeds.

The sun danced off the chrome trim in the snake of traffic ahead of us. She squinted and put on a pair of shades. Her lipstick was crimson. She looked fresh from the shower. I looked like that unmade bed everyone speaks of. Her shoulders were bunched, deltoids of muscle stretched the navy-blue fabric of her blazer. She worked out with weights, I guessed.

"Need a pharmacy? We can stop on the way," she said.

"I'm fine," I said. I shook a matchbox of codeine, Tylenol Extra Strength, and the favorite of prescription pill abusers everywhere, Oxycontin. "Got my hillbilly heroin right here."

She curled her lip in disdain. "Haftmann, if you get pulled over and you don't have a prescription bottle for that, you're going to the pokey."

"I've been to worse places," I said. "I haven't seen a pink Flamingo yet."

She sneered. "Tourist."

"Tell me why Bobbie quit a major paper like the *Miami Tribune?*"

"Let her tell you herself," Sonja said without taking her eyes off the car ahead.

There was a whiff of iodine. My brain felt like somebody had packed it in piss-soaked excelsior. The fierce light was hurting my bad eye in particular.

She told me she worked undercover for DEA in Mexico City before transferring to Miami PD. Did I know that Mexico had produced thirty billionaires in the last decade?

"No," I said.

"This is a country where less than a quarter of the population has eaten meat and fewer who've drunk milk," Sonja said.

"America is ripe for the taking," I said. I attempted a line Pacino made famous in *Scarface*.

"Don't give up your day job," she said.

She wheeled sharply round to the porte-cochére of a Hertz at the intersection of South Bayshore. It was flanked by tall sabal palms.

It dawned on me that maybe Sonja was assigned to watch me.

Just the paranoia of a gunshot victim, I hoped.

"Thanks for the ride," I said getting out of her car.

"I'll be in touch," she said. "Enjoy your flamingoes."

She gave me a toss of her pretty head and a smile and was gone.

The agency office was chilled to frigid temperatures that made me think of a blast of wind coming down from Canada. Shivering, coming out of the heat, my body reacted with bumps of gooseflesh.

A salesman approached me with a smile.

"Where do you keep the Antarctic penguins?" I asked.

"Ha-ha, no penguins, sir," he said with one of those

phony laughs they teach you in salesperson school.

"Will these do?"

He pointed up to the rafters. The entire perimeter was festooned with salmon-colored plastic flamingoes. Then I noticed each salesperson's cubicle was adorned with more of the same, all cloned from the same gooseneck-shape model. My old grandmother had a saying whenever I proved myself to be a troublesome boy.

Beware of what you ask for.

~ ~ ~

Morning traffic had picked up and the rumble of cars leaving for work downtown showed the hive was awake and active. Office buildings partially obscured my view of Miami's skyscrapers reflecting back a white-hot glare off glass and chrome. The young woman behind the Hertz counter had given me a flyer with my receipt, advertising this month's Pompano Beach Fishing Rodeo and a Grand Prize of $80,000.

In the parking lot someone had pinned flyers to the wipers of several cars including mine. A fourteen-year-old runaway from Fayetteville, Arkansas named Rebekah Lynne Kimpel was being sought, a reward offered for information.

My Camry held the after-effects of a driver who smoked and liked cologne. The engine turned over at once but it provided as much torque as piss turning a pinwheel. The air conditioner was broke – at least, that's what I inferred from a tag on the knob: *AC refrigerant malfunction.*

Great, a Freon leak, I thought.

The heat of day had built up by midmorning, my blood pressure was zigzagging from too many pills and too much coffee. But I had a clear sense of direction from where I was to where I was going: Toni DeCamillo's apartment.

I pulled off at a pay phone outside the Grand Bay Hotel. A valet watched me fumble with coins until he was sure I wasn't actually going to try to enter his establishment. An embossed matchbook in gold and black advertising the Ciga Lounge was shredded to pulp on the ground below the phone. On the embossed cover was a woman with fleshy 1950's proportions lounged poolside without her top; her cone-shaped breasts defying gravity. Back home, Tico had spent a fortune on a crate of these advertisement matches which Marta tossed into the garbage the next day.

I got Bobbie's answering service and said I'd call back, but didn't leave my name.

Toni's apartment complex looked bone white in the glare.

I parked in the shade of a Gumbo Limbo and watched the foyer, but no one came in and no one left. There was more graffiti since I had last been there. Somebody had tagged a different wall with spidery letters in glossy black paint that indicated *Mara Salvatrucha* territory. MS-13 and motel maids were El Salvador's contribution to America's melting pot.

I saw no light from Toni's kitchen. The chirrup of cicadas was louder, somewhere an infant or very young child cried in big gulping wails. My scalp tingled from the heat blasting up from the pavement.

I walked over in my best nonchalant style and ducked into the foyer's shadow.

The cards were the same with the difference that Singer's name had been crossed out. I listened for a while and then hit four buzzers and mumbled when asked to identify myself by a couple of voices. Nothing happened, so I jabbed my thumb on Markwright.

A deep male voice responded and I mumbled something back. He repeated his request and I mumbled louder. This time he buzzed me through.

I headed toward Toni's apartment and tapped my pockets as if looking for a key.

What I brought out, however, was something that looked like one of those anglerfish at the bottom of the sea with its lantern dangling above its head to draw the prey. Mine was designed for locks like hers, but because I have such poor depth perception, I had to jimmy it this way and that. My sweaty palms were making it tougher. I heard voices behind some walls and that squirted some adrenalin into my system. Finally, I got it to open.

Inside Toni's apartment my heart's blood surged in the valves. *This is where it all started,* I thought.

Cat-like I am not, so I moved slowly. The air was stifling; the a/c hadn't been on in a good while. Her place was its usual mess, and I thought of the blowsy woman herself, black roots and all, in a morning robe surrounded by the tokens of a slovenly life. The air was ripe with the sweet scent of garbage, yet my nose picked out a wisp of her musky scent, a cloying perfume – then *wham*, right in my olfactory sense, it hit me strong, an unmistakable smell among the overpowering household odors. Everything appeared in shadow or outline as it was on my last visit: dirty dishes, clothes, newspapers, even the photos on the wall exactly as they were, undisturbed since I had touched the one. *That could not be.*

I slowed my breathing. I didn't dare hit the light switch. The futon: the plastic had been removed and it was sticking about three feet away from the wall opposite her ratty couch.

The buzz of flies from the kitchen. I imagined some of the rotting food lying about had grown beards of mold by now.

I was listening hard to everything. Footsteps – a man's – walked past her door, Markwright checking out who had buzzed to get in?

I pushed one end of the futon aside and saw a

small, crusted-over pool of blood. The outer circumference had deepened to rust brown and a darker shade of mahogany enclosed that ring like the growth ring of a tree, and then a burgundy shade closer to the center that contained the uncongealed blood that the carpet's nap had not yet absorbed.

Flies had positioned themselves around the far edge of the pool like savanna animals around a watering hole at dusk. How much blood was hard to say, but from my kneeling position it looked like a lot, too much for a human body to let go of and not be fatal. The smell was ripe now. I was feeling a rush from my gonads through the top of my scalp.

Could be arterial blood, I thought. *Maybe she ran off to die in her bedroom.* The heart won't stop pumping until the body is vacated of blood. I saw more crimson droplets not yet oxidized by the heat. Flies, stench, coppery smell of blood ... *Think, get a grip.*

Had to find her. Fear prickled my skin like an itchy rash; seconds were like minutes. More spatter along the baseboard of the west wall too, but the heaviest concentration was in the pool on the carpet in front of the futon. "*I bought that for Raina...*"

Down the hallway I found a couple drops separated by several feet. She wouldn't lose that much blood in the living room and make it down the hallway without the walls looking like an abattoir. It could come from someone who flicked it off his fingers walking toward the bathroom but not the victim – unless somebody else's blood, the attacker's maybe. Toni was jail-hardened, not an easy mark. I was tramping around in a crime scene violating a sacred rule: "A victim is killed once, but a crime scene can be murdered a hundred times." Every room you walk into, you leave something behind for forensics to find. I was writing my signature for cops to nail me with later.

The bedroom door was off an L-shaped divide at the end of the empty hallway – not a picture here either. I had no gun, no right to be there, and all my commonsense screamed at me to get out *now*. Still, I had to see it for myself.

I nudged the door open with my foot and felt the chilled air against my pant leg.

A separate window unit for extra cooling – on arctic setting – it thrummed away indifferent to any human chaos in its vicinity. Old Doc Harris back home kept it like that: morgue air.

I slipped inside past the light into the room and felt my back scrape the light switch. I let my eyes adjust to the darkness and boxed the room. A shape on the bed, human, a woman's legs were splayed open, uncovered, but a bedspread was rucked up around her midriff and extended up to her neck. I could not see where her head was propped against the bedstead, but I knew it was her without seeing her face. I could see all the way up to the darkened apex where her thighs joined; the trimmed wedge of her dark pubic hair seemed like a dusting over her crotch.

Nothing else was clear in the darkened, windowless room, and I felt like one of those victims of schizophrenia who cannot see the outlines of furniture clearly and whose eye-brain coordination refuses to make sense of the human face.

The bed, the dresser, a night table, clothes strewn on either side of the bed. The stained terry cloth robe hung from one knob on the slatted doors of a small closet. My hand found the light switch and I turned it on.

Goddamned animals.

Her face was a grotesque, lumpy, death's-head grin of rictus.

I walked unsteadily toward the bed and pulled the

sheet from her. She had been tied down. I could see where ligature marks had bitten into the skin – wrists, torso, neck. Lividity spots on her back and behind her thighs.

I started mentally recording like a cop before I knew it: body in east-west position, head toward the west. I could see the way the homicide report would read. Bruising on the mounds of her breasts, her right one showed the scorching where a cigarette may have been touched to skin below the nipple. Some fresh needle marks in the crook of her left arm. No quantity of blood to explain her death. I looked her over without touching her. Some feces protruded below her cleft of buttocks – a sign of grievous head injury. Her bangs looked pasted to her forehead, matted from dried sweat.

I looked at her face again – something wrong. At first, I thought she moved, spoke, her lips seemed to move.

Then it hit me: a razor-thin penciling, like the merest line of shadow, surrounded her face and ran under her jaw; it was obscured by her damp hair. The planes and angles of her face made her unrecognizable.

I took out my lockpick and touched her face and felt it give like sponge. Her facial skin had been peeled off and replaced over her dead face like a Halloween mask.

Yellow globules of fat at the perimeter of her face had oozed from the precision cutting. A spackling of blood droplets about the pillow, her ear lobe, neck. Her hair was greasy with more than sweat – sere and skin tissue had dried and the mask of her face had been tamped back into place. Somebody wanted her discovered like this. Peeled off like an apple rind and put back for the first person to find her to see.

I experienced an icy intake of breath that filled my

lungs: she was alive when it happened. More ooze puckered from the wound around the cuts. She had been cleaned of blood while the incisions were made. Needle marks were injections to make her tractable while the torture went on and kept her thrashing to a minimum. *They wanted her to know what was happening.*

I was shivering now. I could hear the buzz of nearby flies, those nasty ones that find a corpse within an hour of death and start to lay eggs in the wound or in the corners of eyes or inside nostrils. It's no wonder I hate Latin. The four-eyed pathologist at the academy dinned in our ears about the blowfly family of *Sarcophaga bullata*, the grey fly, and the *Calliphora vomitoria*, the bluebottle fly, all the lovely little flesh-eating flies of death.

Before I retraced my steps, I checked every drawer with my hand wrapped in sheet of paper napkin. Nothing but clothes and personal items, no scratch pads, paper, or calendar. I did the same to the bathroom. The medicine cabinet was full of cosmetics and prescription drugs: Restoril for sleeping, Ionamin for waking up, a bottle of Redux for dieting.

In the living room I thought hard about what I had touched.

I wiped the photo frame on the wall and checked the glass for prints or smudges. Nothing I could do about any fibers I had brought in with me. I checked the telephone on the wall divider in the kitchen to see if she had written anything on a notepad. Nothing. The kitchen was all clutter, nothing to write on.

From the kitchen window I could look out into the parking lot. The glare off my Camry windshield, the inkblot shadow cast by the palm leaves. I saw a dog scratching its shaggy behind on a wire fence. An old codger with knee-length white socks was cutting his grass with an old-fashioned push mower in the heat of the day. Traffic looked normal in all directions. *All is quiet in sunny, prosperous Coconut Grove.* I was in an upside-down world.

I pushed the futon back to cover the bloodstain, checked the cushions of both couches. Nothing under them. I reached my hand down inside the couch but felt nothing but more evidence of Toni's slovenly housekeeping. A few coins and fragments of food hardened to rock-like consistency.

"The robe," I thought. I went back down the corridor and entered the room. Without looking toward the body, I reached for the pockets. Nothing. *Toni, I know you hid something for your rainy day – where, where?*

I was returning to the door when I heard two voices talking outside. I stepped to the kitchen window and peered out. A cruiser was sitting outside and a cop was talking to a tall, balding man in his fifties who was shielding his eyes against the sun and pointing right at the window I had just looked out. A second cop car with turquoise and cherry lights flashing turned into the lot, killed the lights, and pulled up next to the first cruiser. The bald man gestured again, raised a bunch of keys in his fist and turned toward the foyer. The two cops lined up on either side and all three disappeared into the lobby foyer leading to the apartments.

I tiptoed back to the living room and pressed my back against the door, listening to the corridor. I heard a clatter of keys scratch at the lock when another voice intruded: then a deep, basso profundo growl.

The man with the keys, the apartment manager, spoke to him in a higher pitch, but I couldn't make out the words. The deep-voiced man said something about a man, a man barging in, demanding something. A third voice: one of the officers said something to Deep

Voice and he answered back brusquely. This time I heard it clearly.

"I've asked you to do something about these lowlife kids and their spray paint before," he said.

My shirt was glued to my back and I couldn't suck in enough air to counter the surge of blood hammering away in my temples.

But Markwright saved me. He said his name twice to the police officers. One of them made him spell it. He identified another name as his lawyer. I heard the words *sue* and *lease* mentioned again, and the apartment manager's voice climbed all the way up to a falsetto of protest. The keys were jangling – he must have been slapping the ring against his leg in agitation. More conversation – everybody talking now at the same time. Voices rising in pitch.

Then silence. Footsteps. The cops moving off, I hoped. My radar was so fine-tuned at that point I think I heard the creaks of leather from their gun belts. The apartment manager, very clearly: "I won't take responsibility for this."

I slumped against the door as my legs bowed at the knees. Pinpricks of light popped at the corner of my eyes. It was all about taggers and their gang logos decorating the sides of the building.

I waited a couple more minutes until I was sure everybody had gone. The lock made a clicking noise like a pistol dry-firing that I thought could be heard all over the complex.

I opened the door and walked out. It was that easy, after all. Sometimes when you're up to no good, what Micah used to call the Fate Sisters collaborate to help you out.

My legs nearly buckled: I stood in the blinding white light of a South Florida noonday sun and felt myself one lucky man. I headed right for my vehicle while the blood sang inside me.

Opening the door, a blast of trapped heat washed over me and stuck my shirt to my back. I sat there but I didn't turn the key. Instead I got out again and ducked back into the foyer. I told Bobbie Gersack I played long odds. This was going to be a big one. I was playing in the maw of the lion's den.

I took the elevator to the fourth floor and hit Markwright's button.

"Yes?" The metallic amplifier made a growl out of his deep voice.

"Sir, I'd like to speak to you for a minute."

"Who are you?"

"It's about ... it concerns Miss DeCamillo, a neighbor of yours." "I asked who you are."

"I'm a private investigator, sir. I just need a moment of your time."

A silence as long as my wait outside Toni's door ensued, the seconds falling like dominos.

He buzzed me in. I went through the door again and felt the sinking in my belly nearly take me down as I climbed the stairs to 4 D and knocked. The door opened immediately.

Roland Markwright stood in front of me in his socks; six-foot six, rail thin, deep sockets around his eyes, and a rust-colored toupee on his head. One strange bird in a strange land. He extended a long arm to me that seemed to unfold from his side and I shook his offered hand.

"What do you want?" he asked in that remarkably low voice, but he didn't invite me inside.

"Nothing for me personally, sir, but you can do something for
Toni DeCamillo."

"What is that?"

"Tell me, if you wouldn't mind, what it was you said to the police just now."

"I'll do no such thing," he snapped. "Who the hell are you?"

"I have to tell you something, some bad news, I'm afraid," I said.

"Any business between Toni – Miss DeCamillo – and myself, is none of yours, sir," he said and was about to slam the door, but I shoved my foot in there and let the side of my foot take one for the team.

"She's dead," I said.

He tried to slam the door again, his eyes wide in fear.

"She's dead," I repeated.

"What? Get your – you're mad!"

His eyes widened and bulged like a mackerel's. He stared at me with his mouth open. I stared back and hoped he wasn't about to go ballistic on me. I noted the dark smudges beneath his eyes, dingy like the skin of a frog's belly. He hadn't been sleeping well lately.

"This is outrageous! You must be an idiot or deranged to come here – "

Once again the door, once more my foot into the breach. *Damn, that one hurt.*

"This is absolutely ... wicked! Is this some kind of sick joke?" His face was all blood-gorged surprise.

He was about to get another one. I had to do it.

I threw my shoulder at the door and backed him into his own apartment. I flipped my Ohio license at him fast, once, without letting him see more than a glance. TV does get it right once in a while.

I said, "I am not joking. I know you're a friend of Toni's because I heard you tell those cops to leave her alone just now."

He was cutting his eyes from side to side like a cornered animal. *Still thinks I'm a loon...*

He backed deeper into the room and reached behind him. I saw what he was going for: his cell phone lay on a stand next to a La-Z-Boy recliner in front of a TV.

In for a penny, in for a pound...

I clipped him on the jaw with a right. He stood there blinking at me. At first I thought I didn't hit him hard enough and then I saw him totter like a building whose girders had just snapped. I caught him under the arms and lowered him to the floor.

When he came around and his pupils dilated back to normal, I brought him a glass of water from his kitchen and helped him drink it.

"I'm not here to hurt you," I said, which under the circumstances wasn't the smartest thing to say. His eyes kept darting all over my face and finally settled their gaze on my bad eye. "Wh-who are you?" he asked.

"I'm a private investigator working a case. I'm sorry I had to hit you."

"Toni is ... dead. You said—"

"Yes, she is."

"Oh my God. Oh my God. Oh my God. Oh my God..."

I had to interrupt this irritating Gregorian chant of grief.

"I want you to talk to me and then I want you to call the police," I said. I wasn't sure I was getting through. "Was it an accident?" "No," I said.

Shit, he thinks I killed her.

"Mister Markwright, I had nothing to do with Toni's murder."

"Why-why should I believe you? I don't know you! You could be some psychopath—"

"Sir, if I had anything at all to do with Toni's murder, would I be here talking to you now?"

That calmed his agitation a little. *At last some progress, I need to work fast.*

I told him I was looking for someone and Toni was helping me – no harm in that lie now. The same people who killed Toni, I said, might kill her too unless I could locate her."

"Call the police," Markwright said. "That's what they're for."

"I just want to get her back home to her family," I said. "I need your help."

He seemed calmer now.

"How did she die? Oh God, I must see her."

I said, "I don't think you want to see her now."

He urged me to call the police again. He started to rise to his feet, slowly, and I kept my distance. It was like watching Bambi on ice.

"Help me," he said.

I hoisted him under his armpits. He was all bones and knobby edges, but finally he stood. His hands were shaking, and I asked him if I could make him a drink.

"We must call the police right now," he insisted.

"Not yet, sir. That's what I want you to do – after we talk. When I'm gone, you call them. Tell them about me. It'll hurt my investigation if you do, but it's all right. This girl I'm looking for doesn't have much time." Something besides his shock at my news of the murder of his neighbor told me he was someone who didn't want to get involved with cops.

We sat at his polished dining room table. He was a neatnik unlike his dead friend. We were an odd pair: a lonely bachelor and a private eye. Me, a rumpled stranger with my hair-on-fire news; he in his crisp, bone-white shirt and old-fashioned gabardine slacks, hugging himself with his bony arms, sickened from the noxious vapor of death I had brought into his tidy life in my wake.

I must have looked a fright to him even before I decked him. I'm not exactly camera-ready in my sweaty shirt and wearing this face. A psychiatrist working for the Cleveland PD with the unlikely name Terd Porn Matrooshian tried to take me off the streets after a clean shooting. A crackhead with a long knife made the mistake of violating that twenty-foot rule cops go by – that's the distance it would take an assailant to cover who intended malice aforethought against you. I saw the report later when a friend of mine glommed it from his desk.

Markwright gathered his elastic arms about himself like a praying mantis, and answered my next questions without guile or hesitation. He was in unknown territory and I was his only guide. I needed him to believe that. When I left him hunched over at his table, waxed so well he looked like a man staring at his own reflection in the water, he mumbled something about "pondering his next course of action," which I took to mean the decision about informing the police. I shrugged. "Fair enough," I said.

I learned little about Toni's dark side, only the side that found occasional solace in the company of Roland Markwright, retired middle-aged accountant, a gawky bachelor who kept an immaculate apartment. He had moved to Florida from Texas seven months ago because he "needed a change" after his wife divorced him.

Some ancient Greek philosopher said change is the only constant in life. I thought of Markwright at his shiny table, unable to comprehend the horror three stories below. A man who knew almost nothing of Toni's other life, her "night life side," as he quaintly called it. I told him as little as possible about her connection to Pavelic, and he didn't seem inclined to want to know it, as if her reputation still mattered. In a sense, I suppose it did. He had his image of her that was completely different from mine. I couldn't waste more time on him now. I had to control my own nervous exhaustion. I felt it creeping into my voice, infecting my stamina, going after my brain. If I was going to find Raina Toivela and get her away from Pavelic, I needed that part of me more than the rest.

Part of my gamble did pay off big: Markwright mentioned two visitors to Toni's apartment last week. He'd passed them on his way to the manager's office.

Large men, he noted, Hispanic, one with a Clark Gable moustache, wing tips. The other was bigger, looked like a weightlifter, and wore black brogans, shiny as new dimes. *Amezcua, Odio.*

"When was this?" I asked him.

"Just a couple days ago."

That would fit the condition of Toni's body. I had missed Pavelic's killers by that much. A lump of ice settled in the pit of my stomach. I wasn't eager to bump into these heavyweight bookends again anytime soon. It would be Miguel, not the excitable Amezcua, calmly cleaning his knife blade after he had just carved off a woman's face.

~ ~ ~

Everybody likes insurance. I've busted dozens of lowlifes, all with their little hidey-holes. One 300-pound mafia bookie stuck his little black book in a waterproof jar and tied it off to fishing line and stuck the thing in the toilet tank. "Dumb fuck," hooted my partner when he searched the bathroom and came up with the goods. "You're gonna use monofilament, asshole, use invisible, not blue!" The blue line was clearly visible wrapped once about the flushing handle and stretched taut as it disappeared below the tank top cover.

This was the second time I hopped out of my car in the now broiling heat of midday to rap my knuckles on Markwright's door. He answered after five minutes. His careworn face and deep-set eyes told me he hadn't recovered from the shock yet.

"Toni's little black book," I said. "Give it up."

He hesitated a fraction too long and that's when I knew he had it. Toni would have known she was in danger before those two thugs rolled up to her door. She'd have given it to him for safekeeping, taken it back every so often, and shared a morning or late-night cappuccino from his espresso machine. She said it was something she didn't want in her apartment because of her long absences from home. Confidential information about clients, she said to him.

Markwright knew of her career as an office designer and believed it explained her odd hours and late nights on the town. She was, after all, "a very attractive woman" and clients frequently showed their appreciation. He had told this to himself, no doubt, but the truth was etched in his basset-hound look. She was too much woman for him, a heady wine he couldn't resist.

"We were not, uh, romantically involved," Markwright whispered. "But I had hopes."

I figured he was a sideline project to DeCamillo, a hobby, nothing more. She'd have skinned this prude like a dead jackrabbit and tossed him aside when she had his PIN number, her name on life insurance beneficiary policy, and his Topps' baseball card collection, if he had one.

Her intuition told her she could trust this man to hold her dynamite. While he went to fetch it from its hiding place inside a cut glass filigreed bowl in the China cabinet, I paid silent tribute to a woman's courage. She didn't give this up. Maybe she knew it wouldn't have saved her life if she had. *I hope she spat curses at them with her dying breath.*

Toni's black book turned out to be a cheap, cloth-covered teenager's diary. It was blue damask in paisley design, not black, and bound with a clasp that would pop open from the slightest pressure. "Did you open it?" He looked offended.

"Of course I didn't! I would never betray a confidence," he snapped.

He handed me a scrap of paper with a pair of phone numbers. His long finger tapped the paper delicately as if it were the last Fabergé egg in existence.

"I don't know if this is something, but Toni said I was to try to reach her at this number first," he emphasized by tapping the folded paper. "Then, if I couldn't reach her there, I was to try a second number. She insisted it was important I call the numbers in that order, so I kept them separate just to reassure her."

He wasn't the first man to play country bumpkin to a bad woman and he wouldn't be the last. "Do you know what's in it?" I asked him, indicating the diary.

"I never looked," he said, his bass voice returning by degrees, a little quaver at the end indicated I had once more insulted his integrity by asking.

"I only meant did she tell you what's in it?"

"No," he said with finality. "Please leave. The sight of you does nothing but disturb my equilibrium at the deepest levels of my being."

"Did Toni say what to do with this if anything were to happen, say, in an emergency?"

"Sir, leave."

Micah used to say I had skin thicker than a nine-banded armadillo.

He held me in his stare a long time, but I didn't move. Being disliked carries as much weight with me as being stoned with popcorn.

I had a job to do.

He sighed from somewhere in the deepest cockles of his being.

"She told me she had a sister I was to call," he said. "I was to tell her that Toni wanted her to have the book. The sister would know what to do with it."

He got up and went back to the China cabinet where he lifted the lid of a smaller glass bowl, its facets catching the light and shimmering. He plucked out a second piece of paper and brought it to me.

I gave him my card and hotel number. "I might need to call you," I said.

"Don't even think of it," he huffed.

When I looked back from the doorway, I thought more than ever of a praying mantis; the male only lives to consummate a union with the larger female; then the female eats the male's head during copulation for sustenance.

Markwright was at the stereo fiddling with the knobs, tuning in a classical station. Maybe it was a ruse to drown out his conversation with the police, so I left him there, but I listened at the door, a caricature of an old-style gumshoe from the pulps. I heard sobbing. Then, said to the walls or whatever spirit world he thought his deceased paramour might be inhabiting just then: "I knew you weren't any good. You deceiving bitch. God damn you!"

I knew he had looked into Toni's little black book. We all want to know what's behind that door, even if it stomps our hearts flat in the dirt.

Going down the metal stairs into the searing light, I heard mournful violins coming from his apartment, played much too loud. A beautiful voice sang: "'O Mio Caro Babbino.'" We were all somebody's beautiful baby once.

~ ~ ~

The day's heat was at blast-furnace level now, and I was weak from lack of food, and in need of a clean shirt and shower. The painkillers were wearing off and I felt the vertigo that sometimes swept over me as if I'd been poleaxed.

I drove to a nearby strip mall and parked behind a Duke & Duchess gas station. I could see the corner of the lot and Toni's building.

After twenty minutes, I heard the first sirens. I counted six squad cars coming from the direction of Main Highway, where I guessed Coconut Grove maintained its own trendy substation. Their wailing of the sirens shredded the afternoon's tenuous peace creating a refrain of their own running through the already dissonant composition of the day's events.

Feeling dehydrated, I started to get out of the car to buy a soft drink but lost my footing and slumped to the ground before I made it to the curb. I saw a fox-faced cashier eyeball me behind the plate-glass window with her mouth opening wide. The distortion of the glare made two dots of her eyes. I struggled back into the car and nearly blacked out.

Somehow I drove back to the Holiday Inn with a drunkard's memory and reflexes. I stumbled toward my room amid the confusion of the lobby personnel and managed to avoid too many more staring eyes.

Inside my room, I tucked the book from Markwright into my luggage and headed for the bathroom where I vomited strings of ropy saliva, stripped, showered, and shaved, after which I slept for two hours with a head pounding like a monkey sitting on my pillow whacking away at my head with a tiny silver hammer. I felt like those poor, doomed muck rabbits in the sugar cane that poor whites and blacks in the central part of the state clubbed to death with Louisville sluggers and sold for a couple bucks apiece.

The tremolo notes of the room phone brought me out of my daze in a hurry. I knocked it to the floor in my thrashing. Bobbie returning my call at four in the afternoon.

She said she might have news of Raina. We agreed to meet at a Waffle House on Virginia Street next to a bar called Biscayne Baby. That would give me time to shake off the logy feeling and get some food into me. I had had nothing but the coffee since early morning and my stomach had enough acid to dissolve ten yards of railroad track. I found a place called The Unicorn on 6th Avenue and ate two specials, one after the other.

The waiter was a Vietnamese girl who bowed slightly before she served each plate and carried cups of steaming coffee in her hands. I ordered garlic crabs to start and she presented me with a wooden mallet. I wolfed down tofu lasagna, broccoli-noodle parmesan, and a vegetable-cheddar nut loaf with all the sides. I washed everything down with two pots of black coffee. She asked me if I wanted dessert, and her almond eyes got big when I said yes. Back in the kitchen, I heard her musical voice enjoined by two others, both Vietnamese males, and then much giggling. I was creating a minor sensation among the staff.

I dropped enough traveler's checks to cover the bill and stuck a twenty beside the free peppermint they give you.

~ ~ ~

"Not a chance, old boy, sorry."

Bobbie was giving me that pouty look, but on her it didn't mean sexy; it meant *fuck off*. She was ill-tempered, biting her nails to the quick from the minute she sat down opposite me.

"I'm not asking to be let inside," said as sweetly as I could. "Jesus, what have you had for lunch? You reek of garlic." "Sorry," I said.

"No," Bobbie repeated.

"I've got to see if she's there," I said.

The waiter brought me another coffee, but my pores were open, and I felt the sweat beads rolling down the side of my face; overdosing on caffeine while my internal refrigeration system was trying to establish some sort of equilibrium was giving me the heebie-jeebies.

I must have looked oddly at her because she stopped talking in her tracks and stared at me.

"What's wrong, Bobbie?"

"Nothing. Everything. I feel like something left over from the sixties, like a retrograde hippie."

"I've had days like that," I said. I could have said *months, years*.

"Let's start over," I said. "All I want is the address. You owe that much for Toni's little black book."

"It's in code, Haftmann. I can't make sense of it."

"I just want to see if she's there," I pleaded again.

She leaned back in the booth and cocked her head to one side. "Stop batting your eyes at me like a lovesick teenager."

"I didn't know I was," I said. "That was my pretty-please face."

"God," she said. The corners of her mouth twitched, maybe a smile forming, but she killed it before it matured. "Are you superstitious, Tom?"

"Hell, no," I said, "I'm an existentialist."

"I doubt you can spell the word," she scoffed.

"It's not very fashionable to be one in these degenerate times," I said, "but it suits me."

"I did a story on Santeria in Little Havana years ago," she said.

"Some of the old ones believe in *mal de ojo*."

"Same as *maloccio*, right?"

"I'm surprised you know it."

"I've got a library card."

"Yeah, sure. And there are no drag queens in Key West," she said. She was lightening up a bit and that was good.

"I get a bad feeling sometimes. I'm getting one now in the pit of my stomach." She ran her hand through the mop of her hair.

"My ex-wife used to say that a lot," I said. "That's why you brought up the Evil Eye?"

"You were a cop once, right? Then you know reporters don't give up their sources."

"Bobbie, you've got her book of names. In time, you'll get it decoded. Not to belabor the obvious, but people are *dying* all over the place. I've had half my limited stock of IQ points blasted out of my head—"

"– and that's another good reason why you should let it go! Go home, Haftmann. This thing is getting worse. I think somebody's watching my place, tracking my comings and goings. Shit, I'm scared."

"Then you can't afford to play ostrich in the sand, Bobbie," I said, too loudly. Heads swiveled toward us but turned quickly back to their meals and conversations.

"Keep your voice *down*, please," she shot back and fixed me with a glare. Her lips got puffy when she was riled.

Maybe the little Cleveland shrink was right about me.

Bobbie had used her connection in the Miami PD to trace Toni's safe numbers. One was a contact to be used only when it was real emergency time, but Toni had run out of time...

I moved backwards, assumed a relaxed position. She cut her eyes right and left to see if we were making a scene, but the diner was more club than restaurant.

I tried to distract her. "I'm sick of Florida. All these bright, happy colors. Who's happy? Oh goodie, look, line dancing."

"You're an idiot," she said. "That's not line dancing."

She looked where I pointed toward a bunch of Happy Hour twentysomethings lined up in some kind of dance formation at the horseshoe bar in the next room.

"You're right," I said. "It's the Macarena."

She snorted. "That's deader than Julius Cesar. Speaking as a transplanted Midwesterner myself, you're a little behind the times down here."

"Not true," I said. "I'm a regular fashion plate. My ex-wife insisted I dress for success."

"Then she was as color blind as you. You think

acting the fool will work, don't you? Look, I've been played by real pros. You're an amateur in this game."

"Help me, then. Please," I said.

"Jesus, you really do have *un mal de ojo*."

"No, it's just a bad eye socket," I said. "Weakened muscles around the eyeball. I got cracked in the head there when I was young."

"Live-and-don't-learn Thomas Haftmann, huh?"

"Yep, that's me."

"Look, I can't keep asking Sonja for help. It's too big a risk.

She's done enough."

"What about you, Bobbie? Have you done enough?'

"Don't tug at my guilt strings like that. I know there's a lost girl out there in a very dangerous place."

"You're right," I said. "I can't ask you to take any more chances. Those two bastards who killed Toni are roaming around looking for me by now. You did what I asked. Thanks for checking those numbers against the Pavelic file. Thank Sonja for me, too."

She sighed. "What more can I do?"

But I had already asked her for it before she sat down. She gave the tip about the two men Markwright saw at DeCamillo's place. The cops would knock on Markwright's door, and he'd give it up. I liked the idea of pressuring them for a change.

"I don't like the idea of holding out on Sonja," she said.

"Sonja's taking the long view," I said.

Bobbie told me her cop had traced the second number to an empty flat in Liberty City, "where nobody knows shit from Shinola."

"You say the first one is a Miami Beach number, private, and

I'm thinking this might be the guy mixed up in kinky sex parties."

"The one you said is connected to Raina, but you never said how you know this."

"Just let me have the address, Bobbie."

"Sonja will cut me off forever," she said. I had no doubt she knew Sonja was the source for the ringmaster in the porn film.

"I'm not going in there with guns blazing," I said.

She relaxed a little more. "I know this will sound a little insensitive, but why didn't you call me at the *Courier* after you left DeCamillo's apartment? It's all over the news. Three TV stations are there right now doing updates for the eleven p.m. shows." I didn't know what to say to that.

She looked at me. "I'm sorry," she said. "That was a lot insensitive. Forgive me, I'm a trained monkey. The job, you know."

"Toni's a back-page item, a fifteen-second sound bite. She played with a rough crowd. Don't pity her," I said. "The real story is Pavelic."

"Now who's being insensitive?" She narrowed her brown eyes, lasering me.

"How did you manage to get in and out of there like the invisible man? They find one of your prints, you'll be lucky if all they do is tear up your license and make you *persona non grata* in this state."

I asked her if the cops were giving out the manner of DeCamillo's death.

"Of course not. They won't release that for all kinds of reasons.

I leaned toward her again. "Just help me get on the property. I have to see if she's there."

"I'll do what I can." Then she looked up at me. "Wipe that shiteating grin off your face." I grinned even more.

"Take some advice, Thomas. Don't go running around like a rutting buck, spooking up the place, because word gets out. My reputation will be shot."

"I swear to you I am simply going to surveille the house, follow Raina if she comes out."

"Why not just call the cops – you do the anonymous tipster bit? Have them do a check? Tell them there's a runaway girl being held inside – make something up," she said.

"Can't do that," I said.

"Why not? Male pride? You have to be John Wayne in *The Searchers* or some shit?"

"Never saw it," I said.

I didn't have time to explain why warrants and jackboots didn't always work in life the way they did on TV. I held up some fingers in what I hoped was a Boy Scout salute. "Promise I won't get out of the car. If I see anything unusual, I'll call the cops and vamoose."

"Better make the Sign-of-the-Cross. You could use the extra help."

She gulped the dregs of her iced tea, crunched a cube, and left me to call Sonja. She had told me she was working on some hush-hush interview with a confidential informant who was ratting off a competitor in the Miami construction industry. I watched her go make the call to Sonja.

A couple twenty-year-old males chatting up girls noticed her walking past; one gestured to the other. I tell myself comforting lies from time to time, such as: *I'm not responsible for this world and all the whoredogs in it.* I know little girls have to grow up too fast in this sleazy culture. There were no knights-in-shining armor like the songs promised them. Micah told me there was an angel of death in the Qur'an called Kafriel, who brought a rose to innocent girls. This culture won't admit to suffering.

Let it be, Haftmann, I told myself. *You've done enough to make it this way.*

I didn't realize until that moment I wasn't trying to find Raina to close a case anymore. If I had any stupid notion about finding redemption, I had better wake up and apologize to someone. That's always a mistake in my book because you can't forgive yourself.

Bobbie came back ten minutes later while I was still wallowing in my own dark thoughts. She sat down, and before I could open my mouth, the muffled ring tones of her cell phone went off.

"Go ahead," I said. "Take your call."

"I know who it is," she said. "I'm ignoring it."

"What song was it playing?"

"That's Duke Ellington's *Mood Indigo*. What do you have?"

I told her what my ex had put on mine, an old Black Sabbath tune from the seventies. She looked surprised and said it didn't suit me.

"'Roll Out the Barrel,'" she said with a smirk. "That's more you."

It figures, I thought, the standard polka song of every Cleveland wedding since the fifties. I wondered if Frankie Yankovic felt any relief before they lowered him into his grave: *No more requests for that, please God.*

Micah had only two Yiddish expressions: *Genug iz genug*. ("Enough is enough"). The other I heard more often when I was being a little moody. "To a worm in horseradish," she would say, "the whole world is horseradish." Looking at Bobbie who was grinning at me in a familiar way, a different folk expression popped into my head. I thought: *We were both running with the wolves and neither one of us had better trip.*

~ ~ ~

Raina was becoming the center of attention for a small but influential group of people whose parties floated from the gay section of Lauderdale down to the wealthy condos of Miami Beach.

Sonja's source among these revelers informed me she was "bottoming" for Pavelic's sadomasochistic friends now. These rich freaks were passing her around at these parties. The next one was day after tomorrow, if they held to their Thursday night routine. Sonja must have the guy's balls in a vise if he gave up this kind of detail. For all I knew, though, it could be a jealous wife or partner.

The man who owned the phone number scrawled in Toni's wildly cursive handwriting was an associate of Pavelic and exporter of flowers from Holland. The Dutch were America's major fresh flower exporter along with Ecstasy. Mexico was another country where flowers and drugs seemed to run in tandem. This particular member of Pavelic's international set, however, had a bent for marking up the nubile flesh of young girls and leaving them to be discovered in public places like abandoned buildings or tied up in motel rooms. Reading about it in the papers the next day enhanced his sick pleasure. Another was a Belgian entrepreneur of chocolates. He had an Interpol file, Sonja said, and he carried wads of cash all over the world so he could buy his way out of trouble anywhere.

I finished the last of my cold coffee and wondered if Micah was right about my choosing to be a cop because it was easier to fight demons in other people's messed-up lives. She might have been pleased to know I was finally out of my depth in this sunny clime ruled by rich predators, and I made as much sense to be in the middle of it as a skinhead in a mosque.

~ ~ ~

Bobbie had confirmed my fears about the botched investigation of my shooting. I was wrong about the cover-up, she said, but I argued with her from my cop's experience. Every shooting generates reports. Nothing generates paper like homicide, but two dead park rangers means the FBI steps in.

Then the other shoe dropped: *Fuckola. Booth.*

That dapper little man who liked to shoot his solid silver cuff links to put rube cops in their place might be behind this. I had handed it to him, after all. Now it made sense.

When I told Bobbie about how many people would have to be involved in a cover-up of this magnitude – the sheer number of forms, log-ins, reports – she said the D. A. declined to prosecute after a cursory investigation of my "case," which turned out to be nothing more than a polite interview with Pavelic in his office.

This was murder of two federal employees in a national park, never mind some shot-up gumshoe from Hicksville.

"What about Manny's corpse?" I asked her.

"Never found," she said. "He's listed as a missing person."

What about incident reports, gunshot wounds? Amezcua took one in the shoulder in the moments before Miguel put the gun to my head.

No Miami hospitals reported a description that fit. Not that there weren't any Hispanic males with gunshot wounds that day. Eight, count them. S.W. Calle Ocho – *Little Havana* – *to you gringos*, she said – always jumps at night.

"Not your man, though," she said.

"Why didn't your district attorney's office go after Pavelic on my say-so? One citizen's word against another's still gets investigated." Pavelic's reputation alone would have grabbed ink.

She rubbed her forehead and took a deep breath. "There's no easy way to say this. It's you. They couldn't go forward because of you. The case would have fallen on its ass."

I thought she meant because I was so incapacitated by my head wound. Then I realized she meant because I had done time in West Virginia. An ex-con. You can't go to court on a convict's word of mouth against a prominent citizen like Raymond Pavelic. A first year-law student would know that.

I gave her Micah's favorite lawyer quotation: "Deeds plotted in hell do not have angels as witnesses."

But it was my psychiatric profile that would have clinched it. After my partner's death in a botched shooting, the Cleveland suits ordered me to take a psychiatric evaluation – standard procedure – except that the individual who gave it to me was a small man with nut-brown skin from Thailand with the memory-indelible name had me fixed and pinned to his wall of certificates. I wasn't crazy, but I was nearly certifiable by the time that little Freudian jerk completed his questions and I had taken a battery of idiotic tests ... *Now, Officer Haftmann* ... hissing like a basket of vipers – *this one is called the MMPI, and I would pliss very much like you to draw a picture of a house, and a tree, and a man...*

The feds accessed it along with the prison shrink's report.

What Booth had said to me: *You're on a list in case you were in doubt on that score.*

That wavy-haired, ass-covering fed was running his own game through the Miami office. He could have been in on it right from the beginning, maybe a part of Sonja's Intelligence operation. The feds could have been linking up with Miami, probably the CIA, because their mandate is internal and exclusively domestic counterintelligence. Who knew what was what in a post-Nine Eleven world of warrantless wiretaps and satellites picking out phrases in phone conversations all over the world?

My throat felt dry as desert air. All those State Department, CIA and FBI bastards went to the same schools, swam in the same country club pools, married the same women, and kept their kids safe behind the same gated communities.

When Booth left for reassignment to New York, he didn't leave it on a demotion as he had hinted to me. I racked my brain trying to remember whether he had ever mentioned a connection to the Miami office. He could be calling important shots down here if his new post required it, but hell, I was way out of my bailiwick as it was, and I had to keep looking over my shoulder for Pavelic's killers.

"That lying sack of shit," I thought. *He had me believing he was knocked down to handing out towels in the New York washroom.* He never reacted to Pavelic's name when I dropped it.

I was disgusted with my own stupidity for trusting him and believing what he told me. I felt like a barefoot hillbilly in a room full of rocket scientists. The last call routed to the Cyber/Ops office meant he was one big fish. In his own impeccable way, he was as warped as John Edgar Hoover in drag.

Booth was the only human being on the planet who had the clout to drop my report on the right desks. If being a convicted felon wasn't enough to put the kibosh on it, being an ex-cop with three shootings, one good, and a psychiatric evaluation that had "incipient schizophrenic" written on it was more than enough.

The *putz* had sold me out – *but why?* No one bothers to fill in the tethered goat. Then I began to wonder: just how big was this operation? Was I being paranoid? Had my brains been scrambled too much for me to think straight? If Sonja were right, and Pavelic was acting for unseen powers or interests like corrupt banks, what did that make me in the scheme of things?

Mother Machree, what had I gotten myself into?

Was it too late to snatch Raina Toivela out of the midst of this before it blew up into a maelstrom and everything went to pieces? I was nothing, a tiny mosquito lighting on a Venus Fly Trap. I didn't want to be part of the shit on the walls when it did blow up.

I sat there and resolved my next move with all the brain power of three gerbils.

She returned from her call, a long and a tough one that showed in her face. I felt it in the air between us, a silent communication of her intense eyes boring into mine: *Tell me.*

The skin of her face was the color of squeezed dough.

"Sonja's being transferred up to Raiford, the men's prison," she said. "You want to hear what a plum assignment they've given her?"

"Listen, Bobbie–"

"Teaching gang graffiti to prison guards, you asshole."

"Bobbie, I–"

"Just who the fuck are you, Haftmann?" And then she was gone.

I wondered if Typhoid Mary ever got asked that question. But I would have one of my own for Special Agent Booth when our paths next crossed. What do they call paranoia, after all, but heightened self-awareness.

~ ~ ~

I wasn't far from where all my Florida problems began. I stepped outside into a lush evening with an exotic scent of jasmine lingering in the air. Taxis were plentiful now that the nightlife was picking up pace. The world was still bathed in incandescent light, the windows of office buildings looked as if they were about to explode into fireball brilliance, yet the sun was on its last legs and would soon sink beyond Key West to the silent approval of gaping tourists.

There were two worlds in Florida, like North and South Korea seen from a satellite view: half the peninsula was darkened in gray and black except for the capital; the other half was lit from one end to the other as garish pink and green neon light up the night sky ... some lusty moths come out then to play. Romantic devil that I am, it was the exactly right time for me to get a gun.

I missed a turn, cursed, rode the clutch too hard, but I was soon looking at the gym where I had confronted the fast hands of El Lagarto. I felt my body change in response to the danger that place meant to me. My palms sweated on the steering wheel and I had to suck in several mouthfuls of air to calm myself.

I sat across the street and watched the comings and goings of people. The tourists were still in evidence – shoppers and late diners mostly. The beach garb of youth had mostly been replaced by the chic clothing of Bonwit Teller and Saks. A yuppie on his cellular was parked in front of me talking animatedly about his latest killing in the market. He wore a tan silk suit, black shirt without a collar buttoned to his neck, black loafers without socks.

I could see a blonde inside his Infiniti staring at him in boredom. A couple times she would hunker over something in her lap as if caught by a sudden fit sneezing; then she would straighten up, and vigorously wipe her hand across her face like a mad woman playing a tuneless violin. Nose candy, getting ready for the night. Finally, he stopped talking, swore, and hopped into his car with a flourish. They sped off into the glitz of nightfall leaving behind a plume of white smoke.

Then my opportunity knocked – rather, it stepped out of a beat-up Silverado so hammered by the tropical sun that its original color was bleached away and the blue-green patina of copper left behind. It came in the form of Alshamoon, chump pugilist with the fat rolls who had taken the pummeling from Emilio in the ring on the same day I had taken mine outside it.

I doubted he was still in the business of helping train Emilio. He called something behind him to the driver who dropped him off and laughed at the response. He carried no bag for a change of clothes and I could see a pair of gold chains stand out in relief against the mocha flesh of his thick neck.

Sometimes you have a feeling about things before they go right and you know they will. I had that feeling and I was grateful to Alshamoon for it.

I walked through the door as if I belonged there. I saw no fight poster of Emilio on my way past.

Alshamoon was talking to three other blacks, all in street clothes. I saw them scatter like fish when I approached with a snap of my single-fold leather case. Florida cops badged the malefactors this way before they bent them over the hood.

Don't ask to see the badge, you mutt—

Alshamoon's huge toothy grin disappeared the second he turned and saw me grinning too.

"Yo, what up?" he said.

"You holding tonight, Alshamoon?"

"Hey, motherfucker, we ain't been introduced yet."

"Then let's go downtown, see what's up, cuz."

"I ain't holding, motherfucker—"

"That's detective motherfucker to you, asshole." I gave him my baddest nigger-hating cop stare.

"Fuck you mean? I holdin'? Who sayin' that shit on me?"

"I am. You're selling out of this gym because I've had you under surveillance a long time."

"Fuck that, man. I ain't sellin' shit."

"Your own boy says that just isn't so. Says to me, 'Alshamoon dealing like a motherfucker—' roids, coke, meth — boy got a pharmacy on him.'"

"Who the fuck say I'm selling?"

"The camera likes you, Alshamoon," I said. "Come on, let's take a walk."

He was looking altogether different, not the creampuff who provided Emilio with some bodywork. Twenty pounds lighter, he walked with his big head swiveling side to side with neck-snapping speed as if he expected his homies to come witness this white man's lunatic behavior.

"Emilio, man, he says you are," I said, watching his face to see if he was buying.

"That white nigga lyin' on me because I ain't sellin' shit to nobody, man. Word, motherfucker! I'm a straight-up fighter, fool." "Sure you are. Let's go," I said.

"You keep messin' with me on this boolshit, you gonna get hurt, motherfucker."

One more try and then I was going to call off the bluff and scoot. I could feel the presence of the others nearby, although I couldn't see them all. If he had a posse and he signaled, I'd get a stomping before I knew what hit me. My fake cop armor was all I had going for me.

"Emilio says–"

"That motherfuckin', lyin' 'Rican motherfucker. Hey, you fuckin' bring that motherfuckuh to my face, motherfucker! You show me he sayin' that to my fuckin' face, motherfucker!"

"OK," I said. "I'll do that."

"Fuck I know, man," he said, sniffing, smelling the trap maybe.

"C'mon, Alshamoon, let's get this thing settled. Maybe it is just a mix-up –"

"Damn straight it a mix-up. Somebody sayin' some mad fuckin' lies on me and you fools goin' for it, shit." Puffing out his chest, he could feel the heat coming off.

"Sure, that's gotta be what it is," I said. "Now give me Emilio's address and I'll go take care of this thing for you right now." Waiting, waiting ... *Come on, you fuckbrain, give, give –*

Finally. He squared his shoulders and did a Mike Tyson neck roll. Had to let me know this wasn't like giving up a brother.

"He living around here?"

"No, man, he say he in Lauderdale now. Getting' him some college pussy. He in town tonight – yo, Skates, where Emilio at tonight?"

I heard a voice behind me say in a slow, even drawl: "He at the Three Sailors tonight, man. Likes dat reggae shit."

Alshamoon turned to me and gave me what I guessed was his war face.

"OK, motherfucker, now you go gets him befo' I find yo' mama and feed her some of dis ten-inch tube steak."

He grabbed his crotch and danced around to the crowd's laughing approval.

"Way to be a soldier, Moon," one of his admirers told him.

~ ~ ~

On my way up Grand I found a sporting goods store. I found the bats in the back and looked at the 32s and 34s. The newer models were up front with Adirondacks in the lead (five Albert Pujols, followed by Rawlings, three Alex Rodriguez, a couple Derek Jeters and a single Barry Bonds). I pushed aside the aluminum models because it wasn't bat speed I wanted. I'm sentimental about wood, even though I didn't recognize most of the names. One Louisville Slugger in the far back, neglected like a redheaded stepchild, had its head swaddled in yellowing crepe paper. It had lost its polish over the years, but my existentialist heart gave a leap when I read the name of that outfielder scrawled across the meat of the bat, long forgotten except to die-hard Tribe fans. The *Plain Dealer* once called him The Ticking Time Bomb of the Cleveland Indians.

Just about badass perfect.

The Three Sailors was off Grand. I parked out back in a parking lot that crunched under my tires and approached the building from the rear. I stepped on the bodies of millions of dead mussels. The air outside was sweet with musk, patchouli, and marijuana.

I heard jazz, not reggae, when I paid the ten-dollar cover. The man who took my money had a tufted crescent of red chest hair tumbling out of his denim shirt. A black male next to him was the club bouncer. He had a weightlifter's build and a brand of Greek letters scorched with a hot coat hanger on one massive bicep; he looked at me in an unfriendly way. Biceps said, "Two-drink minimum," as I passed him to enter the bar.

Like every other place in South Florida, the decor was two toned. Pink and burgundy collided in a way that looked as though the cow intestines had exploded against the walls.

Emilio Vasquez was sitting at a table close to the stage with a couple young women, one white, one black. Both late teens, maybe early twenties. They were laughing and talking, not paying attention to the band. On stage a whippet-thin guitarist sat on a three-legged stool and did solo riffs of rock tunes on request. Someone behind me called out an old Aerosmith tune and he said something mildly obscene that made the bartender laugh.

I walked over to the bar and ordered a club soda with a lemon twist from a bartender with cornrows and colored ribbons. He wore sunglasses inside the dim bar. He took my ten and gave me back three ones with my drink and resumed an intense conversation a couple stools over with a goateed male whose moustache was a blonde fringe over his lip.

A pale girl who must have had a good ID because she

looked seventeen at most hooked her arm through the young man's while he engaged the bartender in an intense conversation. The talk seemed to be about whether John Mayer was as good at blues-rock as the late Stevie Ray Vaughan.

The young man was afflicted with sialorrhea. My cousin Spider had it when we were kids – a raspy-throated gurgling erupted every time he spoke, his vocal cords greased with excess saliva. He gave out spit spray like a sparkler with every other word, and I wondered how the bartender could hold his unblinking posture so close to him until I saw the pale girl, ginger hair and a dusting of freckles across her nose, make a separate kind of eye contact with bartender while her beau expostulated in Mayer's favor. He leaned his big body over the counter and nodded his head, but it was clear to me he was flashing his wolf grin for the little lady.

There were fewer than twenty people in the bar and it appeared that Emilio had the monopoly on the female patrons that night.

I could see his gold chains dangle in the muted light as he leaned toward one of the girls; his shirt opened a couple buttons to expose the smooth hairless planes of his chest and the bumps of his pecs. The black girl wore something diaphanous that exposed the contours of her pear-shaped breasts and the darker area of her nipples.

The rest of the band came back on stage and the guitar player quit goofing for the audience. He got quiet and then his hands moved over the sound hole just casually strumming and then he picked out a four-note theme after a while, or he let it find him, but whichever way it was, he knew when he strained it, so he circled back to it after cheating a little, and just when he began to show off for the audience, the bass fiddle picked it up and settled him down. Both their heads bobbed in time to the meshing of the notes. The saxophonist wiped sweat from his face with a towel, but the piano player looked off, bored or inscrutable, above his chin whiskers.

A waitress walked past with a tray of mixed drinks, headed for Emilio's table. Her white sleeveless blouse was bunched around her waist and loosely tucked into her black shorts. There was writing on her shirt I couldn't make out that might have been the bar logo if a toucan, hovering over a buck-toothed pirate, formed it.

Emilio made a big show of his tip, holding aloft a creased bill for her to fetch from his hand, which she did with a wide smile that lasted as long as it took to turn her back and she moved off to another table. He handed each of his companions a short stubby glass with party straws crooked over the edge. He toasted each with a big smile and a laugh which each of his dates reciprocated with a clink of glass. I pretended to be entranced by the music on stage.

I don't watch reality TV because it's a fun house mirror to life; comedies usually depress me. Overhearing the conversations of young people in bars, which I necessarily have to do a lot of in my job, makes me even more depressed. Besides, I'd need an interpreter to follow most of what I was hearing that wasn't downright insipid: "So-and-so's a skank. So-and-so's a tool." I ordered another seven dollar soda and sat back to let the racing in my heart settle into a steady thrumming in the veins.

At about ten o'clock Emilio hustled his two girls up and out the door. My kidneys were about to burst from the sodas. I followed him out to the lighted parking lot and kept a dumpster between us so that I could watch which car he drove. The girls were showing the effects of their drinks by now, lots of giggling and bumping as they walked. Emilio had an arm around each.

They stopped in front of a Jaguar Vanden Plas so that Emilio could exchange long, deep kisses with each girl while the other waited her turn.

I looked up at the night sky and found the constellations blooming overhead like a great cobalt canopy stretching across the horizon, that habit from my days in the merchant marine. I made the big W easily from Regulus to Alphard, up to Procyon, down to Sirius and completed the last leg with Betelgeuse. I was Capricorn, the goat. An old memory tugged at me like acid eating the sheath of protective memory. "Alphard is Arabic," Micah said once with childish glee in her voice, propped up in bed with her books.

"So what's it mean or am I supposed to guess?"

"It means *El Fard*, the 'Solitary One.'"

For some reason I'll never know, that made me sad and I told her so. What she said back I've forgotten.

Before more synapses could fire down those buried channels, I turned back to the amorous Emilio and watched him practically undress his companions in the lot. Whatever people can do in motels, they'll do in parking lots.

At last Emilio pulled himself out of his embrace with the white girl and held out his hand. The car warbled its disarmed signal and they all piled in, the black girl with her high butt strode around to the other side. The big smooth engine of the Jaguar growled once and caught, and the 80-watt stereo system soon drowned it out as one of them pumped up the volume on the CD player. Some reggae tune blasted the night air apart with a full-throated roar. The volume decreased just as abruptly, and I heard laughter from within the car's interior, all supple leather and burled walnut, I imagined. Emilio was in the bucks. More likely, he was being lavished by his benefactor for his success in the ring. I wondered who his new trainer was;

since Manny's "disappearance," Emilio had won three straight club fights and was moving up in the rankings. The morning *Herald* said Angelo Dundee's former gym on 5th Street in Miami was rumored to be following the cruiserweight's career.

I heard the croaky voice of some Caribbean singer and then Emilio floored it with a plume of shells rooster-tailing backward ricocheting off the metallic dumpster. He made a left onto Grand and roared off down the highway.

I raced, cursing, to my Camry before they were out of sight, and it was close, as they took a right onto Bayshore and I lost his blinking brake lights semaphoring in the darkness. Emilio changed lanes to make an extra three seconds' time to the next red light. If he weren't preoccupied with whatever was happening inside the car, I would have lost him. On an open highway, at night, with my poor vision, I'd have had no chance to stay close. Alshamoon said he lived in Coral Gables, and that was where we were heading.

Warm, moist air fragrant with the scent of bougainvillea blew through the vents in a backwash that soothed my ratcheting nerves.

I saw the Jaguar, three or four cars ahead, pass Ponce De Leon and hit the brakes hard, switching lanes to make the turn on LeJeune. I thought he might have figured somebody for a tail the way he drove and changed lanes at a whim, but it was more than likely just the booze, the women's musky presence and his cock urging him to give his ride so much unnecessary speed. He punched it up to sixty, sixty-five, seventy and got in the left-turning lane. I caught up with him at the light, cursing the Camry's worthless acceleration, and sat about ten cars behind. We all made the light, but I needed every watt of the yellow to avoid oncoming traffic catching me in the middle of Eighth Street. I stayed well behind when he went down Granada as fast as he had come up LeJeune.

I was nearly clipped by a Jeep Patriot passing me. I saw the mouth of the driver like an O as he went by in that slo-mo time of near-misses. My swivel-headed attempt to compensate for my vision in daytime driving is nothing like my nighttime experience; it's like comparing a facial tic to Parkinson's disease. I fishtailed a parked car rounding another corner and kept going despite the ringing sound of metal scraped free. In the Camry's side mirror I saw the crimped metal of its fender. *Fuck me.* That would come out of *my* fee, not Paul Toivela's pocket.

Vasquez must have felt himself secure because he drove up Coral Way in a leisurely road-hogging manner, keeping the James Bond bit going to impress the girls. Emilio driving a car he could never afford as a second-rate pugilist was the first line I had to Pavelic since the swamp. I knew, without actually knowing, Emilio was going to take me somewhere.

We were soon past the commercial district of shopping plazas and eateries and were coming up on complexes of apartments and resort-style landmarks. A large glowing sign said something about the Merrick mansion ahead, but my reading anything at night from a speeding vehicle is hopeless. We drove away from the chrome and glass structures that, like a vast arrow from outer space, pointed directly toward the black ocean.

We came to Coral Gable's old residential district, but not its toniest location, mostly modest bungalows and family homes built before the last boom. The Jag went down Coral for about half a mile more and braked hard in front of a sloping yard with loblolly pines and profusions of jacaranda growing on either side of a small one-story house. Bougainvillea had overgrown one side of the driveway but, careless of the damage to his finish, Emilio barreled down it and pulled into a garage that had opened just in time to clear the Jaguar's roof. Rubber squealed on concrete – no doubt, a practiced maneuver, one last time for the ladies.

Sonofabitch, I swore aloud. I nearly sideswiped a parked Mercedes coupe as I watched him perform his garage-door stunt. My night vision was wretched, almost no peripheral, little depth perception. Ohio joggers had probably blogged me dozens of times without actually knowing my identity because of the close calls with these late-night athletes. Even cars sometimes bloomed out of nowhere in front of my limited vision. I hadn't hit anyone yet, but if I were to lose my driving ability altogether, I'd be a cowboy without a horse in the Old West; it wasn't just transportation, it was my lifeline.

But if I lacked the gun to complete the cowboy comparison, the Louisville slugger bouncing around the back seat, would do fine. I drove up a few hundred yards more up Coral Way and turned around in the next cul-de-sac I came to. I had tossed the only sports jacket I brought with me onto the floor behind the passenger's seat. It wouldn't pass muster at most of the ritzy hotels and restaurants I had passed, but it would do to hide a baseball bat.

I pulled up facing away from Emilio's house and cut the engine. There was a big incandescent moon in the sky that I could do nothing about, but the leaves of the pines and thin traces of cirrus cloud scudding past would keep things reasonably dark. I had already broken the door light with the bat, so there were no other small tasks to perform.

I waited in the dark and thought about what had brought me here to this place at this time. How many chance events had to occur in time to make it possible? Existentialism gives me some comfort in this vast, black meaningless universe. *Maybe as much as I deserved,* if that sort of speculation wasn't something to make Sartre spin dizzily in his urn.

The Camry had a seat lever, but it was broken. I couldn't move the seat back any farther and the wheel was rubbing my thighs. I still didn't know how Emilio fit into Raina's disappearance, but I had puzzled things out a little more at the edges.

Pavelic and his killers were on the move out there in the dark as well, an Intelligence operation targeting Pavelic for an international connection I still hadn't fathomed, and Raina Toivela herself – was she a willing pawn in these sadomasochistic parties? I understood motivations like greed, power, and revenge but not girls who run away from good homes. "Raina," I said to myself, "where are you?"

I closed my eyes and tried to relax my neck muscles which were knotted from the drive. I moved my legs up and down to keep the circulation from cramping me later. *So quiet...*

I heard a voice.

One of those street crazies you see in every city ranted about the end of the world. This skinny, disheveled old loon simply popped up under a streetlight in the middle of the road, reciting his dire prediction; he came in my direction, a wad of papers clutched in his grimy fist.

Shit, I thought, *a Jehovah's Witness. That's all I need...*

He stumbled up to my window and peered at me. His scarred, dirty face was mottled with age spots and wisps of tangled hair bleached of all color. I tried to hunch lower in the seat, but he knew someone was behind the glass and began spewing more religious gibberish, stippling my windshield with his spittle. He was going to blow my cover any second. His burning eyes, saliva streaming from his mouth like an open wound, this mad prophet gibbered in the deserted street in a cracking voice about "unrighteousness, fornication, wickedness..."

All crazy eyes and broken teeth, he zeroed in on me sticking his face above my windshield. He spat out the catalog of God-defilers destined to burn for eternity: "...haters of God, despiteful, proud, boasters, inventors of evil things..."

Never be crazy, not like that. Shoot myself first. My body was running on reserves after so many adrenalin rushes.

Except for this goofy Nostradamus, the street remained quiet as a tomb. Not a dog barked, no noise except for the insect life of the trees and shrubs. My heart stopped its thumping, and I checked the time by holding my watch next to my work shoes. The luminous paint on the hands, those minute green waves of radioactive decay, told me it was exactly 11:07.

I looked up and saw the old man wandering off down the street, still ranting about the Apocalypse.

OK, plenty of time enough for everybody inside to get nice and comfy.

I wrapped the bat in my coat and stepped out of the car and moved across the street into the deepest shadows cast by the trees. I worked my way to the side of house where sumac obscured most of the stucco. A small veranda led around back where the bougainvillea had been trimmed back to allow for a small patio made of fieldstone and a redwood-stained deck. Hurricane fences separated the lots. One yellow pane of window shone above the wainscoting from a house one street over. A night-light, maybe, but anyone looking out could see me plainly despite the sumac that had grown up around Emilio's fence.

A gas barbecue grill occupied a corner next to a dying or dead ficus. The open light came from the torn fragment of moon in the sky and a rectangular slat created by the sliding glass doors. I saw sheers over the doors and a screen door left open to catch the breeze. I couldn't see it well from my vantage, but I heard it hiss and sputter: a box air conditioner had been jerry-rigged onto a platform propped by Y-shaped two-by-fours at the far end of the house.

That, I guessed, would be the bedroom.

Music – a nervous salsa rhythm – poured from speakers close to the screen door. *Emilio, the considerate neighbor*. His house or somebody's borrowed fuckpad, I had him cold.

A wisp of cloud like an old man's windblown hair stretched across the moon. I saw a part of the Scorpio overhead and its brilliant centerpiece in the misty light just above the tops of trees, *Cor Scorpionis* – "Scorpion's Heart."

I set my suit jacket with the bat on the deck and peered inside the house. The blonde girl had her back to me. She made slight ticking sounds on the glass and was nude except for her bra. She bent over a small glass table and did a line while I watched and then rubbed the side of one nostril vigorously. Bent down, did another line, nostril two, rub. Emilio and the black girl were nowhere in sight. The Latin rhythm came from a stereo system and a TV. I saw a plain lemon couch or daybed was facing the other end of the house. No other furniture or photos on the wall. The blond girl snuffled on her knees and began to rock to the music, settling into her dope groove.

I touched the screen: fiberglass, not metal.

I could put my finger through this stuff. Instead, I took out my Swiss blade, and while the girl kept cocaine time to the music, I slit the screen from top to bottom directly behind her.

I picked up the bat, and stepped into the room with

the handle palmed inside the coat behind my leg.

She turned at once, still on her knees, and I saw her eyes get big. Some owl-blinking, trying to recognize me. Her nostrils were coated with powder and her eyes had that look that said the limbic brain's message of *Uh-oh, trouble* wasn't getting through. Her irises were shrunk to pinpricks and she weaved on her haunches like a cobra.

I smiled. She smiled back.

"Y'all a friend of Emilio?" she asked in big-eyed wonder.

I nodded.

"You wanna hit?" She purred, completely unselfconscious of her nakedness. The tousled blonde hair was belied by the dark pubic triangle between her open legs.

"No, thanks," I said. "I'm just going to say hello to Emilio."

She laughed at that. "Him and Sharisse are, like, gettin' it on in the bedroom, man. He won't like that." She giggled, her bra slipping off her thin shoulders.

"Oh, that's all right," I said. "He won't mind."

More giggles. I was a funny man. She looked about fifteen in the light.

"Where's the phone, sweetie?" I asked.

She pointed at the wall. I saw it. "Thanks," I said.

I slipped the bat out of the coat once I passed her and debated whether she would bolt and decided it wouldn't matter in her condition. I leaned the bat against the wall while I twisted my finger around the cord. One tug and I freed it.

The blonde was still smiling at me. One cup of her bra had slipped down and exposed a white breast with a brown, eraser-sized nipple. She had a nipple ring too. She looked down and laughed at that and fell back on her haunches throwing wide open the pink slit between her legs.

"Oh man, am I fucked up!" she laughed.

I winked at her and turned toward the hallway. The surge of new strength was like a drug filling up my arms and chest.

There was no noise down the hallway. I turned the knob and waited a moment for my eyes to adjust to the different light. Something sheer and saffron-colored had been tossed over the single lamp in the room – *mood lighting by Emilio*.

The bed was directly in front of me and there was a thrashing of light and dark, a blur of white-chocolate mousse of human limbs. Like the pixels of a TV screen, the confusion of dots and lines sorted itself out in an instant so my brain put it all together and I saw it as one image.

Groans as Emilio bucked into her doggie style, his back to me. Sweat glistened off his muscular back despite the air-conditioning. His buttocks were pumping hard and the ropy gluteal muscles clenched with each thrust. He even wore his gold chains to bed.

She was obscured from my view, on her stomach, her face in the pillow but one long slim leg dangled over the edge of the bed. She made small noises in her throat in the pauses between thrusts and the slapping sound of skin. I could have come into the room pushing a piano with an entire SWAT team, and he wouldn't have heard a thing, so deep was he in his stud performance. The room stank of sex. I stepped behind him and picked my spot. I had to step to the side and take a chopping downward swing because of the low ceiling, and the timing of his jackhammering rhythm, but my aim was true.

He screamed, bucked off the girl as if lightning had mysteriously struck him. The force of his sudden ejection slammed her head into the wall and he went over the top of her back. They lay like that for a stunned moment while he struggled to find air and untangle his limbs from hers.

"Whaa-whaa, whaaat, baby, hunh–" was all she managed to say.

I took a bead on his neck and watched him turn toward me.

Emilio screamed again and roared in pain. His black eyes found me. I covered the space between us and held the bat poised aloft for him to see.

"You make a move and I'll smash your fucking brains in," I said as calmly as I could, but I nearly gagged from the adrenalin.

He reared back and kicked the black girl away from him, as if looking for room to battle. She hit the floor hard. Neither of us looked at her.

"Oh God – you broke my – Who th' fuck are you?" He said it in one breath.

I wagged the bat menacingly at him, making little circles in the air with the meaty part.

"What the fuck you doin' in my crib, you fuckin' crazy *maricón*–"

"Easy, easy. Don't move a muscle," I said evenly between my gritted teeth.

I held the bat beyond his reach but close enough to his face to make the point.

"You fuckin' broke my fuckin' shoulder! I kill you, motherfucker–"

He squeezed his eyes shut and I waited a tense second to see which way he'd go. Part of me wanted him to charge. I had the X marked on his forehead where my next swing was going. *Lights out, fucker, for good this time.*

He groaned instead, lay back growling, sputtering a volley of curses in Spanish that my buddy Tico would have had a hard time keeping up with. His fighters' hands clenched and unclenched, his tight stomach muscles glistened where moisture pools had collected in the crevices. Even while his body was getting him ready for war, his penis was semi-erect. The black girl started to get up on hands and knees, and I hoped she was as coked up as her blonde friend in the next room. I stepped on the middle of her back and shoved her flat to the carpet without taking my eyes off Emilio.

"Tell her to stay down on the floor, Emilio," I ordered. I double-pumped the bat in front of his face. "You remember me now?" I said. "You remember meeting me in the gym? Look at me!"

His eyes were slits like a jungle cat's. "Yeah, I know you," he said. "You came in looking for some little fuckbitch – " He bit back whatever else he was going to say.

"What else do you know, Emilio? You know about what happened to Manny?"

I made an involuntary move with the bat toward his head. He flinched.

"I don't know nothin' about that, man. You broke my goddamn shoulder, you fuck."

He brought one hand up to his shoulder and held it at the place where the bat struck. No bone showed through. The arc of my swing had torn a groove in the ceiling plaster and slowed down the momentum. "You know everything, Emilio. Your Pavelic's fuckboy."

"Joost a minute, you asshole. You talkin' like you think I can't take that bat out of your hands and shove it up your ass right through you fuckin' mouth."

He was bunching his muscles now, getting ready to spring.

"I know you can take me even with your bad arm but I swear to you I'll hurt you bad. I'll end your fighting career. I'll end your pussyhound career with it. Everything will go. They'll dump you into some shithole place for pensioned-off fighters. They'll spoon-feed you and wipe your ass for you for the rest of your life."

It was a long speech and I was gasping for breath by the time I finished it.

The girl started to groan on the floor and tried to get up again. "Stay down, bitch," he ordered her without looking in her direction. "OK, fuckface. This between you and me," he said. "You better fuckin' lissen a me too, because I am going to kill you even if he don't."

"I want to know where she is," I said. "You've got this one and only chance."

"I don't know the bitch," he said. He was tough.

He started another litany of cursing at that point so I made a move to tap the damaged shoulder, already swollen. The threat of a prod from my bat was too much – he held up his good hand and then cast a glance at the place I meant to hit where blood blossomed like an angry pustule coming out of his shoulder. A little yip of pain came from his throat like something from a wounded animal. His eyes were wet. I saw fear of more pain in them.

I raised the bat again and hoped he was past this macho insanity. He flinched despite the black furnace in his eyes.

"Just tell me where the girl is," I said.

"She's – she's in Boca Raton, I dunno where. The big man, he keep her in his condo. Thass all I know, man, unnh – "

"Where's Luis live?" I asked. "Pavelic's driver."

"He stayin' with her. Her bodyguard. He bring her, take her, man."

His head lolled on his neck. He was close to passing out now.

"You know what happened to Manny," I said.

"Gator food, shithead. Like you soon." He was still flying the flag of machismo and gave me a smile of bravado.

"Where's your gun, Emilio?" Fighters, slaughterhouse workers, mussel shell divers – they all keep guns in the house.

He looked at me, then at the bat. My hands ached from gripping it. He jerked his head toward the wall: *garage.*

"In the Jag?" I asked. "Where?"

"Under ... the seat."

He groaned again and his body writhed, rolling his face into the sheets. "Oh God damn, it hurts. It hurts bad. I gotta get to a hospital, man!"

"Soon," I said. "Get on the floor. On your stomach. Slowly." He did it while I kept my batting stance with his head in range.

"Put your hands behind your back and lace the fingers. Both of you."

The girl complied at once, whimpering. She had been listening.

He groaned. "Can't move ... arm, you stupid shit motherfucker."

Sweat beads had popped out on his forehead from the effort to move. I felt safer, but I was still afraid of his strength and speed.

I stepped over them. The lamp had been flung off in the melee, so when the door opened wide and the blonde girl stood there nude, pouty breasts cupped in her hands, she was like a corrupt apparition of the *Birth of Venus,* all bemused wonder and nubile flesh, stepping from her shell of innocence.

"Hey, what'th'fuck's, like, goin' on in here? Can I join?"

The hairs on my neck prickled and I turned just in time to see Emilio's good hand reaching for the drawer of the small table. I wheeled and brought the end of the bat down on his knuckles just as he pulled the drawer open to expose the gun inside. There was no doubt this time – bones shattered across the entire hand. He clutched it to his chest, the gun forgotten in the frenzy of pain; the whites of his eyeballs were golf-ball size. He fell backwards and writhed on the floor.

I flung myself at the drawer and grabbed the gun. It was a blue carbon steel .357, a model with combat-style grips, a very bad gun to turn my back on.

The stoned blonde was still nonplussed by the action, still trying to compute it inside her fogged-out gray cells. I might as well try speaking to a bushman in the Kalahari Desert. I leaned toward the girl on the floor, shaking in hysteria, and praying to the Lord to save her from this.

"When Emilio wakes, take him where he wants to go," I said. "The cops will be interested in you girls if you're minors, so you might want to hold off on calling them." I added for no apparent reason: "Better ditch the coke."

Emilio was passed out, a part of his head lay under the bed. His legs were splayed out exposing hairy legs and genitals. He had shaved his bag and a crescent strip over and around the base of his flaccid penis like the men in Sonja's first porn film.

"I'm taking this with me," I said, meaning the gun. "Get dressed."

She got up, her whitened, enlarged eyes fixed on me and the gun alternately. Her mouth parted, slightly opening to gulp air, as she stepped into her panties.

Behind me her blonde companion was still giggling, rubbing one leg with her ankle, when I jiggled the latch of the screen door and gave up finding the locking hasp, so I kicked my way through it ripping the screen wide open. I hit the deck running, that salsa rhythm behind me replaced by some happy-horseshit from Bob Marley.

I tossed gun, bat, and sport coat in the back,

jumped in, and cranked the engine. I bolted down Coral Way back toward Miami and the city's brightest lights. I still hadn't seen the ocean, but I smelled the rancid odor of decaying fish and black swamp mud.

Emilio had Pavelic's long-armed reach to back him so I wasn't convinced he'd make the call to the police. But, hunter or hunted, I was running out of time in South Florida.

The moon was gone, hidden fast behind a veil of coastal clouds that had moved in and swept it away leaving a blanched pink light in the sky from the city's reflected glare. I had not taken a painkiller in six hours and I was feeling the nervous exhaustion of someone who has been running in a maze without a hope of finding the way out.

I drove all the way down Coral past the University of Miami, past my motel turnoff, jumped on I 95 and joined the frenetic stream of traffic going north. I bypassed the East Flagler exit on a hunch and took the next exit at Fifth Street.

A sign said Port of Miami. I followed the arrow past the bright lights, glanced at the chrome and glass behemoths of the Southeast Financial Center and headed for the sea.

At the turnoff to the Dodge Island Causeway, I followed the road to the Bayside Marketplace and drove on until I ran out of road. I picked out a narrow tarmac road and followed it for a half mile toward the booming sounds of the docks. I passed deserted and rotting warehouses with broken windows and rusted-out tin roofs with so much broken glass and masonry strewn about that it looked like an abandoned fortress, overrun by some berserk army of vandals who left only ruins and graffiti behind.

I found a dirt road leading up a knoll overlooking the water – two tire tracks angling off where the saw grass had been so bent back by the chassis of cars that it reminded me of figure skaters doing laybacks with their arched spines.

I pulled over near a cluster of pepper trees growing in the midst of this deserted place and cut my lights. Maybe a deserted lovers' lane in bygone years when lovers felt safer outdoors under the stars than in sleazy motels.

I smelled the oily water of placid Biscayne Bay and saw the blinking lights of the harbor, watched deck lights of ocean-going freighters coming and going. Because of the lights, I could see few stars, but there was Orion's belt, clear and plain to the eye on the lower horizon. I could make out Bellatrix, a yellow second magnitude star like our sun. Another insignificant star in a small solar system at the ass end of the disk galaxy we call our Milky Way.

My brain couldn't take any more. I fell asleep to the soughing of the breeze off the ocean punctuated by the shrill shriek of the gulls disturbed in their rest and the laboring groans of the big cranes removing cargo from ships. My eyes throbbed, my head ached with too many questions. Nothing made much sense. My last thought before I fell asleep at the wheel was that planting morality chips into human brains was a bad idea only if you never drove dogwatch in a patrol car, never scoped a bloody crime scene, or never observed people at their worst when they thought they were getting away with evil shit. Whoever said it was all smoke and mirrors forgot about the importance of light in sleight-of-hand.

Those high, cold stars burned in an endless tug-of-war with gravity in trillions of simultaneous atomic explosions and converted hydrogen to helium. Some would grow into red giants and white dwarfs in billions of year life cycles. *What did it matter what I did tonight?* Yet I hated myself for what I did to that punk. I felt dirty beyond all cleansing and I wished I could go back in time, start over, never leave my yard, my house, my things. Live in some timeless moment that would abolish time and memory of all that I had become.

Markwright's words rang in my ears like the tinnitus that afflicted me since my head wound, keening for his lost woman. Was I any better? Moaning the loss of one, trying to find another before some behemoth's jaws clamped round her and took her down beneath the water's surface like the fat little trainer in a death roll.

CHAPTER 10

The sun on my face woke me. It was only as big as a CD disk, but it threw shafts of light in all directions across the water and every flat surface – bouncing off the tops of cranes and masts of ships in the marina beyond my limited vision.

I saw hundreds of small craft moored to pilings and berthed in docks below. Stones about the size of the pyramids at Giza formed a semicircular breakwall held back the ocean and kept the tiny boats rocking gently next to their berths at the piers. The water out beyond the bay was blue and turquoise – except where white caps showed currents rolling ashore, not a serious chop for boaters or swimmers. The sky was powder blue except where the underbellies of the clouds were lit to a saffron glow. *Another gorgeous day in fucking South Florida.*

Traffic was roaring somewhere behind me, and I knew Miami had not overslept even if I had. The Causeway traffic was glimmering in the far distance like a wrinkled oil ribbon as the sun bounced off windshields and chrome. I smelled diesel fuel from the harbor and heard the tiny *whirrp-whirrp* of winged insects coming alive in the tall grass. Now and then one would hit the fender or the wheel cap with a *tunk*.

I touched my face and my hands came away with blood. Mosquitoes had penetrated the Camry's myriad cracks and vents. I looked at my face in the rearview mirror where lumps from the bites were beginning to itch. Just before dawn I had gotten up to piss and felt the tiny marauders jabbing everywhere. I got up to relieve my bladder again. My mouth was cotton, my head throbbed from a bad night's sleep, and I had acquired numerous bruises and bumps from last night's scuffling. The little finger of my left hand was swollen. My right pants leg was torn – probably from that burst through the screen on my way out when I couldn't find the latch to unlock it. I must have hit the aluminum side of the screen door too. I had a vague recollection of jerking the entire frame off the castors when I made it through.

"Better move," I thought. Some rent-a-cop or maybe even a real one might come across my car, sitting there in plain sight. Cops love to coop near docks and deserted warehouses.

I wasn't hungry. My grandmother used to say I was more insect than human, and that one side of my gullet was packed with food stored for energy later. Right then I did feel like a bug. I wanted to get back to my room and clean up, shower, grab a few hours of real sleep, and nip this headache in the bud before it incapacitated me for the day. I had set the fuse going last night and no calling it back.

I checked my pockets for painkillers and remembered I had put them in my suit coat pocket. They were probably scattered all over Emilio's deck right now. *One dumbfuck move, that.* If there had been serious trouble and the cops had come, those pills would be pointing straight to me like a big neon arrow. I touched my face again and felt the stubble of a two-day beard working its way through the swellings of the mosquito bites and aggravating the itching.

I drove back to the Grove on South Miami, then to the Brickell exit to Bayshore.

When I pulled into the Holiday Inn lot, I saw a navy blue Mercedes Benz I had not noticed before. One of Haftmann's rules is to make yourself familiar with a parking lot, and while there were plenty of luxury cars in this lot, that one stood out like a nose oyster on a white linen tablecloth. The windows were tinted opaque like a state trooper's wraparound sunglasses and the car had been backed in next to a dented white Camaro with racing stripes. I cruised past trying to avoid swiveling my head too obviously, just a customer looking for a vacant spot.

I was still exhausted from the adrenalin surges of the night before, and hunger had been squirting enough insulin into my system to blur my vision and spook me at every passing car where I expected to see the two silhouettes of Pavelic's bad-assed gofers. I needed to be clear-headed more than at any time in my life, and this was not the way to do it. I took consolation from the Tribe slugger's name on the bat. He had come through for me and it helped to buoy my flagging courage with flashbacks of Emilio cringing before me and my upraised club while he spluttered his rage.

Neanderthals R Us, baby. How do you like it now, Emilio?

I booked. At Bayshore I did a little backtracking to see if I were being tailed. I stopped the car at a McDonald's on Grand where I had a view of all directions and lifted the engine hood. Nobody seemed interested in me. If I were being tailed, it was by better surveillance than I had ever known in my life.

I had my clothes and personal effects to retrieve from the hotel. Nothing I couldn't replace except the money I had secreted in a pair of socks. Everything else that mattered to the case was on my person or between my ears. I wasn't going to make anything easy for anybody like bribing the cleaning woman for a peek inside my room.

After twenty more minutes of wasting time, pretending to fiddle with the engine, I gassed up at a BP station, checked out of the Holiday Inn and left Coconut Grove awash in translucent light that gave off a pearly sheen. I drove back to Miami on the A1A. I wasn't going to make it easy for Pavelic's scouts to spot me, and I figured that Miami was the obvious place to hide in plain sight. I was sacrificing sleep for security, but I had to have a base of operations and I had been in one place too long. A couple hours of shuteye would do me good. First, I had to call Bobbie right away to see what she could do to get me into that party tonight.

I found a bed-and-breakfast off 13th Street near Simpson Park. I left my car in the street and walked up to a renovated two-story house with sidewalks bordered by peonies, dahlias, and purple irises; there were climbing roses on cross-shaped trestles under all the side windows. If it weren't for the seashells glued to the lintels and above the picture window, this could have been a typical house in Jefferson.

I paid the proprietor downstairs, a widow named Mrs. Tanenbaum, who bore an uncanny resemblance to a popular TV sexologist who loved to talk about the proper ways of sexual intercourse. Micah made me watch her once and listening to the aged crone wax eloquent about some woman's "bodacious tatas" filled me with squirmy distress.

I paid for a week and went to my room. I told her I needed sleep after an all-night shift at my new construction job. Having just arrived in town, I thanked her for the offer of the grand tour but declined, saying I needed to catch up on my sleep. I showered without soap in the common bathroom at the end of the upstairs hallway.

Mrs. Tanenbaum had lined all the sills in the house with glass gewgaws and one, a swan with folded wings captured ruby light in its center, and refracted it like a pool of congealing blood.

I returned to my room down the hallway sopping wet because my new landlady had not provided me with towels; still, I was grateful she let me into her establishment with little more than a nod of her head at my flimsy tale.

At last, I dropped facedown onto a crinoline-stiff pillow on a bed too small for my length so that I had to stick my feet between the brass dowels of the bedstead. The widow had placed a quilted afghan over the lumpy mattress. I could barely make out a few homely sayings stitched into the diamond-shaped panes, but it reminded me of my grandmother who used to stitch little sayings and tidbits of folk wisdom into her own quilts. I kept her last quilt in a closet back home because she had slipped all her cogs by then and what she meticulously labored at putting into it would shock the most depraved. Even Micah with her shrink books didn't know what to call it.

I didn't need to set an alarm. The automatic alarm in my brain worked fine despite all the other problems that slug was causing me. I would get up in a couple hours, eat somewhere, and get to a pay phone.

I remembered my grandmother's fanatical devotion to her Catholic faith and her white leather bible. When I was a teenager, I told her angels were just demons in another dimension of light. I still remember the hurt look in her face. This was a year before that mad quilt business.

It wasn't my anxieties lulling me to dive into a black sleep; it was my ex-wife's face coming up to me like those fat little cherubs on Christmas cards. She smoothed the damp hair from my brow and pressed my eyelids closed with her fingertips. The last thing I remembered was her telling me it would all work out. *Liar, Micah. You said that about us, too...*

~ ~ ~

Rain. I heard it, smelled it a moment later. A Miami spring rain, not the precursors of the summer monsoons, but a light drizzle pattered against the upstairs windows. It did not refresh me, nor did it stop the little man tapping with metronomic beats inside my skull with his ball-peen hammer.

Groaning, I rolled off the bed and surprised myself. I was still nude. I didn't remember undressing or even showering. I stretched stiff muscles in my back and shoulders from last night's batting practice on Emilio. I wondered if I weren't getting too close to the edge again.

But I had an urgent call to make regarding the next round, no time for Micah-style introspection.

First, I had to get this itchy stubble off my face, get into town and buy some more clothes, so I put my old clothes back on, went downstairs for some towels and asked Mrs. Tanenbaum if I might borrow a blade to shave, some throwaway, a Bic or something. She gave me a cool look as if I'd asked to see one of the winged monkeys of Oz, but she shambled off to the kitchen and returned to tell me there was nothing like that in the house but there was another guest upstairs. Perhaps, she intoned, as if we were conversing between pews in church, I could borrow one from *that person.*

I thanked her and went back up the narrow stairs and thought, *Why not?* I had heard a television or radio playing in the room two doors from mine. I listened at the door and heard an announcer say that the Miami Marlins were taking on the St. Louis Cardinals at Roger Dean Stadium in Jupiter. Albert Pujols wouldn't be coming to town, however. The Cards had put him on the auction block for 240 million. *What if I had taken his bat last night instead of my Yankee-killing Tribesman?* I hate it when my existentialist credo is spooked like that.

Then a gabble of voices and snips of pop tunes melded together; someone was fast-turning an old-fashioned radio where you twisted a dial instead of punching buttons.

"Niggers think they own the fuckin' country." A masculine voice with a thick Southern accent, followed by a barely audible woman's voice, measured, accentless, scolding him for the n-word.

I took a chance and knocked.

She opened the door. I scoped the broad-shouldered, shirtless male in his late twenties standing just behind her. He wore jogging pants with FLORIDA STATE stitched down one leg and the Seminole Indian mascot on the thigh of the other. He looked me over with a hard stare and I nodded to him but spoke to the attractive brunette in front of me.

"Hey," I said, affecting a good-old-boy *shtick* to put him at ease. "I'm your neighbor just down the hall. I had some trouble at the airport and lost all my stuff including my shaving kit. You folks have a spare razor I might borrow?"

She smiled. Pretty, ten years older than the college boy. She wore a flowery shirtwaist dress and a pearl necklace. Teardrop pearls dangled from her lobes. Her chestnut hair was fashionably cut around her face. Her smile was bracing, unexpected – perfect teeth.

Without looking behind her, she said, "Hon, get him one of mine."

"Fuck it at?" he asked.

He had that heat-flushed complexion that would never tan, a third- or fourth-generation Southern boy from the Deep South.

"Carry-all, babe, in the corner next to the reading lamp," she said, still without a backward glance. I liked how she kept her eyes on me.

He handed it to her with a smirk on his face, not to me.

She gave it to me, a Lady Schick, and I thanked her

and said that I would return a new one as soon as I had a chance to get to a store and replace my lost things.

She said not to bother, keep it.

"Oh, by the way," she said. "Your landlady came upstairs with some towels for you, but I saw her take them right back downstairs. I think you were sleeping," she said. Then that same pretty smile. "You know, these old houses aren't plumb. You should make sure your door is shut all the way next time you take a nap."

Ah, that would explain Mrs. Tanenbaum's frosty reception a moment ago. A glimpse of my hairy backside must have sent her scuttling backwards.

I said I'd bear that in mind, thanked her, and shook her hand.

"I'm Tom."

Her grip was firm, dry, business-like. "Anne," she said.

I went back to my room and counted the money I had left, gathered everything I needed for tonight. The bat was in the Camry's trunk along with my papers, sport coat and Emilio's gun. On my way down the hall to shave, I heard the redneck's petulant voice again. He was saying something about my weird-looking eyes. Thinking of her knowing eyes as she handed me the plastic razor, I knew she was down here to cut loose. *Fuck you, Junior,* I thought. *You're nothing but a cum stain to that lady.*

The rain had stopped and steam hissed from the sidewalks. It was going to get muggy by mid-afternoon. Despite the refreshing shower and the hot needle spray I directed under my arms, I needed deodorant, aspirin. I had to get to a pharmacy and get some supplies before I looked and smelled so bad that cops would bag me on one of those mopery-with-intention-to-gawk charges Jack and I made up as we went cruising Cleveland's west side for the ne'er-do-wells of the city.

I flipped on the radio at five minutes to noon in case there was a breaking story or news about last night. The DJ said something about the Porno for Pirates' "Under the Tahitian Moon," so I shut it off. *Information overload.* Boomers reaching for their canes and walkers, Generation Xers with middle-age spread, Generation Y in its thirties – it was all around me. I thought of the sweet oval face and high cheekbones of Raina... then an image of the little girl in the film grinding down on her.

Lost, lost – all of us.

I found a Rite-Aid on Eighth Street and bought supplies and ointments for the bites. Across the street was an Army-Navy store. I crossed the intersection and bought clothes – pants, socks, T-shirts, underwear. All of it overpriced but I would have paid triple just then. I bought a decent pair of field glasses – cursing myself for leaving my Zeiss binocs at the office – and a fishing knife without serrated edges for filleting. They sold rifles and shotguns in the back and apparently were a cops' outfitting store because I saw handgun accessories and body armor.

I bought a black thigh holster for Emilio's gun. It had Velcro that wrapped tight around the leg with a boa-constrictor grip. The hammer wasn't shrouded, so I didn't want a shoulder rig and have the thing get stuck. I looked longingly at the bullets in the display case. Mostly standard stuff – .9 mm, .10 mm, .40 S & W, .45 ACP – but I'd bet every dollar I had on me the proprietor could fix cops up with the newest technology in hollow points: fragmentation bullets that burst with 90 percent disintegration. Hit any part of the human anatomy and it's like blowing a grapefruit-sized hole in a mound of Jell-O. I used to love guns, their weight and heft, the recoil down my forearms. All that satin-nickel and bluing finish, the laser-dot sighters and tritium night scopes were an aphrodisiac to me.

I saw a pair of handcuffs "ideal for saltwater environments" and bought them too. I bought a Desert Storm camouflage poncho to wrap my hardware in. I asked the salesman if he had any tools like shovels, rakes. He pointed to some small shovels on a rack next to silver hatchets and hunting bows. The lettered sign called them *Combat Emplacement Evacuators* instead of shovels. I tossed a street map of Miami Beach onto the pile next to the register.

By the time I left, Paul Toivela's retainer money was almost gone. I would be down to credit cards soon. I could risk some gumchewing clerk taking my card and cutting it in half in front of my face but not the paper trail that would lead back to me. Time was too short to discard the cell phone even though landlines for the calls I had to make would have been the smart thing.

I used the fishing knife to cut price tags and identifying labels off everything I bought, threw the receipts from the drugstore into an alley bin, and tossed it all into the trunk. I drove to a Gulf station and used the rest room to clean up, dab my face where the mosquitoes had bit, and change into clean clothes. I left my old clothes and battered triple E's in the station's green dumpster.

One more thing to do: tie the feedbag on. I could have eaten gravel right then.

In the middle of the Miami design district, I found an English style pub. The oak beams traversing the low ceiling looked plastic but were real. I picked up a sliver in the webbing between my thumb and index finger proving it.

I ate a Chicken Florentine and then ordered steak *au poivre flambe* before I had finished the last of the scallion-and-mushroom crepes. Micah thought I had compartmentalized stomachs like a cow. The waitress cocked one hip at me and raised an eyebrow as if she thought I was putting her on about a second dinner. Starvation trumped common sense. I repeated the order calmly and told her to bring me a dark Columbian coffee. She gave me a tart look when she left and I noticed some white-haired tourists gaping at me.

I was tense from the anticipation over whether Bobbie would come through.

Everything told me I was getting closer to Raina, but I was also drawing Pavelic's attention to her as a liability. He wouldn't sit around waiting for me to make another move. His liquid voice warbled in my memory like a saw blade. I tried to read the papers I had bought outside the eatery, but the words dissolved in my neocortex as soon as processed. I wanted a cigarette. I wanted a shot of whiskey. I had lost so much edge over the years that my one-sided battle with Emilio was still debilitating. I had lost some of my stomach for violence.

People still come to Florida to retire, but all I saw were flesh mannequins arriving to expire in the sunshine. Dead people putting forks into their gaping mouths, having conversations in corners with other dead people, rich perfumes and spicy food smells wafting over the sweet rot of death. Paradise or hell, which was it? We're nothing more than corpses on reprieve, as someone said once.

The waitress set my plate in front of me with a rattle, and I tried to smile up at her to apologize, but she was gone when I looked up. Another wraith soon to be gone to early death; she just didn't realize it. I pushed the plate aside, my appetite suddenly gone. I dropped one of my last remaining twenties beside the steaming plate of uneaten food.

~ ~ ~

"I could kiss you!" I roared down the wire at her. I

225

was at a pay phone in the Rumcake Lounge of the Howard Johnson's on Second Avenue.

"Don't even think about it, Buster." Her tone was still angry but I detected a little less of it since she had left me in the diner. "Haftmann, I'm not blaming you for Sonja. It tells me we're on to something big."

"Good. I can't thank you enough – "

"Can the bullshit, please. This isn't just about your runaway girl anymore."

"Ah, can we say Pulitzer?"

"Stop dicking around. This is serious." She meant *dangerous*. We both knew it. "I've been running amok all over town for you," she said. "I've called your cell six times already."

"I've been on the run," I said. "It's charging at my new place right now."

I told her little about the last twenty-four hours except that I had relocated to new digs.

"I think your Raina's in too deep," she said. "Things are happening."

You have no idea, Bobbie, I thought. I could almost see her holding the phone with that pouty look on her face.

"How bad do you want this guy?" she asked.

"I want to *annihilate* him, do you understand me?"

I think she did. Her face had blanched at the restaurant when I told her about Toni DeCamillo's death, without the details of her execution. I didn't know how this would go down over the phone, but she had to know that the stakes had gone way up; maybe it was time for her to get out of the game.

"I'm still in," she said. "What are you going to do with a gun?" she asked in that sharp way she had of clicking her tongue off her palate.

I told her that Luis Amezcua was Raina's bodyguard. The gun was insurance, last resort and *not* cowboy time, I assured her.

I thought she would try to talk me out of taking it, but she said nothing.

"Two more things," I said. "The guy, Markwright. He's seen DeCamillo's little book. God help him if he copied it. Run a computer check. Start with vitals, marriage, credit. Find out how he pays his bills, whether he's registered to vote – liens, anything."

"Who cares about that dude?"

"The way Pavelic cleans up after mistakes," I said, "I don't want him on my conscience."

"You said two things."

"Run this number with your cop at BMV."

I heard her muttering curses as I read out the Jaguar's number from my slip of paper.

"Wait, damn it. Give it to me again."

"Got it?"

"I'm not sure which of my contacts are safe now," she said, pausing, the timbre of her voice betraying fear.

I told her I was going back to my B & B. The chow was making me logy, and my blood pressure was walloping me like a closed fist. I needed to be rested up for tonight. Wealthy people have more security from the local precincts on top of their own security.

"Listen, Tom," she said. "I've got everything on a disk at work – if, if anything happens. Get it to the D.A.'s office."

"That's being a touch melodramatic, don't you think?"

I tried to lighten it up, but it felt like the pot calling the kettle black. Some kind of revenge-from-beyond-the-grave dialogue from a cheap thriller hanging over our words.

The party was tonight nine o'clock, invitation only, at an address in Miami Beach. She gave me directions from the Tuttle Causeway. A place off Arthur Godfrey.

"You should try to look like you belong in that neighborhood," she said.

We both laughed at the same time, knowing that was completely hopeless.

~ ~ ~

Good traffic flow let me make it back by 3:00. Mrs. Tanenbaum was working near a trellis in the front holding garden shears and wearing thick gloves. I complimented her on her roses. She didn't say anything as I passed her. My forehead was glazed with sweat and I needed another change of clothes.

I climbed the steps to my room. My mind was racing ahead to what I would have to do that night. I never gave a thought to the fact that the bathroom door was shut. I stepped in with one hand on my fly.

She hadn't bothered to lock it. Anne was standing in front of the mirror with a towel covering her breasts and I almost had to snap my neck rigid to keep from looking at what it didn't cover below.

"This isn't a communal bathroom, hon," she said.

"Oh, I'm sorry," I blurted, retreating.

I headed off to my room. I had terror about the immediate future – what the next few hours were going to mean for me, Bobbie, Pavelic but mostly Raina Toivela. I sat on the bed. I was also thinking about Anne's body and how long it had been since I held a woman in my arms. My weariness and anxiety were forgotten for a moment.

I lay back on the bed and closed my eyes. The throbbing behind it was keeping time with my heartbeat. I saw the image of Emilio rampant, cavorting and bucking at the flanks of the black girl. I felt old, tired, and burned out with ambivalent desires. I thought about moving out, finding a new place, just my grabbing my stuff and running for the hills.

I looked at my wristwatch. I needed sleep. "Just a

few minutes," I said to myself. "I'll get everything together."

A comforting fib, that. Pinocchio's nose grew with every lie, but it wasn't my nose growing as I fell asleep wondering what Anne's body behind that skimpy towel looked like.

~ ~ ~

Her knock at the door jolted me awake.

Christ, what time is it? Sleeping all this time, shit McGee.

My inner alarm had failed me for the first time in years. I must have looked shocked. She was dressed in business attire – a kind of epicene ensemble favored by the female corporate elite: charcoal gray pleated skirt, bone-white blouse with feminine paisley tie, blue blazer with subtle pinstripes and padded shoulders. Nylons, black heels to torture the feet and to accentuate the calf. And I had pegged this woman for a notch above trailer trash, a cougar on the prowl in bars for younger studs.

She held two drinks in her hands. One was held out to me. I took it just to be polite. "I'm off the sauce but thank you." "You don't drink?" *Meaning: was I a reformed alcoholic?*

"Just for today, maybe tomorrow while I'm down here working," I said.

She raised her glass to me. I raised mine, slopping some amber fluid on my wrist like the gangly teenager Tom Haftmann, klutz, on his first date.

I hoped she would leave before I made a bigger fool of myself. All that tortured erotic desire had fled. Nothing left behind but a panicky feeling in my guts. The sun slanting through the trees told me I had overslept badly. I felt unequal to whatever was coming my way soon. I was worried about meeting that rat-faced Amezcua in the dark. A more effective antidote to desire

I could not then imagine.

She shrugged her shoulders but stayed in the room and came over to sit next to me. The room seemed to shrink. Gulliver among the Lilliputians except that she wasn't larger than life; she was confident, poised, inwardly laughing at my distress.

"You do look nervous, hon. Relax. It's sunny Florida." "I've been here before," I said.

"Oh, a regular, huh? Disney World?"

"No," I said. "I've seen the Everglades."

"Look, is this a bad time? You seem... distracted."

"Actually, yes," I said. "I have an appointment in an hour. I have to get ready."

She laughed. "I have to tell you. When our landlady saw you lying on your stomach naked as a jaybird, snoring to beat the band, she ran down the stairs like the house was on fire."

I said, "Look, I don't mean to be rude, but I really have to be somewhere soon." An attractive woman in my room, the first in ages, and I was throwing her out. *There is no design to the universe,* I thought sadly.

She stared at me and her expression changed.

"Sorry to have bothered you," she said, snatching the drink from my hand and walking out without another word. Her tight skirt hissed from the thigh action. She was the second woman I had insulted that day. Things come in threes, as the old superstition has it.

Mrs. Tanenbaum's voice called from downstairs. A soul-numbing dread crept into my guts and squeezed stale air out of my lungs like one of those albino pythons they've been letting loose in the Everglades.

That old law of biology: Exotic strains drive out domestic. I hoped that wouldn't apply to me in the next few hours.

~ ~ ~

"Who was that woman?"

Sonja Andersen, not Bobbie.

"My landlady," I said. "I didn't expect to hear from you again." "Did I strike you as someone who buckles under pressure?" "No, not at all," I said. "I feel responsible for your transfer.

Bobbie told me."

"Drop it. I've got that information for you. Bobbie is out of her depth on this one."

The unspoken assumption was that I was too.

I jotted on a pad Mrs. Tanenbaum kept next to the downstairs phone. There was no surveillance on the party house, just the usual patrols at regular intervals of an hour and fifteen minutes, Sonja added.

I asked her about Markwright.

He was a blank sheet, a nonentity. No voting record in Broward or Dade. He owned a 2011 Taurus. No liens, no mortgage, no other properties besides his rental, no apparent aliases. Paid his utility bills online, drew on an account at the First National Bank and Trust of Miami. No criminal record (not surprising), no traffic tickets (very surprising). No military record. He sent a patron's support check for $100 per month to the Purple Rose Theatre Company in Chelsea, Michigan.

I asked her if there was anything suspicious in that.

"No," she said. "He has a daughter, Miranda, married, twenty five, a costume designer for the company. He also has a son in Texas."

She could get me information on the insurance company that employed Markwright by faxing the Secretary of State's office in Jacksonville. "If it's owned by a holding company," Sonja said, "I can get information about the officers, board members, stockholders from the corporate charter. Do you need it?"

"Let it go," I decided. He was just a civilian in the wrong place at the wrong time. But get me what you can on his son in ... Texas, you said?"

"Yes," she said. "He's an accountant like his father."

"Let's hope he hasn't followed too far in his old man's footsteps," I said.

"Bobbie tells me that bullets bounce off your skull," she said.

"So far," I said.

She told me Pieter Beudert, host for the night's activities, had a habit of showing up in the files of some bad guys and their KA's in Interpol's database. "Smuggling of one kind or another." Sonja said he probably had personal security. He wasn't the type to stint on cost and hire some Lauderdale bikers for bodyguards.

"I'll take care, thanks," I said.

Traffic on the freeways and causeways would be at its worst. I returned upstairs to change into my olive khakis and black work boots with steel toes. Earlier, when Bobbie had asked me what my plan was, I'd said I had none. I could hear the mockery in her voice again. *That's a great plan, Haftmann, or should I say, Peeping Tom Haftmann? You're going to skulk around in the bushes and pop out at her when Raina comes out, is that it?*

That was it in a nutshell. It wouldn't be the first time I underplanned something and wound up flat on my ass. Now I had a gun, but I didn't like the odds.

On my way down the steps, I noticed Mrs. Tanenbaum's gloves and pruning shears. I grabbed them on a hunch. Micah and her logical lawyer's brain would have sneered at the idea of it, hunch or no. What better symbol of my deepening lunacy than me with a pair of pruning shears running off into the dark like a half-blind creeper from a campy horror flick?

CHAPTER 11

Traffic, even for a weekday's post-rush hour evening, was frenetic in both directions. The light glinting off bright metal of expensive cars was bothering my good eye now.

I realized I had finally found a state with my kind of driver: the old were completely hopeless and disregarded all turning signals, the young professionals had cellular phones glued to their ears, the idle young in the IROC-2's and Porsches were speed-crazed and texting at the same time. I wondered how many fatal car wrecks had smartphones lying on the ground with incomplete phrases like *Where R u?* or half-formed words waiting for the next letter when the message was interrupted by a head-on collision.

"Not nearly enough," I thought with some bitterness.

I passed tourists in Winnebagos and silver-bulleted Airstreamers looking for signs, exits, campgrounds. I ignored the organized chaos of traffic around me and tried to focus on those intangibles waiting to pounce on my first misstep.

Miami's labyrinthine freeway system was no more complex than any other city, but I drove slower than the traffic allowed and ignored the drivers ballooning in my rearview and the impatient yuppies blasting horns behind me.

From the causeway I could see the honeycombs of terra cotta roofs of the Miami's privileged island dwellers. Tall palms and pines obscured much else.

I discounted the notion of a thorough reconnoitering of the area once there. That went against my grain and my training both, but the moment had come too soon, and I was not prepared, so better not to push my luck with too many drive-pasts. This was not going to be like last night's party crashing of a couple teenagers at Emilio's. If I managed to make it home in one piece, I'd pay that same boozehound from Tico's Place to stencil Specializing in Seat-of-the-Pants Operations next to my name on the glass.

I opened my driver's side window for air and accelerated across the causeway, savoring the salt-air sting; a trickle of perspiration coursed down the left side of my face. The sun was still high, a hand's width from sinking into the ocean. The light would dim soon, softer after the afternoon's harsh glare, and the world would feel different in a tropical night.

Pieter Beudert lived on Pine Tree Drive between 37th and Arthur Godfrey. He was right on the water of the back bay. You can probably see the top of the Fontainebleau Hilton from his backyard. I imagined what a yard it would be, too. Pristine lawn cut to a uniform half-inch in all directions, maintained by teams of Mexican or Haitian landscapers. More exotic flowers than a parrot jungle.

I drove past Beudert's house number and thought his place undistinguished from his neighbors' homes, give or take a million bucks' worth of real estate here and there, that is. Bobbie said Miami and Miami Beach were different worlds. "Most people think rich men hold their pants out in front of them and jump into them in the morning," she said. Tico used to tell me stories of life in Guatemala City, whole families occupying a single ramshackle hut with a tarpaper roof. Lives spent in a stinking ravine where death squads tossed the bodies of the *desaparecidos* at night. The perpetual haze of that stinking blue smoke from the ever-burning fires of the garbage pit made even the elite of Guatemala know what the truth of their lives consisted of.

The ten miles of Miami Beach's Gold Coast and the Atlantic Ocean were close, but I had no time for sightseeing. It was 8:05 and the party guests would be arriving soon.

I kept driving, not too slowly, but too fast for people to wonder. His Mediterranean house was at the less-crowded end of the island. I did a loop between Arthur Godfrey and Twenty-Eighth Street as the outermost points of the box and then I circled it once more, passing Beudert's house again: 8:32. Two cars in the horseshoe-shaped, caliche driveway: a black Mark VIII and a mint green Alfa Romeo convertible. Palms and mahogany trees, the obligatory manicured lawn. Oblong beds of bromeliads stretched in front of the veranda. An overgrown Wandering Jew depended from an eyelet hook. The leaves of a plantain were visible from the back of the house, and some kind of Plexiglas glazing canted at a forty-five degree angle from the other side. Maybe a small solar greenhouse for orchids.

The houses on either side of his address were similar. I checked my watch once more and decided to improvise.

I drove the speed limit down Pine Tree and swung east on Dade, cutting off a switchback to the first of the large buildings ahead. I pulled into the Garden Center and Conservatory maintenance entrance and asked a security guard with gold piping on his coat for permission to use the phone. He eyefucked me good first and then sent me to the lobby where a tanned girl sitting behind the Information desk pointed at the phones.

Bobbie picked up at the first ring.

"Get me the names of the residents on both sides of Beudert's place as fast as you can."

I gave her the street addresses of his neighbors to left and right.

She came back after ten minutes. "My computer's locking up on me."

"Bobbie, come on, it's almost nine o'clock."

The names she called me were all clichés except for *douchebag prick*, which I thought was novel as it goes.

"Hurry up, Bobbie."

"Shut up, you! Here they are."

She read off the first name and profession. "What *exactly* are you looking for?"

"Keep reading. Who's next?" I had no time to explain.

"Keep your shirt on. Next is, uh, lost it... OK, here it is. Roger

James Craik. No profession listed."

"Give me another one, quick."

"Bite me, Haftmann."

"Bobbie, for fuck's sake – "

"G. W. Keller, no other information besides the address. Here's another: Eaves, D. C. T. Eaves of Eaves Enterprises, Import-Export. Got an office in the Four Arts Plaza, Palm Beach."

A possible there, I thought. "Who's left?"

"Keep reading."

"Lovejoy, Davis R. Rehabilitative and cosmetic surgery – " *Bingo*.

"Call his house on Pine Tree. If you get the machine, call his office to see if he's still in. Then call me right back, you got that?"

"What the hell am I supposed to say if he answers?"

"Pretend you're a patient looking for the doctor. Call me back at this number."

Nine agonizingly long minutes later, she rang back. Is he home?"

"No, he's not. No answer at home. His office

answering machine gave me three numbers to reach him in an emergency, all different from his house number. I got a recording that said he is at a convention in Richmond and is expected back in two days."

I drove back, pounding the steering wheel in frustration because of heavy incoming traffic. I hammered the horn and intercepted a line of traffic of sleek luxury cars. I drove my Camry between a stretch limo and a Silver Ghost Rolls. I got off Dade and made it back in time. At exactly 8:57, I pulled into the driveway of Davis Lovejoy, plastic surgeon.

I stepped out, my sunglasses slipping from the sweat around my face despite the cool ocean breeze. I went right to the trunk and began removing all the equipment I had bought that afternoon. I hesitated about leaving Emilio's gun loaded. If a cop came by right then, it would be ex-con carrying, never mind CCW without a license, the caboose for me, no questions asked. The store sold speedloaders, but I had resisted the temptation. If I'm ever in a place where I need that kind of firepower, I'll know I am well and truly fucked.

I lay the poncho on the grass and started to toss tools onto it as if it were normal. I felt as inconspicuous as a cockroach on a bridal veil, but maybe my gardener act would buy me a little time with any suspicious neighbors. I didn't want to get too close to the house in case this Lovejoy had his place rigged with light-motion sensors. These people didn't stick private security stickers in their bay windows like the proletariat. They didn't need to advertise what they felt was theirs by right and they knew how to protect what they had from the rabble. I hadn't seen a security vehicle yet, but there were squad cars near the convention centers on routine patrol. I just needed a little time and hiding in plain sight was the best I could manage at the moment.

I pretended to be examining the quality of the peat

moss. Someone made a half-hearted effort to plant flowers near the columns of the veranda, but the peat was dry enough to be flammable. Davis Lovejoy was clearly the black sheep of the neighborhood as far as progressive gardening went. Both his neighbors had high shrubbery fences with arched gates. His was the only accessible yard as far as I could make out. I kept myself busy as if I knew what a landscaper was supposed to do. I putzed around with the tiny shovel and Mrs. Tanenbaum's garden shears, snipping away at a butterfly bush, trying to look for all the world that it was up to my artistry alone to restore it to beauty. At least my car looked like somebody's idea of a working-class vehicle.

From what I could see of Beudert's place in the last gray light of dusk before the tropical curtain fell, no activity was in evidence. Nothing moved except a macaw perched by an open downstairs window. He was so still he looked stuffed, but I saw his crimson blue-yellow, saber-shaped tail dip against the white sheers.

Then the beautiful people came all at once. They came in nondescript small cars and without escorts or chauffeurs. If I expected to see tuxedos, scooped-neck gowns and bare arms dripping with jewelry, I was to be disappointed. These looked like suburban, married couples from Pepper Pike, Cleveland. Singles and doubles, mostly between forty and sixty in age. Gray heads, bald heads, toupee clips and expensive hair transplants – all coiffed and barbered smartly. Two young women, classy in their nonchalance, one with golden hair in a French twist, in their late twenties, arrived at 9:15 in a Porsche and went up the driveway where all the cars had parked on both sides.

At 9:15 she came.

Her profiled high cheekbones were outlined against the car's passenger window of the titanium-gray Intrepid. The driver must have figured there wasn't enough room to squeeze all the way in, so he dropped her off and she went up to the veranda alone.

My heart hammered wildly in my chest and I had to resist the temptation to run straight for her and grab her in my arms before she reached the door.

I had a good sideways look at her while on my knees scooping out a small gingko Lovejoy or somebody had planted five feet from the painted address on the curb. Raina wore something so sheer it was gossamer next to her long legs and sienna skin. Her hair was cut and feathered to her oval face. I was afraid that those limpid blue eyes would pick me out, but I had to look long after I knew it was Raina Toivela.

Amezcua was looking for someplace to park his sleek car, dying light glinting off its side like a barracuda's flashing form under water. The door was opened before she had to knock or even stand there.

"Welcome to the debutante's ball," I thought sarcastically. I heard a deep male voice greet her.

Ten seconds later Amezcua trotted up to the door. He wore black pants and a black knit shirt, but he still looked like a monkey in a tuxedo. He turned a glance in my direction, and I froze in place for a long second before I remembered to get the pruning shears back in action. Apparently satisfied with who I seemed to be, he headed right up the caliche driveway and knocked on the door with a couple sharp raps.

The sight of him made the blood pound in my veins. Something Tico used to say about braggarts in his bar came to mind: "That guy, see, Tomás, *se da paquete*. Big shot.'"

I took a couple deep breaths. The gun was stuck down my pants with the barrel pointed at my testicles.

For him, there was a gatekeeper. I heard voices, a different voice from the one who had greeted Raina. He wanted to know what time to come back, *que hora volver*? I strained to hear but the voice didn't carry far enough. Of course, my directional mic back home in my office closet would have been nice to have handy; the catalog said you could bounce off glass windows twenty-five stories up. *What the hell was this?* Amezcua was trotting off now.

"Something's wrong with this picture," I thought, but I kept my face looking into the dirt at my feet and scraped more soil back and forth with my shovel. Mr. Lovejoy's butterfly bush was too desecrated to be fit for any discerning butterfly, but I worked it like a professional landscaper.

Dusk became night with finger-snap speed in the tropics, and my ruse was on its last legs unless gardening in the dark is the latest fad among rich folks. Automatic timer-set lights were popping on all over the neighborhood. My guts turned to water when the first cruiser rolled past at 10:02. I pretended to be packing up my equipment, but I felt cops' eyes rip tiny holes through my back, and they'd brace me on their next pass, I was sure. A white van pulled up across the street at the address.

Do something, Haftmann, you coward.

I slammed the trunk lid and got in the car, revved it, and backed down the sloping driveway. As luck would have it, I almost hit the taillight of a Karmen Ghia parked in the street.

Fuck it, I figured. *Better go for it.* If I left now, I'd never see her again.

I hit the Ghia, crunched a fender and broke the taillight. Pieces of it tinkled into the street. I sucked in some more air for ballast and walked up the long driveway to Beudert's house. The sight was cutting a furrow into the skin of my right thigh with every step, but I felt as if I were floating.

I knocked.

A big man with black eyes and a five-o'clock shadow

so heavy it started under his eyes and made his skin look blue around the jaw opened the door.

I stammered an introduction, said I was landscaping the Davis place over there, and could I please speak to the owner of the little sports car in the street? There's been an accident, and I'd like to exchange insurance cards.

He shut the door without a word, and three agonizingly long minutes passed before it opened again. This time the man who had spoken to Raina was there with the big man who had moved behind him and to the right.

I repeated my story, all abject working-class humility. I said that my company would be responsible for the damage. He spoke over his shoulder to the younger man and told him to get Guy Fitzmaurice down at once. He pronounced *Guy* like *Gee*, with a hard G.

The big man disappeared.

I said, "Mister Beudert, I do apologize – "

He cut me off at once. "How do you know my name?" he said.

"We did some landscaping for you a couple years back," I said.

"What is the name of your business?" he asked.

His voice had Pavelic's silky resonance and a smile to go with it. His English was grammatically precise, accentless. His dove-gray eyes were looking into mine. He flicked his gaze over my bad eye once and then back to my face.

I said, "Up-to-the-Minute Landscaping. I'm sure we've done work here before, sir."

He continued to smile genially at me, but his eyes were cold and flat. He said with an affected lisp, "I have never done business with you. What did you say your company's name was?" I repeated it.

"I thought you said *minette*. I thought you were joking with me." "Why, no, sir."

"That is slang for fellatio in French. Do you know the language?"

Jerking me around, the snob.

"*Non parle vouz Française, monsieur.*"

He gazed at me differently now, uncertain, sensing something off. I didn't look like the typical Mexican or redneck gardener he was used to seeing.

"Maybe I should call the police," he said.

I said nothing but I was seething inside.

The big guy came back with a woman who looked about thirty-five. She was petite with hair so black it had a blue sheen, very thin, except for her round bosom. She wore black stretch pants and a black blazer with gold braiding like a sailor's chevron on the sleeves. Her slender physique and the jerky motions of her head and the black cap of hair with a widow's peak made me think of an organ grinder's monkey.

"Guy's, uh, busy right now, Pieter. He said for me to see what the problem is. Giorgio said something a moment ago about an accident," she said.

Beudert never took his eyes off me while she spoke. "Jeanette, please put on your shoes and go with this gentleman. See to it, whatever it is."

He smiled at me again and shut the door. I heard a rapid Italian spoken to Giorgio.

The light from the foyer was poor, but I could see Jeanette's eyes were bright when she opened the door, cursing mildly as she hopped from one foot to the other putting on her sandals.

"Well, let's go see the damage," she said.

Her walk was a little unsteady, but she didn't appear too far-gone this early in the evening.

I kept up a steady prattle of apologies, playing the rube to my betters. She ignored me.

When we got to the street, she looked at the car, bent over to examine the taillight better and said,

"Well, this is no big deal. Let's get this over with. I've got Mister Fitzmaurice's card and I'll fill out the information for you."

"Never a cop when you want one," I said with a smile. *OK, enough fucking the dog. Let's do it.*

I got around in front of her with my back to the house lights and pulled up my shirt so that she could see the gun. I watched her eyes watching me in curiosity and then widen in fear as I pulled enough of the gun out to show her it was precisely what she thought it was.

"What is this? W-Who are you?"

She was working up to a scream, I thought, so I calmed her. "Nothing to do with you or anybody else in there," I said. "I want the girl, Raina, who's in that house. *Now!*"

She looked back at the house but there was no one coming to help her.

"I don't know who you mean! Oh, God help me!"

"The young girl inside, twenties, blonde – Beudert's guest. Where is she?" I motioned with the gun again.

"The girl at the piano, you mean? She's working with Guy. Pieter said they're performing tonight – "

"I'll bet they are," I said. "Where *exactly* in the house is she?"

"Are you a cop?"

"I'm a private investigator. I'm here for the girl. I'm taking her home."

I heard a car coming down the street. I had left just enough room to squeeze past my car.

She gave me the layout of the house and told me where Raina was. I frog-marched her back to the house before she could cry out or run. The gun barrel in her back did my talking. She kept her mouth shut.

The door was left unlocked. We entered a white

room and I pushed her ahead of me into another white step-down room where a dozen or more people were standing in groups of two or three, some drinking, a few looking toward us – including Pieter Beudert and his man Giorgio – standing near the piano.

I shoved Jeanette ahead of me into the middle of the room.

Everybody looked at me and the gun and all the talking stopped at once. Although I had mentally prepared for this kind of entrance into their midst, I was almost mesmerized by the surreality of it... the abrupt silence of murmured conversation halted in mid-sentence, eyes boring into me, and the sound of a piano filling the vacuum left by the voices.

The walls of every room were eggshell-white, the furniture was white. A monstrous white piano slightly smaller than Hitler's Mercedes Benz dominated the far corner. A group of people parted as I came toward them. Raina was seated at the piano, her long fingers splayed over the keys, and she was playing with a rapture I had never seen; it was as if the piano was sucking her inside it. She was oblivious to the people around her and to the commotion gathering around me.

I focused on Raina, willing her to turn, break her concentration, to see me – *to recognize me and know why I was there*. Her precise, powerful movements over the keyboard were the only sounds in the room. As I got closer, keeping an eye on Giorgio and Beudert, I heard light conversation outside and splashing in the outdoor pool. A woman's legs dangled from a diving board at eye level over a rectangular patch of shimmering blue water. I heard laughter. A light breeze ruffled the bottoms of the sheers of the glass double doors leading to the back. Wink of glass and cutlery, time could not unfreeze, and I felt that odd calm in the eye of the hurricane.

Serene, poised, confident – she looked nothing like my last image of her in that sordid film.

Something in the air, some communication against the stillness caused her to twist her torso just enough to take in the new scene. Our eyes locked; she knew me.

Her mouth gaped in recognition. I could not tell what emotions were passing through her contorted face – what my ex would have called a Jungian jungle of emotions. All I remember in that terrible instant of time stopped like a bug in amber is that we were alone in that crowded room, Raina and I. Both of us were going toward the bottom of the same river except that I was diving while she was falling.

"Come with me, Raina," I said. My voice choked it out.

If anyone had moved toward me in that fragile moment, I would have shot to kill. I walked toward her, slowly, slowly. I touched her shoulder.

She stood up quietly and looked at me once. I guided her through the onlookers without so much as a sound or whisper of protest. Her blonde head was bent slightly and she walked slightly ahead of me. Beudert's face had that same aloof smile; Giorgio's face was without any expression at all.

"Leaving now, Raina? Raymond won't be pleased."

I wanted to smash the butt of my gun into his handsome face, see if he could speak that precisely through cracked teeth and a bloody mouth.

She stopped in front of him but said nothing. Then she spat at his face. It struck his chin and I saw a slobber of her phlegm on the knot of his silk tie. He flinched in reaction but his expression remained unchanged, and even as he took out a handkerchief to wipe his face, the smile was fixed in place, the gray eyes calm.

I moved her past him with my hand at her waist. I

kept my gun hand showing for Beudert and Giorgio to see all the while.

Like some kind of slapstick farce, a man without clothes wearing a Zorro mask across the eyes strolled into the room from the other wing of the house. No one laughed. The only sound was the *whap-whap* of the swinging doors he had passed through.

He saw Raina walking toward the door and looked at her. He was in his late forties, early fifties, gray, flabby, sallow skin. His long, thin penis bobbed against his scrotum sac.

Beudert turned to him. "Guy, your partner for the evening is taking leave of us."

Guy Fitzmaurice's smeary blue eyes looked at her, then me through the mask holes.

I bellowed, "Get out of the way, shithead!"

He protested in the high voice of an effeminate homosexual. When he saw the gun, he stepped aside.

I was crossing the foyer when I heard the first shot. It struck the ceramic bust on a table under a window. A sliver caught me in the side just above my hip, in the fat. The second shot glanced off my boot and ricocheted through a pane of glass near the iron filigree stand with the macaw.

By the time I had the gun sighted at her chest, Jeanette was dry firing the little two-shot derringer in her hand. I had my weapon aimed at her torso in a two-handed combat stance. The pressure on the trigger was close, very close.

Stupid, crazy bitch, I thought.

Who else would pull on me?

Her tiny gun kept going *snick-snick-snick* in her fist until I stepped up to her and took it out of her hands. She had zombie eyes. I put it in my pants pocket and turned back to lead Raina out the door. No one in the room moved but the macaw squawked and bobbed his head up and down. The room stank of cordite, fear, and expensive perfume.

Beudert said in his quietest voice. "Brava, Jeanette."

We both walked out of Beudert's elegant house without anything else happening.

We were home free. I squeezed her tricep hard enough to make her yip. "Don't turn around," I commanded her. "Keep walking."

She turned her face to mine. What she gave me instead of the look of fear I expected was a smile so sweet and pure that I felt my own face burn with shame.

Now and then, the gods let you get away with one. But I wasn't turning in my existentialist card just yet.

~ ~ ~

We headed for Dade Boulevard. I couldn't outrun anybody in this heap even with good eyes and perfect reflexes. Raina sat beside me, silent, with her hands folded in her lap.

I don't know why, but I thought it might help to get her talking while I drove as fast as possible out of there.

"What were you playing back there?"

"Beethoven's *Eroïca*. Pieter wanted the *Egmont,* but I told him I couldn't."

Micah's territory: classical music.

"Dubravka Tomsic herself tutored me in Youngstown. She has such, such *lightness* in her fingers! She wants me to choose the Schumann's *Traumerai* for my senior recital."

"That's good," I said. *Crazy, crazy...*

I was swiveling my head about without trying to alarm her: ahead, behind, side mirrors – everything was a blur. I half-listened, but I knew she was talking about music.

"Look out!" she yelled and thrust herself

backwards against the seat. "You almost hit that man walking his dog." "Sorry," I said.

My body was dealing with the after-effects of the last five minutes. I was a quaking shell of myself and anybody could beat me up now. My imagination had concocted some ugly scenario, a *Götterdämmerung* that the Miami papers would have fed off for weeks, guns blazing in an upscale home, Amezcua and Odio blasting away at me, the collateral damage of dead and dying upper-class libertines bleeding all over expensive carpets...

It could have been brutal, I thought to myself while Raina hummed beside me, oblivious to what we had just escaped. Yet here I was, driving off with my prize in tow and only a scratch on my hip and a nick on my shoe to show for it.

"Jeanette tried to kill you," Raina said suddenly, as if she had come awake from a dream.

"I should have shot her," I said. "It was stupid of me to hesitate. Those damned derringers come in four shots, too."

"Jeanette's a man. Did you realize that?"

"No, I didn't."

"His come tastes bitter," she said.

I could forecast years and years of therapy ahead for her, but she was alive and young. None so resilient as youth.

My side was beginning to burn, so I tugged my shirttail out and saw blood. Maybe I had a slug in me, not a ricocheted fragment. Going through my flesh it would have cauterized the nerve endings for a while. My shirt below the beltline was stuck to my flesh.

I was goddamned sick of my flesh being used as a pincushion for hot lead projectiles. The scorching of my side was starting to affect me. I didn't dare black out. I knew Raina would flee into the night forever.

I rolled down the window and took a blast of sweet-scented night air into my lungs.

Invisible below me in the black were the Sunset Islands and somewhere directly below the Venetian Causeway were the Japanese Gardens. I saw a spackling of stars through my dirty windshield and Mercury low on the horizon. Raina was brushing away strands of her golden hair from the backwash of wind swirling about inside the car. It had grown out several inches since I brought her home at the end of that summer. When she saw the blood on my shirt, she smiled that same angelic smile as before. Nothing mattered to her, nothing was real. She was what my Bible-crazy grandmother would call a *whited sepulcher* – beauty outside, all rot inside.

~ ~ ~

I called Bobbie from a payphone on East Flagler. I didn't tell her about being shot. I told her to meet me in the parking lot of that Denny's on Bayshore where we first met. She said she'd be there in twenty minutes.

Raina sat quietly beside me and listened to my plan. I told her she would spend a day, two at most, with the woman who was coming to meet us. Then I would take her back to Ohio. She nodded her head without looking at me and said she understood. She shivered in the damp air and hugged herself, so I retrieved the poncho and told her to put it on.

She did it without protest, a thick hank of honey hair falling loose from its plait. She still looked like that girl of the family photos, a teenager out past her bedtime. Inside the restaurant mostly older men sat drinking coffee while being served by younger women. I watched one man eat what looked like pie and talk to a second man. Crumbs spilled out of his mouth and he waved the fork about. I felt tense, sick to my stomach, woozy from blood loss. As more nerves came back to life, the pain increased.

Bobbie pulled up beside me and left the motor running. She looked over at Raina and then cut her eyes to me.

"What happened?" she asked.

"Nothing," I lied, giddy. "She needs a place to stay until I can take her home. My car was spotted. I'm going to dump it. Can she go home with you?"

"You look like shit," Bobbie said. "Don't tell me nothing happened. What's wrong with you?"

I must have looked nauseated. No more conquering hero stuff.

I was shaking and nerve-shot.

"I'm OK. Will you take her home and watch her?"

"All right, she can come with me."

Raina smiled shyly across me at her, and then she looked at me.

"Go ahead," I said to her. "Bobbie will take care of you. Do what she says, Raina."

I looked hard at Bobbie and pointed two fingers at my eyes.

"Watch her."

"You'd better tell me what's going on, Haftmann."

"Later," I said. "Call me tomorrow morning before you leave for the paper. Lock her in. Tie her up if you have to. If she tries to leave, does anything, call me. You sense anything wrong, call me. Any time, I don't care."

I watched Raina get into Bobbie's car. She was the key to the whole goddamned thing. Whatever deep conspiracy Sonja had hinted at was somehow connected to this runaway girl.

They drove off. I sat in my car trying to feel something about my accomplishment, but like the empty night sky overhead nothing came to me except the droning pain of my side; a rodent gnawing away where before had been wasp stings.

"I'm tired, people," I said to the night owls inside

Denny's. If they looked into the parking lot, what would they have seen? A girl gets out of one car and gets into another. No one looked in my direction. They ate their food, drank their coffee, and talked about whatever people talk about in restaurants in the shank of the evening.

I drove back to Mrs. Tanenbaum's in severe pain, my mouth dried of spit. I had forebodings of worse to come. This was too easy, even with a bullet wound in my side. I tossed Jeanette's derringer out the window and heard it shatter into pieces against a curb in the blackness. The wind whistled past my ears, indifferent to my lucky night moves under Sirius, the Dog Star.

~ ~ ~

A bare light bulb surrounded by a flurry of small insects lit the side entrance. No one was to come in the front after 8:00 o'clock in the evening, my landlady said, when she gave me a key.

I went upstairs holding on to the walls and stripped off my shirt in my room. It was wet from the armpit to the tail, and when I pulled it away from the hole, I caused it to bleed slightly.

It didn't look all that bad in the mirror, however. I felt as if somebody had lit an acetylene torch and held it to my skin. A .22 shell doesn't look like much, but if it gets inside, it'll bounce around and do serious damage.

I didn't want to make a mess of Mrs. Tanenbaum's floor, so I stripped all the down to my shorts and stepped into the bathroom. She had one of those old-timey jobs with the claws. I was drenching the wound with iodine when I must have slipped and hit the side of my head on the porcelain. I cursed too loudly because a few minutes later someone knocked on the door.

"Are you all right in there?"

251

I panicked, looked for my gun: back in the room under my pillow. I recognized Anne's voice. She pushed the door open a few inches. Then she saw the hole in my side with the hot-pink abraded skin surrounding, resembling a tiny papier-mâché volcano with lava in the center.

She sucked in her breath: "Christ, you've been shot!" I said yes, indeed, I had.

She looked at my face and then back at the wound. "Have you cleaned it?" she asked.

"It shouldn't get infected. Just hurts like holy hell."

"You should go to the ER. I'm not kidding. You don't want to take chances."

"Tomorrow," I said. I tried to walk past her, but she grabbed my arm.

"Let me help you back to your room. You look as if you're going to faint."

Her breath had a sweet licorice flavor, minty schnapps.

"I just slipped a bit," I said.

"I thought for a moment maybe you and Mrs. Tanenbaum were having some risky sex."

"In her dreams," I said, through tears. "I think getting her in bed would be as easy as arranging a lap dance in the Vatican."

"By the way, she said you stole her gardening shears. You'll hear about that in the morning."

"I'm sure I will. Good night, Anne," I said when we reached the door of my bedroom.

She wore a slinky white number that clung to her hips like tulle and showed bosom you'd see on a beach rather than the street and not in the upstairs of a B & B run by a middle-class widow. Her skin had a musky scent, a slight odor of cigarettes over that.

Barhopping, I supposed, and it made me feel sad.

"I'll help you to bed if you feel like it," she said.

No double-entendre there. Just a woman playing Florence Nightingale to a shot-up, badly aging private investigator.

She led me to the edge of my bed.

"I've got the identical Tanenbaum décor," she said and smiled at me. That meant a wicker chair and the obligatory seashells on the windowsills.

"Honest to God, that woman," she said. "You know she had dried seaweed with that crap? I threw it out before the cockroaches nestled in it. I thought she was going to have a conniption." "You shouldn't have told her," I said.

I wanted desperately to lie down, but I had thrown her out of my room once. Twice in one day was unthinkable. Even card-carrying existentialists won't provoke fate that much.

I asked her why she came to a place like this when Miami is glutted with hotels of every size and description.

"It's the privacy. Hotels are so impersonal, you know? Everything they do to make you think it isn't only makes me realize how fake it is. Besides I get tired of every male in a business suit trying to put the make on me in the elevator."

Courtesy demanded I ask her about her work, but I didn't care, and I didn't want to get dragged into a long conversation. She asked me what I did, and I said insurance investigator, my standard response to that question on the road. She surprised me by saying that sounded interesting. She said Mrs. Tanenbaum had a laptop downstairs with a screensaver that presented a row of cattle, sides of beef, actually, rolling along the top, and as each one hit the end of the screen it would fall to the bottom of the screen and turn into skeins of sausages, racks of ribs, or quartered chunks of meat.

"Sounds relaxing," I said. "Like watching goldfish."

"Join me in a nightcap, kind sir?"

I agreed to get her out of my hair. I heard the door of her room open and shut a few seconds later. She entered my room without knocking and stepped over my luggage on the floor. She had a couple of those tiny bottles the airplanes give you for serving booze. She had a clear one and a dark one in her hands. I chose the clear one. My ban on alcohol, like everything else, was shredded but I felt the circumstances of the last twenty-four hours warranted a drink.

"What shall we drink to?" she asked.

"Absent friends," I replied. *Amezcua, Odio, Pavelic,* I thought. *I beat you all.*

I apologized to her for my rudeness that afternoon. It was business, I said, a stakeout on some guy who claimed to have a bad back but was working at a car dealership. The booze was enough to finish me off in my state. My eyes closed and I lay back on the bed. When I opened them, Anne was staring at me with a crooked smile on her face.

"Good night, Tom," she said. "Get that wound checked out tomorrow."

I said good night, thanks for the drink from my supine position, but it came out all mushy-voweled and unintelligible. You'd have thought I had just stumbled out of the Gobi Desert with grit still stuck in my teeth.

The last thought I had was a tickler: *Why didn't she ask me how I got shot?*

~ ~ ~

In the early morning, hours after dawn, I awoke in a fever. I downed four more aspirin and found a painkiller at the bottom of my luggage. I tossed it down with the rest. I didn't remember sleeping. One time, I was drinking beer with Reggie, my judge pal, in some shitkicker bar on the Lake when he told me the brain secretes an enzyme at night to paralyze you so the body can go to work on cell repair. I needed a coma to fix me.

The remainder of the night was full of dreams, misshapen faces and specters from my past, voices loud, vile, and abusive. I relived my cousin Spider's death the summer after high school, his arm wrenched off in a sprocket of a conveyor belt, bleeding to death while his foreman vomited helplessly on his shoes. Max, a vicious watchman on my first lakeboat as a nineteen-year-old deckhand, pulled a knife on me in an alley near a black bar in Lackawanna. Deadasses, misfits, criminals from my cop days all lined up to get a piece of me. A long list of worthless human trash.

But when Amezcua began roping me to the tree, I shot awake with a gurgle of phlegm choking me.

I had to get up, get dressed. Go to Bobbie's house. Instead, I fell back on the bed and slept.

When next I awoke, it was midday.

I fell back asleep.

I awoke for the third time. It was night. I tried to get out of bed. I had to piss or explode. I made it to the bathroom, urinated like a horse, and stumbled back to bed.

I awoke again. I had forgotten to recharge my cell. Bobbie must be worried sick.

I closed my eyes again. When I opened them, she was there. Anne, holding my head in her hands, calming me with shushing noises the way you calm a frightened child. She had turned the light on and was dabbing at the perspiration around my shoulders and chest.

"Bad dreams," I said.

"I know," she said. "I have them too."

I sat up squinting in the glare of the lamp so that she could wipe the moisture from my back. "What's that?" she asked me.

She saw my tattoo, something I did for Micah when

we were first married. It was a Chinese ideograph, shaped like a capital H or like an old-style football goalpost – except that it had two bars evenly spaced apart, above and below. Micah said it looked like a fortress seen head-on with the drawbridge lowered.

Anne asked me what it meant.

"It doesn't translate easily," I said. "It means 'the deep within the deep.' It can also mean the depths that confront you on either side."

I didn't tell her what the old man, the tattoo artist – a loquacious old Taiwanese – said to me when Micah left the room to escape his cigarette smoke. He slurred it like an incantation or maybe like a poem:

Everything is dangerous.

He is never at rest. His struggles will plunge him into the chasm within the deep.

She climbed in my bed next to me and held me, her slightly soured whiskey breath on my face, her skin warm and smelling of soap and perfume.

And then we were kissing, our tongues locked, and stabbing in our mouths. I was greedy for her. Lazarus come back from the dead. I craved every inch of her flesh, every crease and mound and dimple of her sweet flesh. I had my head between her legs, and she moaned in her throat as I licked the salty wetness of her. We fucked so hard that the bedstead banged against the wall.

Hear that, Mrs. Tanenbaum?

I fell atop her sweaty body in a panting, exhausting climax. All the fear of the last few days blasted away with my seed and we were left like that – strangers and lovers, two misfits who went through the right door at the wrong time.

~ ~ ~

My side was not only tender but it was swollen to a blistered hillock now. I could have stuck my index finger into the hole. Great, I thought, blood infection. By the time I get to the emergency room, I'd be told I had twenty-four hours to live. ER docs are obliged to report gunshot victims. That would mean cops. That would mean the end of my case. That would mean my exit from the sunshine state, with or without a state trooper escort to the state line – Adiós, Haftmann. Just another clock ticking down to doom except that I was carrying this one inside me.

She gave me a last kiss on her way out the door, a little of her tongue like a promissory note on a check to be drawn later. I promised her I'd go straight to the emergency room.

I looked at the wristwatch on the night table. Better get dressed, shower, call Bobbie and face the music.

First, some aspirin for the pain. I wrapped a towel about my waist and headed for the bathroom. Mrs. Tanenbaum caught me as I was entering.

"Mister Haftmann," she said sternly. "I must talk to you when you're decent. I'll be downstairs."

Decent, I thought. *That'll be a long time from now, considering.*

I knew what was coming. Stumbling up the stairs at all hours of the night, the stolen shears, that noisy romp in my room. I could hear the words on her lips before she spoke them: *"This is a respectable house, Mister Haftmann, not a bordello."* Did people still use that word nowadays?

I found her in the kitchen peeling potatoes. The smell of bacon and coffee made me realize how hungry I was.

She said, "This note was slipped under the door of the parlor this morning when I arose. It had your name on it." I opened it.

Who uses a typewriter now? The font was from an old ribbon with the letters unevenly spaced, and tinted in one of those sepia tones like a washed-out lavender ink that didn't exist anymore.

It said:

"We are like lambs in a field, disporting themselves under the eye of the butcher, who chooses out first one and then another for his prey. So it is that in our good days we are all unconscious of the evil Fate may have presently in store for us."

Schopenhauer is exactly right, Haftmann.

Beneath that, an inch-high signature like a swordsman's flourish with its ascending first letter oddly balanced by the descender with its curled tail like a seahorse. The *e* looked drawn backwards – a child's *e* – in contrast to the jagged scar of the remainder of his name.

Why didn't it surprise me he used his surname only?

Pavelic.

He was simply welcoming me back to hell

~ ~ ~

I could not get an answer at Bobbie's number nor could I get her work phone. Apparently they had it rigged so you got patched around. I spoke to Nikki in Society, and she told me that "Ms. Gersack is away from her desk." She said she was a couple desks over and could see her computer on, so she must have come in, but was probably out on a story. Could she take a message? I told her to have Bobbie call me at the new number – it was urgent, I said. She asked me to repeat the message because of some loud talking behind her. I heard laughter, a young woman's and two male voices in counterpoint and the soft clicking of her keyboard as she spoke. Multitasking, there's another pet Micah-word. It meant fucking up because you can't do two things well simultaneously. I was proof of that.

What to do first? I was anxious about Raina

foremost. I couldn't risk driving there and leading a tail right to her. Pavelic's note could be a ploy to set me running. My side was hurting worse, which meant I had to get to the emergency room sooner or later. Bright pink skin, hot to the touch all around the wound, which had changed colors in the night and had the texture of pigskin.

My khakis from last night were blood-spattered and flecked with dirt from mucking around in Lovejoy's lawn, so I put on some lightweight chinos. Any contact with the skin of my hip was unbearable, which meant I notched my belt a couple eyelet holes looser and let my pants ride low, a plumber without his tools. *No*, I reckoned honestly for once, *a private eye on the skids, reaching out for the end of his tether*. It was insane to risk a blood infection. I tossed five aspirin down my gullet after the coffee to thin the swelling and ate a couple pieces of toast standing up.

In the chaos of the last several days I had neglected to check in with Raina's father. I gave him the short version, and I told him I'd have her on a plane or I'd drive her myself "within the next forty eight hours." I also said I had to have some more money due to unexpected expenses.

"How much more?" he asked.

"One thousand, if you can spare it," I said.

I waited. I flicked sweat out of my good eye.

"I'll expect a detailed itemization," he said.

He didn't understand why I couldn't start back with her at once, but he took my hesitation to mean her condition rather than my own balking.

"You said she's all right," he asked me again, the fourth time.

"She's fine. Be patient a little longer. There are a few minor complications I have to unravel before we can head back."

Minor complications. My lying tongue ought to be

dipped in bronze and enshrined at the Smithsonian.

I gave him Mrs. Tanenbaum's phone number and the address of the nearest Western Union from the phonebook and asked him to repeat it back to me.

"It'll be there this afternoon," he promised.

I had just financed my stalking horse with a father's love.

So who was the whited sepulcher now?

~ ~ ~

Finally, at five minutes past eight, Bobbie rang me. I couldn't get through because her line was constantly busy. She had been phoning in a story on a couple Atlanta Braves picked up in a brawl at a steak house on Biscayne Boulevard.

"I'm a journalist. This is how I make my living," she said.

I cut her off: "She's all right?"

"She's fine. I'm not an idiot. She hasn't been out of my sight."

I told her that I tried calling, but we'd told Raina not to pick up unless it was three rings and a callback, as we had agreed in the Denny's parking lot.

"Nobody else called?"

"Just work," she said. "I told you my condo has concierge service, twenty-four-hour security. Guests have to check in. My number's unlisted. She's fine. She knows better than to leave the place."

I doubted that, but I said nothing. I told her what I had in mind.

"Haftmann," she said solemnly. "You said you were taking her home."

"I know," I said. "I have to get my prescription changed at the pharmacy," I said. "Then I'll drive her home. Just a few more hours."

"I want Pavelic, Haftmann. We have a deal."

"I'm not reneging, Bobbie. I'll help. I've got to get

this girl home first."

"I've been thinking about this Markwright," she said. "I think he's involved right up to his asshole."

"He struck me as too clean, too," I said.

"My theory is he and this DeCamillo were trying to run a scam, blackmail – I don't know."

"Toni's little book of names and kinks," I said.

"Maybe one of her blackmail victims turned her in to Pavelic like you thought."

"You're not listening to me, Bobbie."

"But it was too late. DeCamillo, of all people, knew Pavelic played hardball, but she must have figured she had a foolproof angle."

I told her you don't do that to someone's face to get information, that it's punishment.

"Pavelic wants the book back," she said. "And he's got something going bigger than sexual blackmail."

"Bobbie, listen to me for a second here, would you?"

"Markwright, that schmuck, doesn't realize he's neck-deep in bloody water and a great white shark named Pavelic – "

"Pavelic's too big for him to take on," I said. "He's a retired accountant from Texas. They're as conservative as church mice."

"He would if he thought he had all the angles figured," she replied.

I said, "Pavelic buys and sells people like Markwright. He doesn't need a slash-and-burn policy for the little people."

"All right, so what? Maybe he just went over the deep end and wants to let the people behind him, his backers, know he can't be fucked with in Miami."

She had that obsessed sound cops get when they have a red-ball case. She wanted Pavelic. I wanted out of Florida, get Raina home, and heal myself up.

"It makes as much sense as anything else," she said, bulldozing over my protests. "Look, he's not going to turn anything over to a cartel when this is through. He's going to run it. He's not doing spadework for people who won't get their hands dirty."

"Bobbie, the world is a rotten place because of people like him. It's always been that way and it'll never change. I'm all through with crusades. It doesn't pay the rent," I said.

"You're a quitter and a coward. Is that what you mean?"

"In a word, yes."

I had not mentioned Pavelic's little calling card but it was on my mind just then.

"He can't resist an opportunity to show who he is," she said. "What good is power if you can't make people afraid? All that lickspittle I had to write about what a class act he is – "

"Let it go, Bobbie."

"What's wrong with you? You're grunting and moaning like a pig."

"I have to get some medical attention," I said.

My plan was to exchange rental cars, drive back to Bobbie's place, scoop up Raina, get the fuck out of Dodge. Pavelic could wait. On my way to her, I'd stop at Mrs. Tanenbaum's, pick up my stuff, including the gun I had rolled into the poncho and tucked away inside my luggage. Once I was across the state line, I'd take the first exit, get to an emergency room and get all the penicillin they could inject me with. By the time they filed a gunshot report on me, I'd be back in Ohio. I was congratulating myself all the way over to Mrs. Tanenbaum's.

Mrs. Tanenbaum had her own plan, however, so when I pulled up to the curb behind the beat-up Crown Victoria, my plan was knocked into a cocked hat because who drives a Crown Vic except a cop?

The old bitch had called the fuzz on me.

The unregistered gun hidden upstairs, last night's shooting, kidnapping a girl from a home, aggravated menacing, not to mention battering a local boxing hero with a baseball bat – *shit almighty*, the list could go on and on.

It turned out to be about the garden shears. Mrs. Tanenbaum had called the cops on me for stealing.

Sometimes it's hard to be an existentialist when there are so many signs around that make you believe in luck and superstition. I thought of the Dog Star, Sirius, raging in last night's pre-dawn sky. Despite my existentialism, it was trying to tell me something and I just wasn't listening.

~ ~ ~

The cop bought my story that I had walked off with it to help a friend with his gardening chores and forgot to return it. I offered to pay Mrs. Tanenbaum on the spot, which satisfied the officer but not the landlady. She wanted me booked. The officer, however, wasn't going to do that and convinced her to take my money.

"You'll be leaving immediately, Mister Haftmann," she said while the officer looked on.

"Right away," I said. "I just have to pack up my things."

She was still muttering behind my back when I came downstairs with my travel kit.

"You've ruined the carpeting on my stairs," she said. "Look at the walls."

I looked behind me. I was a forensics specialist's dream criminal: blood droplets, some with tails, tiny clumps of dirt and peat moss, smudged palm prints where I had steadied myself going up the stairs – and that's before you get into the microscopic stuff.

"I apologize, Mrs. Tanenbaum. Please allow me to

pay for the cleaning."

I handed her a crisp Ben Franklin from my roll, fattened as a result of Raina's father not letting me down.

I hotfooted it over to the car rental and turned in the keys.

They were not pleased at the condition of the Camry, and two of the staff spent a long time looking at the damaged fender. I spent about forty-five minutes explaining and filling out forms. A fat supervisor in the service department said, "She looks like shit, partner. Gonna have to charge you for repair, maintenance and clean up."

Finally, I grew weary of being jerked around by the fat man in his bolo tie and sweat moons under his arms. In his tiny office, I rucked up my shirt and showed him my side.

"Look," I said. "I'm getting blood poisoning by the minute while you're dicking around over that shitty car. Now take my money or my credit card number and let me get to the hospital."

I called a taxi and told the woman behind the wheel to drive me to a reliable used-car lot. I wanted a discreet place where I didn't have to answer a lot of questions and fill out a bunch of papers. Did she know a place where they don't hassle you?

She said that I could get a good deal in Davie down Federal Highway 1. Her stepfather owned a car lot and wasn't too particular about seeing whether the pink slip was in the glove compartment. I told her to take me there as fast as possible, and I'd double her fare, and pay any speeding tickets. She smiled with her eyes in the rearview mirror and that was the last communication I had with her until I paid her. We barrel-assed down the highway, weaving in and out of traffic, as if she were driving a Ferrari instead of the dented yellow heap with the rump-sprung seats.

I watched as the hotels, restaurants, racquetball clubs, shops, and multinational offices gave way to houses and southern colonials and villas were replaced by bungalows and ranch styles. Then the crowded traffic of the roadway became open space, and I saw horse farms and farmland where bean sprouts, tomatoes, and cucumbers were already flowering in the spring air. I asked her to double back once, and she did without any question. She looked Cuban or Indian and wore a man's flannel. She had webbed fingers, and she drove like a state trooper with her hands fixed at the ten and two o'clock positions.

We arrived at a small car lot in Davie where all the cars were at least five years old and cheap. I gave her fifty plus fare, and she thanked me and wished me luck.

She honked her horn twice while I walked toward the lot. I was looking at an '01 Plymouth that had CHEAP and $2000 written in chalk across the windshield.

A Florida Rodeo Championship sticker was faded and peeling loose from the trunk where it had been slapped at an angle.

I heard a door slam off in the distance. I saw a concrete block house painted pink about fifty yards away in a cluster of loblolly pine, and a white-haired man about sixty walking down the steps toward me. He wore a faded red, white, and blue T-shirt that said Brakes Are for Pussies. He spat a gob of chewing tobacco juice near the Fury's front tire.

"You can have it for eighteen hunnert dollars, cash money," he said, "but I ain't gonna negotiate. I got me a got-dam problem over to the house and I can't stay here dickerin' in the heat like no fuckin' Arab."

We went inside a ramshackle shed to get out of the heat. He had an American flag on the wall with Final

Solution embroidered into the center. I saw a poster of a starving Somali boy inserting his hand into a steer's anus to extract corn kernels for food. The legend said *Dinner Time.* Other posters warned of ZOG and World Jewry.

"Man oh man, this heat like to shrink an alligator's dick. Ya'll serious about gittin' you a good car today, son, ain't you now?" He was already regretting he hadn't jacked up the price. His cowboy boots were glossy black with elegant stitching across the fronts: a rattlesnake coiled for striking adorned one boot, the other showed what looked like a panther rampant.

I gave him all my remaining hundreds, added five hundred in traveler's checks, and asked him if he would sell me a license for use while the paper work was going through. I was getting low, I told him, and I needed money myself right then, but I would make it worth his while.

He looked at me and said, "Can't do that, son. It's against the law."

He spat another gob of amber juice at the Plymouth's other tire. He counted the money twice in his hand and turned to look at me once, briefly.

"That damn Phillips must be over there under that black Mustang 5.0 what just come in. I can sell you that plate – for a hunnert.

The front one's gotta be soldered off, seems like."

I peeled out of the dusty lot in a sandstorm of brown haze.

On the road I doubled back and sat for long stretches at intersections where I could see traffic in all directions. I jumped on I 95 for good measure and cut across lanes to exit. Nobody followed me; nothing but my own yellow fear at my back.

I called Bobbie and told her I'd been delayed. I was on my way.

"Where are you?"

"I just bought a car," I said.

"We have planes, trains, and Greyhound busses down here, you know."

"You've also got law enforcement down here that knows where people like to go when they want to get out of town in a hurry," I said. "How's Raina?"

"She's a little bored, she says. She wants to play a piano." "So let her."

That wasn't worth responding to, so she hung up on me.

~ ~ ~

A pair of flies snapped out of their torpor and harassed me all the way back from Davie, but I couldn't wave them out the windows whenever they buzzed my face. The vehicle was malodorous, reeking of onions. I'd watched the cabbie's stepfather tossing out paper bags from fast-food places and wipe off the dashboard with a filthy rag. Maybe I was giving off a secret signal: the flies had found me, smelled my blood, and were anticipating the feast to come.

"Not yet, fuckers," I said.

I sped off and drove faster than I should have, but I had stopped sweating and that was worrying me. Getting heat stroke would upset the old apple cart for good. My body used to be my friend. Now I didn't trust it. That young doctor at the Clinic said I was aging faster than a man my age should. He was lecturing me about accretions on the spine that press on the nerves *and atypical meningiomas that put pressure on the pons.* I told him to get out, my head hurt, and doctors were worse than lawyers.

The flies kept pestering me at every intersection and stop sign, but I couldn't shoo them away from my face.

Crossing the Miami River at Seventh Avenue, I had a flashback of my last runaway case: a young man, 19, had left Ann Arbor and wound up on the Strip. I found all his friends and everybody he knew in the short time he was in JOTL, local shorthand for Jefferson-on-the-Lake. But nobody had seen him recently, and so I had run around like a two-headed dog in a meat market up and down the Strip, in and out of bars, tattoo parlors, biker joints, and video arcades. I kept missing him by just a hair. Three, four days passed, and it was driving me crazy because the place isn't big enough to stay hidden in for long.

Then one of his new acquaintances gave me the clue I needed. He'd somehow fallen in love and been rejected by a girl in the three days I was hunting him down and all that time was lying in the saw grass near Mariner's Point. Shot himself in the head with an automatic. But the .9mm Parabellum he used to shuffle off the mortal coil deflected and exited through his sinus cavity and merely knocked a tooth out of his mouth. His head was full of maggots and that's what saved his life. They ate the dead tissue and prevented gangrene from setting in. I don't know what happened to him afterward. His parents fetched him home.

All my cases are like that – unfinished. I don't know how their lives turn out. I don't know how anything ends except that we all die someday.

~ ~ ~

In the foyer I received no answer to my buzzing. I pawed the others, but nobody called out to me. I thought of getting the manager and making him admit me. I went back to my Plymouth and sat in the heat and watched the apartment. All was still in the broiling afternoon heat of the parking lot. My clothes were stuck to my back and thighs. Fat cumulus clouds rolled past but the sun was unhampered and sent shafts of light dazzling off everything that could reflect it. I used my fingers to pinch the sweat away from my eyes but it was hopeless because the light glinting from every surface was like a dagger in my bad eye. The humidity was worse, nausea inducing, and it made my discomfort worse. A little voice in my head was chiding me for delaying the hospital treatment, but that being the X-factor in my escape plan, I had to put it off. The sky was swollen with moisture like a distended water balloon that refused to burst.

The lacy shade of the palm was doing me no good because of the sun's angle, so I sat and sweated and felt the wasp's nest churning louder in my side.

How much time did I have left? My mind drifted. At the Cleveland museum I saw a painting by Winslow Homer that Micah hated, *Gulf Coast, Gulf Stream,* something like that. A slave in a wrecked skiff surrounded by sharks. I saw her curl her lip in distaste when I bought a print of it.

Whatever made you buy that? I remembered her words and smiled.

"That's me," I said to her, looking at the figure sprawled on the deck of his sinking craft. A waterspout in the corner a last final insult to the poor bastard's final moments of life. We die alone, no matter how. She tried to give me some psychological claptrap about shark's teeth and the male's fear of women in her Latin: *vaginum dentum.* I told her sharks were realists, not given to psychoanalysis when they saw prey in the water. The next day she came back with two more prints and down went my shark picture. Eakins' *The Gross Clinic* and Rembrandt's *Carcass of Beef...*

"Micah, you call these an *improvement?*"

Jesus. Lost in a reverie so real I was talking to my long-gone wife. I snapped to. I had nodded off in the car.

More memories, unbidden, came. My amigo and

barkeep Tico told me how he had to leave his family in Guatemala City after the military police, the death squads, came for his brother. His mother found him in the Book of the Dead weeks later. Then a sister raped and tortured, her uterus ripped out of her body, her three-week-old baby half-buried in a pile of human shit beside the road.

Damn, I had nodded off again. The sun was beating down harder.

I checked my watch. Just a few minutes had elapsed. I was becoming delusional. I had to focus.

I took the lock pick from my pants pocket and palmed it.

Can't wait any longer.

The outer door was harder, and I was visible for all to see, but at last it popped, and I was in.

Markwright's lock took less time than Toni's, but I wasn't getting better at lockpicking. Someone had been there before me.

~ ~ ~

When I smelled him, I was pretty sure his death had taken a long time too.

I shut the door quickly and let my heart stop pounding so that I could hear. Spread-eagled on his back across the dining room table and all four limbs tied down with nylon cord and tied off at the base.

I left him there to check all the rooms before I went up to his body. It was Homicide 101: *the body stays dead a long time; it doesn't go anywhere. Check the perimeter.*

Sure that his killers were gone, I moved toward the body. His pants had been pulled to his knees. The arctic air conditioning kept the slobbers of blood a reddish-brown where he had bitten through his gag. The pulpy flesh of his genitalia was a blackened crusted lump of putrid flesh burned beyond recognition. They must have taken the bottle of lighter fluid with them. I saw no attempt to clean up.

I wondered if drugs were given to Markwright during his torture. It was too soon for a toxicology report for DeCamillo, but Bobbie would get her hands on it eventually. When the cartels torture for information, they sometimes give histamine shots to make sure their victims feel the pain and scopolamine when they need some time to keep them sedated. It was an advance from chopping off hands and heads and burning torsos in fifty-gallon drums. *Better torture through pharmaceuticals.* Even the cop humor at a grisly crime scene was a knee-jerk reaction to horror. I remembered the tiny cotton fibers around Toni's mouth which would have come from a towel shoved into her mouth to stifle her screaming.

I turned his head with the tips of my fingers. Pupils fixed and dilated, the black swallowing up the color, evidence of petechial bleeding in those little red pinpricks around the iris. How had they subdued him coming through the door? Maybe a Taser. I wasn't about to vacuum the carpet to see if there were any telltale dots scattered about the floor. Two raw and purple ligature marks were seared into his forehead where he'd strained against the rope. Hours more before full rigor, but it sickened me to think I was dozing and daydreaming in the sunshine in my car while Markwright was in here cooling off a degree at a time.

His toupee had been knocked off, the last indignity. It lay upside down like a fuzzy aberration in the swirl pattern of the carpet.

Markwright had found terrifying death in Florida instead of whatever he thought was there for him in his golden years – a new start with bright skies and blue-green waters. Like that poor wretch sitting on the wrecked boat in Winslow Homer's painting, surrounded by shark fins. He's looking into oblivion, thinking (I always believed) his lonely thoughts surrounded by ocean. I wondered if he thought about how it was going to feel when that shark bit down on his flesh. I wondered what his final image would be before the pictures in his brain faded to black.

CHAPTER 12

As before, I wiped down everything I touched and got out of there as discreetly as possible. I was pretty sure Pavelic wouldn't set me up. He had something more creative in mind. I drove a distance and pulled over but kept the place in sight. I phoned Bobbie at her condo in our code, but got no answer. I left a message. I called her paper, sure she'd take Raina with her to work. But she wasn't at her desk, and I got passed on, handed around and finally wound up back to Society.

This time Nikki's response was abrupt. "I don't know where Bobbie is. G'bye."

I called her home number again to change the first message, but Raina picked up. "Hello, Raina, it's Tom Haftmann here." "I was hoping you'd call soon," she said.

"Listen to me, I don't have much time and this is important. I've spoken to your father today and he knows you're coming home soon."

"When can we leave?"

She didn't sound very eager. I might have said we were going for a stroll on the beach later. My unlicensed shrink of an ex-wife would have described it as "a flat affect."

"Where's Bobbie? Did she tell you where she'd be?"

I was fuming inside, desperate to keep panic out of my voice. Leaving Raina alone like that caused a red mist to come down over my eyes.

"I wrote it down so that I'd get it right."

"Good girl. Where is she?"

"'On a story breaking this moment, the Intracoastal.' Looks like 'Near Hallandale Beach.' It says to take a right at Gulfstream Park and 'head straight for the water. She said something about an explosion."

What the fuck?

"One more thing," Raina said. "You're to call her at the paper, if you miss, uh, connecting with her, she said."

I'll connect with her all right. My size-12 triple E shoe and her ass.

"OK, thanks, Raina. I'll be right over." I tried to keep the panic out of my voice.

"Can we go home now?"

"As soon as I get there," I said. "I'll buy you clothes on the road."

Please stay put ... please...

The hospital would have to wait. My side wasn't hurting as much because of the pills I swallowed every twenty minutes. *I'm more likely to die of bleeding ulcers.*

I was going to get us on the road pronto, call Bobbie from North Georgia and tell her *thanks for nothing, friend, now kiss my ass in the crack.* Of all the wrong times to go traipsing off on a story when a major shitstorm is brewing, ready to come down around my ears any second like a house of cards under strobe lights.

Killing Markwright in the same apartment complex where DeCamillo was murdered was a powerful, vicious way of saying, "Fuck you, cops. Fuck you, world. I can do anything." That kind of guy is scary, and I *was* scared. Anybody connected to Toni's little book of names was on a short leash and they weren't all going to get engraved invitations with philosophical quotations like me.

I knew Pavelic could find her, murder her just as easily up North. I had to make sure Raina's father understood the danger his girl was in. "Create your own Witness Protection program, sell off everything and go," I'd tell him.

There's no live-to-fight-another-day theory left in my book. You just need to live. Get into the wind, as the bad guys on TV say. My boxing pal in Detroit told me he asked Roberto Duran, long after the *No más* fiasco, why he was still fighting on undercards with no attendance and short money. "The wind is old," the tough Panamanian said, "but it still blows."

After last night's failure to kill the transvestite, I knew I lacked the stomach for where I was going. Getting into a firefight with Pavelic's boys was not on my to-do list any more. Enough pain to the old corpus. I told myself. *This is not what you're paid for, Haftmann.*

You went to Florida to fetch a girl home.

But how do you keep things simple when life won't let you?

I drove fast to Bobbie's place, still cursing everything connected to Florida under my breath, myself most of all, but slowed when I realized my erratic driving could attract coppers. How would I explain my presence at two grotesque crime scenes?

Something more frightening than talking to cops in a small room was nagging at me as I pulled into Bobbie's parking lot.

What if Toni and Markwright were just appetizers?

That would make Raina the main course. That would qualify me for dessert.

~ ~ ~

I met her at the apartment door after using Bobbie's name to get past security. Because I wasn't on a list of preferred guests, I had to show him identification. He wrote down my driver's license and thumbed me toward the elevators.

Raina must have seen me through the peephole because she opened right away. I told her to grab an extra set of clothes just in case.

"In case ... what?" she asked. Her blue eyes were clear. The drugs, whatever made her docile last night, seemed to be gone. She hadn't bolted on me – the best sign yet.

"In case we have to spend the night on the road," I said.

Hallandale. Where the hell was Hallandale? I took my map out and checked it. On the way to Davie but well south of it.

Shit on a stick. I was going to say goodbye to Bobbie. I owed her that, and I was worried for her. Markwright's over-the-top murder put things on a new level. The papers had speculated that Toni's "lifestyle," a newspaper euphemism for prostitution, was the cause of her sensational killing, the theory went, but you don't do two of these in the same place and call it anything but a full-tilt boogie. I was going to insist Bobbie get protection – no more Lone Ranger and Tonto.

Raina wanted to drive after five minutes with me on the highway. I refused. I know how bad I am, but I'm even more afraid when I'm not driving.

My cabbie had made it to Davie in less time than I made it to Hallandale, but I got there and took a right at the horseracing park, as she said. I found the beach, but there was nothing to see. Raina was fanning her face, hot and bored, listening to iTunes on her MP3 player.

I took a chance and pulled into a Walmart Supercenter. I forced Raina to go inside with me. I asked the smiley man where a pay phone was and called the sheriff's office in Hallendale. I said I was looking for a reporter.

"Who is this?" came the response.

"Can you put me through to the sheriff?"

"Who is calling?"

"A private investigator. I can give you my Ohio license number.

I have some information for the investigators." I gave her my number to run through her computer.

Five long minutes later, another voice came on the line – a molasses-thick accent that sounded more like the red-dirt hills of Georgia than the polyglot Northern transplants, Hispanics, assorted Midwesterners, and retirees you hear everywhere down hear.

"OK, Mister Huffman, you said you had information about a murder."

"Sheriff, before I tell you what I have, I need to know whether a reporter named Bobbie Gersack has contacted you."

He told me she left right after his office gave out the statement, and as far as he knew, she was heading back to Coral Gables to file her story.

"You have information about a murder?"

"Yes, sir, I do, but it's not in your jurisdiction. The victim's name is DeCamillo."

"I'm aware of it."

Big cop understatement, that.

I had nothing to lose, so I asked him to tell me what happened with the explosion.

He hesitated, irritated I wasn't forking over the goods, but knowing it's wiser to be patient with an informant. Besides, if he wanted, he had me by the short and curlies with my license number. But it was my dime.

"Cabin cruiser was blown up on the Intracoastal," the sheriff said at last. "Gas fumes. Didn't bleed the air out of the engine hold like they should have. It happens. Nice boat, too."

"Anybody killed?"

"Like to make a cat sob, you lose a boat like that for some dumbshit reason like not blowing your fumes out with your ballast.

Chris Craft, a real beauty."

"Anybody killed, sheriff?"

"I heard you the first time. One guy, we fished him out of the water – not too badly burned. Concussion killed him. M.E. said his lungs was shredded."

"Has he been ID'd?" I asked.

"Victim's name was, uh, let's see, Gi-or-gio Braschi. Big sombitch too. We had to wrestle him up topside and that was no easy thing to do. Boat's registered to somebody else, another foreigner name of, uh, Pieter Beudert."

He pronounced it *Pie-ter Boy-Dirt.*

"Now whatchu got for me?"

I hung up without saying anything.

We're really not in Kansas anymore, Toto. Time to book

~ ~ ~

Raina was hungry, so I stopped at a Wendy's and ordered for her. My stomach was in no shape for food – far too many aspirins – and I was feeling dizzy. She bit down on a sandwich oozing Thousand Island dressing and looked at me.

"Do you know what they call Florida chicken?" Without waiting for a guess, she said, "Armadillo."

Seeing me wince, she misinterpreted it, "Dumb joke, huh?"

She seemed to be going backwards, becoming younger, acquiring some of the silliness of teenaged girls you see everywhere. But I knew there were layers to her, and deep down, I imagined at puberty she was one of those rare, thoughtful girls who paused in the mirror from time to time, not to admire herself, but to ask herself: *Who am I?*

That's Florida, I thought. *It's a reverse Shangri-la where you age backwards.*

She was wiping her mouth with a napkin – those long, tapered pianist's fingers looked delicate but they belied a strength I had seen with my own eyes at Beudert's party. She was lunging at that huge piano with a passion. I blocked the film of her debasement from my head before it started up. In time, she'd get over it. I had known a few drugged-out, brain-fried Cleveland hookers who pulled themselves back from the abyss at the last second. A fraction of the victims drugs destroyed but it gave me hope. With love from her family, which she had in abundance, I was sure she'd recover.

I let her drive so I could think, clear my fuzzy head. Pavelic takes care of Beudert and his thug without skipping a beat. Payback for letting me waltz off with Raina last night? Why wasn't Amezcua there to intercept me? Sonja said Beudert would have protection, but one bodyguard for him hadn't been enough, either. I realized, not for the first time, how lucky I was to get in and out of there with my life, let alone Raina's. Had the she-male been a better shot, one time, everything would be different. I looked down at my boot where the bullet had scored a shiny furrow, a metal streak that glinted through the leather.

Both Bobbie and Sonja were agreed on one thing: Pavelic was wired in to everything going on in the state. Why not Sonja's Intelligence department too? Maybe he knew I was coming and was setting it up for me. Maybe Beudert had been on his list and I was playing a part in things. He never figured on me crashing his sex party and making off with – what was she to him? A prize or a possession?

The nausea was welling up in me. The car still

stank of onion, and was recirculating fetid air from outside to mix with the already rank air of the car. Raina had complained of the smell as soon as she got in.

I was having difficulty focusing my vision.

"See that turnoff over there?" I pointed. "Pull over near the phone."

She did, with her sure quick wrists and perfect coordination. I had a hard time getting out of the car because of my swollen side. Some kid with a hoop earring was coming up to the phone at the same time, but he saw me approaching and veered off. I dialed Bobbie's work phone and her answering service put me through.

"Sonja called me about Beudert, and I no sooner got back here than I had to cover a story. Listen to this quote I got from the sheriff – it's a gem. *'It was like a vortex of bloodlust and arson. It was consuming them. They couldn't get enough.'* Great, huh?"

"Bobbie, we have our own crime wave going on," I said. I put an edge into my voice. "How could you leave her like that?" "Keep your panties on," she said. "I *had* to go. The guy who does Police Beat says an expensive Jaguar was found torched at the old Coconut Grove Hotel on South Bayshore. Some of the after theater crowd frequent the bar there, Cafe Brasserie, and came out and saw the flames. Registered to – " "Pieter Beudert," I finished.

"You should have trusted me more," she said. There was an edge in her voice.

"She's more important than your revenge or mine," I said.

"Oh, says who? You're the one leading with the chin, so don't lecture me, Haftmann. You weren't exactly forthcoming in your explanation in the parking lot. I had to find out in case you were in trouble. Raina was safer at my place."

"We'll finish this conversation later," I said. "What have you picked up about Emilio?"

"Pavelic's fair-haired boy seems to have vanished," Bobbie said.

"His head will roll up on Miami Beach one of these days," I said.

"I'm curious to know how you're going to help me get me my story on Pavelic now that you're leaving. I'll be back," I said.

"That was a shitty Arnold Schwarzenegger, if that's what it was," she said.

"You never laughed much when you were a kid, did you, Bobbie?'

"We're both whistling past the cemetery, pal. I'm scared, but I can't stop now."

"I trust you, Bobbie. You're the only one I do trust," I said.

"The authorities are going to want Raina back when they resurrect the case against the dead park rangers."

"We'll cross that bridge later," I said.

"You're done when you deliver her up there," she said. "So stop playing God."

She was right, of course. I wasn't very good at the job. Another six billion years, I thought and question becomes moot. The sun will use up its fuel and the world will shrivel into an icy darkness. Better to let it burn to a cinder right now.

~ ~ ~

Back on the road, speeding north on Interstate 95, I felt better than I had in days, despite the throbbing pain. I looked over at Raina's sure-handed concentration on her driving; her tanned profile and golden hair made those sickening films impossible to believe. I had never known anyone on junk to be able to kick like this. It was baffling.

While she drove us through a late-afternoon

tumult of rain falling from thick black-bellied clouds to the Western Union so that I could pick up more of her father's money – that I'd no doubt go through like a wino through cheap port – I read Bobbie's *Courier* picked up from the stand outside Walmart.

There was a back-page piece on the Hemingway family's saga beginning with the Nobel laureate's own father's suicide. It followed with Mariel's sister Margaux, who had committed suicide after another long bout with pills, depression, and bulimia. A color photo depicted the troubled actress lying on a bed with her pale green eyes staring back at the camera. The story ended with the suicide of Hemingway's son, Gregory, addicted to fetishistic transvestism. He had called himself Vanessa, and underwent breast implant surgery before killing himself after a humiliating arrest and incarceration in a Dade County jail. The article noted that fetishistic men who didn't have a social role as a female often committed suicide after sex-reassignment surgery. The piece ended with a ridiculous reference to the annual Ernest Hemingway Lookalike contest in Key West.

"Chaos, disorder, despair and then you get a dollop of irony to go with your miserable life," I mused. I was a wise man to my shaving mirror sometimes. "Welcome to the club, Papa."

Bobbie's byline on the teenaged terrorists was on page seven. I read the quote she had given me over the phone. Bobbie wrote that the teens had planned the ultimate "crime of chaos." *Like a vortex of bloodlust and arson.*

The piece ended with the quotable sheriff's query: *"Could these be our kids?"*

I sneaked a look at Raina, beautiful young woman, and wondered how and why she had summoned her own vortex behind that smooth brow. I didn't think long about it because I never get far when I think of motives. Cops don't need motives anyway; we have the crime. That's what matters. I looked out the window at the indifferent trees rolling past our car – cedar, sugar maple, Carolina ash, camphor trees – more than I could name. They were just fighting for their place in the sun like the rest of us.

An hour later, that bright blue sky had darkened to an ugly ochre that reminded me of pus-filled boils about to burst. In minutes, the rain pummeled down on the highway's caravan of cars speeding north; sonic booms of thunder rumbling in the distance. The humidity was worse and condensation fogged up the windshield. I used my hand like a windshield wiper to smear a line of sight but nothing affected Raina's superior driving. I thought of back home, the shifting light over Lake Erie, my own inland sea. Jagged yellow flicks of lightning illuminated the oily pewter sky, but the worst of the thunderstorm was over.

Another hour passed. I was feeling a sharp stabbing in regular intervals by then.

"Raina, I don't know if I can make it all the way to the state line," I said. "How does it look?" I pulled up my shirt for her. Whiplashes of pain had begun to flicker across my vision, that calamity of the swamps that would never cease tormenting me. I felt as if I was giving birth to something, some tiny monster would come tumbling out of the hole in my side like in those horror films. She looked at my side, then at me. Her eyes were hard to read.

Then she did a U-turn with the same G-force as the Devil Drop at Cedar Point, and before I knew it we were going back in the other direction.

"We passed a hospital back there," she said. "I'm taking you to the emergency room."

I said, through the veins in my neck and with

precise articulation, that *We Were Doing No Such Thing*.

She was inflexible. It was a hospital – or she pulling over and refusing to drive. I was convinced she'd do it, maybe jump out right here and hitchhike back to Ohio. I agreed to it as long as she agreed to come into the room with me, never leave my sight. I squeezed her hand until she yelped.

"No waiting in the lobby," I said. "No phone calls, no restroom – nothing."

She agreed. We didn't speak until she pulled into the hospital parking lot.

I signed in and we sat in those bingo chairs near a receptionist's desk. When my name was called, I limped through a metal detector with Raina by the hand and dragged her through behind me. The ER nurse scowled but said nothing and I gave her my fiercest I-Dare-You-to-Say-Something look. We were directed into a small cubicle sectioned off with green curtains.

The doctor who saw me was in his late twenties and looked haggard, but his eyes gave Raina a quick once-over. I told him we were cop and suspect and she had to stay with me at all times. He shrugged and then fixed me up with a couple needles' worth of something that felt like liquid fire going in.

He ordered me to stand in front of a mirror so that I could see the veiny red radii of infection worming away from the wound in four directions. He lanced it, drained some of the pus away with a small metal tube that looked like a trocar's little brother from a funeral parlor, and then, in disgust, he squeezed it with latex fingers and about a half-pint of foul-smelling pus came out.

He wrote me prescriptions in gobbledygook and told me to fill them all at once at the hospital pharmacy.

I told Raina to wait for me by the stand-up magazine rack where I could see her, and I left her reading *Marie Claire*. I told her I had to fill my prescriptions. She nodded her blonde head, barely looking up from the magazine.

I was there fifteen minutes by the wall clock, and Raina was constantly in my view. I had to walk a couple steps from the pharmacy counter to see her still reading every other minute or so. Her blonde head was still buried in the magazine.

When the tech assistant took my money and handed me the bag, the pharmacist looked over her Plexiglas wall to ask me if I had any questions. The name on her tag said Khan and she looked Vietnamese. She must have meant about the medications but it seemed creepy, as if she were reading my mind in some devious way. I had questions about the whole Florida mess but nothing for her, so I thanked her and paid. I grabbed my white bags of pills and turned the corner – the blonde head was still reading as a host of visitors, patients, doctors, staff, and medical personnel passed by her on their way to one section of the hospital or another.

As I approached Raina, I noticed frizzy streaks of frosting at the tips that weren't there before. Closer yet, I smelled a different perfume. Another blonde, Raina's age and size, and close enough in physical likeness to fool a man with bad eyesight. She looked up at me as soon as I invaded that threshold of her private space. I must have scared her by the expression in my face when I went from fear to a mortifying shame at being so easily duped.

The girl scowled back at me and said in that irritating California lilt they all learned from one another in their nasty middle school cliques: "Like, man, what-*ever* is your prob-*lem*?" She put the magazine back and clip-clopped off in bright rubber sandals.

My problem? I'm the biggest fool on the planet, little girl.

But I had no doubt about the specific problem staring back at me in the hospital lobby. Raina was gone ... just plain gone.

CHAPTER 13

No one in the waiting room saw her go; the nurses at the reception desk were too busy to notice her presence, much less her absence. I was badgering people to the point that security had to be called. I bolted through the pneumatic doors in a near-blind rage and frenzy.

I had the Plymouth's keys, so I was sure the car would be where she had parked it beside a royal palm in its cubicle of landscaping.

Not Pavelic. No, I'm not ready for him ... Nothing for it, nothing to do but return.

As an ex-cop, I knew what a colossal waste it would be to report her missing.

I drove back to Coconut Grove and looked for an inexpensive motel. There weren't any vacancies at the three places I checked, so I drifted up to the Gables and wound up near the University of Miami on the canal. On Riviera Drive I saw a blinking neon sign and aimed for it. A landscaper near the sign was tending a palmetto, its gorgeous leaves shone like crimson blood drops on green baize. The air was muggy again despite the heavy afternoon downpour.

The night manager at the Riviera Court, an Iranian or Paki in his twenties with a complexion dark as cocoa, had Valentino eyes and hickeys on his neck. Youssef said he had what I needed, an efficiency. The place had no bar, restaurant, meeting rooms, tennis court, sauna, playground, or pool. I was sick of South Florida heat and decadence. Sick of its black-hearted *cor scorpionis*, Miami. I just wanted to lie down in darkness. I was in the blackest despair I had known since that gun was placed to my head.

I used my real name when I signed the ledger.

Youssef typed with fast fingers; then he stopped to look at me again. He moved a can of Red Bull he was using as a paperweight near the computer.

"Ah, Mister Haftmann," he said. "There were two men here asking about you."

I stared at him. "Cops?" I asked.

"They said they were FBI agents."

"When was this?"

"Two hours ago, maybe," Youssef replied.

I believed they were real FBI agents as much as I believed in Irish mermaids. I asked him to describe them and in a few clipped sentences he gave me a pretty fair outline of the stats for Odio and Amezcua right down to Luis' pencil-moustache.

The pills were making me really woozy by now, so I kept the curtains of my room drawn, the room dark. I told him to call me if "the agents" returned.

Here I am, again, I thought. *Back in the lion's den, wounded, gun in hand, nothing to show for all that mayhem. Not the plan, Haftmann, you fool,* I said to my mirror self.

I pressed my stupid face into the pillow and recited every obscenity I had ever heard from the foulest-mouthed sailor on the Great Lakes and every cuss word I picked up from Tico. I was Sisyphus watching his rock roll back down the hill.

I called Bobbie's numbers but no answer. I left a curt message with Paul Toivela's answering machine stating we had been "temporarily delayed but would leaving Florida soon."

I called Mrs. Tanenbaum's B & B, disguising my voice, and pretended to be from the gas company. I asked to speak to Anne, if she was still there.

Anne came on the line and recognized me at once. She had several tender but lewd suggestions for our next rendezvous. Before all the blood in my brain surged south and I forgot myself in the warm tide of her lustful whisperings, I refocused. No one had visited the premises looking for me, she said, no calls or messages, no mysterious prose passages left near Mrs. Tanenbaum's Royal Poinciana out front. Despite my complete and utter sense of failure, I felt that tingling in the loins that made expulsion from Mrs. Tanenbaum's Garden of Eden the bitterest pill I had swallowed that miserable, long day

~ ~ ~

"I – we, uh, can't make that flight, sir. I can't explain things right now, but I will soon."

"Listen to me, Haftmann. I'm your employer. I am Raina's father. I demand that you tell me why you can't put my daughter on a flight this very evening."

Pacing uselessly in my room, no calls from Bobbie returned, I had finally given in to the pressure of my mounting guilt and called Paul Toivela.

"Things are happening here that I can't explain right now but I'll call you soon," I said. I didn't want to lie, but I couldn't throw gas on the fire by telling him the truth – that his daughter had given me the slip.

"Haftmann, if one of two things doesn't occur in twenty-four hours I am calling the appropriate authorities. Namely, the county sheriff's office, the Cleveland FBI, and the state Attorney General. Either you put Raina on a plane or you get her in your car and drive her home *NOW*."

"I intend to do that second thing very soon, sir." I hoped I sounded more like the archetypal Snake in the Garden instead of the lying-ass dog I felt like.

"I hired you despite the rumors about your character floating around town," he said.

What rumors? My wife had left me, run off with another man, I was broke, and I practically lived in a bar on the Strip. Those weren't rumors, they were the truth.

"I've heard of scams like this, Haftmann," Paul Toivela said, his rage unabated by the abject humility of my weak responses. "You keep calling for money, promising to deliver – "

"Where is Raina *now*, Mister Haftmann?" His wife on the extension.

"Hello, Mrs. Toivela," I said. "I can't tell you that, but I promise I'll have her with me very soon."

"Liar! Bastard liar!"

They double-teamed me like this for twenty hellishly long minutes. I couldn't blame them.

When the whole conversation ended on the dismal note of Mrs. Toivela's sobs, my hand was shaking and my palms were wet. I had been on the giving end of good-cop/bad-cop many times, but this was my first time on the receiving end by a middle-class couple.

I couldn't sleep. My head was on a roller coaster and my body was detached, somewhere floating off on its own. When they did get together, my thoughts twisted around one another like a ball of snakes. The air conditioner beat chilly dead air back and forth. It was too cold but I didn't have the energy to get up to do anything about it.

At four in the morning, I got off the bed and went in search of a vending machine for coffee. The air outside stank of diesel fumes and magnolias. I heard the lazy drone of mosquitoes hissing like lost souls.

My existentialist saints, Albert and Jean-Paul, had abandoned me for good.

~ ~ ~

Still no word from Bobbie. The absence of news was almost worse than too much.

I called Sonja and left a message on her answering machine. I told her I was coming over about nine o'clock, on an "urgent matter," I said.

I called Mrs. Tanenbaum – *and why not?* I was in

my most accommodating masochistic mode. I would have subbed for Judas Iscariot at the Last Supper if he'd asked me.

She sniffed when she recognized my voice.

"Well, you have a lot of gall, I must say."

I asked her to give a message to Anne. "Tell her I'll call her soon."

She hung up without saying anything more.

I called Tico's Place.

"Tomás, fuck you doon', man?"

Micah said listening to Tico's English was like being dragged across a barbed-wire fence.

I told him I was fine. "How's things with you?"

"You need money? I sen' you some. Much you need, man?"

"No, no, thanks. I don't know why I called you, in fact." "Thass OK," he said calmly. "You in trouble, Tomás?"

"No, I'm OK," I lied with as much cheer as I could muster. "Everything's going great."

"You can't afford no more knocks on the head. You go blind, man."

"Hey, if it ever comes to that, promise me you'll finish the job for me."

"I don' like this conversation. I think you better come home."

He gave me a fast rundown of life on the Strip since my absence. A bill collector for the hospital had stopped by looking for me. One resort councilman was caught exposing himself; another member of the town's leading families had a drug scandal hushed up. One of Marta's friends from her parish was caught in adultery.

"You know why Micah left you, man?"

This was strange territory for my sole friend in that forlorn place. He had never once asked me about something like that.

"Yeah," I said. "I know why."

"OK, then," Tico said. "Goodbye."

I had no more idea than the Man in the Moon what he meant about why my wife left me.

I had a few minutes before I'd have to venture out again. I threw water on my face, downed a few more pills to fight the infection. I didn't need to see the map again to find my way to Sonja's house. I'd follow the sonar pings in my head.

I thought of what Paul Toivela had said about me, about my marriage. I knew the whole town wagged its tongue about Micah's infidelity. I didn't care about that; in fact, at the time, I was hoping the talk of her indiscretions and furtive meetings would cause her to forsake her fling and return to me.

The sad, sick truth I had to confront in the mirror was I never would have said anything.

I had spent a lot of time at Tico's afterward until I finally drank myself to the bottom of the bottle and then I quit for a while. Gave up the smokes, too. My place was too quiet, my life too full of prolonged silences and empty places. I spent weeks looking at Micah's dictionary on top of the fridge before I could bring myself to touch it.

I watched the lengthening shadow of a sabal palm's leaves wave at my window like arthritic fingers.

I put on the last clean shirt I owned, buckled my pants so that they canted across my hips to avoid contact with the compress. I'd need to change it tonight, and then I put on my wristwatch, this time strapping it on upside down, with the watch face on my inside wrist. Guns in people's hands, especially when they're aimed at you, mesmerize so you shoot at the evil thing before it can hurt you.

That's why there are so many gunshot wounds to

officers' hands. The old limbic brain and its atavistic response screams across the centuries its single message: *Survive, survive, survive ...*

Stepping out the door into another humid, salty Florida evening scented with the sweet rot of flowers, I thought: *Nobody ever changes.* Not in time, anyway.

~ ~ ~

It was 9:45 by the time I got there. Slow traffic on University Drive slowed everything to a crawl. I hadn't seen so many cops rousting so many kids in cars since the last time I was in Detroit on a Friday evening on Gratiot Avenue.

The woman who came to the door was Hispanic, about twenty five with olive skin and long black hair in a single rope braid, brown eyes with gold like tiny glitter flakes. She wore some kind of long wraparound nightdress in Aztec design that tied over one shoulder in a knot. A pungent whiff of peanut oil heating reached me just as Sonja appeared. She wore a white silk robe and her smile was more a bemused regard. Her blonde hair had darkened to a ginger tint from the shower she had just taken; she arrived at the door buffing her hair with a towel.

She called the girl I had met first Isobel and told her that the chicken was ready for serving. She arched an eyebrow toward me, but I declined with thanks and apologized for arriving unannounced. She disappeared with a grace of movement accentuated by her clingy robe.

"I just got home," she said. "I'm filling in for some people on vacation," motioning me to a seat. I chose the same one that I had sat in when she showed me the films of Raina.

"Sure you aren't hungry?"

"No, thanks."

"You won't mind if I nibble a bit of chicken? I'm

starved."

"Sorry to blunder in like this," I said, "but I don't know how much time I have left. I need your help again, Sonja."

She nodded, as if expecting no less; she led me into the living room.

I told her what happened.

"Does Bobbie know?" she asked.

"No," I said, "I can't track her down."

"Don't," she said. "At least, not yet."

Why?" I asked.

"Did she tell you why she wants to get Pavelic?"

"Yes," I said. "I thought that was a deep secret."

"It is, but not how you think it."

"You mean the woman, Bobbie's lover?"

"Yes, I mean her. It was because of Pavelic and, yes, she was Bobbie's lover."

"What am I missing?"

"That woman was Bobbie's lover, but she was going to leave Bobbie for me," Sonja said.

"OK," I said, "and the point I'm still missing..."

"I thought she'd get over it. We stopped speaking. She never returned my calls. Quit the *Tribune*, tried to pick up the pieces. Then you showed up and now I'm worried again."

"I'm sorry." *The past is a wilderness*, I thought.

"When she, this ... other woman committed suicide, it nearly destroyed Bobbie. She still blames me in part. I was afraid she wasn't going to make it."

Revenge, I thought. *My own familiar demon.* I wondered what Micah expected me to do when she dumped me – or whether she cared enough to think about it.

"I don't know whether you understand women," Sonja said, looking at me.

That was an easy one. I knew as much about

women as I did breeding pure salukis.

"No."

"I don't want her to get hurt," Sonja said. "She's aching inside, but I suspect she believes you can help her get revenge."

"What do you think?"

"I think the two of you will get yourselves killed. This isn't about her writing an exposé any more, not for her. What is it for you?"

I didn't have a ready answer.

"Find your runaway again and get out of here," Sonja said.

Isobel came back into the room and took away Sonja's plate and handed her a cup of tea. Her dress of brilliant colors made a swishing sound.

"I need you to help me find Emilio Vasquez," I said. "He mentioned a condo in Boca Raton where Pavelic kept Raina."

I asked her to pull his rap sheet for addresses and aliases. I was betting he was aware of his own value to Pavelic, if the two murders on the Intracoastal meant anything. I told Sonja about the two girls he was with that night. I seemed to remember the black girl's name was Sharisse.

"If they're minors, they won't have yellow sheets," she said.

"Maybe if one or the other has been reported missing," I suggested.

"I doubt if we have information on five percent running around this half of the state."

"She had a girlfriend with her," I said. "A white girl, blonde and blue, five-four or -five, looked about fifteen, already a rockhound. Your gang section might have information."

Sonja gave a toss of her damp hair and squeezed the ends. "We don't list K.A.'s on teenagers, and if we did, the information would be outdated in a week."

Teenagers on the loose were like unstable molecules: they formed and dissolved alliances in a fraction of the time an adult did. A week was an ice age in their world.

I gave her my new place and number.

"One more thing," I said at the door. "Pavelic's chauffeur drives a gray Intrepid. I couldn't see the plate number at all, but can you check BMVs for Dade and Broward?"

She looked at me with her unruffled gaze before she spoke. "You ask a lot," she said.

The misfired synapses of déjà vu were snapping in my head as I left. I had an image of a woman from another time, another place, troubling me – a woman in a robe eating Thai chicken licking her fingers

~ ~ ~

I drove back to my motel in a light patter of rain that became a torrent. The humidity seemed no less heavy and the air in the car pressed in on me and dampened my clothes to my skin. I checked my watch's phosphorescent button: time for another dose of pills. I had forgotten the numbers and combinations by now. Lightning crackled along the horizon and the monotonous whump-whump of wiper blades seemed like a code beating its own rhythm into my brain.

I made it back at midnight, grateful the traffic had been slight. Driving at night in the rain to me is like driving along a mountain road in West Virginia with the windows painted black.

I was hungry, my side was throbbing, and I didn't know which way to turn. It was clear I wouldn't get another dime from Raina's father, and Pavelic's men were hunting me. I was too tired to think about what to do next. Truth was, I was halfway resolved to pack up and leave this state at first light. Take a job as dishwasher at Tico's Place to pay off Toivela. *Screw it, give up, go home.* Even runaways should have the right to choose their own damnation.

My room changed all that – or, at least, the part about packing up. There was nothing to pack that wasn't shredded and cut up in sections. Even my new shaving kit was missing. The room had been ransacked as well as tossed. This time the mattress had been completely upended; it lay propped, sagging in the middle like wet pasta, against one wall of the small room. It brought home how little time was left. This was no professional job, which Pavelic could have ordered if he chose; it was done by somebody wearing the same fuck you shoes as the DeCamillo and Markwright killings. Tufts of cotton wadding sprouted in a random pattern from the mattress' side facing the wall. Pavelic might as well have written his name on the walls.

He goes where I've been and leaves messages for me. I was the groundhog to his fox.

Then the light bulb lit up, a forty-watter, but illumination all the same.

Pavelic thinks that book is still out there. It was even possible he thought Emilio might have it. That thing wasn't insurance or blackmail anymore; whoever had it or got near it died. If Pavelic knew that book was in a file somewhere in Bobbie's desk or home, would he cease the rampage? *Bobbie, she was in big trouble.*

Years ago my lawyer wife told me what a corollary was, so I add them to my own rulebook from time to time. One that goes with the rule that everybody lies is this: Everybody tries to hold something back for that rainy day.

If some of Pavelic's girls turned up missing or dead from his action, Pavelic could only benefit. Sex parties for wealthy degenerates just didn't add up to reasons for murder; nobody risks life imprisonment or a date with Old Sparky for that. It made me angry to think the rest of my life would be plagued with headaches and blurred vision because I had interfered with his business by trying to return a runaway girl to her family.

I ground my molars in sheer disgust. All this time I'm using one person after another to get to Pavelic to find the chink in his armor, and it's been me all along who was being used as a cover. I hated his guts as much as my own blindness. Everything right in front of me from the start but I misread all the signs as if they'd been written in Greek. What chance did I have of finding and returning Raina now? Short of calling in a strike on his villa by Phantoms from Homestead AFB, I had not much chance of getting to him. Even then, he was probably having dinner with the people who gave orders to the base commander. What did I have going for me – a banged-up private eye running on empty? It was a minor miracle I wasn't on my way to the Glades a second time.

I looked at my destroyed room one last time. I put a twenty for the maid next to the nightstand. She would have the mess to clean up in the morning.

~ ~ ~

My new place was a dump on Eighth Street. It was well short of the commercial district and many miles before the Tamiami Trail turned into the color and piquant favor of Little Havana. The desk clerk was an unshaved slob with a chewed pencil clamped in his teeth. The place was off the road and only half the neon sign was lit. His tiny cubicle of an office was airless and dirty. He told me to sign the ledger and jabbed a thick finger at the line in case I had never checked into a room before.

"Unit seven," he said around the cigar. "Key's on

the counter."

He slapped the key down in front of me in case I had never seen one of those before either.

"No drugs, dogs, or women," he said as if we both knew that was a joke. "Check out time's at ten."

I racked my brain for a bit about the dog part and left him there. I could hear the crackle of a small television set from one of the rooms fronting the road. The night air was full of the drone of mosquitoes, and a small cloud of black insects danced over my head as if a tiny tornado had sucked them up and kept them revolving in its centrifugal force. I swatted them away from my face and looked for my unit. It was in the L-wing of the structure at the end farthest from the road. The paint on the door was flaked like alligator skin from facing the sun.

A single light overhung the roof and cast its lemon beam on the dirt path leading to the last rooms. A single tree surrounded by arching fronds and candy stripe phlox was caught in the light's shaft; it was weeping a thick, viscous sap from long vertical scars in its bark the way a corpse in the heat too long will bloat and burst through soapy skin that has lost its elasticity.

Inside the small room, the smell of must was thick. The light sent a few cockroaches scampering. *Sorry, fellas, I'm moving in for a while.* I saw a can of Trade Winds air fragrance left on the windowsill but no bug spray. The wastebasket was full of rubbish – paper wrappings from fast-food places, the Panama City daily with yesterday's date, and a glossy magazine called *Juggs* showing a blonde with an enormous bosom held in check by a pair of red suspenders. Her name was splashed across her midriff in boldface and probably wasn't the one she was born with unless Kleavage is part of some forgotten Scandinavian clan. I picked it up carefully by two fingers when I saw it had served its purpose: dried semen had pasted it closed at the midsection. Under the bed was a can of warm Coors. A mosquito bit me on the neck. *With my luck, it'll be carrying the West Nile Virus,* I thought.

Despite the surroundings and the mess left by my predecessor, I fell asleep in my clothes and shoes as soon as my head hit the pillow.

I dreamed of faces at the window peering in at me. They were faces of the people I knew, as if gazing at me sleeping signified some momentous event in their lives and mine. I saw them all in the crazy logic of dreams, viewing my corpse-like remains. The pug face of Luis Amezcua was the last gazer before I awoke in my new digs to face the light of a new day.

I saw dust motes dancing about the dirty window. Dry-mouthed and baking in the morning heat, I yearned for the cold of the North. Sweat coated my chest hairs, and I thought I was going to gag from the nausea in my stomach – too much medicine, not enough food. I made eating my first resolve after a cold shower.

Despite my wretchedness from the previous day's events, the strong desire for getting out of town had lessened. Something had resolved itself in my mind. All my years had taught me nothing. I was unable to turn back. It wasn't about saving Raina. I imagined her at the white piano again, fingers gliding over the keys in a glissando of liquid notes. Then I recalled another memory, sodden in grief of many years gone. The funeral mass of my grandmother and how I shivered next to Micah as the organ pumped out the solemn, brassy notes of the *Requiem for the Dead.* I had a sharp memory from my boyhood of stories my deranged grandmother used to tell me of those terrible Envious Sisters of mythology who made the trees bleed.

PART 4

Being filled with all unrighteousness, sexual immorality, wickedness, covetousness, maliciousness; full of envy, murder, strife, deceit, evil-mindedness; they are whisperers, backbiters, haters of God, violent, proud, boasters, inventors of evil things ...

- Romans Bk. 1. 29-30

CHAPTER 14

The next day I relocated to a flophouse on Collins. My theory of a moving target being harder to hit was put into practice.

Someone had pasted up old cinema posters around the room, mostly teenaged stab-a-thon horror flicks from the last decade. Jason Vorhees stared through his hockey mask at Michael Myers on the opposite wall, while an indifferent Hannibal Lecter regarded Tony Montana.

My arrangement at the new place, with the night clerk Ernesto, was solid. For twenty bucks, he would hold all my messages. I had no intention of using my current dive for any kind of outside communication, even if there had been a phone in the room. It was the kind of dump cops would keep an eye on just on general principle. I left more messages for Bobbie at work and with her answering service. No word at all.

Sonja, on the other hand, had been busy despite her own mixed emotions about twice being co-opted into my investigation. She said that Pavelic was no longer being investigated by the Miami PD for the park ranger killings, that the case was left open under the euphemism of *Pending Investigation*. Hell would freeze over before that file label would change. Her own intelligence-gathering operation was still on, but she clammed up when I asked for details. One more whiff of me would kill her career for good, but she'd said the Raiford transfer wasn't for two more weeks yet. I needed her if I wanted to stay beyond Pavelic's reach.

No word of Sharisse, if that was her name. Emilio was still in the wind, his whereabouts unknown since he showed up at the hospital in Coral Gables. He hadn't tried to outrun any cops yet and nobody had picked him up. All the information on his rap sheet before he took up boxing was useless. I didn't want to risk surveilling the gym in Coconut Grove. My guts told me either Odio or Amezcua would be sitting on that site while the other cruised around looking for me.

Emilio's car turned up some possibilities. There were twenty-six late-model gray Intrepids in Broward and twenty-nine in Dade registered to Hispanic males between 25 and 40. One Emilio in Dade and three in Broward. I didn't get my hopes up. Pavelic wouldn't let his minions have their own registrations. Those people didn't exist on paper. I asked Sonja to have her contact at the BMV winnow that number down, use the Grove as a benchmark and move outward. I had a feeling that the way Emilio drove the day I had my brains trimmed in the swamp was because he knew the area so well.

Pavelic would use people like tools, and putting the big men on me had nothing to do with it. One of those addresses or phone numbers might be a hit, a step closer to Raina. Sonja would get me the printout tonight after work. I was to meet her at El Tio Pepe's on 40th Street.

I called Bobbie at the *Trib* and got Nikki in Society again. This time she cracked gum in my ear; she *yeah*'d and *unh-huh*'d me as if we were old buddies. But she would (*sigh*) leave (*crack*) a message (*pop*) for her to call me on her desk. I wanted Bobbie to get me all Pavelic's phone numbers – front companies, houses, flats, condos, offices – in a radius of a hundred miles from Miami. Maybe one of those would match up to a number on Sonja's printout. *Let Pavelic feel me coming,* I thought, a little too bravely. My rule here is when you're hit, hit back harder.

Then there was my job. I was going to check as many malls as I could, beginning with Coconut Grove.

I mentally kicked myself for not even being curious about where her clothes had come from since her panhandling days. I'd check out a few trendy boutiques and trattorias hoping she had shopped there, maybe with that lug Amezcua in tow. Her outfit at Beudert's had that expensive look you don't get from the Chinese sweatshops of Walmart. I had a slim hope that somebody seeing her photo might remember her. Gorgeous young blondes were thick on the ground in South Florida, especially in season, but not many of them trailed stubby Hispanic bodyguards with flat-black killer's eyes.

It was either do this much, or sit in my room brooding, thinking about driving over to Oceanside Boulevard with my wooden friend in the back seat.

I spent my first day looking at Mayfair. None of the young females at Ralph Lauren, Berenka or Charles Jourdan recalled her face from the one of her at the piano. I was in and out of thirty shops by mid-day. Footsore and tired, dizzy from breathing the perfume of so many sales associates, all pretty girls and young women. I found a restaurant that served me a Dagwood grinder and fried ice cream. Then I went back to another couple dozen places until I had sampled about a third of the shops.

I went back to my room, took a shower, changed into clean underwear, and I fell asleep within minutes, listening to the drone of the air conditioner.

Waking at 6:30, I called for messages for Thomas Haftmann: none. I dressed, turned in the key to Ernesto's replacement, and drove to meet Sonja.

She was already seated with Isobel, and I joined them. I ordered paella, black bean soup, fried plantains and a Cuban coffee. Sonja took the list out of her purse and slid it across to me; I folded it without looking at it and put it in my pocket.

At one point, I was aware of a lull in conversation and looked up to see Isobel staring at me tucking into my food with curiosity in her light eyes. I told her that I had done a great deal of walking that day and had worked up a huge appetite.

"You should have had the specialty of the house," she said. "El Tio's famous for its baby lamb *segoviana*."

I ordered it at once while the two women were finishing up their meals. Before they had finished their flan and dessert, I had enjoyed the last garlicky bite.

I had worn out my welcome with Sonja by then, but she was a professional. Isobel seemed amused by me and asked me how I kept from putting on weight, and with her Latina flamboyance, she blew out her cheeks to simulate a fat man. She mimed my eating my second dinner and we both laughed.

I said, "I have a theory. Nothing I like is bad for me."

"Do you have other theories besides those with food? Maybe, say, books, art, films – anything like that?" Gold flakes glittered in the deep brown of her irises, her handsome oval face propped between her long fingers as she eyed me shoveling down the last morsel of my plantains.

"Nope, not much of a reader," I said. "My work keeps me busy."

"No books? I can't believe it!"

"Somehow I can believe it," Sonja said. I detected a whiff of rebuke in that.

It was Micah who gave me any smattering of book knowledge I might possess. When she left, she took that with her along with everything but my existentialist props. I didn't think of the random couplings with women I picked up at Tico's Place. Micah was my compass, and when she went, I couldn't understand some of the things I did or the new habits I acquired, like binge-eating spicy foods. Ironically, Micah was a hopeless cook who burned everything from hamburgers to standing rib. I stung her to the quick during one of our fights when I told her she could fuck up a baked potato.

I gave Sonja a dispiriting progress report, and I told her a few things I had been holding back such as the fact that Pavelic's boys were sniffing the trail behind me.

"That doesn't sound good," she said matter-of-factly.

I said, "It's worse than you think. The forces of darkness are still pitching a shutout and it's the ninth inning."

When the dishes were cleared, Sonja and I talked business. There were rumors in the department about more assignment shifts, and at last, some news on my damaged pug. Emilio might have wound up on an incident report in the southwest district for beating an Hispanic male outside a Cuban supper club. Even used the cast on his hand to sucker punch him and then kicked the guy unconscious. The victim gave a good description, especially of his attacker's bum wing. *Calle Ocho*'s full of these hot bloods every night. They reminded her, she said, of Mexican *federales* – young and cruelly handsome like TV soap stars.

I told her what else I had been doing all day and what I would be doing tomorrow. Sonja's silence told me all I needed about the value of this kind of needle-in-haystack approach to detection. Isobel asked me who this girl was, and I took out Raina's picture, a little dog-eared by now from handling.

"She is very beautiful," she said. "One can see it. A beauty in one so young is remarkable, even so. She has the kind of face an artist would want to paint."

Images of the kind of posing Raina actually did

came to mind, but I said nothing, merely agreed that, yes, she was pretty and her parents were very concerned about her. I told her briefly about her aborted music career in college.

"Ah, does she like art as well as music?" Isobel asked. "You might try some of the galleries in those malls."

I thanked her for her suggestion, but my stomach lurched at the thought of adding more places to the number.

"I meant, if she, this girl, were interested in a certain kind of art, you would reduce the number to a handful," Isobel added.

I knew nothing about Raina's possible interest in art, but I knew that there were those close to her who did: Pavelic and Beudert. My mind flashed to Beudert's place as if I were filming it from inside my head. I recalled walking in his house – the white walls, Jeanette being shoved ahead, Giorgio's eyes taking me in, Beudert's smirk, and Raina, flesh and blood, at the white piano. I could even see the gun dangling conspicuously from my hand in a nervous twitch, the knot of people hushed as I passed them. Then, something else my eye and brain had taken in automatically, but that I had not processed until now: two photographs on the wall.

One right on the wall where that idiot in the mask, Guy Fitzmaurice, had made his farcical entrance through the swinging doors. I couldn't get the camera in my brain to zoom in on it. But the other was clear, unmistakable, and I remembered it. A portion of a woman's back in black leather, skintight over shapely buttocks, hands placed on each cheek with the fingers extended – only the tips of her fingers free. The garment cinched in back with eyelets and laces and exposed the long, shadowy crease of her womanly rear behind the crisscrossed laces.

How many galleries could there be exhibiting that? I figured that, between Dadeland which was on my list for tomorrow, and Miami Beach's Worth Avenue, there must be at least that many Nieman-Marcuses, Lord & Taylors, and Saks Fifth Avenues alone to tramp through. And I had already been thoroughly raked with what Micah called "a trenchant stare" from crown to sole by dozens of the salespeople and valets I had queried about Raina today.

Outside the restaurant we said our farewells. The balmy air reeked of diesel fuel and citrus. I watched them walk off and again thought of that singular photo. By a not too complex process of associational logic, I found myself thinking of the warmth of Anne's scent. I wondered if Mrs. Tanenbaum ever bothered to give her my message.

~ ~ ~

My mind was adrift, like the car. I strayed across the cat's-eyes in the road several times and drew a caterwaul of car horns. I didn't feel like returning to that rat hole of a motel, but there was nothing else to do that would bring me closer to finding Raina. What little of the sky I could see between the graceful swan-necked streetlights arcing over the street was barren of stars and blank as gunmetal.

I parked down the street and walked up. As I turned the corner, I noticed the overhead light had been turned off. I was used to the sight of the strange tree and its open wounds, the gothicness of it. Phlox surrounded the tree – the oddness of a little patch of dirt on one of the busiest thoroughfares in Miami – made me wonder why it had escaped notice from the developers and commercial entrepreneurs or been bypassed during one of Miami's prosperity phases.

I was pondering that when the nape of my neck

prickled with heat, only it wasn't real heat. It was a warning. I stepped close to the rooms in the shadows and retraced my way with slow steps back to the corner and peered in at the top of Ernesto's gleaming bald head from the lobby. He was in the same position, the *exact* same position.

I saw no one else in the lobby. The usual freaks and squatters were missing. All the action was outside beyond the glass where the panhandlers and street people, the evening partyers, and some of the genuine urban night-types were milling about.

I went inside slowly, cautiously working my way toward the front of the chest-high lobby desk. I took a peek over the counter, spied a gun lying by his shoe. He died in a half-standing, half slouched position; he had time to pull out the gun before he died, a .44 Magnum. Some of its ammo lay scattered on the floor when the gun hit and the drum opened. Most of the back of Ernesto's head was missing, but there was no entrance wound in his face. Someone had clobbered him from behind while he was facing a threat in front of him. Something made him reach for his gun.

I felt like someone looking into a baby bassinet and seeing the squirming of eels instead.

The dark would help me now. I exited the lobby and checked for a tail.

Traffic continued to whizz past, but I saw the wink of cherry lights as a car suddenly braked to a halt, and a white moon of a face with a pencil moustache looking in my direction.

Come on, you bastard. Stick your head out. Give me a look.

No doubt though – it was Luis Amezcua.

I heard the unmistakable sound of a clip being jammed into place and my guts turned to water. Amezcua leaned his torso out the door and sent a fusillade of lead in all directions. Citizens, deadbeats, drifters, panhandlers – we all scurried off into every direction in a blind panic. Amezcua screamed something, but I was too busy running to the parking lot for shelter to hear it. When I risked a look over my shoulder, I saw a large figure in a black ski mask beside Amezcua send a burst of flame and spitfired bullets in a semicircular sweep of his arm moving ever closer to where I tried to shrink myself behind the tire of somebody's car.

I was hunched down but not completely shielded from his view, and I could see him well enough to recognize Odio by his bulked up torso. If he lifted the barrel six inches over the side higher in my direction, he could have riddled me with slugs.

Hi-low sirens warbled in the distance, getting louder but a couple blocks distant.

Sensing it was now or never, Odio raised the gun and spat fire and burning muzzle gases a foot from the barrel; the thudding and thunking into car metal, shattering glass, and tearing chunks out of concrete buildings. The burst was barely audible above the gun's ragged syncopation.

I flattened myself to the ground behind the wheel well. Cars and tires were squealing in every direction, as if traffic flow going in both directions had gotten the single message at once: *Maniac Ahead. Drive with Caution.* From beneath the chassis, I glimpsed the bottom portion of Odio as he jumped into their car and in seconds darkness swallowed them. The image in my retinas stayed long afterward, the muzzle flash of the silenced gun in his fist, the *bip* of the sound it made, the loose tail of his *guayabera* flapping behind him as he dove into Amezcua's car.

I tried to stand, but my legs had an action of their own in mind, and I felt the earth slip sideways. I was struggling, using my elbows mostly, to pry myself from the dust and tar of the parking lot when a surge of vomit forced my insides out until my huge meal came back and burned its way up my throat and out of my mouth.

A half-minute later, the cop who pinned me to my stomach wasn't taking any chances, and I felt his weight squeeze air out of my lungs until I nearly blacked out.

By then, of course, the block was sealed off. The lot where I had parked my car was teeming with cops and sirens, and a mob of people of all kinds. Motel people and their children, the street people with their assorted looks and faces, sable wraps, mink furs, and expensive jewelry rubbed shoulders with tattooed bikers on hogs who stopped to take in the carnage. The headlights all around dazzled me, but I could make out blacks and whites standing side-by-side with Cuban-Americans and Haitians, Latinos and a sprinkling of Vietnamese, Cambodians, and some third-worlders. Young and old, toddlers, babies and the aged – everybody was drawn to violence in an orbit of darkness on an urban street.

It was a language fiesta from what my ringing ears could detect, mostly English and Spanish but also a polyglot of slurring and glottal stops, guttural with sibilant. The babel of a cosmopolitan night crowd spectating some unreal, impromptu street theater.

And me in the center of it all, emergency lights whipping beams of cherry-turquoise-cherry into the flat black night.

I was a dark star pulling everything toward me with the centrifugal force generated by the small mass of my being.

I was equidistant from the yellow plastic perimeter holding back the crowd, night, infinity – except that it wasn't a perfect circle, more an oblong because it had been taped or fixed to the sides of the smashed hotel doorway. Strangely, I felt abandoned by everyone for the moment while a hub of activity by cops, uniforms, detectives, and paramedics competed in the organized chaos of a crime scene, went on all around the circle's perimeter that reminded me of my high-school torture in geometry class – " *r fucked,*" I thought.

I managed to work myself up to a sitting position; a couple cops nearby stopped talking and checked me out to see what was doing.

My shirt was torn and stained with my own vomit. One side of my face was bruising from being pinned to the ground, and I was wearing cuffs, my pants had been ripped almost off from the frisking I had been given. I was dopey from the shellacking my body had experienced in those few, but hellishly long, moments of purest terror. If it's possible to relive the horror of that day in the swamp, I did in those seconds when I had gone from a quiet walk to digest my expensive dinner, to this.

I heard some cop yell, "Wait for the wrecker, God damn it!"

Another booming voice ordered a couple of the uniforms to help the paramedics get the body out of the motel room.

Ernesto had a white sheet thrown over him, and the crowd *oohed* when his body was handed off to several pairs of EMT personnel. The sheet was bloody where it covered his torso.

A captain overseeing the transfer of the corpse let out a stream of profanity at the men. When they regrouped and lifted him back onto the stretcher, the final indignity of Ernesto's life occurred as what remained of his brains slipped out of the back of his skull and fell onto the sidewalk. The captain somehow achieved the impossible in reaching a pitch of rage at this unbelievable insult to his command, or to the further incompetence of the men on his watch, or maybe just unnerved by the unbelievable shattering of this peaceful evening, that he almost stepped on the sodden mess in front of him.

I thought of Dr. Bhargrava back in Cleveland: "... everything in the body or on the body is extremely important as evidence and must be handled carefully by the attending officers ..."

My reverie at this blasphemy to every forensics rule going was broken by a veteran cop in the background whose beer belly sagged over his belt. He was trying to hold back a crowd of people swarming him with their cell phone cameras held high. His face was expressionless but, to me, he looked just then like a drunken priest trying to bless a rowdy congregation.

CHAPTER 15

The problem with getting bagged on a weekend is that the cops get to spend a little more time with you than the Constitution says is acceptable. Good for them, bad for you.

"Your arraignment can't take place until Monday when the judge comes in..." Or "Sorry, your bail bondsman's gone for the weekend." I've heard them all and I've used them all to get an extra few minutes of interrogation time in. I don't take the perp's point of view in this easily because it goes against the grain. Cops have a single fixation; they want you to go to jail. So when you get Mirandized, the rule is simple: *Shut the fuck up* and call the best mealy-mouthed lawyer you can afford.

Trouble was, I didn't have one. At the station house, I used my call to Mrs. Tanenbaum, hoping desperately that Anne's word about staying until Sunday was good. The old bird's pause after I told her my name was expected: *Haftmann, the boarder from hell*. When I gave her the number to write down, she grudgingly did. I held my breath in fear that she would hang up. There was a large black male with a do-rag, a trustee named Curtiss, who glared at my back while I spoke, and it appeared from his aggressive body language and guttural noises he wanted the phone. Finally, she came back and picked up.

"All right," she sighed. "Give me the number."

Curtiss muttered behind me, "C'mon, motherfucker, I need that got-damn phone."

I said, "Police Substation Southwest, corner of West Flagler and – "

I had no idea what Anne could do for me or what I was

expecting from a one-night stand.

The stationhouse lighting was fluorescent but only every other tube burned at shift's end.

The cops had questioned me three times already. I gave them little, way too little as far as they were concerned, and though they didn't call me a liar or hit me with a Miami phonebook, I knew they'd be back with more questions. It was a game like chess. I'd move, they'd countermove, until one side quit or won. Right now, it was still a genteel sacrificing of pawns. No middle game in sight, nobody bringing the knights or rooks up yet.

I told them several times I was a private investigator working a case, looking for a man's daughter rumored to be hanging out on Calle Ocho. That's why I was in that sleazy joint in the first place. I said I had just begun looking for her and was coming back to my room when I heard the noises and saw a man shooting from a car.

"What kind of car?"

"Didn't see it, sorry. I was ducking for cover."

The cop who wrote that story down the first time never interjected a comment. We were sitting at his cubicle. The questions began with the second interrogation – only, of course, the homicide cop who led me to a small, mustard-yellow room, didn't imply it was *that*, of course. I was a material witness to a shooting which resulted in multiple homicides. But all his questions were obvious ones and mostly about me, so I gave him everything I knew they'd try to confirm before the next session.

"Word is," he told me, looking up briefly from his notepad, "you puked on yourself. You were that scared?"

"Hell, yes, officer, I nearly walked into a massacre," I said. "What was it all about, anyway – drugs?"

He grunted noncommittally and didn't bother to answer. The cocaine cowboys were long gone. Being a civilian in the center of the shitstorm might not be written off as coincidence. But nobody mentioned the big name. I knew they'd run my name through the databases six ways to Sunday, but so far I was just another tax-paying citizen of Ohio.

"We have just a few more questions. As an ex-cop, I know you won't mind cooperating."

Forty-five more minutes passed before the door opened and he returned with three other officers with him. The tiny room was swallowed up by cops at one end of a cracked table, me at the other. I looked at each pair of eyes and they looked right back at me. Cop stares.

He started by mentioning each man and woman in the room by rank. The date and exact time was noted. It was one thirty-three in the morning, and if I had a lawyer next to me, he would have stopped the proceedings on the grounds of sleep deprivation. A good psychological gimmick as well as legal necessity to suggest my cooperation, mutual search for the truth, proceeded from that point. I parroted the bit about no coercion, *nossir*, and I was cooperating of my own free will, et cetera, et cetera. Then they got down to business:

"Do you know either man involved in the shooting?"

"No, I never saw either one before tonight."

Long pause there, but my face gave nothing away. This was not the place or time for truth-telling.

"How long did you know the hotel clerk, Ernesto Reyes?" "I saw him only once when I checked in the night before last. Actually, early in the morning, so it would be the same day."

"You had no prior knowledge that establishment has been a frequent source of police calls for fights, domestic violence, drug transactions?"

"No, I did not," I said. "I wanted to be close to the

places where my client's daughter might show."

A second officer tapped her eraser against the table, signaling, I suppose, she was taking over for a while. The ranking officer, no doubt.

"Haftmann, your client... the girl. This Raina. Did you find her tonight?"

"No, ma'am, I did not."

She tapped her pencil tip a couple more times, and then said, "Describe everything you saw from the moment you left your room to the moment you returned. Tell us what you ate, where you parked – everything – take us through the last twelve hours of your life, leave out nothing that you might think inconsequential. We want to know exactly what happened."

I spoke for twenty minutes. I kept to the story's main line and embellished trivial details that would make no difference if checked. These were good cops. They all looked at me with that flat disinterested stares, but they knew I was holding back. No one interrupted me. When I finished, I looked at all three officers and waited. No one spoke, perhaps deferring to their senior officer for the group.

Without a signal being exchanged, or a word spoken to me, not so much as a nod of the head at the conclusion of the story, the female and one of the male officers at the end of the table got up and left the room.

The cop who said he would bring me a coffee flipped his eyes to me and smiled what had to be the world's fastest smile, or maybe, in my clapped-out state, I interpreted it as a smile when it might have been a knowing grin, one cop to another. *That dog won't hunt, buddy. Try another fairy tale –*

"Now, I just have a couple more questions to clear up – "

I could have done something stupid and screamed

for a lawyer, or said I was too tired to go on, or it was too late, any number of other things that would have been logical and reasonable, but I acted my part of the innocent bystander and answered questions for another twenty minutes. Just as I was completing my list of bars and restaurants I had scoped out that day, he glanced at his watch, stood up, and left the room without a word. At the door, there was an animated conversation on his part with the woman officer insofar as I could tell, and then he walked away.

She watched his back for a moment, and I looked at her profile.

She had a widow's peak, thick, black hair with a streak of gray over her right temple. She wore make-up too, I noticed, and a navy blue knee-length skirt and dark sweater.

They released me. I got the standard warnings about staying available for "further questioning." Told me to call the station in the afternoon, ask for Lieutenant Talbot, Crimes Against Persons. As I was leaving, I heard the desk sergeant speaking to a uniform about the killings that night.

"Jiminy Crickets, Stevie, the killer poleaxed the poor guy's head, busted it open like a watermelon."

The young officer laughed, "So what? We don't print heads."

Traffic slicing through the slate-gray mizzle of 4 a.m. on Calle Ocho closed off the sergeant's response to Stevie. All my nerves were jangling now that the fierce concentration of my responses was past. I wasn't going to dwell on their investigation; my goal was to keep myself out of it. I had things to do and even less time now. Those twin killers, Odio and Amezcua, were out there like Castor and Pollux in the night sky, but they were out of my hair for a while.

For the first time, I felt good about something.

Pavelic was indulging his flair for sensational violence in a way that was only getting worse, and he had everybody on high alert now. My old grandmother would have leveled a quote from her dog-eared bible, something about eating the bread of wickedness and drinking the wine of violence

~ ~ ~

I drove to the Riviera Court and found my man Youssef with the debauched face just getting ready to end his shift. His dark eyes and unshaven jaw mingled a look of sleeplessness that almost made him seem profoundly older than his twenties. My own eyes throbbed from lack of sleep. I saw him do a double-take when he saw me in his lobby again.

I told him I wanted a room, now. He started to stammer something about his manager's instructions if ever this John K. Mahan showed up looking for another room in his motel.

I had a pair of twenties under my hand, and as I leaned toward him to make a second request, he palmed them from me with the expertise of a corner drug dealer. I paid for a week and tipped him an extra twenty not to report to anybody asking for me. I gave him my new alias.

"Sure, Mister, uh, Eye-de-ota," he said.

"It's Greek," I said.

Youssef screwed up his face and asked me whether my "party friends" were likely to come back to see me.

"No way," I said and gave him a weary smile. "They're sleeping it off by now."

"I'll have to call the police, you know," Youssef said. He looked miserable, the bearer of bad tidings.

"No problems," I said, "but if they do, I hope you fare better than the last guy who booked me a room."

He looked at me less sure of his decision but handed me my room key and some slips of embossed stationery with Riviera Court logo as letterhead. I went back outside to move the car, thinking I was no closer to Raina than the day I arrived in this godforsaken state.

Tomorrow, I said to the little voice in my brain. *Nothing more to be done now. Too many mistakes have happened.*

I wouldn't have to wait long for oblivion because my brain was already on auto pilot, heading vectored in on the nearest pillow. I swung my car around to the back of the parking lot overlooking a grove of cypress and willows, made sure it couldn't be spotted by the highway. The undersides of their leaves were silvered by a misty rain. High up, pink and peach clouds caught spires of light from the rising sun. Such wasted beauty. A new day, the air was changing but my biorhythm clutch was still in overdrive, gears refusing to mesh. The canal banks loomed like silver ribbons in the distance through the green swath of the campus owned by the University of Miami. Nuisance alligators, I had read in Bobbie's paper yesterday, were crossing the highway in greater numbers.

The darkened, monkish cubicle of a room waiting for me beckoned and I took labored steps to get there.

Inside, I peeled off my clothes like dead skin. They were filthy with dirt and sweat from the night's bloody débâcle. I opened the collar of my shirt and felt the rasp of a two-day beard. My fingernails, now blackened from grunge in the parking lot where I tried to claw lower to the ground, were sore. There's a popular myth that people won't give up: when we die, our fingernails and hair continue to grow. Here's the truth: when you die, you're gone for good; everything stops growing.

Men die and they are not happy.

I had to recharge my mobile. Sonja left three messages, yesterday's date, all after midnight. She would have heard of the shooting, even before Bobbie's newspaper cronies, I figured. She was following Machiavelli's adage about keeping your friends close, your enemies closer. One of Sonja's messages was slightly encouraging, however: "BOLO still out on Emilio, but Sharisse is in county."

My brain was awhirl with a jumble of thoughts, terrible, bitter, and keen like razors. Hope fought despair for the briefest of moments; then my head, three times its normal weight, sank deep into the plastic pillow, sucked down by gravity, and I crossed over once more into a place so dark and heavy light couldn't escape from it.

CHAPTER 16

Iawakened, gasping for breath, expelled from the Land of Oblivion where I wanted to remain.

I guzzled warm tap water from the sink, cranked up the air conditioner, showered, and dressed in some of the same clothes.

Youssef, good lad, had followed my instructions precisely.

My cell wasn't yet recharged so I asked to use his lobby phone on the wall. Someone had scratched a Coconut Grove number beneath the words *Blowjobs Available*.

The precinct first – cops could hobble me if they wanted to start squeezing. I had to look as if I wanted to play straight for a while. I spoke to a Detective Sergeant Terry Moreau. He wanted to see me at three. *Could I be available?* It wasn't a request. "Just a few matters to clear up," he said.

The *Trib* was next on my list. I was worried about Bobbie. Same thing: answering service said to leave a message so I did. *Call me at the Riviera, ask for the guy with the Greek-sounding name*, I said to it.

I was running in circles now. Pavelic could find me wherever I went. My trusty bat was leaning behind the door, much readier for action than I was.

I called Broward County Sheriff's and asked for their visiting hours. I could get there if Moreau didn't hang me up with questions. Maybe I wasn't going to get a chance to walk out of there. I couldn't think clearly enough to guess what charges they could bring.

I checked the map again.

I had a little more time to wait for my cell, so I went out to my car to open the windows. It would be a solarium by the time I needed it if I didn't. I went back into the lobby and dialed Sonja's private number. I asked her to use her clout to make a call to New York for me. I gave her the motel number to use. I could see him in his FBI office downtown Manhattan, sitting behind his polished walnut desk twenty-three floors up on the east side.

Twenty minutes later the phone rang.

"Hello, Booth," I said as soon as I picked up.

It always pissed him off when I didn't use that Special Investigator title.

"I understand you've been busy lately," he said.

"I know you're keeping tabs. I'm busy now, so let's come to the point. I want you to put in a call to your Miami office and get some agents to help me."

"No can do, Haftmann. This isn't an escort service and I'm not the Miami SAC."

"I can use your name when I make the call," I said. Hoping that would prick his vanity.

"Goodbye, Haftmann."

Sonja called back. The hunt for Intrepid registrations came up zilch.

"You said Emilio's girl's in county lockup. Can you get me in to see her?"

"I'll make a call," she said.

"What's she in for anyway?"

"Mall security nicked her for shoplifting, her third offense, she'll get thirty days."

"Where's Emilio now?"

"He should have stayed safe behind bars," Sonja said. "But he's out on bond for the Calle Ocho beating. One of Miami's best firms sent a man down yesterday afternoon to spring him."

"He's really stupid, isn't he?"

"Like a lamb to the slaughter," Sonja said. I didn't like the sound of that. Pavelic's private note came to mind.

It was possible Pavelic hadn't yet twigged to

Emilio's treachery – or maybe the boy was counting on that. I asked her if we could get the bail bondsman to fork over the address, but she beat me to it. It was the same house where I had broken his hand. *Like me, 'The dog returneth to his vomit,'* I thought. Sonja's computer said it was owned by a Gerhardt Benn of Tampa Bay. She would run a check tonight.

"Widen the Intrepid search too," I suggested. "Extend it to Hispanic males to fifty." I gave her another name to check out.

"That a last name or a first? How do you spell that?"

"A-L-S-H-A-M-O-O-N. He's in the Grove somewhere. I'll call you at work tonight."

I asked her about Isobel. She was miffed I hadn't leaped on her suggestion to call art galleries, so she took it upon herself to call some for me. I figured that checking out every chichi gallery in every mall in South Florida had as much chance of picking up Raina's scent as the Miccosukees had of taking Florida back.

"Thank her for me," I said. "Isobel must not be impressed by my sleuthing skills."

Sonja didn't respond to that.

Thinking of Micah at the other end of America, I thought she was lucky. A second chance in love must be rare.

Fate's capricious Wheel had rotated slightly in my favor because Isobel learned that the most prestigious galleries like Gloria Luria and the Barbara Gillman didn't handle that kind of fetish art. "They just wouldn't," she said. Isobel had also told Sonja to forget the Kane Concourse galleries in Bay Harbor Islands.

Sonja told me that Isobel was an anthropologist with a specialty in Mayan art and a degree from the University of Mexico. It stood to reason, Isobel told Sonja, these people, "these degenerate ones," in Isobel's delicate phrasing, would value that kind of art as well. Maybe Pavelic or Beudert made a purchase. Maybe Raina herself bought something at a shop close to the gallery. Somebody might know something or have a receipt with an address.

"While I'm waiting for technology to stop screwing with me," I said. "Call me here again if you or Isobel learn anything." The lobby phone rang a couple minutes after I hung up. Youssef raised his head from time to time from his Sudoku puzzles to glance at me. While I waited for phone calls, we chatted and I learned he was a doctoral candidate working on wave propagation theory.

The trill of the phone interrupted us. I snatched it off the wall, hoping it was finally Bobbie.

Sonja again, but excited in her voice. She said Isobel had just called her, too, and said she'd just left some places in the Esplanade and got a tip from one of them. She located a gallery in Coral Gables which catered to that kind of art on a regular basis.

The last thing Sonja said to me was: "Bobbie needs to send over that little book."

"That's the first thing I'm telling her when I catch up," I said.

"Do you remember an old comedy called *It's a Mad World* – something like that?"

"No, I dislike movies," I said. Every movie I ever took Micah to when we dated had one objective: to get her into bed.

"There's a scene where everybody is tripping over themselves to find loot buried under crossed palm trees in the shape of a capital W," Sonja said.

"Uh-huh," I said. Micah told me once that geishas painted a white W on the backs of their necks to simulate a woman's sex.

"You remind me of that," she said, before hanging up.

I tried calling Bobbie again. Nothing. This time Nikki wasn't at her Society desk to pass on a message. The voice I spoke to passed me up the line to an assistant editor who queried me about my interest. I clicked off. Maybe Bobbie hadn't checked in and they were concerned... or maybe Pavelic was checking on me through one of his paid whores.

I had no time to speculate without facts; things were rolling, and as bad a hand as I was holding, I had to play it out.

~ ~ ~

Detective Moreau looked like a drag queen, but he was only sporting the orange hair I had seen on many middle-aged South Floridians who used cheap hair dye. The sun bleached it orange no matter what the container said. Box fans were running all over the homicide squad despite the air conditioning. An early heat wave had set in and the temperature was going into the high nineties.

"How you like this weather we're having? I heard it's a nice cool sixty up in Cleveland right now," he said. We were sitting in the muster room, which was a relief.

"I don't live in Cleveland," I said.

"Right, you said. Where is this Jefferson place?" I told him. *Fuckola.*

We went around and around for two hours. Same questions as last night, mostly, just to see if my story had changed. He mopped his forehead with Kleenex so often little bits of it stuck to his chin where his beard snagged it. His bored tone told me he really had better things to do than waste time on a jamoke like me.

I told him I had an appointment.

That perked him up fast. "I'm not done with you yet," he said, rising out of his chair and slapping his hand flat on the desk to make the point.

"Look, I've cooperated fully, but I'm down here on a case."

"I don't give a shit."

"Let him go."

It was the lieutenant from last night. She was dressed in a similar outfit as last time except the sweater was gone and her sleeveless blouse showed crescents of perspiration under her arms; her eyes zeroed squarely on mine.

"Lieutenant, I was hoping *Mister* Haftmann would tell us what his – "

"I said cut him loose." She never once took her eyes off me.

I stood up and hitched my pants where they had stuck to me. I nodded to her in passing. She was twisting a bright yellow topaz around and around on her ring finger.

"You may find you will want to speak to us, Haftmann." No *Mister* this time.

I tried not to limp out of there. My wounded side had stopped suppurating and the drugs had taken care of the infection. Still, I was tender there and every bump and rub hurt. I walked once more into blazing sunlight. Every chrome, glass, mirrored fixture that could reflect light did like dazzling splinters of glass. Three million neutrinos were zipping through my fingernails every second, but even they couldn't outrun light speed. Yet when you look in a mirror, you're seeing your old self. It takes a fraction of time to travel from the glass to your eyes.

Time – what was left at any universal speed for me? For Raina Toivela?

~ ~ ~

"Look, Sharisse," I said to her through the wire cage. "I'm just a guy hired to look for a runaway girl. I can give you money for a lawyer.

That's all I can do for you."

"I need to get out of here to take care of my babies," she said.

She was wiping her hand across her eyes, leaving snail tracks of tears. She reminded me of a ruffed lemur I had seen at the Cleveland zoo with Micah years ago. Kewpie-doll ruff of black fur surrounding a sad round face, big frightened eyes.

I bit back a quip about not being too concerned about her babies while she romped with Emilio in the sack. *Wrong tack,* I thought.

"Money, Sharisse," I repeated. "Money can help with your legal fees. I'll give you two hundred dollars to tell me where Emilio is right now."

I wagged some fifties at her and watched her sniffling subside. Her eyes were cold and savvy despite the tears and the babies, if there really were any babies.

"I can tell these cops about you, motherfucker. Then you be right in here with me," she snarled.

"But, then, there's no money for poor Sharisse," I said.

The heat in the lock-up wing was unbearable. The air conditioner had blown during an outage I had heard about on the radio on my way over to the Broward jail. The stench of too many incarcerated human beings in too small a space was vile. Flies buzzed. The overlay of stale perfume and body odor made the smell of heated flesh worse. Sweat beads dropped off the tip of my nose as if they were following a plumb line.

"Come on, Sharisse, give."

"They won't let us have no money in here," she said, stalling.

"Where is he?" I persisted.

"He kill me if I tell you that."

"He'll never know it was you. It's hot in here. I'm leaving," I said rising from my plastic chair.

"He say he helpin' take care a some bitch for someone," she said; she watched me fold and tuck the bills away into my wallet. I stood there looking at her.

"He say they s'pose to keep her at this place but they ain't nothin' to do at night on account they only old people around. Rich white fuckers, he say."

"Where do they go when they don't stay at that place?"

"Stop acksin' shit and tell me what you gonna do for me."

"Where, Sharisse?"

"'Bidness' he say, s'all. Fuck, man. You know what I'm sayin'?

He braggin' all the time, that kind of bullshit. I don' lissen to half that that motherfuckin' shit."

"Was there another white girl with Emilio? Someone a little older than your friend that night?"

"Yeah, uh-huh. She run off from some fuckin' place. I ain't seen her since I got busted on that bullshit charge. Man, I was gonna pay – "

"Would you lie for him to protect him?"

"I ain't lyin' for him, mister. I disremember is all. Fuckin' dyin' in here, like, I'm starvin'," Sharisse whined.

"I don't remember being served stone crabs with mustard sauce in the joint," I said. "All I'm asking you to do is remember where the other white girl is right now."

The puddle of sweat on the floor grew larger where I scraped it off my forehead. She probably had one on her side too.

"Mad, fuckin' crazy," Sharisse said. "No air conditioning in a jail, what the fuck." Her big brown eyes were laced with thick veins across the whites.

"Three hundred," I said. "Last offer."

"Five."

"Three or I'm gone," I said.

The bandage on my side was itching like a nest of fire ants had been place in there. The furnace-like heat of the cellblock made me light-headed, woozy. My prescription bottle was back there behind the wire screen when I had been frisked

"They gon' be at Hialeah Sunday, sure. My right hand to God.

Emilio and his boys like to bet. They go there almos' every Sunday." "I'll drop off the money off at your mother's address," I said.

"Don't you try fuckin' with me, neither, white man. That money best be there when I call or I'll dime your white ass out."

She reminded me of a Norwegian rat in a wire cage when she bared her teeth.

"My word is good," I said.

Even I didn't believe that one.

~ ~ ~

The Duhamel Gallery in Coconut Grove wasn't what I expected. Gas lamps and brick pavements outside, salmon-on-pink walls inside. Light, airy, as cheery as a high-class eatery, except for the missing tables and the photographs on the walls, chest- and crotch-high, the sum of which were enough to kill a goat's appetite. Turn-of-the-century crime scenes, asylum inmate portraits, and some that could have been stills from the last Faces of Death sequel. Morgue shots and medical photographs of diseased and severed limbs. An assortment of cadavers, animals, and transsexuals rounded out the exhibition.

I was less intrigued by the subjects, some of which were exquisitely toned; others looked as if they'd been found in boxes in abandoned police stations, than I was by the dark alchemy of the mind that wrought them as art.

I was staring at a portrait of a woman's torso in a sleeveless black gown. Two dark striations cut open wound channels down each breast and disappeared under the black fabric of her dress. I could not describe the look on the woman's face except as the haughty look of a woman proud of her physical beauty.

A woman in her thirties crossed the room to me. She was graceful like a dancer and as thin as a ballerina.

Was I, she asked me, *an admirer of Phister*? I said that I wasn't particularly familiar with him.

"We had a Joel-Peter Witkin showing last week."
"Oh," I said as if I knew the name.

"Fabulous," she said.

I made what I hoped sounded like a fine-arts grunt of approval.

"May I introduce myself? Thomas Haftmann." I flipped out the badge.

I put my hand out lightly and let her squeeze it. *Delicate sparrow bones.*

"Marcia Cendrars," she said, trilling the *r* like Spaniard.

"Marcia – "

"That's *Mar-say*," she corrected me.

"Miz Cendrars, my apologies. I'm in the insurance business. That is to say, the investigative end of it. I'm hoping you would favor me with a few answers to some questions."

"Well, she said. "I don't know. Are these personal questions?"

"You may decide that for yourself. Do you know your customers very well?"

"I know our preferred customers, naturally. Our regulars," she said.

I said, "Did Raymond Pavelic ever purchase anything here?"

"The real-estate developer? Oh no," she said. "Him I would remember."

"What about a Pieter Beudert?" I asked.

"Wasn't that an awful tragedy? Mister Beudert was one of my customers. In fact, he has an original Phister. He bought it from a Swiss museum. You know they're signed with the artist's chop." She drew a Chinese ideogram in mid-air.

"May I tell you something in strictest confidence, Miz

Cendrars? It won't require breaking the trust of Mister Beudert's confidence now that he's... no longer with us."

"If it isn't too personal, yes, I might answer it," she said and sniffed the air with distaste.

I had wrongly assumed from her eagerness to get in on the gossip about the secret life of one of her rich clientele, she would have flung herself through the plate glass.

"Fair enough. First, may I ask if you own this establishment?"

"Oh, goodness, no. I'm not the owner. Sylvia Townsend Duhamel is the gallery owner. She's on a buying trip in New York right now. I'm acting in her stead."

"I see, well, I'm investigating the death of Mister Beudert for my company, you see, because a rather large claim has been put forward in his name and we are required to honor it. We suspect that all may not have been as it may have seemed in Mister Beudert's life."

Wink, nod, leer. You know how it is. I widened my eyes for her in disbelief.

"We have reason to believe that a young woman in Mister Beudert's company may have been involved in this... tragedy," I said. "I'd like to have a discussion with this young woman as soon as possible, but I don't seem to have her address."

I took out Raina's photo and she looked at it as if she wanted to devour it.

"Wonderful facial bones," she said, as she returned the photo.

"Her I've never seen," she added.

"You've never seen her in your gallery?"

"No, absolutely not."

"Did you recall an address for mailing him brochures, announcements of forthcoming exhibitions – that kind of thing?"

"Yes, of course. Often when he was away in Europe,

if we were having an exhibition and he wanted us to hold something for him – in fact, Sylvia told me that we lost a big sale in that explosion because he wanted a signed print of one of Eric Kroll's *Fetish Girls*."

"Miz Cendrars, may I have Beudert's addresses? Any besides his Palm Beach house would be helpful."

She fetched me the addresses on her gallery stationery.

"What do you think happened?"

I told her that Beudert was a notorious pyromaniac from Chicago with a fake accent who blew himself up playing with matches. I left her gaping in open-mouthed wonder and left.

Two of the addresses were in Europe, one was Pavelic's Oceanside Boulevard house, and the other was in Hialeah. That made two intersecting lines in an hour. From famine to feast.

I had heard of the place many times, but where in the hell is Hialeah?

~ ~ ~

I headed for the Tribune next. Bobbie's silence told me she was going solo.

Not a good idea with this particular bad guy, I thought.

I was cruising on Blue doing fifty when I saw an SUV in my rearview mirror about forty yards back sandwiched in a lot of traffic. The driver kept swinging out as if he wanted to pass and then settled back into position. Several possibilities, cops or bad guys, sorted through my mind. I was half-hoping Booth had made a call down here after all and sent the cavalry. The one person I hoped it wasn't, was Miguel Odio. He wouldn't waste time reading me a Miranda warning; he'd simply blow my head off.

The front of the building was locked, so I swung round to the maintenance bay and rolled under the door. The presses were running with a deafening roar. I walked up the iron stairs next to the conveyor belt rolling out today's issue for stacking and bundling. I helped myself to a free one and scanned the headlines on my way up.

More news on the shootings. A follow-up piece on the hotel's sordid reputation referred to three other murders in the last ten years. My name was withheld, but I assumed I was being referred to as the "fortunate occupant of Room 7" and later as one of "several witnesses questioned by the police." They used the description of the driver and shooter as I gave it: masked, stocky, one taller than the other. In a way I was glad they were still out there, assuming they hadn't been sent to Jamaica for a holiday because, if caught and locked up, Pavelic would simply go to his own little black book and look under Dial-a-Thug. I might not see the next one coming.

Beudert had been dumped off to page ten, a single paragraph. "Death by misadventure," according to Hallandale Sheriff's Office spokesman, which was any death except suicide.

I asked someone mopping to point me to Gersack's desk. All the reporters' carrels were furnished alike with the same array of name plaques, computers, printers, phones. Hers was more untidy than the rest, but where the others had personal items like tiny stuffed animals, family photos, and bric-a-brac scattered about, she had stick-'em notes pasted around every square inch of the screen but nothing personal, no pictures, nothing of herself. Being in her familiar space made me nervous as if I were about to step through an open manhole.

I spotted Nikki from Society's desk. Lots of girly-girl, foo-foo stuff, photos of cute shorthaired cats and plenty of photos of her with various people. One of her leaning against a palm tree with a guy's arms around her. Lots of bikini shots. Nikki, hands on a chrome ladder, arising from turquoise water, rivulets of drops escaping from the sides of her bra and between her ample bosom; the name of the Hard Rock Hotel and Casino in Vegas behind her on a square thatch of the islands-style bar they had built right into the massive wading pool.

I spotted a plain manila envelope in a corner of her desk.

Nobody looking my way –

There, got you.

I left the way I came, untroubled by anyone asking who I was or demanding to see my visitor's pass. I was invisible. I hoped it was going to turn out to be that kind of day.

From a payphone around the corner, I dialed Sonja and asked if she'd finished running the Intrepids. No, but she had the address of one Alshamoon Tarvarius Jefferson. I asked her for any males showing a Hialeah address so far.

Bingo. Gerhardt Benn. The same Tampa Bay resident who owned the fuckpad used by Emilio Vazquez, pugilist and shithead. Now this same Benn happened to own an Intrepid driven by that same weasel.

I checked my watch: twenty minutes to spare. I gave it a shot and asked the first guy walking past if he knew where Alshamoon's street was, and he pointed across the street.

"Three blocks, turn right, man," he said.

I drew my wallet to give him money, a knee-jerk habit, but he waved me off with a smile.

One of Micah's psychology bigwigs, Carl Jung, used to celebrate bad times with friends, mourn happy times. I asked her if the guy was disturbed. She said something about knowing bad luck and good luck always follow each other.

The neighborhood turned fast from struggling to black streets long ago flipped by poverty and drugs. I saw a little boy missing front teeth playing in a dusty yard with hydrangea like blue popcorn balls growing beside the porch. I asked him if he could show me Alshamoon's house.

"Big guy," I said, "a boxer."

The kid smiled at me and lisped, "He live over dere in dat white houf."

I knocked. Alshamoon came to the door. He was sporting jheri curls.

"Oh, no, man, what the fuck you doin' here?"

"I want to buy a gun, Alshamoon," I said. I gave him a big smile and waved a fist full of Ben Franklins like party favors.

"Get in here, motherfucker," he said. "Standin' there like you buyin' drugs in a nigger neighborhood, fuck's a matter wid you-all?" That concluded our socializing, and we got down to business. I wanted a Sig Sauer for three of the bills. "Kiss mah black ass," he said. "Eight."

"Got any .10 mms? Five-inch barrel?

"Keepin' dat for myself. Got orders, but ain't got 'em filled yet." He sounded like a businessman in a dry spell.

"What have you got for five?" I asked.

He left me there in the foyer for a few minutes. I heard stair steps groan under his weight above me; a door slammed. The same noises of wood being stressed as he descended. He was carrying a cheap plastic airline bag.

He dumped the contents at my feet. "Lots of nines," he said. "Take your pick."

I took a .45 with a slide-mounted decocking lever. I'd get a blister carrying it concealed against my ribs on my good side, but the Velcro holster he tried to sell me with it was strictly for OK Corral time, and I wasn't anticipating that prospect. I reached in the pile and pulled out a couple extra clips.

"Got some blades too. Really fine-lookin' pig stickers, yo," he said, eyeing me.

"This'll do me." It's one thing to go into a knife fight with a bat but there's an expression for that mistake in a gunfight.

My luck was riding high. I stood on Alshamoon's rickety porch steps and felt like giving the finger to the heavens.

Then my cell buzzed in my pocket. I didn't know the number. "Who is this?"

A voice I didn't recognize said to meet at a place on South 8th Street at four.

"You know where that is?" "Yes," I said.

Calle Ocho – shit.

My good luck was gone as fast as it had come. Suddenly, I was sick of it all, sick of cabbage palms, pink stucco, and mustached parakeets, toucans, parrots on pastel T-shirts, sun-bronzed joggers in synthetic outfits painted like Birds of Paradise preparing for their mating dances, old men with their ugly sunburned shanks. Paradise, everywhere I looked. *God damn you, Florida.*

~ ~ ~

The Malaga was packed and waiters in white aprons and black outfits were running from table to table. I found my caller in the crowd easily; his old-fashioned crew cut looked polished under the muted ceiling lights.

"Agent Booth told me you liked Mex, so I ordered ahead for us both," he said.

I sat across from him and watched him sip his Tom Collins. It reminded me of my time with Booth in Tico's Place not so long ago, except that Booth preferred sloe gin fizzes.

"Agent Booth filled me in," he said, "but this is a

mere professional courtesy from one office to the other. Don't try to take advantage of it."

The card he gave me said he was E. S. Kirk, ADIC. Booth's reach was long. This guy *ran* the Miami office. Kirk crooked a couple fingers at a boy with a tray of steaming enchiladas moving past. The boy's eyes flicked once in acknowledgment.

"I assume we're not here to talk about the Heat's chances this year," I said.

"No," he said. "Why? Do you like basketball?"

"Nope," I said. "Not since LeBron left Cleveland for Miami." "You find that girl yet?" "I've got leads," I said.

"I called that lieutenant, the woman, what's her name, at the precinct," he said.

"I'll bet she loved that," I said.

He ignored that, too.

"She was ... concerned. We don't interfere with local matters."

Local matters, ha – a typical Booth euphemism for bloodiest homicide.

"I have a few concerns, too," I said.

The waiter brought me a tall glass of pink lemonade and set a bowl of black bean soup in front of Kirk. I took in the room – some well-dressed Cuban-Americans on the town but mostly well-heeled Caucasians, bankers and investment broker types. Business consultants who did Powerpoints, fired a thousand people, moved factories to Mexico or China and walked away congratulating themselves on a job well done. The kind who brought supercenters, mega stores and hotels into suburbs and left small-town neighborhoods reeling like Kabul in their wake.

He watched me eyeing the crowd. "Not a mixed bag here, but you should try Islas Canaris on Twenty-Seventh if you're going to be here long." He used his spoon like a conductor's baton. "Are you having me followed?"

He never blinked. "No," he said. "Why would I do that?"

"Do you know where Raina Toivela is?"

"No," he said. "I don't know her or you."

He'd go back to his office, call Booth in New York, and tell him the favor granted.

"We have a situation here," Kirk began...

That sounded familiar, too. It usually meant somebody's dick was about to get caught in the zipper.

Kirk wanted me to see the big picture in capital letters. If Booth were sitting across the table from me, I'd know it was time to dive under it. I also knew I wasn't going to be told much that would help me.

Between bites of food, he explained his version of the big picture.

"Too heavy on the cumin," he said at one point, interrupting himself.

My search for Raina had attracted notice even before that sensational mess at the hotel, but it had nothing to do with the FBI's personal interest, my safety being the least of ADIC Kirk's concerns.

He talked about Castro, not Raina. Mostly about countries which had invested heavily in Cuba at Castro's invitation.

"Right now," he said, "there's an international snafu over this Helms-Burton law that says American citizens and corporations can sue international companies using confiscated American assets in Cuba."

"I thought the President opened up some of this last year."

"Castro is going to go away soon – the guy's ninety-nine percent dead now – Raul is trying to make peace with some of the hardliners in the party. It's going to be a new ballgame," he said.

I told him international law wasn't my specialty and I didn't care who got rich afterward.

"Some powerful people are going to become *personae non gratae* in the US, all because of one old man." He stroked invisible chin whiskers in case I missed the point.

He told me four thousand commercial companies had investments in Castro's Cuba and thousand more wanted in. He named some of the biggest, ticking them off fingers and thumbs: Bayer, Daewoo, De Beers, Deutsche Bank, Glaxo, Labatt Breweries, Mitsubishi, Pemex, Sol Meliá, Toyota ...

"Everything you can imagine," Kirk said. "Over twenty billions so far to prop up Cuba's woeful economy – pharmaceuticals, oil, electronics, tourism."

He was boring me. "So what?"

"But the kicker," he said, "is big American companies don't like this law any better than our allies. The only people who are going to make out are the international lawyers."

He named an American sugar company which had already filed a property claim against Cuba for eighty-one million.

"I can Google this," I said. "I don't give a rat's fanny about Cuba, or free-market capitalism, or politics. The little guy gets fucked no matter who's in charge."

"One of those *progressives*, huh," he spat the word.

"Get to the point, Agent Kirk," I said, checking my watch.

He made these businesses sound like the heirs apparent of the mobsters of the forties – Lansky, Trafficante, and Giancana – all of whom had sunk seed money from bootleg whiskey, drugs, loansharking, and prostitution into casinos and hotels and made vast fortunes before Castro's revolution.

Time takes away the stench of blood from money. I.G. Farben and Bayer used to do business with SS-run death camps to obtain slave labor. One depressing case in my rookie year as a cop was an old woman, an Auschwitz survivor in the care of a drug-addled grandson. She suffered a stroke that left her on her knees unable to rise, so he drove over to feed her and give her sips of water every other day. By the time we found her, conscious and alive, the papery skin of her legs had soldered itself into the floorboards like melted beeswax and we had to cut around her with the Jaws of Life.

Nothing ever changes –

"What did you say?" Kirk asked me, aware I was drifting away from Big Picture.

The waiter returned with some dessert.

"Thank you, Françoise," Kirk said.

"Françoise?"

"That's my point, Haftmann," he said, savoring the sweet scent of the milk. "There's a lot you don't understand. Vigilance is paramount. You'll like this," he said. "*Très leches.*"

Marta's people were also Nicaraguans, and it was a special favorite of Tico's. It was something she made for him in their courtship days in Guatemala, and she wanted her husband to remember those times when they were young lovers in their dangerous country.

Dabbing the corners of his mouth with a napkin, he said, "What we want is to open a copy of *El Jefe* and see the headlines saying Raúl Castro gone."

Moon over Miami came through the speakers. I realized that despite all my time in the state I had never heard the song played. Listening to Kirk and watching him jab bits of delicacies from his fork into his mouth made me think of vultures over Cuba, waiting for the first whiff of rot from Havana that would send them aloft.

He never mentioned the name I was waiting to hear. Pending Raúl Castro's demise, Pavelic seemed to have his own cloak of invisibility. It would all shake out fast after Castro but right now I had no time for international politics. The message to me was clear enough: *don't screw around down here too long*.

All I wanted now was to get the girl and get out. That green light wasn't going to stay green much longer.

He checked his thin gold watch for the time and drew out a wallet that looked soft enough to be doeskin. He left a twenty on the table. I thought that was cheap and said so.

"This is for you," he said as he extracted a folded-up piece of paper from the wallet. He tossed it in front of me.

I watched him shake a few hands on his way out, glad-handing, working the big shots and their trophy wives at the tables.

I opened the paper and read the words. It was from someone signed M. in childish block letters:

Haftmann – Meet me. Tomorrow. Seaquarium. Last show.

Jesus, Mary, and Joseph, as my old demented grandmother would have said. The only M. that wasn't Micah's from her past little notes to me, scolding or tender, thoughtful or deliciously obscene, was one that I didn't want to recognize. This big M was embedded in the neocortex like the bullet he sent ricocheting off my skull bone: *Miguel Odio*. He was the last human being on planet Earth I wanted to meet anywhere, anytime, under any circumstances.

Fool that I am, I knew I was going. It was the coming back part that had my skin rippling with gooseflesh.

CHAPTER 17

Miami's Seaquarium on Virginia Key used to feature Flipper the Dolphin, star of hundreds of television performances.

Micah told me years ago the creature was really a female dolphin named Susie.

"Males are too difficult to train. They just eat and fuck," she said.

It was during one of our bad patches. We were getting along in a stalemate kind of fashion, or more like one of those lulls in trench warfare at the Somme.

The Seaquarium also had a killer whale. We used to have one in our Sea World, too, not far from Jefferson in a little silo town with a pretty name: Aurora, Ohio. Ours was Shamu, one of many, but I don't recall which one; like former heavyweight George Foreman, the burger grill salesman, naming all of his five boys George. The whales were rotated from one aquarium to another, replaced as soon as they died with other killer whales waiting in the wings and ready to gobble up the fish from their tanned, two-legged captors. This spectacular four-ton beast had to remain second banana to Flipper or Susie's successor, however, because rigorous five-per-day-performances exhausted its heart. Lolita was the crowd pleaser – at least at the show I saw along with hundreds of others under a scorching sun. It was Seaquarium's first big week of the new tourist season.

The crowds of shrieking children, the cranky elderly, the huckstering teenagers darting into and out of the crowds like lampreys looking for the fat bellies of carps to suck, selling every kind of overpriced trinket, stuffed animal, pennant, whistle, or balloon. If a parent made eye contact with one of these licensed marauders, he or she was battered into submission and another sale racked up. Let a father hesitate a second too long and the caterwaul of the deprived child shaking a stick of pastel cotton candy like a pygmy warrior would soon sound bring him round.

One luckless bozo, surrounded by a brood of sticky offspring, shelled out twenties like toilet tissue for stuffed or plastic gimcrackery, all of it stamped *Made in China.* And all of this consumerism and exploitation of God's creatures brought to you by the Chamber of Commerce and the Book of Genesis: *Ye shall have dominion over the fish of the sea...*

I yearn for the day human beings disappear from the face of the earth.

The last show ended with Lolita's soaking a couple dozen customers down front with seawater. The crowd squealed delight but the whale seemed intent on scoring the fish it earned for the finale. I watched its monster head, a surreal black-and-white, magnified in the thick tempered glass of the sidewalls. The announcer was still talking while the crowd got up to leave in search of the next event. Light danced on the turquoise water of the performing pools.

Big Miguel Odio had sneaked up behind me, cat-like. "Which way did you come?"

I had to steel my nerves to silent scream in sync with the crowd. "The Rickenbacker Causeway," I said.

"No, fuckhead, I mean here, to this place. How did you get in the park?"

He put a large hand on my shoulder, and I flinched instinctively. "Let's go for a ride."

We exited the park in a caravan of a dozen other cars and campers. I saw catamarans and sloops on the blue waters below.

Dozens of white and parti-colored triangles dotted the

horizon. Following my gaze, he said, "I used to race a sailboat."

His accented English was so familiar in the way the *y*'s came out *j*'s and a slight burring of *r*'s.

An old couple in a pearl Escalade passed and slid a car-length in front of us.

"Them old people," Odio said and I had a sharp memory of that blue Datsun that annoyed him on my ride out to the swamps.

Odio looked at the man's wizened face reflected in the Caddy's mirror. The low angles of the car made it possible for me to see the old man's droopy neck like a tortoise sticking out of his shirt collar.

"*Los viejos* ... these old ones," Odio said, shaking his head; "they drive worse'n Jamaicans. Even Haitians will signal a lane change now and then. But these fuckin' retirees, *marrón*."

It was surreal to hear this psychopath, even without his silenced MAC-10, complain about elderly drivers. His sunglasses hid his eyes. "Where are we going?" I asked him.

"You worried about it, eh? You think we goin' for another ride in the swamp, eh?"

He smiled at me. He was a handsome man but not smoothly handsome like his boss. Hollywood might not want him for leads but they'd love him for the stunts for the leading man, one handsome angel of death.

"I was talking to an FBI agent yesterday," I said.

"I know. So what?"

He had a black silk shirt, the black and white chest hairs sprouting like fur below his neck. He reminded me of a goshawk. His breath blown at me with his words had the slightest trace of fennel. The air conditioner was blowing full force directly at him and the hair on his chest waved. He wore lots of gold on his chest, wrists and fingers. A garnet pinky ring.

"Some trick you pulled at the hotel the other night,"

I said.

He said, "You should have seen my friend's face." He made a slapping noise with his big hands on the wheel; they were covered in black hair that stopped just below the cuticles.

"I never saw him run like that in my life," Odio said. "That was funny, man."

"Why did you kill Ernesto?"

"Who?"

"The clerk in the lobby," I said.

"The bald guy, you mean?"

"How many people do you kill in a week you can't remember them all?"

"I can kill you right now, shithead, so be polite."

He took off his sunglasses and rubbed a knuckle in one eye. He looked at me again, briefly, this time without amusement. His eyes beneath the brow ridge were mocha.

"You're going to be famous. The cops will have your prints by now," I said.

He shrugged his broad shoulders. *Mister Big Cojones.* But I noticed a vein ticking in the side of his neck just above the collar.

"Listen to me, Haftmann, no more questions. You're here to listen, not talk. You know what we can do to her." He blew air out of his mouth, his thick chest deflating like a tire, and then, calmly, eased his grasp on the steering wheel. "We yust gonna have a quiet drink at a place I know and then I'm gonna take you back to your car."

"Where is she now?" I asked him.

"I'll show you," he said. "Sit still and don't do anything stupid."

He swung the car over to the curb and popped the trunk. He took the keys and got out.

My heart was hammering in my chest. I was

waiting for the sound of a shotgun being racked or a slide pulled back. *This time*, I thought, *I won't feel the bullet going into the back of my head.* Murdering me in the middle of traffic weaving around us meant nothing. He had given me proof of that fearlessness already on Calle Ocho.

"Get the fuck out," he yelled from the back of the car.

I got out and walked to the back of the car, curbside in case I had any chance of escape at all.

I saw her trussed inside.

I had to reach a hand out to steady myself on the car. Large welts and bruises dotted her semi-nude body. One breast was exposed to the nipple from the ripped bra. Her lips were split and puffy around the gag. Her eyes bled tears looking up into mine – begging me for help, save her from this nightmare.

Odio watched me, waiting for a reaction. He slammed the lid shut. "Get back in the car."

I did what he said. Hands folded, I stared straight ahead. I was thinking he meant Raina, not Bobbie.

Some animals imitate their prey to survive. I tried to turn myself into granite, will my blood to stop pumping, dry up, free myself of pity or compassion. I tried to do that for her sake.

"You won't have any trouble with me," I said. It came out funny when I said it.

"I know that," Odio replied calmly.

He spoke with the certitude of a man who knew life could not surprise him.

~ ~ ~

He drove to a place on the shoreline near a rotted black pier and parked facing the road. There were a few older cars in the sandy lot bordered by discarded telephone poles bleached tan by the sun and wind. Stunted trees like the cholla of Baja California grew behind the poles but there was nothing else to see except the windwhipped sand and the din of surf. The water smelled of fish and had oil slick in peacock colors where it eddied. This was as close to the ocean as I had ever been. A faded wooden sign above a cement block tavern said: Christine's-on-the Water.

It was a dark bar for serious fisherman. A few older men hunched over their beers at the bar. A couple played dominos in the corner. One of them looked up at us as we passed through and nodded to Miguel. The old guy had a serious case of melanoma developing on his upper lip.

We passed through a narrow corridor where cases of beer were stacked along the walls, past the restrooms, and out the back through a storage room where pool tables were stacked on one another. The place had been an old home at one time before it became a bar. The open patio faced the ocean and part of the porch that had wrapped around the house was intact. The original cedar shingles had been left to buckle and turn gray on this side. The deck we stood on was new and rose from the sand on brick piers. Some Christmas lights were strung up overhead and waved in the hot breeze. Someone had fixed one end to the house, just under an old Palladian-style window and draped the other end over a coconut palm.

There were railings on three sides sprouting with some kind of climbing flower like clematis growing up the sides; their mauve pink blooms were dabbed ruby-red.

Obscured from the parking lot were three small Gulf Coast cottages built close to the water. They had high, hipped roofs with large holes where the shingles had been blown off. Sea gulls perched atop all three and proclaimed their squatters' rights.

"We can talk here," said Odio.

I looked at his heavy masculine profile, a prognathous jawline topped by coal-black hair whipped over his forehead by the shore breeze. I never heard Odio give the order when we went through but a waiter appeared with two bottles of St. Pauli Girl.

"They keep these for me," he said and gave the waiter a twenty, told him he was renting the beer garden for a few minutes. The waiter was a bearded youth with red-blond hair and built like a Viking. He nodded and moved off after setting the bottles, already beaded with sweat, in front of us.

"You already know my name," Miguel Odio began, "and if you aren't half as stupid as you act, you know something about why you're here."

"Pretend I am as dumb as act," I said. "Start at the beginning." He said he was born in Havana a decade after Castro took over. When he was finished speaking, I was told to keep my mouth shut and get out of town. Bobbie would be released. Raina Toivela would be free to stay or go home.

I nodded my head as if I believed every word he said.

~ ~ ~

Odio had been in many places and done many things as a mercenary soldier and gunrunner. As a boy, he supported Castro, wearing the armband of pretend Fidelístos. They, the youths on his street, played at being revolutionary soldiers. They even stopped cars and bullied adults with their swagger and newfound machismo. Boys playing at war. Once in a while they'd beat someone up, a few hard kicks to the enemies from other tough neighborhoods in those early days of Castro's Revolución.

He said they stopped a despised old man from the neighborhood, a teacher at the prep school, at one of their impromptu roadblocks, dragged him from his car and kicked him unconscious.

"I kicked his false teeth right out of his mouth," Odio said with a grin. "That was my last day of school." They even smoked cigars like their hero.

Then block-by-block Castro took away their parents' homes, businesses, factories, and possessions for the state. All the beautiful Yankee hotels along the Malecón were closed or renamed for revolutionaries or union workers. Then the Russians came and the special relationship began.

"My father was a doctor," he said. "My family was rich. We owned a big house with servants in Vedado. We, my friends and I, had been among the elite of Cuba. We did not like being poor."

So he immigrated to America during the Marièl evacuations under Carter. Castro had long since closed off the airport. He lost touch with his family over time, whose financial ruin had begun in the wild celebration of New Year's Day 1959, but he still communicated with a rich aunt who owned a pharmaceutical company in Puerto Rico. He fell in with the anti-Castro faction on *Calle Ocho* and a man recruited him to join yet another of those secret Cuban émigré societies that sprang up like toadstools after a summer rain, all intended "to liberate Cuba from the Bearded One."

He looked older than his years and had a man's body when he was a teenager. Miami was full of girls and women. He slept with rich older women who kept him with money, clothes, and jewelry, and spent it all on his favorite dark-skinned beauties in Little Havana. At fifteen he killed his first man, a *chulo*, pimp, who thought he was enjoying some of his girls for free. Odio took his switchblade, snapped his wrist like a toothpick, buried the knife in his neck and watched the blood spurt a shower over his arms while he watched the pimp draw his last breath.

He thought there would be a second wave of the Bay of Pigs invasion.

"The fucking name 'Kennedy' still doesn't mean shit in Little Havana," he said.

He returned to Miami after his contracts. Then he saw the money in drugs.

"You'd had to be blind not to see the cash those *folloneros*, those hellraising Colombians, were making. Bags of fuckin' money everywhere, man, more than you could count or carry at one time."

He worked for a drug dealer who used to complain about that. The banks were taking it at that time without embarrassing questions from the federal government.

"Took hours to count the shit," he said with his handsome devil's grin. His face was unlined and unmarked except for telltale crow's-feet around the eyes. He did some freelancing besides enforcing for his dealer, ran some guns to Latin America, imported a little heroin with the help of the *federales* in Mexico City under that big thief de la Madrid.

Then a few years ago he got bagged by the DEA flying in planeloads of cocaine. They were in a fight for their lives with Customs, their perennial rival, at that time, and he came, he said, "within a cunt hair" of spending the rest of his life in a Tucson prison. Or worse, hanging out in those hothouse cages in Leavenworth with the rest of the aging Cubans. He made some big busts for them, and in gratitude they handed him off to the FBI.

"When did you go to work for the feds?" I asked him.

"Three, four years ago," he said. "DEA's gonna get swallowed up by a bigger fish one of these days. I just got lucky."

He wound up working with Pavelic, and when the feds realized how big Pavelic was and what he meant to the future, not to mention their own prestige, he was allowed a free hand.

He drank another beer. "They're gonna 'wake me up' when the time's right," he said. "Pavelic, he trustin' me more and more."

He used spook jargon like a delighted child. This maniac thinks he's a CIA sleeper agent. *Oh fuck me*, I thought. *This can't get worse.*

He laughed. "Then you come along, you fuckin' one-eyed *cabrón*, and you fuck it all up."

I asked him: "Do you kill for Pavelic?"

He laughed again. "We use codenames. 'Swan' and 'Eagle.'"

"Answer my question," I said.

He shrugged, took a long slug of the icy beer. "He don' ask me, I don' tell him," he said.

I followed that with a harder question: "Did Kirk tell you to pick me up?"

"He ain't my *chulo*, OK? Your pimp, maybe, not mine," he snapped. I noticed the accent grew a notch with his anger. He finished his second beer and walked over to the rail. He made a show of unzipping his pants; then he took out a long, thick penis and urinated loudly over the side of the fence rail.

Sea gulls *scree*'d high overhead. Despite the ocean breeze, I was sopped with sweat. He looked at me, still holding his member, flopping it on the rail to shake out the last drops.

"Man, I still love to piss outside," he said. "*El meadero.*"

I knew that one from listening to Tico complain about his restrooms: slang for "street urinal." Sad memories of after-hours boozing, pissing in the gutters outside Tico's Place, Marta chasing all the worthless drunkards out with a broom, Tico roaring with laughter.

Miguel was pissing on me. Showing me he was the bigger man.

Why not? He's already killed me once.

~ ~ ~

I don't know what leverage Booth had applied to

Kirk to get to Miguel Odio, and I wasn't sure what my options were. I had to wonder now how deep Sonja was involved. I had no doubt she wanted DeCamillo's book of names, but did her operation intersect with the FBI's keeping watch over South Florida politics? Bobbie was an expendable pawn, and her life depended on me. The rules say a pawn can make it to the endgame and be crowned, but the reality is that they were used to gain a small advantage or distract an opponent. Always the Big Picture.

When Odio dropped me off at the empty Seaquarium lot, his sunglasses and smile were intact. I stepped out and held the door open.

"If I get you Pavelic's book, will you let her go?" "Get the book," he said.

"What about Raina?"

"She ain't my problem. Mez gets to watch over cooze, not me. Pavelic, he can wipe his ass with finer *caheta* than your little bitch any day of the week, so don't waste my motherfuckin' time. Get the fuckin' book."

"What would Pavelic do if he knew you were talking to me?"

"He'd find me a tree in the Glades with my name on it, but that ain't gonna happen."

He wagged a thick finger at me. "Next time I see you, I am going to have to kill you. We fucked up at that hotel. Better hurry, gets hot back there." He jerked a thumb at the trunk behind him.

His sleek machine's fat racing tires screamed against the warm asphalt, the door slamming shut from the torque of his takeoff, and I watched him go in a glint of light on chrome and glass.

~ ~ ~

I drove back to the Riviera Court and lay on my bed thinking in the dark. I squirmed with fear and self-loathing, my mind a pinwheel of thoughts that wouldn't let me string them into a logical sequence.

Odio was insane, delusional, psychotic – whatever those books of Micah's want to call him. A CIA-backed operation involving Pavelic and men of power in Cuba took me way out of my comfort zone, yet Kirk had intimated *something* was happening. None of the pieces were coming together. The one fact I had was staring me in the face: no one but me cared about a kidnapped reporter and a runaway girl. Miguel's last threat was going to play peekaboo in my mind, hide around corners, and cause me to second-guess my moves from then on: when would I next see my suave would-be killer?

I fell asleep with that and a dozen other questions swirling in my brain. I had one of my recurring nightmares of falling in an elevator. As always, I hear the cable snap with the door's closing. Lights flicker, dim, go out. I plunge at eighty miles an hour. The ratcheting *whoooooaaannng* of cambered metal smacking into the sides of the shaft as it hurtles toward the bottom is so vivid I can relive the rocking, side-to-side motion from air pressure below ... But this time I'm not alone in my fall; there's a dark silhouette standing in one corner, laughing, unafraid. He says calmly to me, "Blood is black in moonlight, Haftmann..."

I awoke suddenly, irritable at my own failure to act. I know the elevator is going to fall before I cross the threshold – yet still I get on it. Just once in my life I'd like to dream of lying beneath a cedar tree with leaves the size of elephants' ears, full of golden butterflies, the boughs loaded with fruit the size of jars.

The air conditioner was making its usual burbling noises but not pumping out much cool air. Outside this room, nothing existed but the last of the constellations fading from the night sky. I thought of Miguel's Boy Scout codenames, "Swan," and "Eagle." Deneb and

Altair, the constellation. *Who was who?* I wondered. I couldn't get the image of Bobbie Gersack, tied and gagged in the trunk of his speeding sports car out of my head. She was hurtling through her own private hell while I tossed in my clammy sheets in my elevator dream.

Count no day good before it's done, as somebody smarter than I'd ever be once said long ago.

~ ~ ~

I picked up my messages from the young woman who had replaced Youssef in the morning. She handed them to me and smiled. Youssef must have reassured her I was harmless. I smiled back at her, but despite the smile, she had only suspicious eyes for me.

Sonja called just past midnight, and there was one from Mrs. Tanenbaum. *Probably billing me for more damages,* I thought.

A third message, however, had me pivoting on my heel and returning to the desk. I showed her the number and a scrawled message: "Can you make this out?"

She wrinkled her brow like an old woman. "No," she said, looking at me and shaking her head. "It's in Youssef's handwriting."

I thumbed the numbers on my cell. A woman's voice came on: "This is Lieutenant Annunziata Baddalucco."

"Lieutenant, this is Thomas Haftmann. I'm returning your call, actually."

"Mister Haftmann, would you be available this afternoon to answer some questions?"

"No, Lieutenant, I'm sorry. I can't do that."

"We can do this the hard way, you know," she said.

"No, you can't, Lieutenant. That's TV bullshit. The fact is I don't have to see you or talk to you, and *that's* the law."

Stalemate. I could hear the nervous tapping of her pencil against something like a Tibetan monk slapping his palms to disperse angry feelings. Baddalucco wasn't going to get me in a room to talk about the shooting or debate how many angels could dance on the head of a pin.

I was a heartbeat away from thumbing off the connection when she said, "We found a body inside a dumpster behind a fish market on Cortageña." *Oh no.*

When she told me it was a man, I nearly collapsed from relief. *Not Bobbie.* When I refocused, I realized she was fishing. I could read into her silence what she was holding back. My prints were found on the body, on something – then it clicked – *the stolen gun from my room.*

"We ID'd the body, a Cuban national, Jorge Luis Amezcua. He passed himself off as a Mexican national from Chihuahua, according to INS. No criminal record, as far as we know."

Shit on a stick. I said, "OK, I'll swing by the station at three this afternoon."

I knew there was more coming and I was right.

"An enskid came back with that."

A what? "What's an enskid?"

She repeated it. NSCID: *National Security Council Intelligence Directive.*

Worse and worse.

"It's CIA, you know. It's a CIA order-directing assignment." "I see."

"Do you? Because I don't, actually. In fact, I'm having trouble understanding why a corpse with false papers was found in Little Havana, not to mention .9 mm shell casings identical to the ones we found at the scene of hotel shooting."

"I can't explain that, Lieutenant."

"Can't or won't? Then maybe you can tell me why the Miami

SAC has expressed official interest in the shooting." "I'm afraid I can't help you there, either." "There's one more thing," she said.

My grandmother's dithering, bible-spouting phrases tumbled into the pause. *What next, O Lord, for thy servant?*

I ground my teeth waiting for the shoe to drop. I heard papers rustling.

"It seems a Mister Paul Toivela of Jefferson, Ohio has filed a complaint against you. We had a call from the Ninth District AG up there."

"I know him," I said.

"Good. You're finally admitting to something. We're making progress."

"If you say so."

"Let's make it then, three sharp."

"Maybe I should bring a lawyer," I said. She saw through that one easily.

"That's your privilege. I'll delay turning the complaint over to our bunco squad until one minute past three o'clock, unless I see you in my office with or without your lawyer at which time I'll be forced to issue an all-points on you." "Lieutenant, wait a sec – "

But she'd clicked me off this time.

I thumbed Sonja's number next. No answer at home, her work extension buzzed a long time before she picked up.

"I'm worried about Bobbie," she said. "Her paper thinks something's wrong. She hasn't called in. They asked for a house check at her condo last night. No answer, but the security man said she spoke to him yesterday on the phone, something about a pickup or delivery, he said."

"What did the cops say?"

"The cops were satisfied and went away. Her editor's going to report her missing if he doesn't hear from her in the next hour."

I stood rooted to the ground as if ten-penny spikes were drilled through my shoes, paralyzed with a lump of molten lead in my stomach. I couldn't tell Sonja about Bobbie and I couldn't lie to her, so I told her I'd drop by "as soon as I cleared up a little matter."

"Call me right back, Haftmann." Her tone said that had just failed the sniff test by a mile.

My third call completed the hat trick of my misery. "Hello, stranger, I left a message for you as soon as the old biddy told me you'd called me."

"Anne, I can't speak right now," I said. "I'll call you later."

"Pardon *me* for bothering *you*," she said. "That's twice you've blown me off. Why don't you just make up your mind?" Click, and she was gone. *Holy Shit McGee.*

I sloped off in the duck waddle my aching side had forced on me. I was a one-man hurricane of bad luck dwelling in the calm center, all deadly force swirling around me. I thought of Odio's threat, and I knew that I'd have to leave the eye wall and experience that force sooner or later. With that blinding clarity of our worst convictions, I saw myself as a wandering, luckless Jonah bringing disaster everywhere. Toni DeCamillo and Roland Markwright were casualties of their own desires, so I felt little for them. *For out of the heart proceed evil thoughts*, as my dear dead Grannie used to say.

Raina and Bobbie, they were different. They didn't ask for this. In the deepest cockles of my own black heart, I had a premonition Bobbie was right when she said that bad things always happen in threes. Micah once told me about the Metatron, a fiery Hebrew super angel second only to God. I accused her of being childish, fearful of boogeymen. I asked her what the point was of believing in powerful angels or invisible jinn if we couldn't see them and they couldn't help us. I was looking out the bedroom window at the time, watching a squirrel hang upside-down from the bird feeder by his hind claws. The feeder was bucking and swaying in the wind, tossing him back and forth like a trapeze artist.

I was in a spiteful mood and I felt like a rat. I wanted to gnaw the balls off any good thing she believed in. Micah hadn't darkened the threshold of a synagogue since our wedding. I knew I had hurt her. She said I was the child and I was wallowing in my own locked-in syndrome. Right then, I wanted nothing more than to believe in a prince of demons who came to the dying and dripped the poison from his sword into their mouths. I would have begged for a sip.

Anything to shut out the rancidness of my own existence.

CHAPTER 18

The address Sonja provided was the quayside bar Odio brought me to. I parked the car between two mud-spattered pickups with their four-wheelers tied down by chains in the beds. I grabbed the bat in the back seat.

The same old men were playing dominos in the back. The Viking was inside wiping down the tables. He looked at me, looked at the bat, and kept wiping the table. I walked up to him and casually laid the bat on his shoulder.

"Where is Miguel Odio?" I asked him. "*No se,*" he said.

"*¿Come se llama?*"

"Benicio."

"Benicio, *donde Miguel? ¿Aqui?*"

He shrugged. There was nothing in his eyes – no fear, nothing but a pair of blue eyes fringed above with white-blond eyelashes.

"*Sientese,*" I ordered him in my limited Spanish and pointed to the bar stool at the end. "*No se mueve.*"

I went through the rooms, bat raised, kicked open the restrooms, went into the storage room with my heart hammering in my ribcage and building up a head of steam. Nothing. I went out to the garden. The same ocean, the same sun with rapier shafts of light. The same view across the water of the same buildings and shacks and the same colors in the same pinks, browns, and yellows. The cottages looked the same, the same gulls on the rooftops. The frayed ends of sheers ruffled out the back window of the middle cottage. I blinked salt sweat out of my eyes and stood where Miguel Odio had leaned against the railing pissing into the water at sundown.

I went back inside to ask the bartender who owned the cottages and saw that everyone had cleared out. Two engines were starting up.

My car was left where I had parked it, but the pickups were gone. A haze of gritty sand settled around from their fleeing tires. I saw a dirt track pass in front of the blackened tongue of pier and saw it lead to the cottages.

My car's worn springs took a beating from the deep ruts and puddles scoured into the hard sand but it was a road that seemed to head in the right direction. It narrowed at one point to little more than a four-wheeler path, and I had to plow through cattails and fronds for about thirty yards without being able to see much that wasn't some deep or light shade of green. The calls of red-winged blackbirds nesting cried alerts as I invaded their home.

At last, I broke through onto hard-packed sand again and juddered around a few more ruts and approached these places. Up close, I saw they had been long abandoned and left to nature to wear down.

I saw the gable of the nearest cottage a hundred yards away. The glass in the windows was missing. The paint had been scoured from all the buildings long ago and the wood at the top had acquired a patina of oily soot from the docks. I pulled up in front.

I walked around the back of the second cottage and looked at the ragged sheers fluttering in the breeze like fingers waving. No footprints on the ground. Thousands of crosshatched x's in the sand marked erratic patterns from foraging shore birds. Between the cottages, I saw a pelican regurgitate a small fish and swallow it back. He watched me and waddled off to inspect a crab seeking cover. Birds and animals lived here, but no human beings had been around for a long time, probably decades.

The front door was hanging loose from one rusty hasp so I kicked it free and stepped inside letting my eyes adjust. Someone had put dropcloths on a few tables and chairs but even these were torn and faded yellow with age. Vandals had smashed most of what was left behind. Walls were punched through and graffiti painted on every surface: the same obscenities kids write with spray cans, some of it in gang code that was too cryptic to make out or now meaningless. As I moved along the wall with my bat held ready, I passed a small bedroom; it was trashed knee-deep in paper wrappers and food containers. The kitchen had a steel-framed table in the center surrounded by more litter. Desiccated feces had been dropped onto the table.

One more room at the end on the left, a second bedroom.

Bobbie was trussed on the filthy bed amid the squalor. Blood that had poured from her nostrils and ears was crusted to a brown.

One of her eyes was glazed, unseeing behind a contact lens. The other eye had been blown out. Gunpowder stippling marked the socket in a half-moon like clownish eye shadow. A wisp of her hair fluttered across her forehead in the same air currents that snapped the torn curtains out the window. She was beginning to smell. Her head was slightly ovoid from the impact of the expanding gases. The back of her head was gone, vaporized against the filthy wall where a couple flies were still feasting. I shooed one away from her face. Too soon for maggots. I stroked her hair once more and walked out of the room.

One bullet had not been enough. She had been shot in the genital area too; her exposed undergarments were fouled. Homicide cops know it as a signature in killings where the man wants to punish the woman, humiliate her. They called it a "bitch" shot.

I took a moment outside to look at nature and listen to the sound of my beating heart. I wiped a trickle of blood from my chin where I had bitten my lip. Driving away, I had to clench my jaw to stop my teeth from chattering.

~ ~ ~

I exited Virginia Key and made it to the causeway before I saw a single cop car. He wasn't flashing. I saw no surveillance, but that didn't mean there wasn't one. I called Sonja from a payphone across the causeway and gave her the news without much of a build-up. After a hiss of her breath, she said nothing but words of one syllable – the cop taking over. I told her I'd phone in an anonymous tip from the highway. I heard a sob. Maybe it was mine, not hers.

She whispered something people have been telling me too late all my life: "Take care." How do you do that in a world like this?

CHAPTER 19

I wasn't going back to the Riviera Court. I had to think.

I turned north and drove randomly. Last night's dream of falling was nothing more than brain static. I'd been having that same dream since I was a boy.

I had to eat, put food in the belly. I was on Biscayne drifting with the heavy traffic flow, ignorant of the streets. I pulled over and parked opposite a cluster of restaurants and bistros, with brightly colored awnings that made me think of my grandmother's expression for them, "cat slides." I walked into the nearest one, and found a family Italian restaurant.

I checked my watch: 3:09. Lieutenant Baddalucco would have made her calls by now.

I was down to a couple hundred in cash and the last of the traveler's checks. I needed a change of clothes. I'd all but enslaved Youssef because he was taking my laundry with him and returning it to my door at night for the occasional five-dollar gratuity. At least he'd stopped giving me that twisted, turd-in-the-punchbowl look.

"Big fish eat little fish," I thought. "Everybody uses people – the way of the world."

I heard a pair of British tourists erupt in loud laughter at a table behind me: "That's fookin' brilliant, Roger," one said to his table companion.

I was trying to unwind, to get myself in a frame of mind to think, slowing down to find that zone of calm amid the chaos. A waiter loomed in front of me and asked to take my order. The sharp edge of hunger that brought me to seek food, however, seemed to disappear. I gave a cursory glance at the menu and stabbed my finger at something. I'd have eaten sawdust. "Linguini diabolo," he said. "Very good." "Coffee," I said to his back.

The Brits at the other table were arguing about whether they were in a *trattoria*, a *ristorante*, or an *osteria*. It sounded like a conversation my ex would have liked.

I sat there in a daze, thinking hard but no light bulbs went off. The same waiter appeared at the British table and set dishes in front of them. I heard one of them compliment his *Filettini di cappone alla Piemontese*. The waiter gave a smart click of his heels like an SS officer.

Something rang a bell. *Cappone:* capon.

"That's me," I thought. *A rooster without balls.*

The waiter's blue eyes and olive complexion sent my mind reeling back to the blond Hispanic at Christine's and by some alchemy of free association I thought of Toni DeCamillo and her pseudolover Markwright.

It was coming together too slowly and in the crazy logic of dreams. What I had been ignoring all along – the human factor in all this – emotion, not reason or logic.

The jolt of recognition, my eureka moment. *That was it.*

Toni was hard as nails beneath that woman flesh. She knew a scam on Pavelic was as high-risk as it gets. She had to know Odio and Amezcua, or men just like them, would show up one day and start putting cigarettes into her breasts if she didn't have some contingency plan, a bolt hole. Markwright, that gangly man from Texas with the bad rug and the accountant's training, would have done what any lover would do for his beloved. He would fall on his sword for her.

My waiter set the coffee in front of me and returned

to the kitchen. I saw him greet another waiter coming through the kitchen doors and speak Italian to him; then he nodded his head back toward the dining room, and I heard the word *maloccio*.

My mind was finally moving in a groove like a sliding door on its runnel, and I recalled words from my conversations with Toni in her apartment.

Toni, what else were you hiding from me that day?

The thoughts fizzled out suddenly like a wet sparkler, my flash of inspiration gone. I came back to my surroundings and heard noises. Dishes clattering onto drying racks, plates being set onto tables, unctuous voices of waiters, people just entering being greeted, tidbits of conversation all around me... life, real life, where people didn't walk into rooms and find people like that.

I saw a mixed-race couple with a little girl wearing a party dress and a pink ribbon in her hair. I thought of the portrait of the little girl hanging on Toni's apartment wall, the one she had tried to fake me out with. Something tickled those brain cells that even Odio's bullet couldn't damage. That photo on the wall the day I found Markwright tied to his own table.

I was aware of silence, the clattering of knives and forks had stopped. People were staring at me from all around the room. A man in a white apron making washing motions with his hands was staring at his waiters, shrugging his shoulders.

I must have blurted something aloud. *Losing it, Haftmann.*

I walked out without eating a bite of my meal but I left plenty for it and the tip. They'd spend the rest of the shift discussing the oddball customer and his *maloccio*. I had become too used to reacting and jumping through the hoops set in front of me, running and dodging

Pavelic's gun thugs to remember that I used to be a pretty good detective once.

I needed to make another phone call. More, I needed to call up my lost good luck.

~ ~ ~

Toni had no family. Her effects would still be in a precinct property room, but her personal goods would be kept in the apartment complex's storage facility. I hoped the manager didn't toss them out yet or give them to a charity.

Markwright had two kids that might have his father's possessions, if the investigating officers had released them. Neither was a sure thing.

I kept all my notebooks in whatever car I was driving at the time, and found the one dated for my brief and inefficient interrogation of Markwright. Doodles, scribbles – my usual nonsense to look "professional," but there was a phone number for the daughter in Michigan and one for the son in Texas I had from my last phone call from Sonja.

Bless you, Sonja.

The daughter answered on the third ring, but when I said who I was and what I was after, she grew impatient and told me she had nothing to do with her family back in Texas.

"Your father sent you money every month," I said.

"Not me," she snapped. "The theater I work for. I allowed him to do that much. You can't buy love after your children are grown and gone," she said.

I could hear one of Micah's quotes sailing into my thoughts, but I didn't speak it: *Sharper than a serpent's tooth...*

"Is there anything else?"

"Sorry I bothered you, Miss – " But she was already gone.

I flipped to the next page to find the name of the

town and his son: *Big Springs, TX, one son, married, Norman.*

It figured: the battery in my cellular needed charging just then, so I drove around for fifteen minutes looking for a pay phone. After a brief hassle with the out-of-state operator, I had the number, and a digitized voice told me how much change to feed the machine. I dialed and a woman's voice came on.

She was the wife. I could hear a child's voice calling, "Mommy! Mommy!" in the background, something about a TV show called *Blondo the Clown*. She listened to me and hushed the child alternately, but I managed to explain who I was.

Yes, her husband had his father's effects. Probate just sent them an official letter from Florida, in fact. Still in boxes in the upstairs.

Now the tricky part –

"Mrs. Markwright, I have a sensitive matter to explain that I really should speak to your husband about first. When will he be home?"

"He's home now. Wait a second – "

I heard the receiver hit the surface of something and then a child's voice came on and began some kind of prattle about shooting zombies and mean "montherths."

Little girl, I thought, *don't be in such a hurry. Monsters are all around us.*

Norman's voice was like his father's but not as deep. But he had the same slow delivery and a stronger Texas twang.

The gist was he believed me. I gave him Sonja's number and told him to call her to verify who I was. I dodged around the truth in such a way he assumed I was working for law enforcement in Florida. Baddalucco would have loved hearing that, I knew.

My stomach knotted when he said he'd go upstairs to look.

Markwright's granddaughter came on again, but his mother scooped her up, and I heard her bawling from a distant room. Busy people, normal family life, something I had lost forever.

He came back on.

"I have a photo here," he said. "To tell you the truth, when I first saw it, I thought my father had lost his marbles. You know, bought one of those frames from Walmart with the photo of somebody and just left it there as a joke, maybe. But my father never told or listened to a joke in his entire life. And my wife and me, we just couldn't understand why my father would have the picture of a black child hanging on his wall."

"Norman," I said. "Feel along the back of that cardboard matting and tell me if you feel anything stuck there."

"There is something stuck here. Like a lump of something stuck, I believe. There's a piece of scotch tape where it was opened.

Shall I open it?"

"Please do," I said calmly, half-gagging from the tension.

"It's a disk. There's a written entry on the side. It's in my father's hand. Dated six months ago. It says: 'To TD from RM' with all my love.'"

"Norman, would you be kind enough to FedEx it to me as soon as possible – right away, if you can? It would be a tremendous help to my, to our investigation."

"I will do that, yes, anything to help catch the animals who murdered my father. But I would truly appreciate it if you would tell me what it means as soon as you know or return it to me. It was my father's property, after all."

"Of course."

"One more thing, if you would." "What is it?" I asked.

"I'm not quite sure how to say this but, the police in Florida weren't very helpful about how my father died. My father and I, we didn't have the greatest relationship, you see. He was a moody man.

I never had much closeness, you understand?"

"What is it you want me to do?"

"If my father were involved in anything... *sordid*, I – I'd like to be called first," he said.

"I'll do my best, Norman," I said.

"I'll FedEx this to you as soon as I hang up. I can just make it to the post office."

"Norman, a last favor," I said. "I know this is going to be hard, but I must ask you not to put the disk in your computer. Your father would know – it's highly probable there's a virus planted to destroy the program if – "

"I don't think it works that way but I'll respect your wishes."

Somewhere in Toni's little book, I felt, was the key to unscrambling the code. Without that, the disks would be worthless. Toni's greed started all this, but her lover would use his knowledge of spreadsheets and programming to complete the circuit.

If Lieutenant Baddalucco ever got word of my conversation with Markwright's son, she'd find a way to jug me and lose the key for good.

~ ~ ~

I wasn't through role-playing. I found the manager at home; his face lit up when I badged him, and he was all eagerness to help. I told him that "we" were following up the murders and needed a second look at Toni's effects. "They're still in storage – is that correct, sir?"

He almost tripped twice on the way there, with his keys jangling in his fist and yakking at me the whole time. Told me all about Toni, his suspicions, how that other victim, the big fella, Mark-*somethin'* or other, was wrapped around her finger, mooning like a dadgum schoolboy. "Let me tell you, any danged fool could see she was just a two-dollar tart with big hooters. I even tried to throw her out once, too, but a couple of her big ol' spic friends showed up 'n scared the livin' be-jesus out of me."

"I know what you mean, sir," I said. "There's always trouble in a good man's life."

"Good riddance to bad rubbish is what I say," he said with a smack of a sweat-stained ball cap against his thigh.

He swung the door to the shed wide and stood there, rapt. "What the holy hell?"

I peered over his shoulder into the small storage shed. I knew that my good fortune had just run out. The little manager, all banty rooster and offended dignity, stomped into the midst and kicked a couple upended boxes out of his way.

"Some fuckers has broken in, by God!" he said.

One corner of the shed's door had been jimmied. He pointed to a spot where her belongings should have been.

"Is there anything of hers left?" I asked him.

"Nope," he said. "Nope. They done cleaned it out, all of it. Look for yourself. Just her junk that them cops didn't want."

He was asking me if I wanted him to take down a report, you know, like a theft report, or "whatever we called it," but I was almost out of earshot by then.

Bobbie's place was a greater risk because I wasn't going to be able to run a game on their security as easily. I knew it was too soon yet for the papers to have word of it for the evening edition. In hours it would be slathered across the front pages in all the dailies. No respect for the dead there, either. Bobbie would have been the first to say that was how it was in the business.

I'd just have to ask the right question.

The guard with the clipboard who stopped me

recorded my name and p.i. license number, and asked me my business. I tried a fast bluff. "Have any officers from the, uh, Southwest Precinct been by yet?"

"Just some men from the paper," he said.

He had brought them up to Ms. Gersack's apartment, he said, and one of them stayed in the hallway to talk to him while the other went inside her apartment.

"What were they looking for?" I asked it as casually as I could.

They were going to link up her computer to her workstation.

The guy explained it all to him. It was Ms. Gersack's idea, he said.

"I see," I said. *Fuckwit*, I thought. She would be hooked in to the bigger computers at work this way. She was getting her new computer today, in fact. A "bigger one" than the one they took away, he said. I had actually found someone who knew less about computers than I did.

I asked him if the disks were taken away too. He didn't know. I asked him if I could go up there and look for myself.

"Not without her permission," he said.

"How is it that you allowed those men to go up there without permission?" I asked him.

He looked huffy. "She gave me permission," he said.

"She?"

"Hellfire, yes, pal. Who'd you think?"

"You – you knew her voice well enough?"

"What time did she call you?"

"Very late. About ten o'clock, ten thirty." *Game over*.

Now Pavelic had Toni's book and probably Bobbie's notes on him. The only thing he didn't have was what Markwright's boy had put in the mail for me an hour ago – that is, if he kept his word.

I hoped Bobbie had chosen her confidant in the D.A.'s office well and that this person would move fast once the news of her murder was public.

I had to get to Hialeah. I drove back to the Riviera Court for some clean clothes. I had to look presentable to some geek in the U of Miami's computer science department when I dropped in. I needed a computer and somewhere along the line a code-cracker once I had my hands on Markwright's disk. He was a conservative man in all but two respects that mattered most: he knew zilch about female hustlers and he couldn't see bad men coming.

I was beginning to feel the noose tightening around me once more. The betrayals and combinations were getting exponential. Markwright had been suckered by Toni, yet he had loved her, and she had been betrayed by Emilio and ultimately the biter was bit. It all boiled down to my last piece to move in this demented chess game. Sacrifice the disk for Raina.

First, I had to know its value, how it made Pavelic feel vulnerable enough to send out his marauders. Bluffing rarely works with real gamblers, psychopaths, or cops. I had to *know*.

~ ~ ~

Racetracks are places where two-legged animals throw hard-earned dollars at four-legged ones running in circles. They say people in this state bet a billion on the dogs alone, those greyhounds that fly around the track at 45 MPH Micah and I had gone to see a dog race at Naples once. She loved their sleek, aerodynamic bodies rippling with speed and power. "They touch ground only thirty percent of the time," she said, reading from the track brochure while I was trying to figure out what a bet on the quinella meant.

"That means they're in the air seventy percent of the time," she said, having a little fun at her thick husband's expense.

I watched a couple dogs running in the adjacent paddock, where a man used his weight on the bar to set a stuffed rabbit in motion. Someone else was washing down dogs with a garden hose. Their long, slavering snouts bit at the cool water. I watched her shading her hand in front of her eyes, and I knew, even though I didn't, that our marriage was starting to show cracks. I was confident then my love could save us. I watched the dogs running in circles. She said something to me about which number did I like in the next race. I said I was never going to bet on an animal again, and I haven't since.

Watching them run, knowing what their ultimate fate was despite the happy horseshit in the colorful brochures, I felt mean and small. *Dogs,* someone once wrote with cold-eyed clarity, *are a bridge to nowhere.*

CHAPTER 20

Hialeah was exactly like my little resort town back in Ohio, except it was on steroids. A couple obvious differences besides the brutal heat were the buses following each other in a snaky path toward the entrance gate, and many more Hispanics. The same fulsome catering to bad-tempered old folks near dotage who shambled about with various infirmities holding canes, walkers, and bottled oxygen tanks. The bustle spoke working class all the same. The rich snobs, the art galleries, expensive eateries – they were all back there in Coral Gables.

I took 42nd Street and drove alongside the Miami River all the way to 4th and MLK Drive. It was like old home week. Exchange the palm trees for oak or maple and swap the ratio of Hispanics to blacks, and I was as good as back in Cleveland.

I took my binoculars and scoped the loges, ignoring the crowd and seeking out the blonde heads. I hoped Emilio, not Miguel, had taken over the babysitting now that Amezcua had found his circuit completed in a dumpster. I didn't have the nerve for more batting practice with a hardened killer like Odio, even if he came at me empty-handed. Time to cut bait and run. I was down to hours, maybe minutes.

The late spring crowd was mostly older males with white skin and spindly legs. Pants worn to their nipples; plaid shorts exposing knobby knees and sunburns, varicose veins popping through legs. The uglier they were, the more misshapen their physiques, the brighter their clothes. Torn tickets like confetti littered the walkways. Mourning doves roosted in the trestles under the roof in the upper decks. The air smelled of cigars, cheap cologne, and liniment.

It wasn't until the seventh race that I spotted

Emilio's cast. By the fifth race, my neck had begun to ache from scanning like some loony submarine captain in his conning tower, and I was cursing Sharisse under my breath. I had a piece of rebar from an abandoned construction site rolled in a newspaper that I carried under my last decent suit coat.

Emilio gestured to someone behind him, but he never approached the betting window. I scanned the loge he was in – no cornsilk hair, no high-cheeked beauty, no sign of Raina Toivela. No sign of Pavelic, although I couldn't see him slumming here much less with someone of Emilio's caliber. The buffed physique of Miguel Odio would have stood out in this geriatric crowd.

I waited, knowing exactly where each exit was in case I lost them in the crowd.

He did what I hoped. He took the 4A concourse to the main parking lot with the last race yet to start. I was behind a crowd of people who also wanted to get a jump on the exits. I stayed far enough back to avoid being seen when the crowd thinned in the parking lot. I was moving in a direction away from my car, so I had to gauge the timing exactly. Emilio helped me leg it back to my vehicle by delaying things with his big mouth at the last minute. He waved the cast about and argued with somebody, but I saw the car he was heading for – a silver Porsche convertible.

I hustled back to my car and hoped they'd still be talking so I could get lined up.

It all went as planned coming out on Hialeah Drive, and then I lost him. Emilio blew past lights and traffic with disregard for traffic flow or lives. He owned the road. I gunned it, but he had the lights down Hialeah synchronized, and the Porsche was ruthless and heeled to his stop-and-go, lane-changing, macho antics. I was worried he had one of those Autobahn-tested jobs straight from the German factory that top out at two hundred.

My junker was straining for all it was worth but was hopelessly outclassed. Before we'd gone ten blocks, he was gone like smoke, and I was looking at traffic from the middle of a ten-car pack. I had him figured for Boca Raton, and I knew he'd fly once he hit the 95 interstate. There wasn't much I could do except make fast time for Boca Raton myself and try to pick the right exit.

I was choking with disgust. To lose him like this had me pounding the steering wheel in a black rage.

Then, as if the gods weren't through fucking me over, they blew out my front left tire while I was creeping up on 85 m.p.h.

I fought the car hard all the way until I had it back on the shoulder and out of harm's way. Shreds of rubber smoked around the wheel rim. I put the emergency on and stepped outside into the chickweed and saw grass on the passenger side. I opened up the trunk, saw there was no spare, and kicked the rear tire. If no Good Samaritan pulled over, there'd be a state trooper coming along eventually, and I needed to look like any other ass-scratching citizen with bad luck. I was close enough to the road that the semis blew oily diesel smoke deep into my pores.

Twenty minutes and about ten thousand cars had passed me.

Enough of this shit. I opened the hood, fetched my rebar and suit coat. I had exactly forty-five dollars and sixty-two cents. *What was there to lose now?* If a cop stopped me, it was all over but the shouting, and I knew with gold-plated certainty I had to trust to blind luck.

I walked for ten minutes, and an angel stopped to give me a lift. A genuine Hell's Angel. He was a bearded lowrider on a sassy hog and the patch on his frayed denim said San Mateo, CA. He smelled bad, but I climbed up behind him and felt the thrust of the big engine, and we were in traffic going 70, 80 miles-an-hour in mere seconds.

He took me to Fort Lauderdale, to the Strip between Las Olas and A1A. It was a month after the annual college invasion, but there were dozens of young kids panhandling, making drug connections, and openly soliciting prostitution. I had been dropped off in the teenage runaway capital of the United States. Back home on the Strip, these sad stories were played out through the long summer nights, but it ended with the season. Here were the real McCoys, the lost youth from all over the United States – all around me, as if I were invisible in the midst of their subculture. I couldn't save any of them, either.

I walked on. Maybe I'd walk right back to Ohio in rags and a beard, but I had gone as far as I could. I walked on the boardwalk past cars lining its side. I looked at all the trash paper and syrupy crap where the yellow jackets were drawn by the sweetness. I saw crack and marijuana being smoked under the boardwalk by small gangs of teenagers, a girl who might have been thirteen or fourteen having sex with a fat man with short gray curly hair in his fifties on a blanket. She all but disappeared under his bulk.

"Time for the Apocalypse," I thought. The locusts ought to be over the skies any day. I saw a pale lemon GT 500 Super Snake, a genuine Shelby Mustang, with an orange anti-theft bar across it. That equaled a hacksaw and ten seconds' more inconvenience to an average car thief.

I walked on.

Cannot be – it just cannot be...

Emilio sat behind the wheel of the Porsche while he talked to some girls about thirty yards down on the beach. He was smiling and waving his cast around.

Picking up girls. Girls meant a party. That could mean Raina – maybe.

Suddenly, in my despair, I felt I could do nothing right and I had nothing left to do. I was certain of it right up to the moment I pulled up to within twenty yards of the back of Emilio's car. I watched him thrumming his fingers impatiently on the wheel while some teen girls admired his "whip"; they all seemed to have names like Lexxie and Sookie and exposed the tops of breasts too large for their tender years. All at once, they clambered over one another into the seats, squealing and arguing over who got to ride shotgun.

The timing had to be perfect. I heard Emilio laugh; he barely cocked his head. One girl stayed back, the other pleaded with her to "dog out the ride" with them, but she said she had to be at track practice.

When the girls settled themselves with loud squeals and laughing, Emilio revved his machine. I dodged around to the other side out of his sight. Ten feet from the pier, the drop to the sand was a good fifteen feet. I didn't hesitate and I rolled as if I were practicing for the 82nd Airborne. The guy getting trimmed five yards away behind a pier support was in his forties, a Caesar fringe of hair and a big hairy stomach over his pants. When the girl servicing him saw me appear out of nowhere, brushing sand from my clothes, she opened her mouth and released his member. He was lucky she didn't clamp down in her fright at seeing me.

It may have been the badge in my right hand, but it was probably the steel bar in my left that did the trick. He went soft in an instant. She sprang from her crouch and took off beneath the pier. I told him I was Fort Lauderdale Vice and he was busted. I ordered him to follow me. He did, protesting all the while and putting himself back in his pants

"Are you married?"

He was. Had two kids, eight and seven. On his way to work.

The tears in his eyes were begging me. His wife didn't do *that*, so –

"Shut up! I'm not your goddamned priest. Get up here now!" Begging and blubbering. "I'll lose my job," he said.

He was ready, so I tipped him over the edge.

"You ever hear of 'eminent domain,' asshole?" I said. "I'm confiscating your vehicle in the name of this sovereign state under Lewd and Lascivious Acts with Minors, Section C, paragraph five, one-oh-eight-nine-two point-two-one of the Criminal Penal Code of Florida."

He was screwing up his face now. "Wh-aat?"

Got too fancy with that penal code stuff, I realized.

I heard the Porsche's car door slam and it roared off with squealing tires.

"You're right, fucko," I said, "but I am taking your car. Report it stolen to the police – in one hour – and your wife won't find out what you do before you punch in," I said. "Hunh?"

"I said, give-me-one-hour-before-you-report-your-car-stolen.

Or she finds out."

"The fuck I will," he said. "Fuck you!"

I didn't need his keys. I had the housing peeled back like facial skin at an autopsy, wires crossed in less time.

"Where the fuck're you gonna leave it? Hey, hey, hey!" His fat form in the rearview mirror shrank to doll size and he disappeared.

I had Emilio in my sights again. He got stuck behind some twenty Warlocks riding tandem and had slowed down. You don't pass bikers riding tandem, anywhere, and if you do, you should have a DNR signed and ready at the hospital because the quality of your life won't be worth living afterward. He was going to get the next red light, too.

One more time into the breach, dear friends – or something like that, Jack used to say, quoting somebody no doubt as suicidal as I felt at that moment.

~ ~ ~

Emilio nearly lost me on the A1A, but I stayed with him, well back in the pack. The girls in the car might have slowed him down too; he wouldn't want to answer any awkward questions to the state troopers if caught speeding. If he had gone here first, just ahead a few miles to Delray Beach, I thought, he could have had all the teenaged girls he could cram into the car's maw. Thank God, it wasn't spring break or the beaches would have been packed with bodies of teenagers assembling in the warm south like Markhor on their annual rut.

We never went all the way to Boca Raton, in fact, because he exited at top speed and punished the brakes all the way down the exit. Lighthouse Point, it said. No idea where, but I stayed with him at a safe cruising speed well obscured by traffic. I was the last thing he was expecting anyway.

He was a couple hundred yards ahead. His lunatic driving winked cherry brake lights at me and guided me right to him. Heading toward the ocean. He hit one of those black asphalt roads that cut through the green vegetation, still driving too fast and foot-tapping his brakes every three seconds, hot-dogging for the girls.

Then he braked hard, cutting off to a narrow drive through an allotment with its name in scrollwork on the arch. The gaslights on either side weren't bright enough for me to read it.

We passed some ordinary farm-framed houses in brick or lap siding, and dormer windows, with screened in porches. Then we came to mostly brick and wood two-story jobs with more jazz to them, and finally, following a winding curve through trees draped in Spanish moss, we veered onto a more secluded section where the developers pulled out all the stops. Striking façades in cream villas with porticoes and fountains, Tudor-revival cottages you could drive a battleship through and great places in antique buffed brick with soldier courses, jack arches, and keystones.

I saw his brake lights flutter fifty yards ahead, and then he disappeared into a long driveway in front of an elegant white house with Ionic columns topped with one of those decorative balustrades you could make speeches from to the mob below; that is, if they were ever allowed onto the property.

As I passed by, I saw the girls and Emilio climb out; his cast glowing phosphorescent like St. Elmo's fire under the house's security lighting. The air was dank but spiced with oleander and bougainvillea. I drove past slowly and pulled off to the side of the road, idling, looking at a map in case someone came by. There was a low iron gate that surrounded the property and some shrubs along the ends.

I had to make a decision about the car. I picked a spot ahead where the vegetation had enough space to let me get the car into it. I tapped the accelerator and it spurted ahead a few feet and then rolled into the brush. In a moment it was obscured by thick lime greenery until only the roof could be seen from the road.

I was far enough from the lights to be unseen from the two houses I had to pass, but a dog must have picked up my scent because a howl broke the stillness in back of me. I trotted up the driveway of the house in sight of anyone who might have wanted to look out. *No choice except to risk exposure.* Once past the driveway, I was able to avoid windows and slip around the back. A rabbit nibbling the dewy leaves of a plumed fern in the back somersaulted at my approach and disappeared into the misty darkness. It was all black from behind, not a light except for the opposite end of the house and an upstairs window.

I was looking at a huge garage where the cars, a motorboat and off-road bikes were stored. Some kind of sailing cloth, a windsail for a surfboard, was spread across one wall.

My lockpick opened the door in a second and I stood breathing the smell of new wood inside. I had no idea where anything was and somewhere back there my Bic lighter was gone. I used my cell phone light to see my way. No sounds from inside the house. I hunkered and waited in the dark to get control of my breathing. Blindness is a bigger fear of mine than ever since the shooting. The panic started hammering inside me like an animal trapped in my throat trying to claw its way free. I had to will myself back to calm.

I stood up, stretched out my aching thigh muscles, and felt my way along the walls until I came to a door. It smelled of unpainted cherry. I found the knob and set my pick into the keyhole and gave it a sharp three-quarter turn.

An unlit corridor took me past vaulted ceilings into the main areas of the house. Track lighting in the den and living room, bottles of Dos Equis lying around. It looked like a house where people used to live but were away on vacation.

A spacious family room at the end of the foyer.

Voices above...

I took the winding staircase, the champagne carpeting smothering any sound I made, my hand clammy around the rebar.

The first room to the right had the door wide open and the clearest sounds and voices were coming from it. Emilio, the stallion, was rampant again, and one fast look confirmed it. The girl was obscured except for tanned legs wrapped around his quaking pelvic region.

The second room on the left was empty, a master bedroom.

Two more to go.

I could hear slurred words dribbling out like dropped coins in the next room – somebody giving instructions. Odio was standing ten feet into the room in the nude, encouraging action beyond my vision of the room.

"Lick her pussy," he said, and I saw his hand busy in front of his crotch.

You hear someone say *My blood ran cold* and you always think it's an exaggeration. It wasn't in my case. His gun lay holstered atop a heap of clothing near his legs. It would be a long journey down that carpeted hallway, moving toward the room at the end of the hallway, but I did it, one foot after the other like a toddler learning to walk.

The door was shut but unlocked. A slow turn of the knob, my heart thundering so loud in my chest I was sure everybody inside the house and next door could hear it.

I was inside.

Raina Toivela sat on the opposite end of a bed looking out the dormer window. It was an image fit for a tasteful ad for lingerie in a glossy woman's magazine. She wore cotton shorts and a black bra. Her honey hair spilled down her back.

Then I saw her reach out her hand and spoon some white powder from a dressing table and tilt it into her nostril with one quick, expert thrust. She rubbed furiously and continued to look out the window.

I must have moved because she turned and looked at me. "It's you," she said quietly. Her head nodded as the drug coursed its way through her system, shutting down one section and sparking up others in her brain.

"Thought you ... gone ... back by now..."

A little slurring, but not yet incoherent. "I promised your father," I whispered. "Oh, yeah, you did. My dad," she said.

Emotionless words, dry as desert stones.

She returned to gazing out the window. She was staring at the moon. I saw a silver crescent with Venus almost touching the bottom horn. I walked over to her and sat beside her. I kept the rebar out of sight, but in her raptured state I could have led a dancing bear into the room.

Fuck.

The sight of a gun barrel was digging into the hair at the nape of my neck.

Emilio's voice. "Man, am I ever gonna fuck you up."

One of the girls he had been with, fleshy in her nudeness, walked in on us.

"Hey, where's the coke you promised us?"

A déjà vu moment I thought better of mentioning.

To her: "Get out of here, *coño!* Now!"

She turned on her heel and disappeared through door she had come from. I never even noticed it, so entranced by the sight of my prize.

To me: "Stand up, motherfucker." I stood and he gave me a fast frisking.

He was nude, holding a gun. His black eyes widened in disbelief; he could not believe his luck. I watched his face and waited for him to shout for Odio to complete the surreal tableau.

Instinctively he moved back, too far for me to try a kick at the gun.

Raina said nothing all through this. I didn't see her face. I heard her shift her weight off the bed and then, whether the drug addled her common sense or she did it on purpose, I never got to learn, but she passed between Emilio's gun and me.

But I made no move. I froze in that split-second; the moment passed.

Coward, Haftmann.

I was going to have hours to think about that because I awoke inside the trunk of a car. That was after Miguel Odio came into the room with his own gun held out, took in the scene, bared his teeth in a quick wolf smile. Then, faster than I would have believed a man his size could move with or without clothes on, he moved up like a boxer stepping inside his opponent's reach and snapped out his arm at my jaw. It would have KO'd me even if it wasn't the one holding the gun.

CHAPTER 21

It took me three hours of sweat-soaked, exhausting labor to get the corner of the Porsche nearest the backseat matting loose enough to insert the tip of one finger; it took two more hours to put my hand on one spring. By then I was nearly dehydrated and so weak I couldn't work for more than a few minutes at a time before gasping for air.

It was close to dawn before I had one wire staple free, and three more to go. I had the image of Bobbie lying alone in that filthy, deserted place to keep me going.

Emilio kept the radio on until early in the morning. Three times I heard him get out of the car. When I knew he was out of the car, I worked frenziedly and made as much noise as I dared. Early in the morning, the radio off, I heard him stretch out on the seat – the faintest telltale creak of springs. Then quiet again. I went back to work, breathing through my mouth and twisting my body as far as I could for leverage or purchase. The pain was ferocious and my fingertips were bloody. By then, I knew every inch of my space and could have drawn its outline to the exact dimensions.

Finally, I had the coil free and resting in the palm of my blistered and bloody hand. My right hand was so cut that I was going to have to do this with my left. One left jab, one opportunity. Live or die consequences. I had the narrower top layers worked out to a flatness that my body weight helped to straighten. The wire bit into my skin and the gunshot wound in my side opened up and I felt wetness soak my pants. I still had a bad crimp to work out in the middle, but there was too much risk. It was light enough for me to see dust motes in the pinprick of daylight along one seam of the trunk above my head.

Finally, it was as straight as I'd get it. I worked it inside my pants under the belt on the right side.

Long minutes passed, or maybe hours. My mind was floating in and out.

The trunk lid sprang up with such force that it flooded my space with a blinding white light. I rubbed my face with my dirty, bloody fingers but I couldn't put sight back in my eyes.

"Get out," Emilio said.

I lay there groaning and forced him to move closer. He swore at me in Spanish.

"I need water," I said. I coughed for effect.

"You say another word, shithead, I kill you here and now."

I took all the time I could despite his rapid cursing. I managed to get one leg out of the trunk and then the other, banging my kneecap, and before I could stand upright, Emilio kicked me in the knee and I tumbled headlong into the dirt.

"Look, I need to piss. Please. I can't walk in there after I've pissed myself."

"Fuck you, *maricón* – "

He couldn't stand it. He wanted to tee off on me so badly he did what he shouldn't have; he reached under one arm to jerk me upright with his good arm and I was able to throw my body at him with my left hand in a death-grip around the coil. I felt a stinging along my forearm and registered the gunshot a split-second before I felt the coil's end strike him in the face just below the skin of his eye. It went in as easy as splitting the skin from a grape; it went deep and I felt the shock of bone scraping all the way to my elbow.

Nothing ever felt so good.

He screamed once and the gun flew.

I tottered around trying to manage an overhand right but my legs were so weak and cramped that I stumbled like a drunk in traffic. It didn't matter. Emilio was down for the count. The coil shaft was embedded six inches into his face. He lay on his back, his legs crumpled under him like a ragdoll's, his feet splayed out. From another angle he'd resemble a child at naptime in a romper room. It was a ludicrous, grotesque moment to realize he wore expensive boots that disguised the elevator heels.

I dropped one knee onto his chest. I took a breath and jammed the spring in as deep as it would go. I screwed it all the way into his face – seven, eight, nine, ten inches. His eyeball bulged and flopped out, lying on his cheek with a single thick red vein holding it in to the gushing well of blood. My vision had suddenly become so acute I noticed the back of his eyeball was a spiderwebbed with thin silky veins.

I got off his chest without taking my eyes off his face. His fingers twitched once and then he resumed his child-like pose. I reached down to his neck and felt for the carotid, but my nerves were so shot and my trembling fingers couldn't detect one. One half of his face was swelling as if a football had been sewn under his eye.

I looked around for his gun. Whatever tunnel vision I was operating under let go and I was aware once more of the world and of noises, sounds, and the cool feel of morning air against my burning skin. I smelled water.

Staggering off in the direction of a loon's call, I glimpsed it, a shimmering opalescent pool just feet away. Like an animal, I moved toward it and saw lily pads and bright green algae offshore. I plunged into the water up to my knees and splashed my face. Aware of the intense burning in my throat, I sank my head under and gulped the brackish water as if it were purest spring water.

Then fear did what my will could not. I shot bolt upright.

Water moccasins, alligators.

I got out of there as fast as my legs could bull through the sludge sucking at my ankles.

Emilio still lay where he dropped.

My wounds were minor. In fact, the slug had torn a crease up the sleeve and just the friction of the fabric being parted by the bullet's track had given me nothing worse than a rope burn. My knee throbbed where Emilio kicked me and was swollen but I could limp along.

Better than that, I could drive.

I retrieved my wallet and papers, took his keys and wallet out of his pants pocket, folded fifties and hundreds into my wallet. I giggled from the sheer joy of being alive. I found a machete and a bag of marijuana under the front seat. I tossed the marijuana in the weeds and put the weapon in the trunk.

The Porsche engine cranked and rumbled. I was on a single, desolate road banked by sand dunes and patches of saw grass. I drove back the way I assumed we had come. The road widened, the tall pines and the mowed grass on the shoulders told me I was in or near a state park. The first sign directing commercial vehicles one way and passenger traffic another confirmed it. My internal compass told me I was probably north of Lauderdale.

I didn't want to look at my face in the mirror. My throat was still parched. I saw a pavilion at the park entrance and headed for the men's room, where I washed off as much filth as I could. I filled my stomach to gurgling capacity at the tap. Out of the park, I saw the interstate juncture and headed for it. The Porsche was the finest set of wheels I had ever experienced but it was nothing to the air I was dragging into my burning lungs. I booted traffic out of my way all the way down the pipe and pulled into the Riviera Court just after ten. I was a bum with bloody paws behind the wheel of a two-hundred-thousand-dollar car.

The package was there behind the desk. The clerk who replaced Youssef began to say something but took one look at me and handed it to me without a word.

I tore the cardboard open and handed it to her.

"Would you mind putting this into your computer?"

She turned around. I imagined she was thinking about running, and I wouldn't have blamed her. Then she took it from me, holding it gingerly between her fingers as if it were radioactive.

"I'll have to use the one in back," she said.

She stepped into a back room and I heard the *ker-chug* of a computer being turned on. Then some clacking at the keyboard. She came back with it a moment later.

"It's encrypted," she said. "Maybe they can help you up the street. The computer science building is just off University Drive."

Her eyes were votive candles. *Please, God, don't let this maniac kill me...*

I thanked her and said she should quit her job as soon as she could. Tree trimmers and female night clerks in roadside motels and all-night gas stations have the most dangerous jobs in America.

I bought a paper from the rack outside and drove around to my room.

The investigation into the death of a well-known journalist was in big type font. I saw Bobbie's file photo next to the copy. I scanned a couple paragraphs: "We want to make an arrest for this heinous crime as expeditiously as possible," was the quote from Police Commissioner Jerome Ross. "And we will spare no effort to bring this case to closure."

He didn't have a fucking clue.

I had to wash up, shave, put on my last set of clothes, quiet my stomach with something bland, and get this disk checked out by one of Suntan U's technology experts.

Lieutenant Baddalucco was busy out there, too, with her troops looking to make me infamous.

I wanted to stop. I wanted to drive that expensive car north as fast as it would accelerate. The black-and-white pixels that formed Bobbie Gersack's face in the newspaper said: *Don't even think about it, Buster.*

~ ~ ~

The man I found to help me over there looked at the screen and said, "Hmmm" about six times. I wanted to throw him out the window but we were below ground in some kind of cavernous IT laboratory set up in a maze of phalanxes of smaller labs splitting off one another.

He had been saying that for all of ten agonizing long minutes. But because he was obliging me with his expertise, I had no choice but to cup my chin in my hands as if I, too, knew what the hell he was talking about. It sounded more like a video game with swords and sorcery involved. I heard words like "deep scanning," "bots," and "victims," "masters," and "zombies." All that Google-talk went over my head the first five seconds he began tapping away at his keyboard with flying fingers.

"We need the code," he said finally.

Duh, I thought. *Fuck me, a rocket scientist...*

I thanked him, pocketing the disk, and started to pick my way around his untidy office where a fire marshal would have fined him for the mounds of paper and journals lying in disarray in unsteady piles on the floor. The guts of several computers were lying between those piles and on top of them I saw dozens of tweezers and several soldering guns of different sizes.

He wanted me to leave it with him, but I said no. He was prattling about a new Klingon language version of the world English bible as I headed for the elevator.

The geek shall inherit the earth, I thought.

I had a choice. Turn it over to Pavelic, try to deal for Raina, or give it to the cops and let the chips fall. Try to salvage something out of this for myself to avoid going to jail.

~ ~ ~

No car was parked in the circular driveway in front of the house, but I saw a Honda Pilot across the street and lights in the houses down the street. There was no music coming through the patio doors this time. No naked little blonde hunched over to do a line. In fact, there was no furniture. The house looked abandoned.

The screen was shredded just as it was the night I had gone through it. The patio doors were locked and a wraparound bicycle chain was secured to that. The air conditioner was missing along with the two-by-four prop. The rusty barbecue grill and the now-dead ficus were the only things in their former places.

A dead end. I didn't know what I expected to find there. I flicked my fingertips along the floor where the television set was. Dust, dead skin cells.

I didn't have to choose anymore. It was waiting for me.

CHAPTER 22

I headed downtown. I saw some newspaper racks and stopped to see whether the big Miami papers had any more news on Bobbie's death. Nothing. A back page item already. "Tribune Correspondent's Abduction-Murder to Be Investigated by FBI." Time I called Sonja, time I gave up.

"I've got the disk," I said, as soon as the extension buzzed her through.

Long pause.

"Bring it," she said.

Disgust I heard in her voice.

"We can stick Pavelic with this disk," I said.

"Haftmann, did you hear me? You're looking at charges that carry a minimum – "

"Got to go, see you."

I went back to the car and checked the map, five blocks from the Miami Public Library's computers. As long as I was driving a Porsche registered to one of Pavelic's front men, I seemed to be invisible. It wouldn't last – but whatever in this life does?

~ ~ ~

The carrel I sat in was shielded from the people on either side of me, but I reflexively looked around just to check.

I took out my last two twenties and found a folded-up fifty jammed behind my driver's license. I had forgotten I had it. It was my emergency booze money. After my last bender at Tico's, when I was buying drinks for the bar just before closing, Tico's wife Marta put her hand over mine and said I should put that bill away for some "bad time."

I was hoping the kid wasn't too greedy. He was a

genius, the "best hacker in Miami," according to his sidekick. A bunch of these skatepunks were hanging out using the lot despite the sign at the entrance: NO SKATEBOARDING. When I asked them for a name of the best computer whizz they knew, they pointed at one of the skateboarders in baggy pants at the far end of the lot.

It was a lengthy, annotated list. At least seven hundred and fifty names of not only South Florida's and the Caribbean's most prominent and wealthy citizens but also addresses for a number of cities between Mobile and Dothan, Alabama as far north as Atlanta, Georgia. Another column had dozens of names and addresses for corporate heads, CFOs, lawyers, factory owners, high-ranking law enforcement officers in ICE, DEA, Justice, and some agencies with acronyms I had never heard of. Medical people, bankers, and politicians were designated by their degrees or by their affiliations. Most impressive were the names subcategorized under the Department of State. Somebody had taken the time to note which ivy-league universities and social organizations they belonged to. Not your garden-variety professionals but the people who ran offices, agencies, banks, governments, published newspapers and influenced millions of people.

These were the kinds of power-brokers Pavelic was lining up for whatever kind of move he was plotting. With this kind of clout behind him, he could think gubernatorial race and not be aiming too high. The list wasn't something that should have gotten Toni butchered – unless there was more to it. Any PAC could garner a list of influential names like this off the net. For all I knew, you could track them from cell phones. It had to be something else that left Toni DeCamillo without a face and Bobbie Gersack dumped in a broken-down shanty. Maybe a fifth column of supporters who would use money and influence in Pavelic's behalf, a reverse Bay of Pigs, and this first wave of his future scheme?

A third subset looked like blackmail victims or potential ones. I saw names indexed by predilections that ranged from public masturbation through transvestite fetishes to child molestation. There were names of girls with asterisks after eleven of the entries with a different date and a location; all but two cities were foreign and ranged from Mexico City, *Zona Rosa*, to the Dominican Republic with the names of haciendas and nothing else.

I scrolled to the bottom of the page to find it: *sn. fm. to addressee.*

I wondered at the strange delicacy of a blackmailer who couldn't type out "snuff film."

There was more. Whole pages detailing fiscal transactions at several banks in Columbia, Belize, and the Cayman Islands. A net worth figure was noted after each name. A second, much smaller figure, was entered next to that. Maybe the sum requested from each victim. These were numbers from $2,000 to $50,000.

There were notations after some names that suggested favors performed: influence peddling – several Florida commissioners' names were double-underscored – bribes, drugs provided, prostitutes. Markwright's annotations were elliptical but precise enough to indicate the scope of Toni's net. These were the sex-party degenerates Toni supplied girls to and probably had evidence on, maybe a cache of disks in a Miami vault somewhere. She'd have picked up useful gossip along the way about important citizens, the cream of society, the movers and shakers.

Pavelic had to be the focal point for all these contacts because only he moved in all these interlocking circles. I wondered how Toni had gotten her hands on it, but Pavelic took stupid chances and risks because of his big ego. He wasn't the only monkey who climbed so high he showed his ass, something like that Micah used to say about her courtroom enemies. He didn't think any of the little people who floated in his gossamer wake would have the *cojones* to double-cross him. This entire state was built on a foundation of raw greed and the desire for status, wealth, and privilege. Still, it was mind-boggling. One ex-con looking to score big, a nobody compared to Pavelic, had set all this off by rattling the stick in the swill bucket too soon.

Only Toni had the insider's knowledge of the white slavery and the disappearing teenaged runaways. Markwright, the squarejohn boyfriend, had the organizing ability to put it all into a tidy spreadsheet. It still bothered me Emilio had been the one to take me for my second ride, not Miguel. Odio would never have failed twice.

I had played my part for them all – a stalking horse the day I stumbled into that gym in search of answers to questions about Raina.

And Raina herself. What part did she play in all these betrayals? Was Pavelic her Svengali or had she survived so far because no one thought she was worth killing? I was still fumbling in the dark with parts of the puzzle.

I wasn't even sure that what I held in my hand was worthwhile to Pavelic. I hoped that, when the time came to drop the disk onto the table and these names dribbled out, it wouldn't stick to my hands. If this disk didn't ring true, I didn't have a shekel left to barter. I already had enough experience in South Florida to know what my life was worth and what was going to happen to me.

~ ~ ~

The number on Oceanside Boulevard rang once and an answering machine intercepted it with a mechanical voice that repeated the number I had just dialed and told me to leave a message. I gave it the number of the phone I was calling from and said it would be good for one-half hour before I would change locations.

It rang back ten minutes later. A voice I didn't recognize told me to call back at precisely three in the afternoon.

I sweated through mid-day traffic, itchy, muscles taut as chicken wire, and even my one good eye felt scratchy. I hadn't slept in twenty hours and my head was sagging on my chest through the long afternoon. I parked at the far end of a shopping mall and crawled into the back of the cramped Porsche and took a ragged catnap. I was vaguely aware of faces passing by or peering in the window, but I didn't care. I had to rest.

At 3:01 I made the call.

The same voice asked me if I knew the Art Deco district of Miami Beach. Be at the bar in the Carlyle at 5:00 p.m., it said, and wait for instructions.

"Tell Pavelic I'll decide where and when. I'll tell him – " Click.

Fuck a duck.

~ ~ ~

"I remembered that hotel, the pink one in pastels with the donut hole," I said to the bartender.

"It was on *Miami Vice*," he said.

"You're too young to remember Sonny and Tubbs," I said.

"I'm talking about the movie with Jamie Foxx," he replied.

I was working on another ten-dollar drink. A club soda, again. The bill Marta made me save was going fast. It felt as heavy as a shot put on my stomach. I was down to ten and some change in my pocket.

He ignored me. I assumed he had heard that comment a few times.

"How's your drink, sir?" he asked me.

He was hoping I had run out of ten-dollar bills. The

valet had sent word to the bartender I was OK; after all, a man driving a Porsche 350-SL … but, still, he knew I didn't belong in this set. I never understood how it was that working-class mopes acquired the snobbery of the people they served. There's a footman in all of us, I guessed.

I had shaved in a gas station restroom with a disposable razor, my white shirt showed the crease lines from the cellophane wrapping, the zipper on my Dockers was always an inch short of making it to the top. I was wrinkled everywhere but the ass, and my suit jacket was split under right arm from the rebar poking through it.

If this is a set-up, I'm not dressed for it.

I twisted little wet circles with the stubby glass on the doily. "It's fine," I said.

This time his voice schmoozed. "For you, sir," he said. He handed me the phone and wandered a discreet distance off.

"Haftmann," I said.

"Drive over to Collins Avenue – "

"Stop running me around, fucker. I'm out of money."

"Drive to Collins Avenue from where you are. It's easy to find, or ask someone. Go to the Sheraton Bal Harbour. It's on the beach. Look for a cabana with a striped-yellow awning. Wait there. Someone will come for you."

"Is Pavelic going to be there or is Miguel waiting for me?" "Leave now," the voice said.

I had a look on my face that must have summoned the bartender. He asked me if I was OK.

"Right as rain," I said.

"Maybe too much of that soda," he said. "Never touched the stuff myself." He winked at me as if we were secret blood brothers.

"Try one," I said. "It's the citrus that makes it go." I put my last ten and all my pocket change on the counter.

People are wrong. You *can* tip the undertaker.

CHAPTER 23

I drove down Collins past hotels where aged, brightly dressed, listless shuffleboard players stood with sticks or lounged at poolside like baboons on the Serengeti Plain around a watering hole. Dorsey era swing music from nightclubs and revues poured through air-conditioned doorways into the street. More sunburned or pale flabby flesh, more restaurants, bars, hotels, and discos per square yard than anywhere else on earth. The Gold Coast. He who has the gold, as the saying goes, rules. The Midwest I had left behind was slogging through the worst drought since the Great Depression. Cornfields were burning up and factories were folding up and moving overseas. Even the bloody cartels were feeling the pinch; they stopped buying their own hand-woven blankets to wrap their victims and were using blankets imported from China.

I found the Sheraton. A hostess in a black-and-white outfit like a French maid in a porn film pointed me toward the beach cabanas. I had no money to give her, but she didn't seem to expect it.

I spotted the one with the yellow awning; it was folded up. His was all wood and glass on three sides except for the back. Crystal wind chimes of birds tinkled from one corner. There were wooden Venetian blinds drawn up high over each window.

I opened the sliding door.

"Come in, Mister Haftmann," Raymond Pavelic said.

He was seated at a glass table on which sat a vase of white roses, drinking something dark, legs crossed, looking out over the ocean at the sun dipping into the water.

"Would you care for a drink?" He asked. "I'm having rum and Coke."

There was no one else in sight. No one had followed me down to the beach. I had, however, the prickling at the nape of my neck told me that, if I thought I wasn't being watched ever since I set foot on this expensive white sand, I had better wake up and apologize to someone.

"I've had my last drink in that bar."

"That sounds ominous," he said. "Relax, won't you? In Latin America it is considered boorish to conduct business in the home.

Like bringing dogs inside one's house."

"DeCamillo, Markwright, Gersack, to name just a few. They must have thought a man with good table manners and a fat bank account couldn't possibly be a butcher."

His silk shirt had ruffles down the front; it was open at the collar, and his sleeves were rolled up over arms matted in thick black hair. A pair of gold cufflinks lay on the table, thick as doubloons. He was clean-shaven but the shadow of his dark beard gave the lower half of his face a blue sheen. His expression was blank. He averted his eyes from me, as if I were unpleasant to look at, concentrating instead on the sun's setting than my feeble attempt to goad him. "Where is the disk?" he said casually, bored.

"I have it," I said. "Not on me, of course."

He turned to look at me briefly. "That's not what I'm asking." "I brought these for you," I said.

I laid the folded sheets of printout in my hand onto the table.

He glanced through them briefly. I noticed that his toes and feet in the black sandals were hairy too.

He set them aside, "I didn't ask for these," he said.

He turned back to the combustion in the western sky, a brilliant pink-and-peach fireball descending into the Atlantic. A talky cabbie years ago told me that Key

West sightseers look for a green wink of light when the sun sets during the summer solstice.

He put on sunglasses that probably cost more than I had spent in the state so far.

"I prefer this time of day," he said. "I do my best thinking at sunset."

"You have the soul of a poet, Pavelic," I said. I suppose he wanted me to think that.

"The world is in balance for this one moment," he said. "Do you know Wagner?"

"Yeah, he played for the Pirates back in the dead-ball era," I said. "They called him 'The Flying Dutchman.'" I was thinking that if I had the original Honus Wagner baseball card from that cereal box, I would never have had to drag my ass out of Tico's Place.

He didn't find me amusing.

"... an old civilization perishes in this kind of twilight but we will make a new one to be born from its ashes. *Troya fuit*, Haftmann.

The word of Troy's destruction spread far across the ancient world."

"I feel privileged," I said. "It's like being a witness to – to a moment in evolution when humanity takes a quantum leap forward."

"Stop being a clown," he said. "You show your fear too obviously."

A new world order, my ass. It was the same old world where money and power were wielded by a chosen few. *Troya fuck-you-a*, is what I thought.

I assumed he was talking of Cuba but maybe he meant America. I looked at the beach where sunbathers and tourists crossed into view. Couples young and old strolled along the shoreline. Several people lay on blankets near the shore's edge. A hundred yards from where I was sitting – an easy shot. A sniper on the beach lying on his stomach with a rifle hidden under a blanket could be pimpling me with red dots, and I'd never hear the shot. As soon as the sun dropped, we'd be backlit, well exposed in the cube-shaped room.

"I'm not interested in your plans for the future," I said. "I want to take the girl home to her family. She can't hurt you and she knows nothing. Let her go."

This time he turned to look at me. "You disappoint me. You think those paltry sums on those papers mean something to me?" He jabbed a finger toward the papers. "Insulting, really, don't you agree? Money is a mere conduit, a means to an end. A way to build one's goals..."

"*Goals*? You call a mobile slaughterhouse *building goals*?"

He looked at me, weighing me and finding me too light even with a thumb on the scale.

"Like water, like that ocean out there, I seek my own equilibrium," he said.

"Water's a conduit, too, but it doesn't leave a bloody mess everywhere."

"Not a bad analogy for a man of your ... limitations," Pavelic said, still without bothering to take more than a second glance at me. "Money finds its own equilibrium, too, Mister Haftmann. Trust me on that."

I had to grip the ends of the chair to keep my hands from shaking. I thought my stock of adrenalin was exhausted by now, but a kind of nervous energy was filling me out like my old cop days when caffeine and cigarettes were more important than food. Being close to your own death, or the man who can deliver it, will do that as well.

"Give me the girl," I said. "We'll both go away."

He ignored that as too trivial for a response. Instead, he

sipped his drink and stretched out his long legs. "How is your recovery proceeding?"

"Being the halfwit you just implied I am, I think well enough to make a living. My eyesight is poor but I work around it. Thanks for asking, though."

Stupid bravado ... wisecracking like an imbecile. I was falling into my role.

"Psychologically, too, would you say? Do you come awake in the night and imagine you're back *there?*"

"Yes," I said. "It happens but then I think of killing you and I feel much better."

He laughed, or maybe it was some other reaction that I supposed was a laugh, but it came out like a single grunt. "I'm sure you do," he said.

"So are we done here? The disk for her, and my silence?"

"You mean, cross-my-heart-and-hope-to-die? Like kids? Forever and ever? Your silence isn't a problem for me."

"What do you want from me?"

"Nothing that matters." He turned his face away from me and leaned back in his chair as if bored.

The points of my knuckles were white on the chair. I tried to relax the pressure.

"*Acabado,*" he said suddenly.

Finished. I knew the word. I had heard Tico use it at closing time often enough when he was forced to cut me off.

I held my breath for a long, tense moment, waiting for a round like a copper Silvertip to blow a chunk out of me where I sat.

But nothing happened. I stood up, turned to walk away. "Bobbie Gersack – " "Who?"

I bit my tongue, stifled the surge of bile rising in my throat.

"The reporter," I said. "The woman you had – "

"You mean the one in the papers this morning? So sad. She must have suffered terribly."

"The book on your ... *new world order,*" I said,

barely controlling my rage. "I know you have it, but she would have known to make a copy."

I never knew the name of her contact at the DA's. *Stupid, stupid me...*

His face didn't change expression, and I knew my bluff was limp as an overcooked pasta noodle. Even if she had sent a Xerox over, I could see it filed away and forgotten. Things have a way of disappearing from police storage like drug money and dope. Xerox boxes full of homicide evidence grow legs and walk out of police stations all the time. Pavelic didn't have to physically hold it in his hands. He controlled everybody who would come within a ten-mile radius of it.

I was at the door when I turned back toward him again. His face was still directed at the ocean and he held his hand under his chin.

"How do you know I don't have that file copied on a flashdrive at home – or hidden under a rock or in a bank vault somewhere?"

"Because if you copied it, if I ever *hear* of its existence outside my possession, that girl will have her face peeled off and fed to my Welsh Corgi within twenty-four hours. I'll send it to your cellphone while it's happening."

My stomach clenched listening to that calm voice.

"Haftmann ... one more thing, if I may? Don't be arrogant because I have known Miguel a long time and I know he likes to play both sides against the middle, which I allow. You outwitted a foolish boy in Emilio. Don't make the mistake of assuming you have accomplished anything down here."

I should have shut my big mouth. But people lecturing me all my life has always stuck in my craw.

"I don't think I'm the one here with delusions about himself," I said.

That ruffled his feathers. "You're a middle-aged

wreck, a seedy nobody, a nothing in my book. I won't overlook you again. You can believe that."

I believed him.

~ ~ ~

Raina was waiting for me in my room at the motel. She was sitting on the bed, her hands folded in her lap. Her eyes were glassy, but if Pavelic wanted to give her a hot shot, nothing would have been easier. He was keeping his part of bargain. I wasn't worth killing and neither was she. Youssef avoided looking at me. I didn't ask him how she got there.

I told her we were driving home in the morning.

"Why not now?" she asked me.

"I have to see a man about a horse," I said. I used to say that in Tico's when I had to piss. I was meeting Pavelic's man to turn over the disk. It was the same voice on the phone who guided me to the cabana. I told him I'd hand it to him at noon tomorrow near the entrance to the Walmart in Coconut Beach. I told him I'd be standing next to the smiley man at the door, the one who greets you and checks your packages to see if you're stealing. I didn't think Pavelic would renege on the deal but with maniacs in ruffled shirts, you just never know. I wanted to delay it for another reason. Bobbie's paper was holding a memorial service for her at a local funeral parlor. I saw Sonja and Isobel there. Isobel's eyes were red from crying but Sonja's eyes were dry and looked at me in a way I was long used to; it was Micah's look, different eye color, same stare, wondering and hurt at the same time...

Before I left town and this godforsaken state, I wanted to walk on the beach just like any ordinary snowbird tourist. I don't know how I knew it, but I knew no cops would be lying in wait for me now, and no Miguel lurking in ambush.

That night, Raina and I walked through moon-whitened sand and I stood at the shoreline looking out over the serene water. The froth on the waves looked like soap scum. She linked her arm through mine, a father and daughter on vacation. I thought of Pavelic's note to me: "...like lambs in a field, disporting themselves under the eye of the butcher..."

It was over, then, for good, my pleasure in the surf. Time once more to deliver a daughter to her family.

~ ~ ~

The ride back was no different from the ones before it. The same gaseous reek from the churned up bog matter of the roadside ditches wafted air into the car that stank like effluent from a Bombay sewer. Raina thought her own thoughts and seemed content in herself. I knew better than to pry, but I wasn't going to turn my back on her for a second. The third time was going to be the charm. Time together, so close, traveling north on a ribbon of road that stretched endlessly.

Words – what good are they anyway?

I saw big predatory birds overhead just to break the hypnosis of the road and the heat mirages that appeared and disappeared. I imagined the hawks and kites and falcons folding their wings in headlong dives like Stukas and Junkers in the war movies I watched as a boy growing up in a silo town. I knew they watched me hurtling along from their vantage above.

We barely stopped except for gas and food. I watched Raina even when I didn't have to. While she was in the restroom at a diner, I went back outside to smash the door lock on her side as a precaution. We had one thing in common besides Pavelic. Neither of us trusted happiness. I couldn't hear the demons who whispered to her but there wasn't going to be any throwing herself out of a speeding car while I was driving.

I had enough money for the trip home. It just took Raina's voice on the phone to free up the cash from her parents, so I didn't need to drive at night against my habit. A clearing of cloud in front of the bright moon showed a silver canopy of mossy trees that became pine and tall fir, maple and oak as the hours passed. Abandoned orchards and small farms, swaybacked barns tugged earthward by gravity, homesteads and crooked putty-white slabs of cemeteries. Space and time, matter and energy – weren't they supposed to be the same thing at the most basic level of existence?

The moon shone on Raina's sleeping blonde head. Her pale flesh glowed in a soft, golden light. "Like a fairy tale," I thought. A damsel in distress she might be still, but I was no knight to the rescue. I was glad to be escaping north, both of us safe from the dragon. I saw the bitter smile on my lips in the rearview mirror.

Moonglow, damsels, fairies – *Stop thinking*, I told myself. *Shut up, go home.*

EPILOGUE

MID-SUMMER, JEFFERSON-ON-THE-LAKE

CHAPTER 24

By the time I saw Raina Toivela again, my farmer's tan from Florida had faded to a few dried flakes of peeled skin on my forearms and neck. I was stepping off the curb in front of Tico's after breakfast and saw her in the back of her father's car. I caught a flash of the shape of her head and knew her at once. She had dyed her hair a buttery yellow. The glare of the sun off glass made it impossible for me to know if she saw me.

I waved to the car anyway and limped across the street. I had sprained my ankle playing tennis. It's not a game you're supposed to pick up at my age. My foot hasn't healed properly, so I had to see some podiatrist at the Cleveland Clinic last week. On a whim, I dropped by my young neurosurgeon's office and caught him scribbling notes on a clipboard. When he looked up and recognized me, I contorted my face and began slurring my words and twitching. He didn't think I was funny.

Raina's father returned my itemized bill with the words *Paid in Full* scrawled across it.

I can't blame him for thinking he was cheated on some of the items. A lot of those expenses after Raina bolted from the lobby in Jacksonville were my own responsibility. But I'm still dunning him. Truth is, I'm in debt again and Tico's been floating me a loan to cover me until I get back on my feet. Pun intended. I can't hustle around as fast as I need to in my line of work, so I'm turning away jobs I could have taken. The old cash-flow problem isn't new, and I get that familiar black look from Marta every time I go in her husband's bar. Poor guy, he takes a ragging, but he knows something I never learned with Micah. A good wife is worth obeying. That's a Russian proverb, by the way, and I didn't get it from her.

Here's another from Bulgaria I picked up from an old timer at the bar: *Starving bears don't dance.* The coming tourist season has to bring me some work or I'm going to get out of the private-eye business for good.

I don't know how Raina's life is coming along. I don't know if she's even fighting those demons that drove her to Florida twice and turned her into a willing zombie. Some things you can't ever know. Micah never believed that.

I don't think about Florida much nowadays. I try not to think about Pavelic and his plans for Cuba now that America is getting reacquainted with its island neighbor once more. Miguel gets into my thoughts once in a while. I do get a warm feeling south of the beltline when I think of Anne, long gone from Mrs. Tanenbaum's and from my life. I never knew her last name but I wouldn't be much of a detective if I couldn't locate her. For now, I'm content with imaginary conversations and scenarios I dream up while I'm having a few beers – say, she flies into Cleveland for a business conference, rings me up and we talk. Then – suave devil that I am – I ask her if she wants to see the show at Playhouse Square, something artsy-fartsy. Then I get her into bed.

I have my days where getting myself off the bed and going to the office is tough. Sometimes it's just going through the motions. Sometimes I go down to the beach and watch the water breaking on the shore. I watch the people going by my window. Sometimes they look in at me.

Whoever said it, I don't know, probably Micah with her damned book-wisdom, but it goes like this – or something like this:

Thank you for reading.

Please review this book. Reviews help others find New Pulp Press and inspire us to keep providing these marvelous tales.

If you would like to be put on our email list to receive updates on new releases, contests, and promotions, please go to NewPulpPress.com and sign up.

After such knowledge, what forgiveness?

About the Author

Robb White grew up in Ashtabula, Ohio. He has published three Thomas Haftmann novels and a collection of short stories featuring his existentialist private eye. He has worked in grocery and department stores, a deckhand on three Great Lakes ore boats, a mold puller in a plastics factory, and most recently, as a book reviewer and interviewer for a boxing magazine. He rarely leaves home but he did get to China for a couple extraordinary weeks.

NewPulpPress.com

Made in the USA
Lexington, KY
02 September 2017